The Beautiful
Mistake

The Beautiful MISTAKE

STEVE ZINGERMAN

iUniverse, Inc.
Bloomington

The Beautiful Mistake

Copyright © 2011 by Steve Zingerman.

All rights reserved. No part of this book may be used or reproduced by any means, graphic, electronic, or mechanical, including photocopying, recording, taping or by any information storage retrieval system without the written permission of the publisher except in the case of brief quotations embodied in critical articles and reviews.

Certain characters in this work are historical figures, and certain events portrayed did take place. However, this is a work of fiction. All of the other characters, names, and events as well as all places, incidents, organizations, and dialogue in this novel are either the products of the author's imagination or are used fictitiously. If there are only a few historical figures or actual events in the novel, the disclaimer could name them: For example: "Edwin Stanton and Salmon Chase are historical figures..." or "The King and Queen of Burma were actually exiled by the British in 1885." The rest of the disclaimer would follow: However, this is a work of fiction. All of the other characters, names, and events as well as all places, incidents, organizations, and dialogue in this novel are either are the products of the author's imagination or are used fictitiously.

iUniverse books may be ordered through booksellers or by contacting:

iUniverse
1663 Liberty Drive
Bloomington, IN 47403
www.iuniverse.com
1-800-Authors (1-800-288-4677)

Because of the dynamic nature of the Internet, any web addresses or links contained in this book may have changed since publication and may no longer be valid. The views expressed in this work are solely those of the author and do not necessarily reflect the views of the publisher, and the publisher hereby disclaims any responsibility for them.

Any people depicted in stock imagery provided by Thinkstock are models, and such images are being used for illustrative purposes only.
Certain stock imagery © Thinkstock.

ISBN: 978-1-4620-4959-2 (sc)
ISBN: 978-1-4620-4958-5 (hc)
ISBN: 978-1-4620-4957-8 (ebk)

Library of Congress Control Number: 2011914821

Printed in the United States of America

iUniverse rev. date: 08/16/2011

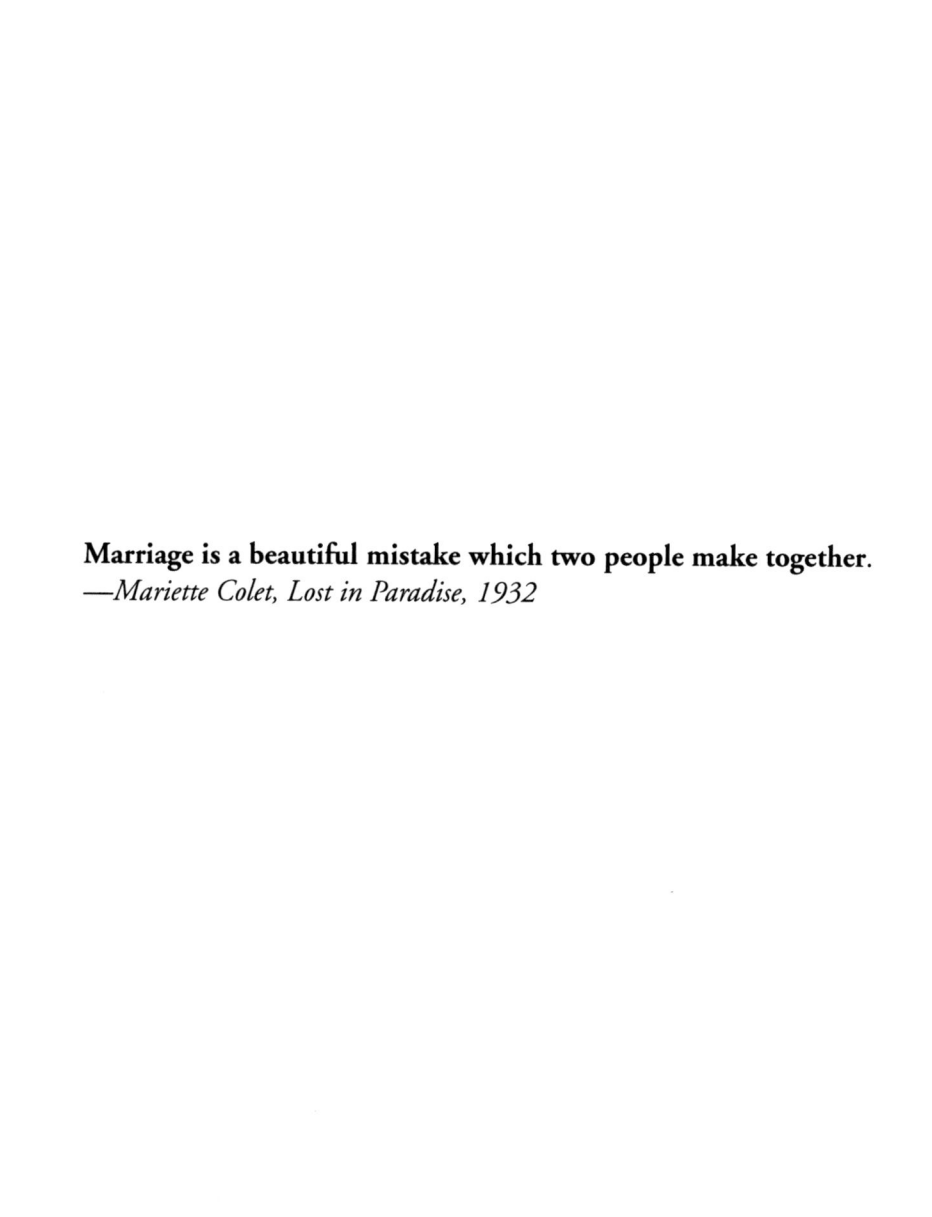

Marriage is a beautiful mistake which two people make together.
—*Mariette Colet, Lost in Paradise, 1932*

Before we heard the whistling, we felt this overwhelming stillness, the eye of our own storm passing quickly. It was muffled—the sound of our banging, pulling, preparing, our fear. Then the planes came. We heard them before we saw them, a squealing like the pigs back home when shoved in for slaughter. In the air, formations of planes known to shoot to kill, to destroy themselves for the sake of the mission. While the instinct was to stare, confounded, at these screaming steel birds of prey, a second wasted could kill us all.

"Hey . . . incoming enemy aircraft! Come on you guys, wake up, battle stations!"

I ran down the passageway hoping to make it to my battle station. As I reached the main deck it exploded in front of me. Everything went black, then white, and I saw the fire rising as I hit the deck unconscious.

"You are one lucky man, Chief Vanderbilt," the doctor said when I regained consciousness aboard the AHS Centaur, an Australian hospital ship. "The steel bulkhead that blew off from the deck above missed you by inches. Wouldn't've been enough'a you to send home for Mama to bury. How d'you feel now?"

"Good, Doc, good as new. Thanks for patching me up but I'd like to get back to my ship if it's not sunk. There's a war going on, y'know."

"Chief, with all due respect, no way. You have a concussion and are more use to the Navy with a working brain than without, plus you're 'bout as dinged up as that ship is. Look at your shoulder."

If I could have turned my head, I would have seen the bandages soaking up blood and ooze covering my right shoulder and bicep. The rest of me was pretty badly scratched with a couple second-degree burns for good measure. Dinged up indeed, but I was given pain medication and was happy to be alive. Doctor's orders, two weeks off for me at 118th General, a US Army military hospital in Australia. My first duty was to write a letter to my wife. The only other chore I could do was start on the memoirs of my life since we got married in 1940.

I thought to myself, *with hardly any schooling, bad handwriting and no idea how to write a story like* Gone with the Wind, *who would print it?* I settled with the knowledge these memoirs would be only for us. Hell, first I had to survive, as the Russians called it, "The Sacred War."

A Sailor's Life

Up until 1932, life was plain hard physical work, low pay, and thankless employers. But that all changed when I joined the US Navy. I hoped to never see the windswept plains of Nebraska again, trading what I knew for the windswept oceans in almost every corner of the world.

Peacetime Navy life was easy, only training and no wars. Rate came quickly in the thirties and soon I was a First Class Boatswains Mate. My ships, up until then, were Great War destroyers, oilers and harbor tugs. Then with the smell of war with Japan and Germany in the air, I received orders to board the *USS Pennsylvania*, a first class battleship. On this ship, it was strictly by the book. If you messed up, you were on a "slow boat to China." By 1939, the war was well underway in the Far East and Europe. The USA knew it was only a matter of time until we became involved. The Japanese were everywhere. The Imperial Japanese Navy didn't seem to care that our fleet was there. The sailing was quiet. We had liberty in Australia, New Zealand and some islands. But something did not feel right. Soon we would know why.

The year 1940 started off a very interesting year. I came down with the mumps. I ended up at Naval Hospital Pearl Harbor while my ship sat in harbor. My three-week stay in isolation was more a pain in the ass than the pain in me. After discharge, I transferred to a job in stores, which is warehousing in civilian life. I didn't know it at the time, but I would never serve on a battleship again. At the time, it was nice duty and a break from shipboard living. We could go out at night to the clubs and movies.

I made Chief Petty Officer in January 1940. The money became much better and the benefits better too. Sea duty for Chiefs could be lesser of a required duty too. That would make it nice for a married man. All I had to do was to find a nice woman and settle down. Hawaii's tourism was big even back then. With perfect beaches, it was not hard to find the right beach, just the right girl. Honolulu was packed with tourists in the winter of 1940. The main island was filled with sailors, which could make the hunt more difficult! Nice girls were leery of sailors, marines, soldiers, and their intentions. However, I was determined to find a mate and settle down to start a new chapter in my life.

Did you ever see a dream walking . . . well I did!

One day in February, I took a ride from East Loch to Honolulu to get away from the base. After about an hour in the sun, I headed up to the bar for a beer. There I saw a group of girls laughing it up. One in particular caught my eye, a pretty woman with bushy brown hair and intriguing green eyes. She was kind of on the skinny side though. Let me put it this way . . . she was pretty, though different. Yes, different is the word and I wanted to meet this girl! I took a deep breath and went for it. I saw her move to the bar to order a drink so I moved in and said hi. To my surprise, she said hi also and we began a conversation the lasted two hours!

Understand I was scared to death of women. I never had the chance to meet decent women because I was in the Navy. In addition, I was not good at talking jive. This boy was a plainspoken Nebraskan.

"Nice day for the beach," I said as I slipped in next to her, unable to think of anything more clever.

"Hello, yeah it sure is. We do not have weather like this in Minnesota, especially in February." She didn't miss a beat, her charm carrying the conversation enough for both of us.

"I haven't been in cold weather since 1936. Don't even own a P-coat."

"A P-coat? Pardon?"

"A winter coat for sailors. May I ask your name?"

"My name is Mystic Bay . . . and yours?"

"Mine is Ethan Allen Vanderbilt, I'm in the Navy stationed here in Pearl."

"Wow that is neat, are you an officer or a pilot or in submarines?"

"No, I'm a Chief Petty Officer which is an enlisted rank. No subs for this sailor, I hate 'em! Are you still living in Minnesota?"

"Indeed I am, Duluth, way up north. You hate subs, I hate Duluth."

"You don't mind me talking to you, do you?"

"Heavens no, let me finish my drink and let's take a walk down the beach . . . if you want too?"

"Say the word Mystic."

"Ethan, my close friends call me Missy, so call me Missy."

The name Mystic fit her well. She was a little aloof and mysterious in a way. However, she seemed genuinely interested in what I had to say and made me feel very at ease. Missy had an enchanting charisma.

She was on vacation with three other teachers, all looking for jobs. All from Duluth, two were Scandinavian in appearance. The other girl wore wire-rimmed glasses, was knock kneed—an intellectual type. Missy was twenty-two and had never even been out of the state until now. They would be here for two weeks. After our walk, I asked her out for an evening in Honolulu. I was hooked.

We went out as much as possible. We seemed to both have eyes for each other, but I was having mixed feelings. Something big was on the horizon because every chief I spoke to coming off sea duty said the Japanese where thick as fleas. More serious reports were coming from the Royal Navy and the Dutch. I wondered if Missy and I should get involved in these uncertain times. Before she left for home, Missy needed to know how I felt. I hoped she felt the same way for me. There was only one way to find out. She wasn't a hard person to talk to so I felt like letting her know would be easy. Otherwise it would be an opportunity lost.

Once we were alone, we started talking. I liked her and she seemed to like me. I asked if we could be pen pals and write to each other. Missy had her address in my hand in seconds. I suggested that if this went well maybe I could come for a visit to her home.

"Oh, Ethan that would be so wonderful, but do you think that could really happen? Duluth is so far and expensive to travel to."

"Missy, I got a feeling it has to happen. Let me work on it. I can let you know before you leave."

Being a career Navy I had accumulated some money because I didn't spend it on the things lonely sailors do. Leave time was also in the bank. We decided that around June 15, 1940, I would take a leave and head to Minnesota for a visit.

The time came for Missy Bay and her gang to head back. Two weeks can feel like months and like minutes in the same quick moment when the time has finally passed. I felt so close to her, and yet it all happened so quickly. All of us went out together. When it was time to say goodnight, Missy gave her friends the high sign to leave.

"I'm going to miss you," I said. "Seeing you again really isn't that far off."

"I will miss you too . . . Your right, June will come fast."

"Missy, you have a cute smile and giggle. May I kiss you goodnight and goodbye?"

"Ethan, you sure can," She hesitated, as if waiting for her blush to fully blossom. "But not for goodbye, just goodnight. Goodbyes are sometimes forever and I hope that never happens."

"Ok, goodnight then."

"Gosh, you kiss really well! I was beginning to wonder if you would ever kiss me Ethan."

"You kiss nice too. Sorry if I kept you in the dark. This is new to me since I have spent a lot of time at sea. Being a sailor, I want you to know I wasn't the type your mom warned you about."

"Ethan, from the first moment we met, I knew you were an okay guy. I might as well have been living in a convent too, dating seemed never to have cross my path much, believe me I understand about being . . . shy"

"I wouldn't know why, you're not hard to look at and have a personality to go along with it." I was so nervous, I tried to stay light-hearted and smiled but wished I could just stop talking and kiss her again.

"You are so sweet to say that, Ethan. Is your eyesight good?"

"Missy my eyes are fine. Wanna stay up all night and watch the sun come up together?"

"Yes, honey, but remember . . . some things can't happen till later. I feel very strongly about that. It's just the way things are. Suppose I fall asleep?"

"I would never push you like that."

"Gosh, that would be so romantic to be in your arms. Now let's sit on this bench and watch that sun rise together. Ethan, if I do fall asleep . . . can I rest my head on your lap?"

"Sure! Oh by the way did you say 'honey,' Missy?"

"Yes, 'honey' is what I said, honey." She flashed me that smile I was already falling in love with.

"Sweetheart, that is music to my big ears."

"Ethan, your ears aren't big but I think you heart is."

My heart was getting very fond of her. The morning of February 18, 1940 came and they headed home.

Back to work sailor!

My new duty was to go out on different ships and evaluate how ready the deck divisions were for war. They were not! The brass was not buying it. That was a bad sign because Navy Chiefs have always been looked as a group that had seen it all and done it all. Most of the Chiefs and Warrant Officers agreed that if something were to happen the services would be in trouble.

Getting into my new job was easy. Eight to five, no weekends or watch duties. *A nice set-up for a cute woman to come home to*, I thought as I made my rounds. Letters from Missy started coming in soon after she got back and mine were getting to her. They were all about us plus small talk. We both knew what the underlying topic really was, but nothing too mushy should be said until I visited. I kept all of the letters she wrote to me. The first one was so exciting to read!

Hello Ethan, Our trip back was nice with calm seas and a nice train ride too. We got home one day early due to good sailing. I told my family and friends all about you and that you will come for a visit. They saw the pictures of us saying what a cutie you are! Mama said you remind her of Joel McCrea! When you get here, I will show you Duluth . . . that will take ten minutes. I have no idea what to do with the rest of your visit. We will think of something I am sure. I hope you really come to visit. I hope you do not mind, I miss you. Be safe and see you soon, very fondly Missy Xoxoxo, sure could use one!

I sure could use a kiss too. Me look like Joel McCrea?

Minnesota Bound

June was coming at a very slow pace. I was making plans for my trip to the States. Part of the trip would be a free ride on the *USS Indianapolis*, a light cruiser that a few years later would represent one of the most tragic events in Naval history. The rest of the trip would be by rail. Until then it would be all work and a lot of daydreaming about her.

Missy said that life for her was good. She liked teaching and going out with her friends. She lived at home with her parents, two sisters and one brother. Her dad was a loader at the docks in Duluth. It was a lake port for iron ore from the Misabe Range in northern Minnesota. Iron ore would be loaded on boats, which would go to places like Cleveland, Chicago and Ashtabula to get iron to steel mills in the US. They sounded like a normal American family. From what I gathered, more upper middle class. Missy was the eldest, her brother being twenty and sisters eighteen and sixteen. In her letters, she said her parents were excited about her meeting me. Perhaps they were quietly hopeful for one chick to leave the nest.

Finally, June, 1940 was getting close and I was getting anxious to get on the Indy to head for the States. Our letters were showing more signs of a desire of being together forever.

The last letter I received from her sounded like either a confession or a warning.

My Dear Ethan, I need to write this letter before you begin your journey to Duluth. There are things you need to know about me. No, I am not an ex jailbird or a hussy. I do have some emotional problems. I have always been the nervous type . . . no, let us call it high strung. I am somewhat hung on fashion, though I buy only items on sale. Never pay retail I say! I suppose too, I have this view that everything should be perfect with no need for much change or interruption. I dream of being married someday, children and with a husband that I can love forever. Yes, I am a bit selfish. When I was little I was a brat. I have grown up a lot though.

In addition, I know I lack certain attributes many women have. I realize I am not a raving Hollywood beauty, but I try to make up for it in other ways. No Ethan, I am not trying to pull compliments out of you! You, on the other hand, are a very handsome man. Yes honey, I am somewhat insecure, however I am working on that.

Ethan, think these things over. I know what kind of man you are. You are levelheaded, a kind and tender soul. We are different. We come from opposite cultures. I came from money and you came from a tough life. However, I could care less about that. I believe all mankind where created equal, I do not judge by what you have or do not have.

So, with that said, if you decide this is not for you, please let me know. I will understand. Missy.

Does this woman think I cannot see some of this? I telegrammed her simply saying, "See you soon!"

On June 15, 1940, I boarded the Indy. The ship was a beauty, sleek in design and armed like a real warship. It was air-conditioned, which was rare back then. We left Pearl right on schedule steaming at about eighteen knots. That would put us in San Francisco in three days. The weather was nice and the sea calm.

In three days, we were there and as usual, the bay was foggy, cold and gloomy. We tied up around seven a.m. We were off the ship at ten a.m. I headed up to the train station. I booked a Pullman for Lincoln. I had not seen them in ages.

My parents were in their early fifties, hard working but poor. My siblings had run upon some bad luck. My sister had polio and was on crutches. She was married with two kids and a bum for a husband. My two brothers were farmers both in their twenties. They too were poor and old looking for their age.

We all met in Lincoln. It was nice to see them. The truth is, I was not close to my family. Things had happened between us years back. Truthfully, most of it was my stubbornness. I held things against them that should have been water over the bridge.

My visit had loosened us up some. It took more than two days to iron out things completely.

The train took me from Lincoln to Minneapolis, then I boarded a local to Duluth. I arrived on June 23. Most of the ride out through there looked like Nebraska with plains and some roll to the landscape. It was real farm and ranch country with no big towns. It was a nice change. Looking at the tropics can get old and the constant heat and humidity gets to you after a while. I sat back, relaxed, and enjoyed the ride. In the dining car you never got your own table so you sat with strangers. Some wanted to strike up conversation and others sat there and gave you the impression you were an intruder. One family I spoke to was heading home from St. Louis. They asked me about the Navy. We got on the subject of current events in the world.

"Do you think the USA will get involved in the war?" one of them asked lightly, making conversation.

"We will get involved in a war," I replied. The parents looked at me like I was nuts.

"FDR will keep us out of it at any price." I looked up and saw their faces were no longer interested but concerned, and I thought it best to step back before my honesty got them worked up.

"I hope you're right." I paid my tab and went back to my room. *Why scare them*, I thought. If war came, their boys might be drafted.

The train arrived on time. I had a three-hour wait until the Duluth local would leave and then a three-hour ride. This journey seemed like it would never end. I walked around town and bought some civilian clothes. I wanted to pick something out for Missy. I never had bought any woman a present. I asked the sales lady for help. A sales girl suggested a pair of the latest style sunglasses.

Two p.m. came with about sixty people on a train that looked like it had seen better days. The ride up was slow with the smokiest steam engine. There were some kids on the train asking if I was an admiral.

"No, I'm a Chief."

"What's a chief?" they asked, looking up at me.

"Kids, he and others like him are the ones that run the Navy," their dad said.

"Sounds like you know about the Navy," I said with a smile I couldn't suppress.

"Yeah, my youngest brother was on the cruiser USS Houston steaming in the Far East." I told him I know the ship well and voiced concern of being in that area. He said his brother told him that a war would break out sooner than later. I shook my head and agreed. Some nut turned around and said war is wrong.

"No shit," I said, "tell it to the Japs and Nazis." I thought to myself, *What a yoyo*. The train kept chugging along making mail and passenger stops in every town along the way. At five p.m., the conductor announced Duluth was the next stop. My heart stopped. I said a prayer and prepared for the big moment.

As the train pulled into the station it seemed like forever to reach the passenger detrain area. I could not see who was outside waiting for the trains. So getting off was the only thing to do. As I got off, Missy stuck out as a spotlight pointed on her dressed like a movie star, all smiles with a beret and a pair of sunglasses, like the kind I bought! The uncertain feeling in my stomach went away. We embraced, kissed, hugged and kissed again. The last kiss took so long that we probably broke a Duluth Blue law! We looked into each other's eyes, smiled, and started to walk away holding hands. Missy said her car was just outside the station.

"You have your own car?"

"Yes I do," she said proudly.

This was no usual woman of the Forties. A car was almost unheard of at the tail end of the Depression for anybody to own. It was no heap either! This was 1940 Ford Coupe! We got in and drove off. It was warm inside the car though not due to the summer heat.

"Why don't I find a place to stay tonight before everything fills up," I said, trying to get logistics out of the way.

"You're staying at our house."

"With a brother and two sisters plus you and the parents? That's a full house, a whole deck of cards!"

"We have plenty of room," she said easily. I couldn't imagine that to be the truth but didn't want to interfere with her family's hospitality. We could work on arrangements after introductions.

As we approached the house I realized she'd proven me wrong. This house was huge, a Victorian home with steeples and all the gingerbread a home could have. As we pulled into the driveway, the whole neighborhood must have known I was coming.

"What's with all the people?" I said.

"You're kind of like a movie star right now." Her sisters were nice as well and cute like her but very Swedish looking with blonde hair and blue eyes. Their names were Eira, which in Norse means the Goddess of Healing. Idonea meaning was, "to renew nature." The brother, Thomas, was a merchant ore boat assistant engineer. He was on an ore run from Duluth to Ashtabula, Ohio and would be gone until August. After introductions, we all sat down for dinner. They asked about my life. Questioning did not seem like a litmus test. They seemed interested in me. What a relief!

Missy's dad, David, was more than a loader. He was the boss and no doubt made decent money. Missy's mom, Annikin, was the one that gave the younger girls their Swedish looks. She had a slight accent, was very attractive and a good dresser. I soon realized who had a hand in that! Annikin, however, was a very talented person in music and writing. Annikin is Scandinavian for grace and she was that indeed.

About eight, we took a drive to the lake. We sat and talked about everything.

That night it was hard to fall asleep because a million things were going through my mind. Remembering Missy's soft lips and the smell of her perfume with her so very cute giggle . . . I knew what I had to do next. I had only three weeks left to do it in!

About eight a.m., Missy came in and said time to get moving. I got up for breakfast and coffee with her Mom and had fun talking.

"Do you wanna go for a drive?" Missy asked once we were all satisfied with breakfast and conversation. "I'll show you where my dad works."

I suppose we kissed at every stop sign. It is a wonder we did not wreck! After a short drive, we entered the marine terminal. The place had huge piles of ore, big loaders, and ten or more lake boats. We left around noon and headed over to Superior, Wisconsin to a store that sold women shoes.

I asked Missy if she is a shoe nut. She replied, "Want me to look nice don't you."

"How are we going to get all of your shoes to Hawaii?" I said before I could stop myself.

"What?" It was the first time I'd made her speechless. We were both dumbfounded. Talk about putting your foot in your mouth! You could have heard a pin drop and probably my heart pounding from embarrassment.

Just Ask Her

We drove around in circles and finally looked at each other smiling. I suggested we go dancing. We ate out at a good restaurant. Around nine, we hit the floor dancing to all the fast swing stuff. Missy was a real trouper. Then the pace slowed down. It was time for all the men to fill their girls' ears full of sweet nothings. Well, that is what I wanted to do . . . I froze up.

We left around eleven pm with me asking, "Do you have a curfew?"

"EA, I'm twenty-two, we've got all night."

That's great, I thought, *what I want to say might take all night!*

"Lets take a walk on Lake Superior," she said suddenly, filling the void in conversation. We walked for about a half-hour and I saw a big boulder on the beach. I picked her up, putting her on the rock. Then we kissed.

"Are you having fun on your leave?" Missy asked.

"This is like being in heaven; I wish it would never end."

"Me too, Chief. Yes, this is the way life should be."

"Missy, do you want to go back to Hawaii someday?"

"Yes I would love too. It is so beautiful and romantic. Do you miss Hawaii, Ethan?"

"No . . . no, not really. I mean, it's nice, yeah." I knew I was stumbling and took a deep breath to get my thoughts together. "Listen, if I go back without you it will not matter where my home is. You know I love you. I am crazy about you."

"I love you with all my heart too. I think about you day and night."

"Well here goes, Missy will you marry me and go back to Hawaii with me?"

"Oh Ethan, yes, I would love to marry you. I might cry I'm so happy!"

"Please don't, I haven't been around many crying women."

"Can't help it Ethan. I am just so happy. One question . . . can I bring all of my shoes to Hawaii?"

"You better . . . There are no shoe stores in Hawaii cause everyone goes barefooted."

"You've got to be kidding me. You are kidding me, I saw no barefoot people there except at the beach."

"Bring your shoes just in case, shoe girl."

"Chief Vanderbilt, I am on to you!"

We went home and said good night. Tomorrow we would break the news to the family, which was perfect because all would be there. We were sure everyone would be happy for us. The next day Missy and I went off and started to make plans. The thing that needed to get first was book the church. Early summer is a big time for weddings. Missy was Lutheran, as was most of Minnesota. I was, well, not much of anything. The pastor was a man in his fifties and knew the family well. We met and he said with a big smile,

"I will get you married next weekend, by hook or crook."

I asked Missy if someone could get a wedding planned that soon.

"You betcha, Sailor!" she said. Nothing was stopping her. I asked her to get me to a Western Union. I would telegram to Naval housing to get a place for us to live.

"Missy, this place where we'll live won't be what you're used to but it will be good enough for now."

"Who cares? As long as there are no rats and the roof doesn't leak."

"I can't promise that!"

At dinner, we all sat down except for Missy. She made her grand entrance in a stunning dress. She looked like a movie star. At dinner, we all talked about everything under the sun. That was good because it made me surer that not only Missy was the one for me but the family too. These were genuine good earthy people. I felt that I belonged somewhere for the first time in my life.

"There is something I want to tell you," she said, suddenly standing. "I want all of you to know that Ethan and I are getting married. We want your blessing on this."

"Good, I like this guy, treat him right, Daughter. Ethan, welcome to the family, hope you like dress shops, shoe stores and hair salons."

"Ethan my Dad is only joking."

"No, he's not. But that's okay, I love you anyway."

"Oh, this is great! When and where for the wedding?" her Mama asked.

"Mom, it needs to be next weekend or time will run out for us."

The sisters giggled and the grandmas became very quiet and her dad looked at the floor.

"Why? Oh, honey, don't tell me," Annikin said softly.

"No, no Mama I'm not in trouble. He has only so much time left on leave so we need to get married. We will be living in Hawaii."

"I know, we are very happy. Ethan, welcome to our family! We will do everything to give you two a nice wedding. I think now I will just cry a bit if you don't mind."

"Annakin," Missy's dad said with a laugh, "you cry over everything including movies and those sad sack radio shows."

"David, our Missy is getting married and I thought this would never happen, I am so excited!"

"Thanks Mama, you sound like no one would ever want me!"

"Missy, no drama. That is not what I meant. Sometimes, though, you are so . . . Oh, never mind, this is so wonderful!"

Her sisters wanted to see her engagement ring. Did I forget something?

We went on the porch and decided Saturday her Mom and sisters would go into town to choose a wedding dress. Her Dad and I would kick back and shoot the bull.

The girls came home near dinnertime looking beat. How does one get tired over shopping? I say, pick the damn dress out, pay for it and head home!

Then, as it got dark, I said maybe we should turn in for the night. We lovingly looked at each other deciding a while longer on the porch glider wouldn't hurt. We talked about how fun it would be to live on an island paradise like Hawaii.

"How do you feel about having children, Ethan?"

"Sure, I want kids. That is one big reason for marrying you."

"That's one reason I want to marry you too. When?"

"When what, Missy?"

"When do you want to start a family?"

"I don't know how about in 1960. Honestly kids do scare me."

"Ethan they are like us only smaller. We have time so we can only enjoy each other for now. Sweetie . . . in 1960 I will be forty-two and too old for babies."

"Yeah, I see your point. Let's take one step at a time."

The next day we picked out an engagement ring and wedding ring. I guess when I asked her to marry her I was supposed to offer her one. I blew that one for sure! She took it in stride with us having a good laugh over it, but seconds later her cheeks were damp with tears.

"What's with all the teary eyes, sweetie?"

"I'm happy and never thought this moment would come for me. You're my dream come true. I love you, darling."

"This is so unbelievable for me too. I thought I would end up lonely or just a drunk with no purpose. You are my dream come true also." I glanced down at the case and blurted out, "These rings are expensive!"

"Ethan twenty five dollars is cheap for a rock like that. You're so funny the way you phrase things like 'lonely or just a drunk with no purpose,' you should write poetry."

"Me, write, yeah that would be nice."

"Now for our song at the reception, what would you like to be played?"

"I am not much on music though one song comes to mind "Always." We danced to it the other night."

"Ethan you romantic devil I love that song. 'Always' it will be! Gosh, I can't wait for you to hold me and dance to it at the wedding."

"Always, as in always, Missy?"

"Yes, Ethan, always and even longer."

The next night we were sitting on the porch talking and, of course, necking. I was in a fog.

"What's the matter, EA?"

"Nothing. In some deep thought."

"You're not getting cold feet are you? You could run, and then again look what you would be missing. Never mind, don't answer that!"

"No, not at all. I know what I would be missing. With this world in such upheaval like in Europe and the Far East, it is so hard to know what is going to change next. The world is a scary place right now. This is a bad time to fall in love."

"Ethan, the world is always changing and we will change too so whatever happens, happens. Think positive and hope there's no war. My parents fell in love during bad times and I suppose yours did too."

"Okay, honey, let's go inside and see what Friday brings. From now on, I'm going to be optimistic like you. You have an optimistic spirit that I don't seem to have."

Our wedding night was at Duluth's finest hotel, the Spaulding. My family wanted to come for the wedding but said it just wasn't possible. Truthfully, money was the issue. My sister really wanted to come. With two kids and a bum for a husband this wasn't possible either. My brothers were both farmers. This was the season to plant, bale hay and bring in winter wheat. I really wished someone could be here.

Since we were moving to Hawaii after the wedding, we went to the train station the day before to pick up all the tickets we needed so we could be sure we had seats. As we were headed to leave back to Missy's house, she suggested we watch the trains for a while. A freight rolled by with two steam engines on the front and one on back. The local came in from Minneapolis and started to unload passengers. There was a tap on my shoulder and to my surprise it was my sister Amelia, her two boys and her husband, Burton.

"What the heck are you doing here? Burton, you don't smell like Carling, what's up?"

"He's been sober for three years and is a conductor on the C B & Q Railroad!" Emily said, visibly angry. "Ethan, if you ever gave us an address to send you a letter we could tell you all of this."

"Ok Sister, I get the point. Hey Burton, sorry about that. Congratulations, I really am happy for you. I knew you had it in you!"

"That's okay, EA. I can't blame you for looking at me as a piece of worthless crap. I am going to show Amelia and the kids I can do it."

Missy had tears in her eyes and said, "Turn around, Ethan."

"Dad, Mom what are you doing here? How did you get here? I mean you are still poor . . . .

"Yes Son we are still poor prairie dogs. This is your wedding, Son. We would not miss this for the world. It's almost a miracle you're settling down."

"Mom, Dad, meet Missy Bay. Missy these are my parents Delores and Jackson Vanderbilt."

"It is a pleasure to meet you. We can tell by the look in your eyes for each other this is a good match," my dad said.

"Thank you both, you have quite a son. I love him dearly. Even more now that you'll be a part of our wedding day. Tonight at dinner, you'll meet my family. They are plain, down to earth people. You'll have a great time."

Missy and Emily were talking off to the side. She was having a good time with her and especially the kids. You could tell that my wife-to-be was mother material. I could see now that children would come sooner than later.

We got them cabs to the hotel and told them when to be at the house for dinner. On the way home, I asked Missy if she had anything to do with this.

"Only heaven knows, sweetheart."

There was a huge crowd at the house and everyone was getting along great. Missy's brother Thomas arrived earlier than expected. We hit it off real well. The Swedish grandmother, Anna got out the homemade glogg, which is Swedish wine. Missy was her favorite granddaughter. Anna was a very loving and fun Grandma. Her Grandmother on her Dad's side brought the gin. Victoria was British. By eleven pm, everyone was sailing. Our families bonded well.

"Honey, I know you told me once before . . . what does Mystic really mean anyway?"

"The name "Mystic" means 'of spiritual ability' or a changeling, like a shaman."

"A changeling, shaman, never heard of that in my life. I got no idea what you're talking 'bout but you're drunk. Do shamans cast spells?"

"Yes they do, here kiss me and when the sun rises you'll forget what even happened tonight."

"Wow, what a kiss! I am in a spell now! We had better call it a night or something might happen that shouldn't. If something did happen, I would remember. I'll bet you are the best . . . ."

"Okay, sailor boy, I hear you." Let's go to our rooms before we have our wedding night in the tomato garden, okay?"

"I don't see a tomato garden anywhere. As matter of fact I see only hot peppers."

"Ethan, yes . . . hot peppers like you! Now help me up the porch. Before we go in give me a kiss like we just had . . . Oh jeepers!"

Our Day

Saturday June 29, 1940, our day had come. The weather was warm, sunny and a good feel in the air. The service was at one p.m., which was good since I had some time to spend with my family. We had a nice visit and spoke of keeping in better contact. I was very curious how they came up with the money to get here.

"Dad, you said that with work and money it wouldn't be possible."

"We received a telegram that gave us instructions with the how's and what's. So that's about it, Son."

"And you paid for it?"

"No, your Bride, son, and what an angel she is. We'll pay 'er back. I wouldn't've taken it but we really had to be here for this moment. The truth is, Missy wouldn't take no for an answer."

"Missy's a great girl," my mother chimed in. "We all just love her. She is different in a way that I can't put into words, if you catch me."

"Yeah, Mom, I can't even explain it."

A message was at the desk saying to call Thomas, Missy's brother. He called me to let me know he wanted to pick me up and drive me to the church. Then it dawned on me—I needed a best man!

"Thomas, would you like to be my best man?"

"Sure. I'd be honored . . . This isn't the best suit in the world."

"Who cares? You're fine . . . She'll get a kick out of this."

It was time for the big moment. The wedding music began. Missy appeared in a wedding dress that looked as it was made only for her. She came to my side . . . we looked at each other and I knew without any doubt this was the one.

The pastor began the service. I am not even sure I heard one word!

Before I knew it, we were husband and wife. Gosh, it did not take long. The pastor said, "You may now kiss your Bride." That is exactly what we did and with me looking at the happiest pretty face I ever laid eyes on. We turned to the congregation and began our walk to the back of the church for the reception line.

After that, we got into her Ford that was driven by her brother and his new girlfriend, Allison. We headed to the Hotel Holland for the luncheon.

"Hey Ethan, she's all yours!" Thomas yelled.

Missy gave both of them the evil eye.

"Mrs. Vanderbilt, I will make him behave. I know how."

"Thomas, do what Allison says and I mean it!"

"Hey Sister, because you married doesn't mean the world has to stop."

"All right you two. Let's be nice and let the new couple have their day."

"Thank you Allison, I appreciate that."

We arrived at the Holland on time. I thought those two would be the next couple to get married one way or another. I was learning fast that these North Country girls all had a wild streak in them. My girl was no exception except she had to have a twenty-five dollar ring first!

"Ethan, Allison looks like trouble to me even though she settled Thomas down. I still have my reservations."

"Honey, go easy on the girl. She might be a nice person. You did say women should let their hair down, right?"

"Yes, she seems quick to let more than just her hair down. I think she is a loose woman. Superior Wisconsin women are like that I have heard."

"So, they're adults too, you know. What the hell does Wisconsin have to do with it?"

"You'll learn soon that Thomas is a nice guy but it is all about what he wants. He is a wild one and a sex maniac!"

"Missy, everybody is that way at times. Sex maniac, I haven't heard that term since my ship landed in a French colony warning us of French women giving the itches."

My wife just smiled and shook her head.

About thirty people waited for us at the hotel. The little band played "Always." It was a sweet moment for us. Missy sang the words in my ear. Wow, was it a turn on! I can still hear the words and feel her warm breath in my ear. After the lunch, we visited the grandparents. They gave Missy some family dowry and of course, advice on marriage.

The Beautiful Mistake

    I had to get my parents on the five p.m. train. We met at the station saying our goodbyes. You could tell they had fallen in love my wife. My Dad told me what an angel she was. He knew and I knew what might happen, meaning a war was coming. He was truly worried. Finally, it was train time, the whole clan got on board, and the train pulled out of Duluth. I felt my relationship with my family would change for the better soon.

    We still had a lot of time until sun down. Wedding pictures were at a pretty spot by the lake. After that the goofing around began. We all played tag, threw rocks in the lake, and chased seagulls. It was funny to see all these dressed up people acting like little kids . . . especially Missy in that wedding dress. Then we settled down, made a little campfire and talked.

    "That fire gettin' too hot for ya, EA?" one of the boys asked.

    "No, I'm fine, thanks." I knew what he was getting at but played it off.

    "I know where one fire is real hot," Thomas said like a true little brother.

    Missy, always with a good comeback, said, "Don't worry Thomas . . . I know how to put it out!"

    The girls blushed. The boys all wished they were in my shoes! When no one was looking, we bailed out.

    We hopped in her Ford and headed towards the hotel. Things were different. The woman next to me was now my wife. For the first time in my life, I was responsible for someone other than myself.

    "Are you nervous about tonight, Mrs. Vanderbilt?"

    "Yes, a little, honey, I am. Tonight will be wonderful."

    As we pulled into the parking lot, we stopped, set the brake, and looked into each other's eyes. We kissed. I asked, "Missy . . . ready?"

    "Yes Ethan, I am."

    We entered the beautiful old style hotel with plush carpets and paintings. Missy and I walked around sightseeing while the bellhop delivered our luggage to our room. We took the lift up to the top floor, which seemed to be empty. I unlocked the door. With a soft light, the room with its rich furnishings left us speechless.

    "This bed is huge, "Missy said, gawking at it. "We could get lost in it. Why are you snickering? Ethan, I must admit something. This might be amateur hour, if you know what I mean."

"Missy, you're just too cute for words. Relax. Your pale face is red as a turnip."

"I know my face does feel like it's on fire. Well heck, I am on fire! So what do we do next, Chief?"

"Could play checkers or monkey around. What do you want to do?"

"I always lose at checkers so let's try monkeying around."

"Missy, one question? Did your Mom say anything about tonight?"

"Sort of, nothing detailed, only love you with all my heart and understand a man's need for some things. I think she knows I know about whoopee."

"Whoopee? Did you take a course in college about whoopee?"

"No silly, but I wished they gave one. It would have been more interesting than dissecting a frog."

I hated, in a way, to see her take the wedding dress off because she looked so good in it. Missy put on a very beautiful nighty, then hid like a squirrel in a tree. I put on pajamas, for the first time ever! This is the way we dreamed our first night together would be. My Bride was radiant! We talked, kissed getting closer. We were now sitting on the edge of our bed. Then Missy broke out a peanut butter jar.

"Missy, what the hell is that?"

"Glogg, honey I need a . . ." Then I interrupted her, took her in my arms, and said, "Sweetheart . . . we need only each other tonight . . . not glogg or anything else."

The Train Trip

The next morning we woke up knowing we needed to get moving to make the train at noon for Minneapolis.

Missy asked, "Gosh Ethan! Can't we just live here forever?"

"No but soon we'll be in Hawaii in our own bed. Where the days are warm and nights are balmy in a paradise for only the two of us."

Then something crossed my mind.

"Listen, I know we wanted to sneak out of town. Call your Mom and have her meet us downstairs as soon as possible."

"Okay I will, I feel better now about us leaving. My mama and I are very close. I know this is difficult for her."

"Missy, we now have a little more time for . . . you know . . . us."

"Darling, I know."

Train time was nearing. All of the farewell party crossed the street to the station. We were all quite nervous, I felt as if I was kidnapping their daughter and best friend.

"I knew this day would come and there will be tears but they want me to be happy and happy I am," Missy said when I told her how I felt.

The station announced the boarding call so we went to the platform and started saying goodbye to all. Mrs. Bay was really trying to hold back so I hugged her.

"Listen Annikin, your daughter is the best thing that has ever happened to me. I will love her, as she deserves. I promise she will be in good hands."

"I know, Ethan. We all love you so much. Go to Hawaii and have the time of your life. At times, you need extra patience with her. Missy is a wonderful warm woman but can be, let's just say, Missy."

"I know . . . we will do just fine. If she gets out of hand I'll send her back to you folks."

Then David interrupted, "No Ethan she's all yours so there is no giving her back now. Missy is a good kid, a little overboard on clothes and strange ideas at times but all sweet just the same. I am very proud of what she as accomplished. She deserves some real happiness. My little girl has had a few disappointments."

"I have found the right girl and I am ready for whatever she brings down the pike."

"Oh no, you're not, this kid is capable of anything!" David Bay replied.

"ALL ABOARD"! We boarded the five-coach local looking out the window. Missy had tears in her eyes. She held my hand. The old steamer pulled out slow with everyone waving. When the station became distant, we looked at each other. I kissed her on the forehead as she sunk into my arms and closed her eyes. This had been a busy two days for my sweet woman.

I guess we slept for about two hours. When we woke up, we felt paralyzed from sleeping in such an uncomfortable position. It took awhile to get feeling back into our bodies. The ride down was uneventful so we talked and let the cross ventilation keep us cool.

"How you feeling, wifey?" I asked.

"I'm happy, tired, and in love all at the same time. How about you?"

"You're next to me. It doesn't get much better than that."

The train whistle blew. We gave each other a big kiss. We walked to the lounge and ordered two root beers to wash the dirt down. We had a good time just being together. The train chugged along. Soon we were close to St. Paul. In two hours, we would begin the final leg to the West Coast.

Soon we boarded the streamliner for our trip to California.

"This is our home till Tuesday evening, and the room won't get any larger."

"It's perfect. Lay with me and let the train rock us to sleep."

The train pulled out of the station. We were on our way.

The next time I woke up it was daylight rolling through Wyoming. I left green eyes sleeping. About eight a.m., she found me in the lounge car. She was all smiles.

"Missy, are you ready for some breakfast?"

"I could eat everything in sight so let's go before it is all gone and coffee, gosh, I need that bad."

"Good, I will get you some, I like a coffee-drinking woman!"
"Suppose I didn't drink coffee, honey?"
"I would make an exception for you."

We proceeded to the dining car. While we ate, a nice couple in their sixties sat with us and we started talking. They were from Bedford, Pennsylvania. They were heading for San Francisco to say goodbye to their US Marine son, who was shipping out to Wake Island in the Pacific.

"Ethan, have you been there?" asked my wife.
"Oh yeah, I've been there several times."
"You look like newlyweds," the woman said.
"Yes ma'am we were married yesterday in Duluth, Minnesota. My husband is a Chief Petty Officer."
"Our son is a Sergeant and is making it a career with ten years in."
"I've been in eight and I will hang it up when I get twenty in. By then I will have given Uncle Sam all I can give."

The couple got on the subject of war. He asked what I thought about the chances of it happening. My answer was clear-cut: only the Germans and Japanese know.

"Let's just pray there isn't a war," Missy said, looking at me. The woman agreed and told us to enjoy our trip and have a wonderful life.

In the room, we got ready for bed and talked then lay down together in a bed barely made for one!

"Kinda cramped with the two of us, Mrs. Vanderbilt."
"Sure is!"

The *City of San Francisco* rolled across the darkened wasteland with that sound of the whistle blowing at crossings and the clickety-click of the track.

In the morning we should be beyond Salt Lake City being somewhere in Nevada. That meant we were on schedule.

"Hey, I have a question . . . How tall are you, anyway?"
"You don't know that after being with me."
"Well, honey, so much has been happening I just never gave it much thought, I know you're not as tall as me."
"Ethan, this is the last time I will ever give you my height or weight so pay attention, I am five feet, seven inches and about one hundred twenty pounds. You'll have to do the laundry to find out anything else."
"I already got the other stuff figured out. I never saw a woman eat so much and be so skinny. Wish I could."

"Ethan, I guess I will never be fat, though."

"Wouldn't matter, just don't stop ever being you."

While we were in the dining car, Missy started taking some stuff out of her purse.

"Sweetie, what's in the purse?"

"This money is for us when we get to Hawaii."

"How much is in there? It looks like a lot."

Missy gets close to me and tells me around five grand.

"Where did you get all of that kind of loot?"

"I saved some of it. When we're alone I'll tell you about my dowry."

"I have a dowry, too. It consists of the clothes on my back, a little cash . . . and you!"

When we arrived in San Francisco, there was time for us to have dinner where I could brief her on traveling on a tramp steamer.

"These ships aren't luxury liners. They are freighters with a few staterooms. Be careful what you do and always stay with me. Don't wear anything sexy because these ships are sometimes manned by bums. You need to keep a low profile."

"I don't dress too revealing, do I?"

"No, you dress great . . . Just stay near me on the ship."

Missy, Nazis, and Storms

We grabbed a cab and headed for the docks.

"This is a pretty good one by the looks of it," I said when we got to the ship. It was an old vessel with empty gun mounts. That told me this baby had been in "the war to end all wars." Missy got out of the cab first and the cat calling began. It soon quit when the first mate on board yelled at them, which happened to coincide with when I stepped out of the car.

"Gosh, what a reception, Ethan."

"Honey, this can't be the first time you ever got wooed at."

"Never like that. In fact, only time was with my sisters. That is who they were probably cat calling."

"Woman, you're too hard on yourself. Blondes are a dime a dozen, you are like a diamond, hard to find."

"Gosh, you should write romance novels."

We boarded and Captain Lewis Noble greeted us. A steward took our bags and showed us to our cabin. It was nice. Missy got her wish, a double bed plus a real shower.

"Sir, your wife's small trunks are aboard," the steward said, "should I send them up?"

"Please, I need some different clothes."

"Sure, we'll make you feel right at home, anything good in those trunks?"

"Maybe sailor man, but you'll have to wait till tonight after the lights go out."

The First Mate came up introducing himself. "My name is Ronald. We have tugs coming in soon so please stay on the vessel." Then the steward came by and said dinner was at six in the Captain's mess.

Missy asked, "What the heck is a mess?"

"That is where you eat, like in a dining room. It's sailor talk."

"Is a 'poop deck' what I think it is?" She flashed me that smile like the first time we met.

"Come on, Missy, I can see that I need to teach you Navy talk, a toilet is called a head."

"Oh, I see, Chief Vanderbilt . . . a head, why?"

"Ask an English sailor, they made up all this stuff."

It was time for dinner so we made our way to the Captains mess through the passageways and up one more flight of stairs.

It had typical décor for the officers of a vessel to have. The space had nice wood panels with trim, plus good cutlery silver and glassware. The table sat twenty. Number One, which is second in command, was at the head of the table while Captain Noble was preparing the ship to get underway. We all introduced each other and began eating with most of the conversation between him and me. Sea stories and general talk like that. There were two passengers in particular that listened but did not say much although I think their English was good. They left after dinner. I asked the officer where were they from. He said Germany, on their way to the Far East. He told me that the Captain had his suspicions about them.

We went for a little walk as the ship was getting underway. I explained what the deckhands were doing. We then returned to our cabin there was a knock at the door. It was the steward with a bottle of champagne, compliments of the Captain.

"Is this ship filled up with passengers?" I asked.

"No sir, it isn't. Several ships left earlier in the week and scooped up all of them so we are about one third full."

With Missy in the other room, I took the opportunity to get my 1911 Colt 45 caliber pistol out and check it out.

Missy came out of the room saying, "What the heck is that for, you going to get rid of me already?"

"No honey it is just in case of any trouble that's all."

"Trouble . . . what kind of trouble, Ethan?"

"Nothing a Bride should worry about."

We had a hot toddy and off to bed we went.

The next morning Missy and I went for breakfast and sat down with the Captain plus a few others. They left so we were in the company of the German couple. They introduced themselves as Stephan and Eva Heydrich, from Dresden.

The woman noticed the shiny new rings on our fingers and said in good English, "You are newlyweds, yes?"

Missy replied in German, *we are*.

"Honey, you speak German?"

"A little."

"A Swede that doesn't speak Swedish but speaks German. Gosh you're a strange one."

"I speak Swede a little but took German in college. Swede is almost like German. French is what I should have learned . . . It's a very romantic language. Who wouldn't want the language of love spoken in his ear? Know what I mean, Chief?"

"When we get to Pearl I will buy you book to learn French!"

"All right, I'll learn it just for you. I'm a fast learner."

"I can see that already, hot stuff!"

They talked while the old man and I spoke about different things though not the invasion of Eastern Europe. He seemed all right. The question I couldn't ask was why they were heading to the Far East while Germany was at war.

It took a total of six days to make the shores of the big island, which was a lot slower than when I came over. The second day was eating, relaxing and being together. We bumped into the German couple and talked over a few drinks, then got on some topics about things in general. Mr. Heydrich said one thing that made me wonder about him.

"You know Germany could never beat the Commonwealth Nations without the help from a nation of equal military power, if you know what I mean."

"And what nation might that be," I asked, a bit weary of the conversation we were entering.

"Oh, I have none in mind. Just making conversation."

"Well, since we're on the topic, why is Germany invading everyone in sight over in Europe?" My eyes met his and I took a sip of my gin and tonic.

"It's a short conflict," Mr. Heydrich said, "Just border protection is all. They'll pull back and leave in peace soon enough."

That sounded nice. I knew Germany never got over the Great War. I said goodnight and shook hands. We went back to our cabin. Missy said she needed to paint her toenails.

"Missy I would love to do that for you, may I?"

"Sure, you know how?" she laughed. "Who cares, just paint!"

I guess that's something girls like because before you know it . . . well, we were newlyweds! We skipped lunch.

When we woke up, I notice the ship was in rough seas. It was really raining and the sea was getting rough.

"Looks like a good storm coming."

"Ethan, this ship can't sink, right?"

"They can all sink but we'll be fine, this isn't a big storm."

"Looks big to me and I've seen some big waves on the Gitshgomee."

"It's a storm but not a typhoon or hurricane."

"Well, that makes me feel better . . . It's just a storm. I'm still not convinced."

We went to dinner then headed back to our cabin. We were sitting on the couch then fell asleep. Awhile later, we both fell off the couch. Missy then screamed. I told her we took a wave with a little roll. We got ready for bed but I told her to stay in her street clothes.

"Why, Ethan? And tell me the truth please 'cause I'm frightened, I can handle the truth."

"Listen darling you need to be dressed in case the Captain Noble wants us to move up a deck or two."

"EA, are we gonna drown?" she asked with tears in her eyes.

"No but I don't want you to have to move in your night gown with you hanging out in front of this motley crew."

"Okay but jeepers, don't leave my side, please. Let's pick out an outfit for me to wear in case we do sink. I want to look good when I wash up on shore."

"I thought you were a brave soul and can handle danger?"

"I'm too young to die! I'll wear this blue dress because it won't fade when soaked. Like these earrings? So how do I look for my upcoming drowning?"

"Missy, you are a real comedian. I am not going to leave you for a second. I'll get you a Mae West life jacket."

"Gosh I'll have big breasts for the first time in my life!"

"Jeepers Missy, just when I think I married a Puritan you say something like that."

We stayed in our cabin through the night and as the storm got worse, so did my wife's stomach. About one a.m. she let it go in the head with her own head over the toilet for a good while. I ribbed her about it but she started to cry so I let up.

"I'll go get some crackers and ginger ale for your stomach," I said in apology.

Ronald was up and said, "Hey Chief, what' ya need?"

"Ronald, I need some ginger ale and crackers for my wife, she's a fair weather sailor."

"Sure, I've been passing them out all night."

"Thanks sir and I'll see you in the morning . . . then maybe in five minutes."

Upon my return I found Missy sitting there looking pale. I had to force her to eat the "seasickness medicine." She started to feel better so I asked,

"Honey, wanna make love now?" Missy turned pale again and headed for the water closet. I headed back to the galley for more crackers. It was to be a long night with Miss Puke of 1940.

The next morning was a beautiful day. It was as if a storm had never happened. My sailor girl was back to normal. We ate breakfast and went out onto the upper deck to see any damage to the ship there may be. Number One was checking out the ship. He said the wireless was out and we had taken on water because of leaky hatches. They were pumping and all else seemed fine. This was our fourth day out and the storm did slow us down so I told Missy to figure three more days at sea.

Missy said, "Well that's okay, just no more storms."

"I think the storms are over with. We should have a pretty day when we arrive in Pearl."

The German couple was out on deck taking in the sun. We sat next to them in deck chairs and said hello. Missy and the Frauline talked. Mr. Heydrich and I started with some small talk then moved to what was really on my mind. The German asked me about my life up until now which seemed innocent enough to me. I asked about his. However, the one thing I really wanted to know was he a Nazi or were the two of them just running away from them.

"Mr. Heydrich, are you pro-Nazis or are you on the run?"

"My dear Chief, Hitler fooled a lot of my country but not all and not my Eva or I. To stay in Germany and stop this madness is only suicide for the underground. Please, dear comrade, I can trust you to keep this secret, we are on your side."

"Are there Gestapo on this ship?"

"No Chief, but in Hawaii that could be another question. This mission that I am on must succeed."

"I will protect your secret sir, but if you're lying I must do my duty and believe me I will."

"Vereinbart," he said. "I understand."

Missy said goodbye to Eva and we went for a walk. Captain Noble motioned us up to the bridge to give Missy a turn at the wheel. Sure was very cute to see her taking steerage commands keeping the ship on course. Captain Noble and I spoke of the German couple, "He seems harmless but let's still keep an eye on him."

After awhile my wife and I took a tour of the engine room. Chief Engineer McGrody and Missy hit it off good because Thomas did the same job on the lakes. Like most engine rooms, it was hot, humid with the smell of oil and grease.

"How does my brother do this for a living?"

"Well, honey, it is either sweat like you're in hell in the engine room or freeze your ass off topside."

"When you retire from the navy we've got to find you an inside job."

"Not me. The fresh air and freedom to move about, that's me."

We then headed to the stern and watched the turbulence of the propeller. My wife's long brown hair looked good blowing in the wind. She looked happy with that beautiful smile. A crewmember offered to take our picture if we had a camera. We did and it is one of the best pictures ever taken of us.

When dark came we went outside and saw a beautiful moon with the sky filled with a million stars. The night air was slightly breezy but warm. Missy had a pretty shawl wearing a nice white flowing dress. She was wearing the most intriguing perfume. Her long shiny brown hair whipped across my face. My wife was so enchanting standing there. Then by chance, we saw off in the distant a large flotilla of warships heading east.

"Are they ours, Ethan?"

"I think so, probably heading for servicing in the States."

"What needs servicing . . . the boats or the crew?"

"Missy, they're called ships not boats. Ships need serviced on occasion and the crew, well they always need that."

Missy laughed, "Read you loud and clear."

Captain Noble announced he estimated our arrival into Pearl around noon the next day. That made everyone happy from the steamship company down to passengers and crew. I knew my wife was happy, you could see it in her face.

The Captain gave us a good send off with good food and wine. Then we all sat down and watched the 1939 Thriller "Confessions of a Nazi Spy" with Edward G. Robinson and George Sanders. It was all about Nazi operatives working in the US. The Germans seemed amused by the movie.

The next morning, the coast was barely in sight but we would be in Pearl by noon as promised. Missy was so excited, she was packed before seven a.m.! My wife acted like a little kid on a Christmas morning. There was no stopping her on getting off this ship. We waited to dock, and sat out on the deck holding hands talking about how we were going to spend our lives together. We were full of beautiful dreams. I prayed some nut from the Rising Sun or Germany would not ruin it for us. It was something I wouldn't want to bet on though.

At eleven, we were in the harbor area of Pearl. We traveled at the speed of a snail to the docking area. Two tugs came out and helped the ship into the berth. When we got up to the dock, all the line handlers came out to begin tying up. Missy came out of the cabin all dolled up with those sunglasses on, a simple cute black beret, wearing a beige colored dress. She was eager to go!

At twelve thirty, passengers could disembark. I said good-bye to Captain Noble and Rodney. I wanted also to say goodbye to the Heydriches, however they just seemed to have disappeared. We never saw them again.

We grabbed a cab for the short ride to Navy housing to check to see what they had for us.

"Honey, ready to go home?" I said as we left the docks.

"Yes I'm ready; you and this moment are my dream come true."

"Me too and guess what: you're in the Navy, now."

In a few minutes, we would be at our new home. We looked at each other, smiled, squeezed each other's hands and headed to Naval Station Pearl Harbor on August 15, 1940. The only things on our minds were we. There was nothing on the horizon that was going to change that.

Navy life with a wife

We headed over to Naval Housing, headed by Chief Warrant Officer Lloyd Timken. Besides my best friend, he was the very best Navy diver the service had ever seen. Lloyd was a Naval Robin Hood.

"Hey, welcome home! Missy, nice to meet you. Anything you need, I can get it. Found you a great place. I think you will be surprised. Plus they left a brand new bed and some furniture."

"So what do I owe you, Lloyd?"

"Nothing. I'll make it up on the next inbound."

"Is this guy a con man?" Missy whispered in my ear when Lloyd turned to his desk for a moment. He sure talked like one, and I knew Lloyd would appreciate the funny remark.

"Now you're catching on, baby. You have just met the con man of all con men!"

"What kind of scam do you run, Ethan Allen?" she said, louder this time. "Something tells me you're the ringleader."

"Oh, I will tell you on our first anniversary."

"Okay EA, I'll remind you of that." Missy said with a curious look.

Timken handed us the keys, directions and a spare car so we headed to the place. The drive over to our home would not take long, though it sure did seem like it was a forever drive. Then we came the sign" Naval Housing next left" so we hung a left, drove three blocks turned right to 192 East Ninth Avenue.

Missy screamed with excitement, "Look that it, our place, it's beautiful! So cute, and with a yard too!"

"This is it and I must say Timken did a damn good job for us."

"You must thank him, Ethan, in some way like have him over for dinner when we get settled."

"Oh, believe me I will. He will bring the best steak you ever ate."

My wife smiled and looking the other way. I don't think she was impressed with Lloyd.

We went inside. The rooms were small as expected but clean and in good shape. The kitchen was adequate. I wondered if my new wife was a good cook. I sure as heck could not cook at all.

I asked my bride, "Do you know how to cook, sugar?"

"Of course I do. All of us girls had to learn. I can cook up some good stuff, just never expect any Scandinavian food. Way too fishy for me!"

"Good love, what's for dinner?"

"Tonight we are eating whatever the nearest restaurant has to offer."

I said let us make out a list of things we need, then head to the base store.

Before we left, Missy said she needed to use the bathroom. It was very small. Missy brought it to my attention that it had no door.

"Ethan, why do you think the bathroom has no door on it?"

"Gosh, I have no idea but I'll call housing. They will put one on after the weekend."

"Honey, I have to go . . . I need a door."

"Can you get by till Monday without the door?"

"I can't go without complete privacy, understand?"

'Yes dear, let me leave the house and you do your business,"

"EA, I can't even go with you outside so could you take the bedroom door off and put it on the bathroom hinge?"

"I have no tools but I'll try."

"One more thing; there is no toilet paper."

"Missy, I will change the door . . . get you a palm tree leaf and you will use it!"

"Yes Chief but a soft one please and hurry!"

While at the store I picked up some uniform items, I noticed the fashion queen looking the uniforms over, and I asked her, "What are you looking at?"

Missy asked, "Who wears blue jeans in the navy?"

"Those are enlisted men's work pants and they're called dungarees."

My wife raised those eyebrows and said, "They're cute . . . Nice material, too."

We then headed over to the beach where we first met. It was hard to believe we had come full circle in this relationship. I know men are supposed to be on the hard side of things but my wife was the love and hope of my life. I did feel awful about being in the service because there would be separation sometime in the future. How Missy would deal with that was an unknown. We stayed out late, danced, laughed, went back to our place and put the sheets on the bed.

"Ethan, before we go to sleep I need something."

"Anything you need so what is it?"

"Could you put the door back on our bedroom?"

"Why, and I can't wait to hear this."

"I like to sleep in complete darkness for a better night's rest."

"I hope you are kidding me."

Of course I am just kidding about the door. Bet you had second thoughts on marrying me, didn't you?"

"You're right about that, Mrs. Vanderbilt!"

"Okay , I am not some brat. Well maybe sometimes I am."

Susie homemaker was up early. She kept checking out the place, writing down things to do and things to get for the house.

"Hit the deck sailor," she said coming into the bedroom, "We got things to do."

"Now where did you learn that phrase 'hit the deck' I wonder? We need to get our own car because this one will have to go back soon. We also need to get that money in a bank!"

"OK Ethan, what kind you want to get Ford, Chevy, or Dodge?"

"No clue, I guess whatever we can afford or get here in Honolulu. I never owned one so it really does not matter. Cars can be hard to get here at times. My friend Lloyd might be able to help."

"Ford is my favorite but Desoto's are nice, especially for when kids come into the picture. Ethan, I like my cars bought on a lot and not hot, so keep Lloyd out of it. We will go into town and see what we can find. Let me change outfits and we will make it a day in the city. I'm dying to see the stores in Honolulu."

"Car shopping Missy, no ladies' stores just yet."

"Yes dear, first things first. But maybe one dress shop or two for a romantic night on the town, ok?" She paused just long enough to acknowledge my big eye-roll. "Honey, with some things I will pester until you go nuts. My Daddy always gave in just to shut me up. His last words before he walked me down the aisle were, 'Daughter this would be a good time for you to stop being a brat. You are not really a big brat . . . just a little bratty at times. So go easy on the poor guy.'"

"Gee, you sure did take his advice! Seriously, we need to get a bank account before you get that bundle of cash stolen. Then we look at cars and then . . . we can take care of you.'

Finding a car wasn't hard at all. We decided on a bright yellow two-door Studebaker. We even named it: "Yellow Baby."

Missy and I picked out a few more household items, then headed home to make the last two days of leave a continuation of our honeymoon. That next morning we packed a lunch, hopped in the Studebaker and drove up into the country. We saw the real beauty this island had to offer other. Hawaii is also more than just fancy hotels and hula girls. This island had mountains and deep valleys with lush forests, waterfalls and beauty unimaginable.

We hiked some, took a nap under a big tree with a mountain breeze. We stayed out all night sleeping on the ground getting away with things that could have gotten me a Captains Mast. We got home about eight p.m., dirty, hair a mess and happy as a dog with a new bone. Monday would start a new chapter in this life of the girl from Duluth with the loner who wasn't lonely anymore.

August 19, 1940 I reported to my old duty station Pearl Harbor to resume my duties at a deck and rigging warehouse. It was just down the way from battleship row.

Everyone was glad to see me and wanted to know about the new woman. It was good to be back. A wonderful woman to come home to at the end of the day made life complete. Missy had the car and she could keep very busy putting the fine touches on our home. Work at the base seemed to be in the groove that it had been when I left, slow and easy.

When I got home, all of the furniture (what little we had) was on the front lawn. Missy met me at the front door with a big kiss and that smile of hers and said, "Like the color Chief?"

"Yeah. honey, it is a nice shade of blue but why are you painting in your underwear?"

"I have no work clothes and I don't want to ruin a nice dress. Don't worry, honey, the curtains were closed."

"I figured that but I would have given you a hand painting."

"No problem! I like to paint and it's done now so let me get dinner finished and we'll eat."

"So, what are we eating? I smell chicken."

"Yes and I hope you like it dear."

"I will like whatever you do."

"Thank you, Ethan, I want to do the best I can for you."

Having fun . . . a lot of fun!

We had a staff meeting one day with some big boys. They wanted to get our opinion on whether our fleet was ready for a war. That was easy to answer: we were not. After the lunch, they informed us chiefs that we might be going to Warrant Officer School. That would be nice.

On my way home, I couldn't decide to tell of the possible jump in rank to her or tell her when it happened. I also was wondering what home project she got into today. When I arrived home, she was painting the bedroom.

"I went to Western Union," she said, "and sent grams to our families saying we arrived safely and were in our home."

"My family will be surprised to hear from me because I don't think I ever sent one to them."

"That doesn't surprise me. I saw a coldness you had with them in Duluth. Why? I don't see a reason you all are so distant. I want to know why because now they're my family too. Your love for me blooms if your love for others does too. This marriage is not about only our love. Understand, honey?"

"I think I understand what you mean. There is a distance between us, but I don't want to talk about it right now. In time, I will explain it. I love my family, but believe me, there are reasons."

"All right, I won't pry about it but it saddens me and I think it does you, too."

We went for a short drive up in the hills parking at a place where probably half of Hawaii conceived. I asked my wife about the money she had brought with her.

"Okay, my ancestors settled in the Duluth area, actually Virginia, Minnesota and soon got big in the iron ore business. They became very wealthy. My relatives made sure that all Swerhenger Brides would have a dowry when the time came. My Grandmothers from both sides of the family put a little more into the dowry. The money I left in Duluth is money I saved from teaching and summer jobs when school was out. I want what we put in the bank used for emergencies. I hope that we can let it grow to educate our children.

"That's good. I will put my money in our account too. It's not much but it is everything I have. Do you want to head home?" '

"Let's just sit here and, well you know."

"Neck in the Studebaker, sure that would be fine by me."

"Lovie, you ever made love in a car?"

"I already told you this is my first car ever."

"That is not what I asked you, sailor boy."

"Oh no, I'm not getting into that trap, lady. I know nothing of your past love life so let's just drop it."

"Ethan, you know darn well you were my first. I hope I was your first. Honey, for the excitement of it all let us do it in the Studebaker! This will be something we can talk about when we are old and wish we could! I want to do things wild while we have no kids. I want to be a little naughty. I'll bet everyone up here right now is so why shouldn't we."

"You're nuts! I hope we don't get caught or I will be a 1st Class Seaman again."

"I would have never married you if you didn't have first class seaman . . . get it? Here, put this on when the moment comes or should I say when we do."

"You're so churchy and proper sometimes, and then you say stuff like that! Where did you get a rubber?"

"Honey, the honeymoon is over, meaning I don't want babies right now. My grandmother gave it to me at my college graduation party. Ethan, I am a woman and will always act like one when I have too. Now with my husband, I am still a woman only moreso. As my Grandma said, 'Mystic, the Victorian age is long gone and thank God. So have some fun while you are young but just use this if the moment arrives.'"

"Your college graduation party, are you kidding? No more talking tonight, I have heard enough." I paused, embarrassed. "It is so dark in these hills . . . ."

"The room was dark on our honeymoon, too. If you need pointed it the right direction I can help. Now let's give Yellow Baby a real test drive!"

Coming home was always a treat for me because she was always full of surprises. Today was no exception. Today she was the landscaper. She had weeded and planted some flowers. Missy borrowed a push mower then cut the grass. She always gave me the impression that if her nails got ruined it would be the end of the world. Guess I was wrong. She looked like she was a dirt farmer from Nebraska, cute with dirty hands and windblown hair.

She came up to me and said, "Hi sugar, how you like the yard?"

"It's nice. I love that planting you did in the front also."

"Thanks. The phone got hooked up but my things didn't arrive."

"I'll check on that tomorrow, it has to be on Pearl."

"EA, I made a friend. She's a teacher at a Catholic school in town. She said they'll hire me if I want a job, what ya think?"

"Missy, if you want to teach, go right ahead. I know how you like it. I say do it, sweetheart."

"I'm glad you're happy. How was your day, Chief, did you have a good one?"

"Yeah, it went pretty good, saw an old shipmate of mine that just got back from the Far East."

"Ethan, I can only imagine what you talked about and can we not discuss it? I know there is a strong possibility of war. I hear enough just mowing the lawn. Germany now owns most of Europe and Japan is walking all over China. Right now, I want to live in our own little world, okay?"

"All right. Being in the service is sometimes like living in your own world or I should say some admiral's world. I see nothing wrong living in our own world."

"Thank you."

The next day I looked into finding Missy's belongings. Sure enough, they were over in a warehouse. Some supply officer got lazy and figured the owner would go looking for them instead. I called the LTJG and told him to get them over to the house ASAP. When I got home, the fashion queen was all smiles.

"You look great," I said. "We ought to go out for dinner and find someplace to dance to celebrate the arrival of your first true love—clothes."

"Maybe my first material love, but EA, you're my first love."

"I love you too, sweetheart; I'll go change into civilians."

"Keep the uniform on, I like you in it, besides we need to update you some."

"Thanks! Hey, I wear uniforms most of the time. I know nothing of men's styles and really don't care."

"Oh, I know you like it when I tease you, you tease me. And don't worry, I'll take care of your wardrobe. You will be the best dressed man at Pearl."

Every day was different and we were having fun just learning about each other. I realized one thing she did not like and that was anything interfering with our little piece of paradise. But we both knew that regardless of whether or not she liked it, things would eventually change.

Good News

As the weeks moved on some events evolved, like Missy got the job teaching at the Catholic school which would give her something to do and a little money also. Letters from home were coming in now with her doing the writing.

Missy said, "Don't you want to send your family a letter in your handwriting?"

"Honey, I can't write too well 'cause I left school at twelve. When I joined the Navy they were looking for seaman, not writers."

"I didn't know, I'm sorry, will you let me help you? You wrote beautiful letters before we were married. Your typing is better than mine!"

"I dictated those to a yeoman friend of mine and he typed. The words are mine."

"You are full of beautiful thoughts. Soon you will be able to put it on paper yourself."

The handwriting lesson began and sure enough, my writing did improve with time.

Word surfaced that three of the Chiefs got their new orders. They would head back to the States to pick up brand new cruisers. I was actually relieved. I decided to keep a low profile because this boy wanted nothing to do with sea duty. I just went about my business and ran the warehouse. The job was quite boring, but it was either that or splash around on a ship in some hellhole part of the world.

The suspense was killing me as to my future. Lt. Commander Carl Finn, a real down to earth guy that could drink more whiskey and beer than anyone else I knew, had me come down to his office for a "talk". I had been on a ship with him earlier in my career. He was an engineering officer. I really had no association with him other than liberty call (shore leave) in my drinking days. He was Irish, had the brogue and would get down and dirty with the enlisted men. How he got this high in rank was a mystery to all.

"Chief, how you been? You look good and from what I hear you brought some Minnesota scenery with yaw, eh?"

"Yes sir I did, but she'll never get around that crew of yours."

"I hear you lad but we're here to talk about you and what we would like to see you do for your Uncle Sam."

"Mr. Finn, haven't I done enough?"

"Yes, you have done your part. We must prepare for wartime Navy. Ethan, you got ears and I know what you been hearin'. It's the same Jap crap ringing in my ears. War is on the horizon even if the assholes in Washington won't hear of it!"

"I know sir, but what do you want me to do, join the Marines?"

"How d'you guess, mate?"

"What, I change services that late in my career?"

"No Chief, not exactly. But this war will be won primarily by air and assault forces in large numbers, on ships of design you can't even imagine. Ethan, you are going to Warrant Officer School. You'll learn the new tactics and be a pioneer in the new Navy. You soon will see ships and equipment that will make your tongue hang out!"

"As my wife would say . . . Jeepers!"

"Aye Ethan, jeepers is the right word for it."

"So when does this exciting new Navy begin for me, or is this not clear yet?"

"We'll be in touch but I can tell you this: you'll be with your sweetie for a while."

"Good. That's some good news anyway, Sir."

I left and went back to work wondering what this really all meant. I got home and my wife looked like she had a busy day.

"Hi EA, give me a kiss."

"I see you had a fun day in town, so what did you get?"

"Not everything is for me; I got you some clothes and just a few things for me plus for the house. Anything new at work? Did they say anything about what you have been trying to keep from me?"

"Honey, I will never keep anything from you but the service has its rules. Say nothing until you can. The good news is I am going to Warrant Officers School and the training will be in Pearl. We are going to be together for a long time plus more money and benefits."

"Ethan, this is so fantastic!" Those big eyes of hers were welling with tears already. "What will be your new job?"

"I don't really understand what's going on with that. Commander Finn said the details will come out soon."

"Ethan, absolutely no dangerous stuff, like airplanes or submarines and positively no being in charge of the Waves, please?"

"I'll be sure to tell them of your concerns. I don't think being in charge of Waves is likely to happen. The only Wave I need is you. You are more like a typhoon. For your information, Waves got the boot after The First World War. Now, as far as airplanes, I doubt it. Submarines . . . no way I hate them with a passion." I must have been hungry because I'd walked right into the kitchen without realizing it and sat down at the table.

"Well that is a relief." I could tell by her tone of voice she still wasn't quite relieved, the buzz of the war was getting her a bit, but luckily the kitchen provided a good change of topic.

"Let's eat," she said after a quiet sigh, "I made your favorite—duck."

"Duck, huh? I didn't know that was my favorite."

"It will be after tonight."

Duck did become my favorite as she said it would.

When we turned in my wife had her hair tied up in little rags. She had cold cream on. She looked very scary. She said this is what she must do to stay beautiful for me. After the shock of that, she asked me a question.

"EA am I allowed being friends with anybody I want whether they are lower or higher in rank than you?"

"Listen Mrs. Frankenstein, the Navy has some stuck up social protocol but if you make a friend and both of you like each other I say what the heck. Not to worry, there ain't any harm in it. I can't really see us going to big parties for the higher ups anyway. Frankly you would show those social butterflies up. Some of the officers' wives are so uppity that you wouldn't want to be friends with them anyway."

"Thanks, I just don't want to do something wrong and they take it out on you. Goodnight sweetheart, kiss me."

"Is that stuff poisonous on your face? Gosh, what you chicks won't do for your vanity!"

She explained that cold cream worn at night was like getting a blood transfusion. Cold cream was as important as having blood!

*

I started WO training in the first week of September. My instinct told me that my new job would be very different than anything I had done before. Commanding a harbor tug or a fuel barge didn't seem to be what Commander Finn was referring too. Amphibious landing operations were not a well-developed part of the service then. It did however involve many types of small vessels, which would be right up my alley.

The basic instruction period of Warrant Officer School was ending. Soon the real training would begin. Our practice would be on landing on Hawaiian beaches. Since I was a boatswain's mate, I would be lending support to the Marines when they launched their landing craft. The Navy's always been a strange animal to figure out. That will remain true until the end of time.

Graduation time came the Navy had a big ceremony for the eight of us becoming Warrant Officers. Our family and friends were invited. Admiral Husband Kimmel who was the headman at Pearl was at the ceremony, an honor in itself, with other brass and wives plus our families. Missy wore a white summer dress with gloves and an orchid flower in her hair. I was in Navy dress whites. She loved my "outfit". I told the fashion queen that we wore uniforms, not outfits. After the ceremony, Admiral Kimmel came over and gave us a personal congratulation for the promotion and our marriage.

"Wow, Admiral Kimmel knows more about me than I figured."

"Ethan, I'm so proud of you and you really deserve this. Admiral Kimmel and I know you are something special, you will make the best WO ever."

"Thanks, this is kind of overwhelming. I don't know what to say."

"Let's go to the luncheon and mix with your friends. White is your color, Mr. Warrant Officer! Oh, I can feel a cry coming on!"

"Don't. You're wearing white!"

"Oh that's right. I'll cry later, then," she said, smiling. "Let's go."

*

October rolled around and it was fall in Hawaii, though you'd never know by looking at the place. To us it meant something. October tenth it would be my birthday. Halloween Night, it would be her birthday. It was somewhat amusing that her birthday was on Halloween because her name is Mystic. It is only a name so I laughed it off.

My training was getting more intense every day. We were practicing with small landing craft with air support. It was kind of fun and exciting although I was not doing what a Warrant Officer was supposed to do. Most WO's were safely tucked away somewhere safe as in an admirals staff! Commander Finn said I would be (in the event of war) the second wave of the invasion force. I would be with others and coordinate material unloading to resupply the Marines.

"Commander, why me?"

"Vanderbilt, you know more about small craft then the Coast Guard does. This job will keep you fit and not fat and lazy like some people in this man's Navy."

"Sir, I just hope it keeps me alive or you're going to have one pissed off bride to deal with."

"Really, Ethan? Ah, don't worry, lad. Everything will be just fine, you'll see."

Now I knew. What should I say to my wife without upsetting her? With Missy, you just tell her the truth because she could read people like a book.

I arrived home around 5 pm a little nervous and concerned that the news I had might spoil my birthday celebration.

"Honey, I'm home."

"Happy Birthday, I'm in the shower, out in a moment."

"I'll be there in a moment." I rushed into the bathroom and wrapped my arms around her before she could turn the water off.

"Well come on in, birthday boy."

"So how was your day, Missy?"

"Good, how about yours, Sweetie?"

"Pretty good, I guess." I put on an extra big smile to suppress the worried look I knew was overtaking my face, but it was to no avail.

"Ethan, you look bothered."

"Finn told me what my new job was today and I'm not sure I like the way it sounds. I will be on the second wave of a landing invasion should the need arise."

"Nice birthday present. Sounds dangerous Ethan, is it?"

"It could be but let's not worry about it because it's my birthday." I grabbed her a towel as she turned the water off, and her small body disappeared inside it.

"Ethan, please hold me and tell me something nice."

"Come here, how about I have the most gorgeous woman in the world, even with soaking wet hair."

"Perfect just perfect, now let's celebrate your birthday."

Halloween came. It was to be a special night for us. Halloween was big on the Island like in the States. I asked her what she wanted to do for her birthday.

"Nothing, Honey. Halloween is my birthday party."

Soon the kids were showing up. I yelled at Missy, "What do I do now?" Even though we were planning on having kids, I was still a bit terrified of them and never knew what to do with them.

"Give them some candy and an apple, they won't bite." Finally she appeared dressed as a witch and what a witch!

"Missy you're a beautiful witch, I thought witches were scary."

"I don't want to scare them. Look at this one coming up the walk dressed as an angel. Gosh, that costume is beautiful. Here little girl," she said when the angel made it to our door, "here's something for you. You know . . . maybe she is a real angel. Maybe she's our guardian angel."

"I think you need a good gin and tonic. She lives two doors down the street, I know her Dad. An angel? Cuckoo—cuckoo."

Then my wife said out of the clear blue. "Have you ever made love to a witch? Hey, don't answer that, sailor. I know you have a girl in every port."

"No, you've got me figured out wrong, Pearl is the port and you're the girl."

She put her witch's hat on and said," Come here handsome, I'm going to put a spell on you that can never be broken."

I don't know if she put me in a spell or not . . . however, she knows what to do with a wand!

Christmas in paradise

Christmas in Hawaii was different for anyone who had always lived in cold climates. Missy, however, fit right in. With the city decorated, she found no real difference between her old traditions and her new home. She loved the opportunity to meet new people. There were many Navy parties. I wanted to show her off. I also wanted her to meet people so she wouldn't feel so alone when the time came for me to ship out. Navy families by tradition stayed close when the fleet moved out for long periods.

Everybody wanted to meet the new member of the naval community. Missy thought these parties were great. Her upbringing made it a breeze to interact with the people. Missy met some nice women her age who were married to Navy, Marine and Army men.

We decorated the house the week before Christmas. We put some garland and lights on an indoor palm tree that Missy dug up out in the woods. School was out so her friends hung around when I was at work. Since she was the only one of the group without a child, they made her the official sitter for all the kids.

I took the hint that she was ready for parenthood. I was too. I left a note on the kitchen table one morning, "I'm ready if you are to do this thing. Go to the doc and see if you're ok to do this."

At bedtime, Missy brought the note up and said, "Ethan, you're so cute! Honey, this "thing" has a name . . . it is called getting pregnant. It is not dirty or shameful so let's talk about it like adults."

"I know, but this is all so different to me."

"I know you are shy about this. You can talk about it. We are husband and wife. Let's be frank, open and honest."

"You're right."

"I want a child with you too, more than anything in the world . . . you're so funny sometimes, gosh."

"I know I'm a real klutz at this sort of stuff."

"No, you're not a klutz . . . just a sweet man. I love you that way."

Christmas Eve came. I've never really been a church-going man Missy laid down the law and wouldn't you know it I was in my Sunday best kneeling on the pulpit. Afterwards we went over to talk to her friend Edith Conover about getting a bottle of glogg for Christmas dinner. I had never met her. She was around twenty-five, unmarried, mostly teaching school or doing missionary work for the Methodist Church. We talked awhile then said goodnight and left with a bottle of glogg.

"This is for tomorrow and is not to be guzzled by you. No drunks allowed on Jesus's birthday."

"I know that. I want our first Christmas to be wonderful for us too. Missy, Timken needs a nice lady friend, how about Edith?"

"Timken? Oh, I don't know, what would he scam her out of?"

"Maybe nothing. He is really a good guy."

"Hah! Well. I'll ask her and see what she says. Maybe for a New Year's party or a get together at the house?"

When we got home, we sat in front of the Christmas Palm Tree. Missy was a real Christmas kid. She said, "I still believe in Santa Claus, honey, do you?"

"Ah no, but if you say there is a Santa I will believe you because you probably have met him."

"You're funny Mister Warrant Officer. Cute too. Wanna give one present to each other tonight?"

"Why certainly, anything I should do before we . . ."

"No honey, nothing at all. Let the tadpoles loose."

"Lady, sometimes you say things in the strangest ways."

Something was telling me that there was a Santa Claus. He was coming to town and to our little mud hut on 192 East Ninth Avenue bringing more than just the regular stuff.

Missy was busy with making the dinner and said, "Honey sit in the living room, I want to model something I bought for myself and I'll be right out."

About five minutes later she came out with her combed down with red lipstick, a nice fitting sweater and a pair of US Navy regulation bell-bottom work pants wearing high heels.

"Well Ethan what do you think, like them, cat got your tongue?"

"Yeah I like them real well. Dear, I just hope the Navy sees it that way, but I must say I hope it catches on with all the ladies."

"With *all the ladies*, Ethan? Remember you can look at other women, I understand that. Even my Daddy looks but as my Mom says, drooling yes but no fooling around or you will be living at the Y!"

"Honey I can hardly handle you, why would I want two women?"

"Good, so think the Navy will make it hard on me with these pants?"

"Not on you but maybe on me but we'll see, just wear them for now."

"I really like them, I really do. Maybe I will start a new trend . . . denims."

New Years 1941 . . . a great year it will be!

New Years was upon us. We wanted to have one that would be a nice memory for us. Lloyd Timken invited us to a party that was at a beach club on Waikiki. It sounded like a real nice affair so I asked Missy if she was interested.

"I would love to go because my new friends are going. Ethan is this to be a drunken sailor's brawl?"

"I think you have been watching too many movies, not all sailors are a bunch of drunken fist fighting woman chasing fools."

"The party sounds good to me, Ethan I know these men are your friends and I want you to have fun but can you not get drunk? I know you told me you had a drinking problem before. I don't want this creeping back on you again. I love you just being you. You're not pleased with what I said are you?"

"No I'm not mad. I will admit it has been creeping back a little so I will watch myself very closely. Alcohol doesn't bode well with me I guess. While on the subject of the party, you tell Edith we will take her to the party. Maybe she'll meet someone."

On the day before New Year's Eve, I was outside washing the car. Missy got the mail and brought it inside. About ten minutes she asked me to come in.

"What's up honey? You look mad, are you?"

"Yes and no. I got a letter from my mom. It looks like Thomas and Allison are going to have a baby in August."

"Well how nice, they'll make a nice couple. Your parents must be excited."

"Ethan, this is not good, they are not going to get married because Allison is married."

"Oh boy, how they gonna to work that one out?"

"Heck if I know. No judge is going to look at this very well."

"They need to figure this one out by themselves. I know it looks like a family embarrassment. Things have a way of working out though, and when that happens it'll be water under the bridge. Once the drama's over everyone'll forget all about it."

"My brother is so reckless. Even if Allison wants to marry in the future, Thomas might say forget it. The baby will be the one that suffers."

"Well baby, let's just put this aside for now and have a nice time tonight, okay?"

"We will. I'll go call my friends, and then go get something sexy to wear for tonight."

"Missy, not too sexy or we might not make it out of the house."

"Ethan, I love parties, we will be there."

"Yeah, and I love sexy dresses." we left the house at eight to pick up Edith. To my surprise, Edith knew how to dress up. She was a very attractive woman. Usually she looked like a nun out of uniform. Tonight she looked like the queen of the ball!

"Edith I knew that dress would be perfect on you," Missy said, lightly rubbing the fabric between her fingers. "Your hairdo tops it all off."

"Thank you, Missy. I knew you were the one to take shopping. Ethan, your wife should be a buyer for Macy's."

"Edith, she is a buyer for Macys . . . on the receiving end!"

"Ha ha, Mister Warrant Officer."

We arrived on time with the party just beginning. The party was all Chiefs and Warrant Officers. Many of the men were married but some were single. Lloyd Timken was there and he made the guest list, which meant some single women were there too.

Timken came over to us and said hello. He was immediately attracted to Edith. She seemed the same too.

"Hey Vanderbilt, who's that fox you and Missy brought?"

"That's Miss Edith Conover, a teacher at the school."

"Not bad, not bad. She married?"

"No, but you got to get through Missy to meet her because she's on to you."

"Like what, I'm a nice guy! Just want to say hi."

"Okay follow me, Lloyd. Let's see what we can do."

I introduced them. Their eyes met and the sexual tension was so thick you could eat it with a fork. Timken headed to the bar with her. We found a table and sat down.

"Ethan I don't know if this is such a great idea," Missy whispered. "Edith is more naïve than me when it comes to men. She might not be able to handle a guy like him."

"Missy, she's a grown woman."

"I hope you're right. She seems so innocent to me and with a shyster like him he might talk her into anything."

"So?"

They started talking then danced then started that googly-eye stuff!

Missy admitted sparingly, "They are good hoofers."

"Yeah they are, so let's dance too."

"Nothing too wild or too fast. All right?"

We held off on the fast numbers. Soon the slow songs began. We got real close with her moving my hands away from her butt that looked so nice in that dress.

"Honey, later," she whispered so softly in my ear I wondered if later could come quick enough. I distracted myself by watching the two new lovebirds dancing.

"Missy, looks like the New Year might be a good one for those two."

"Oh please, she really isn't his type. She's a good Christian woman and he's a nice man but, you know, he's Timken . . . Gangster in the US Navy!"

The clock was nearing midnight. We all were gathering around looking towards the city for some big fireworks. A Chief gave a toast to the effect that 1941 would be a great year for us and would be one to remember. The clock hit twelve . . . we all grabbed our partners and hugged and kissed. I grabbed Edith and kissed her (not bad for a missionary). Missy avoided Timken like a plague. She came back to me wanting to leave shortly. I had sensed all night that she was either under the weather or tired. Whatever it was, she was not herself.

We headed out and drove to our house with her sitting close to me. She seemed to be shaking a bit. I didn't say a thing. I had not seen Missy act this way even in the days before our wedding. At the house, we got ready for bed. Coming out with her hair combed out, pinned up and looking more at ease, she hopped into bed. She could be so sexy with her

The Beautiful Mistake

hair like that. We got into bed and kissed then she sat up saying we need to talk.

"Missy, what is the problem? Are you sick or what?"

"A little of everything. There is something I do need to tell you."

"Can't it wait till morning? Let's bring in the New Year right!"

"We will honey, please wait a moment. Ethan . . . we're going to have a baby."

"A baby . . . when?"

"August . . . towards the end of it."

"This August?" As in 1941?"

"No dear, in two years. What do you think I am an elephant? Yes this year!"

"I don't know much about this reproduction stuff. We only decided to get pregnant last week. Wow that was fast!"

"Honey, it happened before last week. So much for birth control, I guess. You look pale."

"I am. Sorry dear, this is too much excitement for me. So we are really going to be parents, I guess there's no turning back now."

"No, there isn't. If we could . . . is that what you would want?"

"I don't mean it like that. I'm just shook up and kind of scared."

"Oh, You'll be fine, just calm down now . . . pray on it. You will love being a daddy."

1941

The next morning I made coffee. We talked in bed about our future and the good news of last night.

"Missy, you gonna send a telegram or write home about the good news?"

"Write. That way I can give all the details on a three-cent stamp versus a one dollar gram."

"Good thinking, I love that thrifty way about you."

"Me thrifty? Sometimes. I was thinking of getting some new clothes and other stuff. But soon I will be wearing maternity dresses and look like a balloon."

"You could use a few pounds to fill in the voids."

"What do you mean, *voids*?"

"Oh come on, you're beautiful as you are. I'll bet you that you're the prettiest mommy to be in all Hawaii. I can't wait for the baby to come. On the other hand," I paused, teasing her, "little people scare me to death."

"Oh yeah, yeah. You'll get over that quick and be a great Daddy, especially when you change your child's diaper."

"Diapers? Can't wait. You realize there'll be two grandbabies in August, ours plus Thomas and Allison's."

"Ugh, don't remind me."

Time seemed to move slowly in the summer of '41. Missy was doing real well with her pregnancy. Navy training was coming along well. It was now May and we started to get the baby's room ready. Our beach days were few now because the heat bothered her. We went up into the hills where it is cooler. Life was plain nice and quiet.

June would be the first anniversary of our marriage. I wanted to do something special for her. I turned my thinking cap on and gave it a lot of thought. Several ideas popped into my head, though, were just sort of the usual stuff. Then an idea came into my head. I decided to take a moment to see a friend of mine that had a harbor tug command.

The Love Tug Boat

"Permission to come aboard, Chief Nelson?"

"Up your ass Vanderbilt, just come aboard and the leave the Naval crap behind. So how the hell are ya? Congrats on the promotion. Whose butt d'ya kiss?"

"No one's, I'm just good and I need the money to support my new wife."

"Yeah I heard that. I'm happy for you both."

"Thanks Cliff, coming from you that means something. Since I'm here a good idea has come mind."

"Like what? Don't think about taking my shitcan of a tug. This is my little kingdom and I am the king!"

"Settle down man, this is what I got brewin'. How much you gonna charge me to rent this scow for us to have our first anniversary dinner together?"

"Well that is a strange request. I believe we can work out a deal. Let me think on it."

"Nothing illegal or anything that would get us in big trouble, okay?"

"Don't worry it'll be on the level enough. What's your buddy Timken up to these days?"

"At the moment he's fallin' in love with some missionary woman. He's still working on the quiet side. You know, the usual. Cars, steaks, tires."

"Ok I'll give you a call by the end of the week and let you know. So, Timken in love with missionary woman, huh? I can think of one missionary thing he loves about her."

"Thanks, Cliff."

Chief Nelson was an old salt with thirty years service. That meant he enlisted in 1910 when the navy was still using ships from the Spanish-American War. He was well known in the Navy and respected. It was rumored he could get any duty he wanted because he had a lot hanging over the heads of some of the top brass. He married a Chinese woman he met when on gunboat duty on the Yangtze River back in 1914 but left her there. Cliff sends money to her to support their child named Chucky Lee Nelson. Of course, Chucky is all grown up now. Nelson's mind was so flooded with bourbon he thought Chucky was still in diapers. He was just one of those 'lifers' whose faults were overlooked when performance reports come in. He was a good sailor, story closed. It was a classic example of the backwater navy.

The next day, Chief Nelson called saying to take the tug with no strings attached. He said it would be clean enough for captain's inspection.

Missy brought up the subject of what we should do for our anniversary. I said, "Honey you planned our wedding. You made it a wonderful memory, so for this occasion I want to plan this all by myself, okay?"

"Sure I would love that but what are we going to do?"

"Now that's my secret and you won't know until it's time."

I found out what her dad meant when he said she was a little bratty. She almost drove me nuts from not telling her about anniversary plans. Thankfully the day came!

July 28th was here and time for my anniversary surprise. I told her to be ready around seven. We would go to a nice restaurant then to the tug. We went to dinner at a very romantic place. Candlelit tables, soft music and very good Hawaiian food.

"It has been a wonderful year for us, meeting for the first time, getting married; making a home and now a child will be here soon."

"Missy, this sometimes seems like a dream. I am the happiest man on earth and words don't say it all."

"Yes they do, you just said them. If I wasn't so big I would lean across the table and kiss you!"

"That song playing right now is nice and slow; let's dance."

"Sure I would love to dance, just ignore the belly."

"Missy I love your belly."

"Ethan, I love you."

After dinner and dancing, we drove for about fifteen minutes until we reached the fleeting area of auxiliary ships such as tugs, ocean going barges and salvage ships. Ahead was our tug, YTB6.

"Honey this is it, our private yacht for tonight. So, want to stay tonight or head home?"

"Oh Ethan, this is so neat! Are you crazy? This is the best ever. Of course I want to stay here and nowhere else!"

"Good, put on this sailor hat and work shirt, so in the dark you look like a sailor."

"Honey, my stomach is going to give me away."

"They'll just think you're a fat sailor. The Chief of this tug has made sure no one comes aboard until noon. Nobody would rat on us anyway."

"Ethan, I believe the Chief is the one that doesn't follow orders, look."

"Oh no, the dumb bastard is passed out and bloody drunk, now what do we do?"

"Honey, he is sleeping like a baby. He's so cute with that fifth of bourbon under his arm. A toddler carries their bottle like that! Now, let's drag his butt to bed so we can go to bed!"

"All right, I'll drag him inside this space and throw a blanket on him."

"Ethan, will he remember we are here?"

"I'll write him a note and stuff it in his mouth."

The stateroom was nice and clean. The Chief said he would make it fit for a princess. It was. Missy was thrilled and very pleased with her surprise. We got ready for bed and drank a ginger ale for our toast. Then we snuggled and talked.

"Ethan, you are so unpredictable sometimes! You're stuck with me for sure!"

"Good, I love being your boyfriend and husband."

"That's funny, I never thought of you as my boyfriend. Sometimes you are like a boyfriend."

Our time on the love tug was great. When we turned in, we kissed goodnight, letting the gentle bobbing of the boat send us into dreamland.

The Duluth soap opera and a baby

I got orders to be in Long Beach in the second week of July for a week of special training. I would fly in a seaplane. The flight would take around ten hours. This was no comfortable airplane either. It was noisy, rough and no in-flight movies, food or even peanuts. Pack your own lunch with an extra bag to vomit in. Even a seasoned sailor could get sick in the air by the engine fumes alone. I wondered if even my steel plated stomach would handle it. I told Missy about it and she asked what she should pack.

"Pack? Pack the house and stay in it, sweetheart, you're not coming."

"Why not? I could do some sightseeing or shopping when you are in school."

"Honey, wives can't go on these types of junkets. I will try to find something nice for you in Long Beach."

"Ok but I still wish I could go."

"A week will go fast. A little separation might do us good."

"Why? I miss you even when you go to work and come home in eight hours. Are you trying to get rid of me? Do you miss me ever?"

"Yes dear. I have always heard that absence makes the heart grow fonder that's all."

"That is plain bullshit Ethan Allen, plain bullshit! I'm big as a balloon with swollen feet feeling ugly. And you want separation to make the heart grow fonder!"

"Ok, calm down, I just thought . . ."

"You thought wrong, Mister!"

I had always heard pregnant women were touchy! Her saying bullshit had to be a first too!

Day of the flight came and we met down at the harbor where seaplanes take off. I noticed there was no plane in sight. Commander Flynn arrived shortly after and said we needed to go over to Hickman Field to board an Army Air Corp plane. We got there and to our surprise, we boarded a B-17-B four-engine bomber. The plane was large on the outside but when we boarded—man was it small. Very small.

The week flew by, thank heavens. Friday night we on a four engine flying boat. It was a nice plane in comparison to the B-17. Eleven hours we hit Pearl. I unlocked the door and quietly slipped into bed with Sleeping Beauty. Snoring, she never knew I was there until she awakened at ten. She came back into the room and woke me up.

"Kiss me, Missy, I really did miss you. These training trips are dumb and a waste of time."

"I missed you too sweetheart, but as long as it is kept to a week I can handle it."

"You know that isn't going to always happen."

"Drink your coffee EA. Let's change the subject."

"Missy—"

"I know, I know but that's the way I feel. I realize you might have to ship out far away. When the time comes, I will deal with it. I also know there will be a war. 'Til then, it is all about us!"

A week later, a letter came from Missy's mom. She said that Allyson had a baby girl on August 2. Mother and child were doing well. Thomas was there and they named her Juliet Bay. The Bays were happy to be grandparents. They liked Allison very much. However, she was still a married woman. That could be a Pandora's Box. What a mess indeed.

"So, Missy, you're an aunt, how does that feel?

"I have mixed emotions. I am glad that baby Juliet and Allyson are fine. This is such a shame, though, and how it will turn out is anyone's guess."

"What do they want to do? Has that been brought up?"

"Thomas is not real trustworthy when it comes to relationships with women. I think she loves him. Maybe it will work out. Mom says in her letter that he has been with them since the birth. That is good."

"It's not your problem . . . you have enough to handle in the next few months so let it stay in Duluth."

"Ethan, when I have the baby I want you with me in the delivery room."

"What? I never heard such a thing and anyway I'm sure the Navy won't allow it."

The Beautiful Mistake

"Yes you're right about that. That is why I want to have the baby at a hospital off base. I have talked to them and they will allow it. Ethan this is your child also, don't you want to experience this with me?"

"Yes and no, but I might be in the way or . . ."

"Or what, oh I know you're not chicken. Tell me why, okay?"

"I might faint, or maybe have a heart attack or—"

"Ethan, you saying you might cry? Men can cry especially for joy. Moreover, what better place for a heart attack than in a hospital. Please think it over. I need no answer tonight."

The end of August came. We still had no baby so off to the doctor we went. He told us that the child was not ready. He assured us everything was fine.

There were no signs at all until the evening of September 3rd when Missy got her watch out and started taking readings. By the look on her face, I knew this was it.

"Are you ready to head for the hospital?"

"Yes, you grab my suitcase. I'll comb my hair and put on my make up."

"That's my girl. Flood, famine, fire, or having a baby, you gotta look good!"

When we arrived at the hospital, I told them why we were there. They put my wife in a wheelchair and I parked the car. After that, it was like being in the Navy: hurry up and wait and wait and wait. Missy's contractions stopped for three hours. It was nothing but boredom and a sore butt for me in that poor excuse for a chair.

"So Mrs. Vanderbilt, how are you feeling right now? Tell me what's going on," the doctor said.

"I really feel good, considering. The contractions were strong, and then fell off."

"Chief, I hear you're going to be in the room with us. I commend you for it. I feel that the dads should be there if they want to."

"Well, Dr. Humari, I'll be fine, being in the Navy I've seen worse."

"Thanks, I think, but worse than what?" Missy asked.

"Did that come out wrong sugar"?

"Ethan, you are funny but—" she cut herself off. "Oh boy, there goes my water."

Before you could say Mississippi, we were all in the delivery room at our battle stations. I held her hand to comfort her. Then after a short while, the moaning and groaning began with the doc saying push. All of a sudden with one push, the doc said, "Now a little bit more! More, okay?"

There was a little cry then a big one. Then Dr. Humari said, "Well, you two, you've got a son and he looks fine." Missy started to cry. Me . . . well I was in near shock!

"Oh Ethan, we have a boy! He is so beautiful, isn't he?"

"Yeah, he is and he's looking at us, wow!"

The nurse asked, "How about a name for this young man?"

"His name is Todd Allen Vanderbilt", my wife proudly replied.

This baby came out hungry. Missy started breast-feeding him. The nurse came and got him because my wife was in la-la land. I kissed her goodnight then headed home.

I returned early. When I walked into the room, they were both up having breakfast. For the first time since I married her, she looked like hell in the morning. She did look sexy with that beautiful brown hair going in a million directions and I told her so. She smiled. I held Todd for about an hour. To hold a newborn was something I had never done. Holding our own child was humbling. Besides, he was a cool little boy!

"So how do you feel? Was your night good?"

"I feel good, tired mainly because our baby needs fed often . . . very often."

"You're not going to run out?"

"I could but if that happens they'll have to get me a wet nurse."

"Yeah, seems like my mother never ran out with my brothers and sister. I guess that's why she has large breasts."

"Ethan, are you acting silly or just plain don't know?"

"Know what?"

"Ethan Allen Vanderbilt, man of the seven seas, women's breast size has no bearing on their ability to produce milk. If that were true, I wouldn't produce much!"

"I was always told that if a milk cow had big udders she would give more milk than one that had small udders!"

"So these are udders, eh? So what kind of a cow am I, a Holstein, Guernsey or a Jersey cow? Maybe an Aryshire?"

"You would be a Jersey because they have pretty eyes."

"Thanks, now come over here so I can strangle you! Now, wise guy, did you telegram everyone?"

"Yep, last night so they should get our news anytime now."

"I wish they coulda been there too, oh never mind," she said, crying some.

"I know me too, sorry Missy."

"No being sorry. Now this is the way it is but maybe they could come over here to visit."

"Now that's an idea that might be arranged. I'll talk to . . ."

"I know, Timken. Okay, just don't get our family in some mess, okay?"

"Yes dear, it will be on the level . . . at least most of it."

"I know in this world we live in, maybe you need to know a guy like him. Oh, gosh, I can't believe I said that," she laughed. "Forgive me, Lord."

"Ah, come on, you love the guy, admit it."

"Love no, like yes."

Paradise returns, kinda

I went back to training with some nights away from the family. My wife had recuperated well. After about a month, she was her old self. We went out some and of course junior was with us going to the beach or up on the hill for a picnic. Life was different now, though better with a baby.

It became very apparent trouble was brewing in the world. Britain had suffered huge naval losses in the Pacific and the Battle of Britain was underway. It was only a matter of time until the U.S. would have to do something. You could feel the tension that war was coming. The only question was when.

"Ethan, guess what dear, I got my permission slip from Dr. Humari today."

"Permission for what?"

"Permission for you and me to do, you know, the . . . . .well, guess. So what d'ya think, sailor boy? Baby boy is in dreamland so . . .

"Oh yeah." One of life's true joys had returned to 192 East Ninth St.

Things at work were status quo. Many were planning to take leaves over the coming holidays. Many of the battle groups were in port. To see battleship row was an impressive sight. Even my wife thought so. I guess Missy knew that freedom comes with a price. Some of that cost was to maintain a military force that could react if called upon to. Our mighty fleet was ready if needed.

"Hi, honey, I'm home. Where are you?"

"Back here changing Todd. How was your day?"

"Good," I said, kissing her on the cheek. "No news is good news. How about yours?"

"Fine, school was good and Todd did well. He keeps the nuns laughing. He is quite a card with them. I got a letter from your mom and mine. Things seem to be fine."

"Any word on whether your mom wants to come here for Christmas?"

"Mama says she is going to ask your mom to go, isn't that nice!"

"Yeah but you'll never get my mom on a plane or ship. Plus she has no money for that."

"Well we can help with that. I think it would be wonderful for the grandmothers to see Toddy. I miss my mama, Ethan."

"I know. If they can't come here, how about you and Todd go there instead?"

"No, Ethan, my place is here with you and if they can't come then . . . . well."

"Well, what? Come on now, let's sit on the couch and talk, you look upset."

We talked and my wife was truly homesick. There wasn't much I could do about that. Later that night I felt like maybe this was too much for her. Missy said she expected to have low points of living so far away from home. If they could not come, I would get her to the States for a visit after Christmas.

We decided to go up in the hills and camp out with Toddy on the weekend of December 6th and 7th. We wanted to get away from it all. I think we loved the hills more than the beach. There was a shack up there for us to stay in if it rained. It had an old wood burning stove for cooking. This would be a great weekend! Nothing would stop us from having fun.

"Ethan that would be so great, just what the doctor ordered. We need some togetherness and some fresh air."

"Yeap, I have no duty at the base and the weather is going to clear blue skies."

The rest of the week, Missy went to teach school. Her class was a mixture of whites, Hawaiians and some Japanese students. They all got along great. Nobody even back then in the forties seemed to notice they were different in looks. All were good little kids and cute as could be. They were growing up in a nice peaceful beautiful place in the Twentieth Century.

Friday night the "Timkens" came over to visit. There was no doubt Edith loved Lloyd but did he love her? Missy was beginning to believe something was about to happen with them. If Lloyd were going to bite the hook, he sure would delay it for as long as he could. I knew Lloyd even more than I knew my own two brothers. Lloyd and I stepped out to talk.

"So, buddy, when are you taking the plunge?"

"When I know that the shoes fit real well!"

"Hell, I thought you would have tried that on by now."

"Not with Edith, she doesn't budge on pootang at all. I thought this would be an easy one."

"Well, marry her."

"Maybe I will. I ain't going nowhere for a while. There's not much chance a transfer. There's no need for divers right now in Pearl or anywhere else. Last time a ship sunk at Pearl was an admirals fishing boat!"

About ten p.m. they left. We talked some about Edith and Lloyd.

"Ethan, does he love her or is he using her?"

"Neither . . . they're just having fun, which is good enough for now."

"Why wouldn't Lloyd jump on something like that knowing she is such a good catch?"

"Oh, he tried jumping her," I laughed. "You know she is very strict about whoopee with no ring."

"As I was too! And . . . I was not referring to that! I meant she is worth the leap into marriage. Gosh, is that the only thing on men's minds is sex?"

"Yeap."

Friday night turned sour quickly due to baby Todd coming down with a slight fever. Both of us were up doing rocking chair shifts. By the morning, we were both tired. Of course, when morning did come Todd was feeling like a million bucks. He stayed awake keeping us awake. Kid's, have too love them or just go mad! We spent the rest of the day lounging around the house.

We did decide to go up into the hills on Saturday for a day trip. My wife made a picnic lunch. When we got there all of us took a three-hour nap under a tree with a nice Hawaiian breeze. That felt better than a full night's sleep in a grand hotel with air conditioning.

When we got back there was a telegram waiting. It was from Missy's mother. She was on her way here to Hawaii with my mother. They had left Thursday by train for San Francisco. Then they would board a ship for Hawaii. We both kind of looked at each other and wondered how they would do traveling together. My mom on a ship out in the middle of the Pacific would be a site to see. Nothing was going to stop these two now. Their mission was . . . Pearl Harbor.

"Now that was a nice day, Ethan, fun, relaxing and plain nice. Now we have our mothers coming too. What do you think about that?"

"I think they will do well together. I know you need this visit."

She then suggested, "Tomorrow let's go to the beach. Maybe fish? How about being at the inlet early. Let's get there around six so I can catch a real big one and cook it. Maybe invite some friends over?"

"Sure, I like to fish early in the morning. I caught a beauty once that weighed one hundred and twenty pounds with bright green eyes and long brown hair!"

"I am that big catch or am I assuming too much?"

"Yeah I think you were the one."

"Good, well you deserve a big kiss for that, sailor man. I'm gonna lay down with the baby. I still seem to have my days mixed up since the he was born, lack of sleep, him with colic and all. Ethan is tomorrow Sunday?"

"Yeap, Sunday, December 7th, 1941."

The day that changed everything

We fell asleep around midnight after a little small talk. Todd needed fed around three a.m. He took it in fast and fell back to sleep in no time. Something woke me up around four a.m. When I woke, my ears were ringing and I felt my heart racing. I had no clue why, I just felt off key, anxious. I sure hoped it wasn't a heart attack. I didn't wake up Missy. It was fruitless to go back to sleep so I sat outside and stared at the stars. Eventually it was clear that this night's sleep was scrapped, so I went in and made some coffee.

Around five-thirty and on schedule Todd began to cry so I picked him up. I grabbed a diaper then she fed the boy. We hopped into Yellow Baby then headed to the inlet. We set up our fishing gear, threw the first line in and waited for a bite. The sun was rising and what a beautiful day it was. I wanted to tell her about by that strange feeling. I didn't. Why bother her about something silly like that. That odd feeling just would not go away.

About six the little one was sound asleep so we just talked quietly. Soon the fish started biting like crazy. We hauled in a nice one and kept it. Missy caught two in a row . . . she was so charged with excitement. I remember she had this blue bathing suit on. With that rich brunette hair pulled back in a tie she casted again. The woman could cast a surf rod with an eight-ounce weight really far. She seemed to have that knack for knowing when a fish would strike. She teased me about catching nothing. Soon I showed her by pulling in a small sand shark, which scared the heck out of her. I let it go. We took a coffee break. Missy was the best coffee maker ever! We just sat there sipping and talking and playing with Toddy. Man this was heaven. I was sleepy, so Missy said close your eyes for a bit. Before I dozed off, I looked at the clear, calm, so blue skies.

Around seven or so Missy woke me up with a kiss. It was such a great kiss. I was in a good sleep and it took a moment to focus. Then my wife looking down at me said, "Ethan, look at all the airplanes in the sky, there must be oodles of them! Jeepers they are kind of low too."

"Honey, I don't think our military has oodles but yeah, you're right there is a bunch. Wait here, I'll go get my field glasses and see what type they are."

I walked to the car got my field glasses and searched the sky however they were gone. Then another batch came again. Just as many, just as low. I looked into the sky and I almost turned grey. They were Japanese, and not on a social call!

"Missy, grab the baby and run to the car!"

"Why?"

"Run, damn it! Now run and forget the poles, run like hell!"

I ran to her and pushed her and Todd into the car. I drove under a cluster of trees, parked and shut the motor off.

"What is going on, Ethan? Why the fuss? What about our new surf rods?"

"Those are Jap planes, Pearl Harbor is no doubt under attack and I'm sitting on the beach fishing!"

"No! No, you're wrong please tell me so. Oh God please no, not now, not this!"

"Listen, you must be brave and I must get to the base. We will head back to the house. I will get you two hunkered down then head to Pearl. You and the baby get in the back seat and stay down!"

"Yes Sir. I mean Ethan, but . . . ."

"Do exactly what I tell you to do . . . and pray."

"I'm praying, I'm praying. Please God, stop this, please Lord!"

Soon after we left the beach, the explosions began. There was a terrific volume and frequency of explosions. Smoke began to fill the air. This was one big attack by those little bastards. We arrived at the house with no incident. I got my family in the house. Missy was a wreck. She grabbed her Bible, starting to calm down some. I grabbed my forty-five, then called Edith's house to see if Lloyd was there. He was.

"Lloyd we need to get to the base but how without getting killed!"

"Just drive and hope for the best I guess. I'll be over in ten minutes to pick you up," Lloyd replied.

"Honey, are you talking to the Navy?"

"No, Lloyd is over at Edith's house. He is coming to pick me up."

"At her house this early in the morning . . . oh."

"Missy, I love you and if . . . . ."

"No, I don't want to hear it, no goodbyes. Remember what I said about goodbyes when we first met?"

"I remember everything you have ever said. You must remain calm and do what the police or the military tells you to do. I might be gone several days. I will be under orders and I must follow them. You must fend for yourself and take care of our son. If those bastards invade the island, you must drive the car up into the hills. Go where we camp. Let the locals take care of you." I heard a rumble outside and we turned our heads toward the door just as a car horn started honking furiously. "Here comes Lloyd. I gotta go."

Timken drove up with Edith in the car. She would stay with my wife and together they would decide what to do next.

"Hi, Edith I'm glad you came too."

"Ethan, I was in China when these midgets invaded. I know what they're capable of. I'll take good care of your family. Whatever it takes."

"I know you will, Edith. I trust your judgment. Please take care of her." I looked over my shoulder at my wife as my heart hit the floor, and lowered my voice. "Missy is . . . naive on everything. Whatever you do, don't let yourselves get taken prisoner . . . and I mean . . . well you know."

"You be careful and take care of my Lloyd. He thinks he's Superman sometimes."

"I will. He's my best friend."

"Missy, kiss me, I love you so much. I will return soon."

"I love you too, my sweet Ethan. Please be safe, kiss your son and have faith in our God and . . . oh, no I'm going to be sick."

"EA let's take her with us, puke might be the only weapon we have!"

"Lloyd, you are the only one that would find humor in all of this."

"You guy's be safe," Edit said. "Bring back their heads on a stick!"

Timken and Edith said their goodbyes. Missy went back into the house arm in arm with Edith. Lloyd and I went to Pearl to do what we could do on December 7, 1941. We were a nation at war. At this very moment, our lives changed forever. From now on, all of us would play a role in defeating this reign of terror.

Battle Stations, this is not a drill!

Our drive to the base would take about fifteen minutes. With all the noise and planes flying around, it was as though we were already there. Many cars and busses were loaded with servicemen heading for the action. We put eleven men in our car. They were on the hood, fenders, and roof . . . in the trunk too! We drove through the main gate and headed straight down the main road towards the ships. Several ships were already in flames. Navy and Marines had set up machine gun posts and they were sending rounds up into the sky with some results. Lloyd and I decided to get with damage control people (fire fighters) to help put out fires and rescue injured men. Lloyd and I were not fire fighters. For now, everyone was everything. Cooks, machinists, storekeepers, you name it they were doing it. As I look back on it now it was the greatest display of teamwork and courage I had ever seen. No one was selfish that day. Scared, yeah, but not selfish!

    The first thing I did was extinguish an American flag that had caught fire. It wasn't going to save the day but these little rat bastards were not going to burn my flag! It was such an emotional moment for me, I stuffed it in my shirt and still have that seared flag to this day. Timken kept driving on, dropping off men at their duty stations. We safely made it to a fire station and hopped on a fire truck. We proceeded to put out fires burning on the base like vehicles, buildings and debris. We made it where the *USS Maryland* was parked putting out some small fires. I pulled some sailors out of the water. There was a huge explosion. We thought it was an ammo dump. Later I found out it was the USS Arizona. I noticed tugs in the harbor putting out fires and picking up men. I spotted the tug Missy and I stayed on our first anniversary. I needed to get on his boat because it appeared to be undermanned. I made my way around to where the tug was. A Zero fighter plane came in low almost getting me. I signaled Nelson to pick me up. Timken stayed behind working with the base firefighters.

"Thanks Nelson, what do you want me to do?"

"Hell, Vanderbilt the boat is all yours now, you out-rank me, I figured this would happen!"

"Piss on you Nelson . . . you're the skipper so lead on. I'll go on deck and pull people out of the water. Are your water pumps working?"

"Shit yes Vanderbilt, everything works on this tug! You want a good hit of bourbon first. This is gonna be a bloody long ass day!"

"No thanks Chief, Missy would kill me!"

"Hell, man, we'll be lucky today if we don't get killed!"

"Well, shit. Then shut up and give me the bottle, skipper."

We started to cruise the harbor looking for men. Soon I saw a few in the water. The crew and I dragged out four that were in good condition. They wanted back to the fight. We dumped them off near the docks. We went back to the harbor to search again. The attack now was very heavy. Planes were flying low and hitting everything in sight. The fire from the Arizona filled the sky. Then we started to see the inevitable . . . dead sailors. We got near the capsized battleship Oklahoma. We all began dragging sailors from the water. Some were unhurt and others not so lucky. These were just kids, not more than nineteen. It was awful and the worst was to come. One sailor with his hat still on was bobbing in the water. We yanked him by his shirt and hoisted him on. We pulled one sailor that was in half by enemy fire. We covered him up with a tarp. We all stood there paralyzed when a Jap came in at two o'clock and let loose with a barrage of gunfire strafing our tug. Luckily, for us it only scuffed up Nelson's new paint job. His feelings were hurt. He emptied a glossary of cuss words into the sky. The attack on the ships seemed to subside. We then got word to begin only to firefight. Small launches would do the personnel rescues. Our fire party work began with battleship row. We helped the Maryland. Since we were taking water from the harbor, we could hose indefinitely. At that point, we headed to the USS Pennsylvania, my old ship. The Pennsylvania sustained only minor damage. Hit, yes, but still in one piece. The Chief Boatswain Mate that I knew said everything was under control. I headed for a command center, reported in, and documented what I had done in the attack. A Captain said to hold tight. He was getting a crew to take out into the perimeters of the base and scout for downed enemy pilots. Maybe even an invasion force. Soon we had a small detachment. They issued us small arms. Browning automatic rifles, a Colt 45, and some Springfield 03's with plenty of ammo.

After a brief rest, it dawned on me that if an invasion did occur our forces might not be able to hold them back. If that happened, the female population would be in big trouble. These little crapheads would rape and then would kill females like cattle at a slaughterhouse. Nanking China proved that. White woman were in real peril. I hoped that Edith took Missy and our son up into the hills. Missy was so naïve and trusting, she might figure that the enemy just would let them go. This is horrible to say but they would be better off dead. Edith knew what these lunatics were capable of doing. I almost got sick thinking about what could happen.

Our group moved out and patrolled through miles of shoreline. Thankfully, we found nothing. We returned to base. Rumor was that there was an invasion however, that proved to be false. Man did I give thanks to the Lord for that! My wife and son were probably safe. Now I could think with a clear heart.

Now that the attack was over the clean up began. There were still many injured to take care of. Many were dead too. There were sailors trapped below on sunken ships that needed rescue. The battleship Oklahoma had stayed capsized. The Arizona was one big heap of twisted metal. These ships now needed salvage divers, welders, and equipment to extract the living and dead. This was a job for Timken. Lloyd was a very skilled and dedicated diver. He would do everything possible to save our sailors. Then I was to go out with a detail, take a small launch out and gather the dead still in the water. In thirty minutes, we brought back twelve bodies. Until this day, I can see their faces. It was the worst day in my life. Nothing would ever compare.

We worked two days without much sleep or food. Since there was no phone service, I had no idea what was going on with my family. None of us really knew whether the enemy was going to attack again. The base readied itself for another attack. Finally, they started letting personnel return to their homes. As for me, I had to stay. On the third day at sixteen hundred hours, I was relieved of duty. I got on a bus and headed home.

When I walked in Missy was fast asleep wearing those damn navy dungarees with the baby in her arms. I let them sleep. It looked like they got home shortly before me. With mud on her shoes, there was no doubt they had come from the hills. Missy was in need of a bath with her hair a mess. Todd was sparkling clean as I figured he would be.

I sat looking at my two most important people in the world, wondering what had happened. One day we are fishing without a care in the world then the next second running for our lives. Now I realize why I was having all those weird feelings the morning of the attack.

Missy woke up looking happy to see me although fright was all over her face.

"Oh Ethan, hold me and don't let go. I have been so worried about you. What is going to happen to us, our country . . . this world? This is horrible!"

"Missy, I'm here. I'm fine. All the other stuff can wait. Let's just sit here, be close and pray. We have lost many brave young men. We must never forget them."

"Oh, sweetheart, I know. I'm so heartbroken. It has sent me in a spiral of emotion, this must be a dream."

"A nightmare," I said listlessly.

"Do you want to tell me what you did or saw? I will be strong if you need to talk about it."

"No dear, not now, maybe when we're in our wheel chairs."

"Okay, when you're ready. I love you so much."

"Me too dear . . . me too. How are you, what happened here, where's Edith?"

"When all of you left we listened to the radio and heard that an invasion was going to happen. Edith said grab what the baby needs, you some clothes and get the heck out of here. I asked what the hurry was, but she insisted so we packed up Yellow Baby. We drove to her flat, got her stuff, then went to the hills. We went where we camped, as you said to do. We let the locals know. We stayed until the evening of the eighth. I guess if the little bastards had a hold of us we would have become their geisha girls. Edith said they would have killed our baby. Ethan is that true? They can't be that evil!"

"Yes, Missy they are even worse than that. Just ask the Chinese. You're putting it nicely by saying they would have made you a geisha."

"Oh, I see. Then Edith was right. She said they were like a tribe in the French Congo that killed a missionary then ate her. Speaking of, are you hungry honey?"

"Missy, yes and I need a bath."

"I'll make you something good, you look famished. What about our mothers, do you think they're out at sea? They might have boarded on the seventh of December."

"I don't know and I doubt if we can find out right now. If they did, the Navy will turn them around with protection. Let's wait and be patient."

"Yes, Ethan, "I'll try . . . I mean I will."

Missy moved to the kitchen. I heard Todd cry so I went in and brought him into the sitting room. I was so happy to see him. He seemed happy to see me too. Then I thought I heard Missy crying so I asked her if everything was all right.

"The electricity must have gone off. What little we had has spoiled. Ethan, I don't know how to be a navy wife!"

"What are you talking about? Why all the tears, honey?"

"I don't know what to do or say to a man that fights wars for a living. When he comes home what am I supposed to say? *How was your day at the war honey? Go change your blood soaked pants and get a shower because dinner is almost ready.* With me wearing my Betty Crocker apron all prettied up, happy with the kids playing outside!"

"Missy, come here, you need to calm down. Listen to me and listen very well. No one knows how to act right now, this is new to all of us. Everyone is going crazy right now. All this will work out soon then we can go back to being normal."

"I'm sorry; I'm just so scared and confused. Maybe I just should have stayed holed up in Minnesota living like a schoolmarm. Maybe I should have married some professor with a pipe stuck in his mouth being bored by going on vacation to a library or visiting some ancient Aztec village."

"Stop it right now. You are rambling as if you are in a Bette Davis movie. Thank God, you don't look like her. What if we had never met or got married? We wouldn't have had that beautiful child and I wouldn't have you. You, marry a professor? Of fashion, maybe." I kissed her forehead and checked to see if she was smiling yet, and she was, a little.

"I know Ethan, you're right. I am a good catch. This is what I love about you. The way you bring me back to earth with that good plain kind way of yours. I need you so much right now."

"I need you too sweetheart. Now feed the boy and we will figure something out on eating. I will answer the phone."

I answered the phone and it was Lloyd. He was alive and well at Edith's place. He would only be there for a while. Rescue operations were still on and time was running out for the trapped men. I told Missy the news. We bought some food at the store, turned in early then thanked God.

Our friends had come out of the attack unscathed. The island now was under martial law with curfews. Security was as you would not believe. This would pose a problem with the tourist industry. Many tourists were stuck on the island until further notice. Talk of rationing everything was buzzing around. You could figure it would happen because the islands imported most food from the States.

The new week was busy at Pearl. Everyone was trying to get the base back in order. More dead were showing up as we cleaned up. It was so gruesome. How could a nation like ours let this happen with all the warnings we had? The Navy knew this would happen. Now let the blame game begin. The US Navy has always been good at laying blame on some innocent person!

Many of our ships were still burning hulks. Some vessels looked to have only minor damage or none at all. My old ship the USS Pennsylvania would fight again. The days were long, hot and hard. Timken was making dives every day sometimes even after dark. His job was very dangerous. After a few days, it this realized this was no longer a rescue operation.

School resumed and they went back to teaching. It was good medicine for Missy. The few Japanese that attended were absent by government order. The teaching staff did not agree with this decision at all, including Missy.

We heard all ships at sea were safe. I told my wife to assume that the moms were in the US. Missy was relieved, as was I.

The weeks flew by and soon it was time for Christmas. I think everyone was glad to see it come. All of us attended church services then went to our place. Lloyd and I stepped outside to talk. I asked him what he thought his duty would be once the U.S. began to fight back.

"I am sure my job will remain here until we get the Oklahoma righted. We need to figure out what to do with the Arizona. It could take six to twelve months. After that who knows. What about you?"

"I believe I will be dispatched from here to a task force. Then head for action somewhere in the Pacific. I have no reason to think they will send me to Europe or North Africa."

"Have you heard the rumor about the military dependents being shipped back to the States?"

"Yeah, let's keep that one on the QT until it is announced. Also buddy since when did Edith let you in the garden of Edith?"

"What the hell you talking about?"

"The day of the attack you were at Edith's house at eight in the morning and don't tell me you were taking her to church."

"Yeah I was!"

"You're serious? You weren't shacked up?"

"No . . . I wish. Edith is quite a woman. I'm sinking fast." Disappointed in the lack of juicy details, we headed back in the house.

"Edith, I need to talk with you," I said. "Thanks for taking care of them . . . Especially going up into the hills, you did the right thing."

"Ethan, we didn't know what to do. One thing we did know—don't get captured! I know what they would have done to us!"

"Now tell me, did that missionary really get eaten for dinner in the Congo?"

"No that was BS. I don't think Missy understood the seriousness of what was happening. She is the most trusting good-hearted naïve woman I ever met. She needed a good scaring because she didn't even want to leave the house. I hope you understand. I was not going to leave her behind."

"Hey, dinner's ready. Come 'n get it!" Missy yelled from the kitchen. We sat down and said a prayer. My wife gave a beautiful prayer. It was all for our country and our brave warriors out in the Pacific fighting for their lives at Wake Island and the Philippines.

When we passed out the turkey, I just could not resist teasing my wife. When the plate came to me I said, "Honey I think I'll try an arm and a leg." We busted out laughing. Missy looked at me funny saying, "What is so funny? Turkey's don't have arms?" I told her remind me later to tell her what the joke was.

Before we fell asleep, Missy asked me would our world ever be the same. I said no, at least for now. She also asked me if I would be leaving soon for war. I shook my head no. I wasn't lying to her. Simply put we had no strike force to send. Our navy was in very bad shape.

Getting Pearl straightened out was now at full speed. Casualty reports started coming in with high numbers. Some said as high as three thousand. The ship count was getting clearer now. Our losses were high however many of the ships would sail again. The loss of aircraft was very high. They didn't hit fuel and ammo dumps. That was a blessing. No aircraft carriers were in port at the time. This is what saved us from a real bad situation.

One night at home after being at the base for more than eighteen hours, I brought up the subject of evacuation of the island to my wife. The response was not favorable at all.

"Ethan, I will not leave this island. This is where I will be when you return home to us!"

"Missy, you may not have a choice and when the order is given, well, you'll go. Besides when this is over, I might not return to Pearl. It might be anywhere in the U.S. You might as well be in Duluth and at least be with your family.

"I hate all of this, Ethan. Why can't you just put in your two week notice and quit this madness?"

"Now you know I can't do that. Would you really want me to?"

"No, I just want what I want. I'm being selfish darling. I'm so proud of you for doing your duty and the courage you have. I just want us to not have this life we have interrupted."

"Me too and millions like us. I hate that stupid saying, *we are all in same boat*, but we are!"

"I know. If we have to move then I guess Duluth will have to do but I don't have to like it."

"Missy, you are sounding like a baby. Anyway won't this way be better to be at home with your family than alone on Pearl?"

"I guess."

1942

December 7th was now history. Early 1942 didn't look much better. Things in the Pacific were bleak. Many victories for the Jap's were in the bag such as Wake Island, the Philippines plus others in the Far East. Some of our ships were back in the states for repair. Pearl was now looking better. Our military was getting itself together. It would be a rough road to push these bastards back to Japan. They were a brutal bunch. The more we learned about them the more we hated them. Looking back now and comparing them to Al Qaeda, there isn't much difference. These little people were plain nuts. They were pure with evil, as the world had not seen since the days of Genghis Khan. Yes, the Nazi's were bad too. They needed eliminated also. I wanted to get it over with as soon as possible. I had seen too much already.

Edith came over one day in January. She had some news for us and we placed bets on what it could be. I said marriage. Missy laughed.

"Those two get married? I'll wager she dumped him."

"Hi, everyone, how's it going?" Edith said as she walked in the door. She picked up Toddy then gave him a kiss.

"We're good, just very confused about whether we can stay in Pearl. They may run Todd and me out on the first boat. Excuse me, I mean ship."

"Well kids, I've decided to leave Hawaii if they give me the chance. With the school closing soon, I believe waiting around here is probably a waste of time."

"What's a waste of time, Edith?"

"Missy, would you wait around for a guy that will never commit to anything or anybody?"

"I see. Yeah, I guess you're right but does he know about this?"

"No."

"Edith I know I'm sticking my nose where it doesn't belong but . . . this is my problem with getting very involved with a man before marriage. Although I see how it can happen. Look what has happened to my brother."

"Missy, Lloyd and I are not physically involved. That won't ever happen unless we get married."

I broke, in saying, "Missy, that morning of the attack Lloyd was picking her up for church. They weren't shacking up. I forgot to tell you Lloyd picks Edith up for church every Sunday."

"Darn you, EA! You make me feel like a big jerk and a judgmental prude. Edith I am so sorry!"

"Missy, I sort of feel the same as you. I might be more inclined for some intimacy if his resistance to commitment wasn't so vague. He either isn't ready for that or he doesn't love me enough."

"Hey, Edith, he loves you. I know that," I said.

"Well I won't push him and please don't let him know. If he wants me he must come to me on his own."

Edith Jeanette Conover was born in 1909 to the parents of Methodist missionaries. Her father was a preacher and her mother a teacher. Originally they were from Jamestown, New York. Edith had no formal education but was well versed in literature, theology and math. She had been engaged once to a British Army officer. He died in 1938 in Singapore of friendly fire. This put her in a frame of mind that love would never come her way. Time would tell if these two opposites were heading down the aisle or out different doors.

January was almost over. The Battle of the Java Sea was underway. Some people that I had served with were fighting there. I remembered meeting the man who had a brother on the USS Houston. I thought back on the parents from Pennsylvania that had a Marine son on Wake Island. He was now dead or a prisoner. Being dead might be a blessing.

I got home after a long day. Missy was sitting on the couch sobbing so I asked, "What's the matter?"

"Ethan, when someone says 'you're lucky you're not in the Navy or I would send you on slow boat to China, what does that mean?"

"Just what it says, why?"

"I got yelled at by a young officer. I was wearing my Navy dungarees and shirt with a sailor cap on inside out. He thought I was a sailor. I disgraced the uniform, he said."

"Where were you when this happened?"

"In the driveway cleaning Yellow Baby. How dare he think I was a boy, is this man blind?"

"All right don't worry. When I'm done with him, he will be the one on a slow boat to China!"

"I'm sorry. I will not embarrass you again with my stupid fashion ideas. I was being careless."

"Missy, you are years ahead of the rest in style so keep that wonderful brain of yours working. Maybe someday you'll own a line of women's clothes called Missy Clothing Company."

"Ethan, this won't get you into trouble?"

"No, it won't get me into trouble.

The JG that gave my wife a hard time got new orders. There was a written apology. Destination? Take a guess.

Exit

We wouldn't be surprised if the enemy attacked us again. They now had Wake, Guam, and the Philippines. If they got Hawaii, it would be hard and maybe impossible to get them liberated ever again. At that time, all bombers were limited on how far they could fly. They could make it to the islands but would never make it back from the West Coast. An amphibious invasion would be the only way. Casualties would be outrageous. It would be so high our government would consider Hawaii a lost cause. This island had to be defended, that was all there was to it. The only people who would stay in Hawaii would be the most essential ones. Although the order was not official, we all knew that civilian and tourists would have to leave soon.

In February, the order finally came in that all non-essential personnel would start an orderly process of evacuation. Most would head home on a luxury liner. When this was all over, the only people left in Hawaii would be the locals, military and some civilian defense contractors. Missy and my son would have to leave. This would not go over big with her. In war, everyone would have to sacrifice something in order to win this reign of terror that griped the world. Separation from my family was one I hated to make.

"Hey, Missy, when you're done in there come sit with me."

"Yes I will be there in a second. If you have something to tell me that I'm not going to like hearing let me get the cotton."

"I'll just talk louder. You can't win this one."

"Ok, dear, I'm here so let's hear it." She came into the room dressed up for the evening, putting the final pins in her hair. She sat down next to me on the couch and threw her legs across my lap.

"Honey, it's ten at night, why do you have your hair fixed up and lipstick on?"

"I just thought I would clean up before bed . . . for you. Ethan, let's talk next week."

"No, not next week. You need to hear this now."

"I know. I heard about the evacuation at the grocery store."

"Gosh, I wonder what other of our secret plans is available at the store! Anyway, since you know, you two will be leaving sometime in March. You will go by ocean liner for a port on the West Coast."

"Ok, can I tell you how I feel about this?"

"Of course."

"I figure the Jap's won't attack again. You need to tell the brass that. So why not save the taxpayers a whole lot of money instead of shipping us out on a luxury liner?" She was shaking a little, and threw her legs off my lap and leaned over with her forearms on her knees, breathing heavily.

I rubbed her back and she started to cry, complaining about all the what-ifs like being separated, me getting killed perhaps and not seeing Todd take his first steps.

"We will be together again. This war is not going to last forever. We will beat these Nips. After that our lives will begin where we left off."

"Is this ship big enough to take all of my shoes back?"

"Now that's the girl I know, witty with that beautiful smile and giggle. Yes you can take all of them back or leave them here."

"No way, not my shoes. That's like giving my soul away!"

Missy laid one of her soft kisses on me with those perfect lips. Soon we were both in our bed, which to us was more than just a bed. It was our paradise. No one could take that away from us, at least for now.

March would come soon so we wasted no time in doing as much together as martial law would let us. The area was not safe anymore. With rumors of the enemy around every corner, there were many young soldiers, sailors, and Marines patrolling. All were with loaded weapons, some trigger-happy. At times, they would let a few rounds go. Many things were on rationing including gas, meat and electricity. The beaches were off limits. Telegrams sent were almost non-existent. There was to be no talk about an evacuation. The OSS believed their spies were everywhere. They also believed not all were of Japanese descent!

"Honey if I can't telegram my parents that I'm coming home then how will they know I am coming home?"

"They won't. It'll be a surprise. When you get to the States there must be no discussion of the attack or about the evacuation."

"I understand Ethan . . . this is so strange to me. It is like being in a nightmare. One day we are just husband and wife living our lives. Now saying, 'I love you' might be against the law."

"They haven't outlawed that yet so we can still be mushy and lovie-dovie."

"Who will hug me then and tell me everything will be alright?"

"Maybe when you get home you'll want to forget about me and fine someone new?"

"Ethan, you are so close to a good whacking for saying that! Finding a new man is the last thing on my mind. If you think I would ever do that then you just don't see how much our marriage means to me. I feel like . . . . Excuse me Lord, I feel like shit now. Thanks a lot!"

"I was kidding you. I know you better than that so just simmer down. Such language Missy, what would your mama say?"

"Mama would cuss me out for cussing. Please don't tease me about adulterous behavior. We have one of those in the family already. Ethan you could cheat on me when we leave with the girls on Water Street, so there!"

"Sweetheart I would never two-time you. I would rather be lonely than be with those dogs on Water Street! Now, no more stupid talk. How do you even know about Water Street?"

"Well, Ethan we don't have prostitutes in Duluth. I asked Edith to take me down there so I could see what one looks like."

"Okay so what does a prostitute look like? Wait a minute . . . are you telling me that Duluth which is a lake port has no red light district?"

"That's right, no red light district. Thomas would know," she said, rolling her eyes. "I know one thing, boy, those streetwalkers sure don't know how to dress!"

Saturday afternoon we were sitting in our mud hut at 192 East Ninth Street. Then here come "The Timkens" hand in hand smiling and looking like they had not a care in the world. I answered the door then said, "What are you two so happy about? Did the Jap's surrender already?"

"No, however I did. We wanted you two to be the first to know that Edith and I are getting married. Of course we want you two to be in the wedding."

"Lloyd, Edith, that's great! We would be honored", Missy, said.

"Yes, we are honored. I think this is wonderful. I am truly happy for you! When and where?"

"Next Saturday at my church. We will live in my flat until this war is over so I will be staying in Hawaii. Lloyd seems to think he will be in Pearl for awhile as a salvage diver so we can be together at least for now."

Missy broke down in tears. We all knew why. They were to stay . . . she had to leave. Edith took her in the bedroom and tried to console her. My wife came out of it quickly and said, "You will have a nice wedding, so let me know what you need done and I will do it."

Saturday came. When Edith came down the aisle, she was not the same woman! Missy transformed Edith into a gorgeous bride that any man would be proud marry. My wife, knowing proper etiquette, dressed down a bit to give the Bride her moment. I whispered to Lloyd, "Can you handle that head turner, lover boy?"

"I hope so EA, gosh she's beautiful."

The service went smooth. Wartime had brought two lonely people together.

"Missy, you did a great job today. I know this is going to be a marriage made in heaven."

"Thank you honey, I'm glad it went well. I hope they are happy like us. I hope he knows how to take care of her."

"Oh, Lloyd's been around, he can take her through the ropes with no problem tonight."

"Ethan Allen that is not what I meant! I am sure they will do fine with that part. I meant I hope he will be a good husband to her as you are to me. Gosh. Is that the only thing on your mind?"

"Honestly . . . yeah. Hey, don't worry, he loves her like mad. They'll do just fine. It's not hard to treat your wife right when you are married to a sweetheart like I am."

Tears, Tensions and Farewells

February was half over. Still there was no definite time that my wife and son would leave for the States. Everyone was on edge and Missy was not herself. Her heart broke at the thought of having to go home. For all of the military dependents there seemed to be a grey cloud hanging over their heads.

On the last Saturday of the month, the women decided to go shopping in Honolulu. As I changed the baby's diaper, she said, "We are going to shop for a nice outfit to wear for my 'mandatory bon voyage send Missy and Toddy back to Duluth' luxury cruise."

"You are not funny. I think you should be a little more aware that this is not easy on me either. You're leaving me but I will be without you also."

"Ethan, damn it, I hate all of this. I find the man I want to spend my life with and this happens. I am mad but not at you. I am selfish, not for me but for us, please understand my side."

"I do, I really do but this is way beyond our control, so let's just hope this ends soon. We must be patient and enjoy each day we have."

Edith showed up and could not help but see the strain between us. They went shopping and I watched the baby. Feeling sad, I was soon smiling as I watched Todd. He had no clue what was happening in the world. I wondered if any of us did.

They returned about four hours later. She seemed to be in a better mood. As we ate dinner, we listened to the radio. It was The Jack Benny Show . . . nobody laughed. Missy nursed the little boy, rocked him to sleep then hit the sack. We both slipped into bed, me in my shorts and she with hair tied up wearing white-striped pajamas. She looked so cute but romance was not on our minds. We only talked.

"Ethan, I am a woman completely out of control and so ashamed of myself. I need you even if war separates us. I want also to be there waiting for you when this is over."

"I know that this is rough on you and I am not dealing with it well either. Let's just get through this together and when it is over we can move on and live our lives as we want?"

"Yes, that is what I want to do. I promise no more tears or crying about leaving. I am just a brat, guess my Daddy was right."

"Now sweetheart, I expect you to be Missy the woman that should have played Scarlett O'Hara! Have you ever considered acting?"

"Ethan Allen, you are a funny . . . no, I haven't. If I had to do a love scene or even kiss another man I would just turn red and freeze up!"

Missy! Missy! Missy! I thought more along the lines of a Cary Grant-Jean Arthur comedy."

"Gosh, I thought you meant a steamy movie."

"Why don't you just stick to being my steamer?"

"You right, you would not want to see me kissing Cary Grant or Jimmy Stewart anyway."

March 1st we got the word that they would be shipping out on the tenth of the month. We had only days left to be together. I counted our time of being married . . . twenty-one months.

That evening I returned home from work.

"Missy, I'm home. How about sitting down? Let's talk."

"Hi sweetheart, give me a big kiss."

"That is probably a good idea, maybe that's what we should do for the next ten days."

"So it's ten days, eh?"

"I am afraid so. I am slowing dying inside, I could just cry this is killing me so."

"Then cry, I do it all the time, sometimes for joy and sometimes for sadness and sometimes just because. I'm here for you as you have been for me so let it out. Big boys have emotions too."

"I think I will just this one time, but . . . ."

"It is our secret. You are . . . gosh. Such a typical man!"

"You never did tell me what you bought for the trip home. Knowing you it is a nice looking dress with spectators and gloves with a matching hat, right?"

"Almost, except when have you known me to wear a hat? When women stop wearing hats except for a beret they will see how much better they look. Hats take away from a woman's looks. It's been at least sixty years since the Victorian Age. Gosh, when are they going to get with it?"

"You tell them Missy—the Queen of Fashion! So what are you wearing for the bon voyage?"

"Grey . . . because it is the way I feel."

"I understand, so what are you going to wear when I come home?"

"Ethan it will be the sexiest dress and matching shoes. I will put red lipstick that will make you want me so bad. A great hairdo to match that you can mess up when the lights go out!"

"Suppose it is winter and I can't tell you have this dress on?"

"I'm going to wear it anyway. When we get home you'll see it, but not for long! You can count on that."

"Oh woman, you are killing me!"

I was outside one morning drinking coffee and I heard Missy singing. It was the oddest sounding lyrics. I walked in and she had the baby in stitches.

"What's that dumb song your singing?" I said

"It's not a dumb song. Toddy likes it and I do too. It's Three Little Fishes in a Bitty Bitty Little Pool."

"We will learn it together and sing for our twelve kids."

"No, on the singing and no on twelve kids too!"

The next morning Missy and Todd drove into town to shop and get our ration of gas. I stayed home and called Lloyd. We spoke about the war and marriage. The war was not going well for the US, but his life with Edith was great. We made the usual boy talk stuff. To hear us you would think we were in high school. He hinted they wanted to start a family. Lloyd, a family man? I guess he may have said the same thing about me.

We played with Todd when they got home and I said, "These little ones are too much fun. I hope we have more, don't you?"

"Of course, but not while you are away from me."

"I know but Mother Nature sometimes gets in the way, especially when we really use nothing to prevent a baby from happening."

"Well darling, we are going to try and prevent that from happening so I got these for us.

"Rubbers! There are two things in this world I hate . . . submarines and those! I can't believe you had the guts to ask for them."

"People make too much of a deal about stuff like this. I am a married woman . . . it is like buying toothpaste . . . you need it, you want it, and so you get it. Doesn't shame me one bit."

A detail of civilians dropped off a shipping crate the next day to pack all of our worldly possessions. Packing was hard. We gave our two pieces of furniture to Lloyd and Edith. Yellow Baby would stay in Hawaii. Maybe at the end of the war we could have it shipped home. Lloyd would have it to use although it needed tires and those would be hard to find, even for Lloyd.

The days went as slow as we could make them but the sun did rise and the sun did set. Soon, none. The morning of 10 March 1942 came. Missy woke up.

"Good morning, darling," I said and kissed her on the forehead.

"What's so good about it? I leave you tonight and tomorrow morning I will be miles from you. I will be sad except when I look at Todd and think how beautiful he is and much he reminds me of you."

"I know and I will be lost without you. You are my world . . . so deep in my heart. Leaving Todd just kills me. I love you so much."

"Ethan . . . wrap me in your arms for awhile. I just need you closer than close can be."

Heading East

That evening we had dinner at the Lloyd and Edith household. Around eight, Missy changed into her new grey dress. She looked beautiful as ever when she walked into the room. This would be the saddest night of our lives. Edith broke into tears. This was hard on Edith too. Lloyd gave her a beautiful necklace of pearls.

"And just for you, they're not hot." Missy smiled and kissed him.

"You be safe and spend all the time you can with her. While Ethan is in Pearl, be the good friend you have always been."

The Timkens kissed Toddy goodbye. They told me to come back to their flat and spend the night there after the ship left. We got into Yellow Baby and headed to the piers where the ship would be.

"Ethan, I feel like James Cagney when he heads for the electric chair!"

"Well, the suspense of all of this is bad . . . but not as bad as an electric chair," I remarked.

We drove to the docks and sat close. We both fought tears. I looked at the vessel and remarked to Missy that the basic design and size was similar to the RMS Titanic. Just the way she met me, with my foot in my mouth.

"Gee Ethan, the Titanic, really makes me feel good. All I need now is an iceberg to float by."

"Sorry, bad choice of words but it does look like a nice ship. She should ride good and smooth."

The ship was a beauty and a very well known luxury that sailed mostly from the States to Hawaii. It was the SS Lurline, a two stacker weighing in at 18,000 tons and fast with a speed of more than twenty-two knots. Built in 1932, she was a US owned by Matson Lines. With that kind of

The Beautiful Mistake

speed and naval protection, the Japs would have a hard time hitting her. I felt good about my family on this ship.

We took those many steps up the gangway with Missy in the lead. I held Todd. A steward carried the suitcases. When we reached the main deck, we caught our breath and stared at the crowd below also getting ready to board. Missy looked pale, as did I. Todd was being a little monkey. He pulled at my nose, insignias and anything else he could grab.

Their cabin was on the second deck below. The space had a large bed up against the wall and a head with shower and bath plus a sitting area for reading.

"This is it honey. It looks modern for a ten-year-old ship"

"It is very nice. Where's the toilet?"

"Over there, need to go?"

"Yes but my body doesn't know whether to barf or have diarrhea."

"Sit down and calm yourself. Let me help you, do you want a ginger ale or crackers?"

"No Ethan, I want to wake up and find us in the mud hut with no war and no worries. I know that this isn't a dream so kiss me goodbye."

"Missy, we have two more hours together. Let's watch our son play. He is growing so fast."

"He will probably be in college the next time you see him."

"An eighteen-year war? I doubt it. This thing will be over by 1943."

I changed the subject to life when the war was over.

"When this is over I plan to do things with him I was never able to do like play ball, fish or hunt."

"I imagine this little guy is going to have a ball with his daddy. I cannot wait to see you two head out for the day. I'll just stay home by myself and clean the house."

"I can't stand to see a grown woman pout. You can come too."

We cuddled and talked about our time together, like meeting for the first time and our first kiss. Time seemed to pass slowly but then the call went out those not sailing to leave. Missy teared up. I got shaky. This was the beginning of our farewell. The little guy was fast asleep. I rubbed his soft skin kissing him on the forehead. Then I took my wife's hand helping her up and we embraced. I told her how much I loved my Duluth beauty.

It was time to go.

"Ethan, please come home to us . . . do your job well but please be safe. I need you. You are my dream come true. I have such bad feelings about all this and you know how that can be sometimes."

"Mystic, right now I am the mystic and I see us together soon. But you have to stay safe too. There is danger in everything right now."

"I will stay safe darling, you don't have to worry about me. Nothing ever happens in Duluth . . . believe me!"

We kissed and held each other tight. I smelled her beautiful shiny long brown hair and kissed those soft lips. As we held each other, I felt her heart beating right through her clothes. As we continued to kiss, I could feel warm wet tears.

"Missy, I love you and will dream of you every night."

"Ethan Allen, come home soon. I love you too. Remember there is a little boy who will be waiting for you also."

I gently closed the door and heard by wife start to cry. I wanted so bad to go back in. As I walked away and headed down the passageway I heard a voice say, "Excuse me, my I introduce myself?"

"Yes Ma'am."

"My name is Elizabeth Johns. I am leaving for the States on this ship. My husband is Colonel Samuel Johns, US Army. Separation is nothing new to us. First in World War One and now this war. This is hard, I know. If you wouldn't mind, could I maybe be a friend to your wife and help her through this?"

"Sure Mrs. Johns, I know my Missy would love that. She is alone on this ship because all of her friends are on other ones. This would mean so much to me if you could comfort her."

"Your wife and baby will be in good hands I promise. Now you be safe and come home soon."

"Thank you, I feel a little bit better, thank you."

I left the ship then drove to the Timken's house. I slept in the car. The Studebaker had so much of her in it. I looked on the seat and there was a note with her Bible. The note simply said "Ethan trust in our Lord and pray. When we meet again, we will be closer than ever before. Your wife that loves you so much, Missy."

Tears came flowing from my eyes. I prayed, then somehow fell asleep dreaming of Mystic Bay.

Heading West

I soon realized that I too would be leaving Pearl. My destination to New Zealand was to build a landing force. Everything was on the QT. Civilian crews were coming in and freeing up navy men. The war now seemed to be doing well for us. Lloyd would soon go to the war zone.

I left on a transport heading for New Zealand with a flotilla of transports and warships. I am not sure if the brass even knew if we were in safe waters or headed for a showdown. It would take some time to get there and for the first time since we got married I really felt alone. I sent her a letter saying that I had received orders, but due to censorship, my destination was secret. I had no idea how she was doing. Although I knew she was safe, it still gave me the creeps not knowing nothing. When we arrived at our destination, new orders came in. We would be heading soon to the Fiji Islands where practice landings would be. This was in anticipation of the invasion of Guadalcanal.

Before we were to leave, a letter from Missy came in. I was so thrilled. I could smell her perfume on it. Then again, the whole mailbag smelled like perfume!

Missy said that the trip across the Pacific was boring, which was good and she had made some friends. Mrs. Johns was a big comfort and loved helping with the baby. According to my wife, Todd was a hit with the many older passengers. Her letter only spoke of the cruise and said that they were in San Francisco waiting for the train to head east. Missy said that she would stop in Lincoln to visit my family, which didn't surprise me none. I read that letter repeatedly, stared at it like it was her photo. To think how much a letter meant. Such a sick feeling this was to have.

The Fijis' are nice islands. Some of the islands in the Pacific are real hellholes. This was no vacation though and as soon as we arrived, we began landing exercises. Training was day in, day out. Everyone was getting mail except me. Finally, one for me.

Hello my sweet Ethan, I am now leaving Lincoln and did we have a wonderful time. Your family is such sweet kind people and your Mama just loves being a grandma. Dad is so proud of his grandson and you also. They are worried about you and this war but know you are the best sailor in the whole Navy! I know that too and darling my love for you is so much alive even though you are away from me. Each night I go to sleep with your picture next to me and wake up with you. Honey I am scared but do trust that God will bring you back to me. I need to close for the train is soon to arrive. When I get to Duluth, I will write a nice long letter and say things I want to tell you. You are my hero and strength. I love you Warrant Officer Man and you are in my heart always. Love, Missy

After reading that, I went off to be alone.

Soon we were ready for the real thing. On August 7, 1942, we headed towards the Solomon Islands. We landed several days later. Was it a mess! The landing crafts weren't loaded right. There was so much confusion. There was no opposition from the enemy at first. Out of nowhere came the enemy attacking form the sky. That made bringing supplies ashore even more difficult. However, the Japanese believed only one thousand Marines had landed, instead of ten thousand. I stayed there for four days ferrying in supplies and then was relieved. I made my report on the landing to my superiors then waited for new orders.

At a meeting with the brass, they asked me to give a full and honest assessment of the landing. I spoke plain, telling them the truth—we would never win a war with landing operations like these. They agreed.

A Love Letter

Mail had been very slow. I had gotten one letter from her saying that a very excited family met her arrival in Duluth. The Bays were so thrilled to see her and of course their new grandson. Idonea and Eira were proud aunts. Thomas was on the Lakes hauling ore to the now very busy steel mills. My wife was readjusting to life at home. I could tell by her short sentences that she was not a happy woman.

Several more letters came, each sounded more optimistic than the last. Finally, I got the one I was waiting for, a very confident letter telling me that things now seemed to be settling down. My fragile naive wife was going to work at a very large steel mill in Duluth as a crane operator! She was looking forward to do her part for the war effort. My wife as a crane operator! Missy . . . Miss Fashion in a steel mill wearing work clothes with grit and grime. I needed to see that on film to believe it!

A letter from Missy the steelworker:

Hi my Ethan, No letters from you lately and that makes me lonely. As long as the War Department doesn't send me a gram I know you are safe. Everyone is happy about the Guadalcanal win and I just know you were there. We are sad of our losses but I guess that is going to happen. Work at the mill is hot and dirty. Some of the men resent women being there and others are very helpful. I am learning to run a crane in the open hearth where the materials get melted into steel. Ethan I didn't even know steel melted like butter! I only work the day shift because I still nurse little Toddy. I feel I am doing something for the war effort although I'm very tired by bedtime. Oh, honey, I might get my own flat. Although my parents are a great help I don't want Todd spoiled or my Daddy getting too close to him. Reason being when you get home, I do not want the baby being shy with you. He needs to know who Daddy is and who Grandpa is.

Honey I miss you so much and I am still a scared little kitten. I miss your kisses and your strong arms around me. I miss everything we do and I miss that too! I wonder if my letters are conversed. Honey, come home safe. I will be here when you do. Love you so much. Missy Xoxoxo . . . is that allowed Mr. Censor man?

I was back to Guadalcanal in January 43. This time we weren't only bringing supplies. We were now taking the wounded back onto the bigger ships for care. It was a sight like December 7, 1941. The wounds ranged from not so serious to men that probably were better off dead. Burns, loss of limbs and men staring into space like zombies. It was so sad. The dead would remain there until the war was over. I saw no Jap prisoners. Word was that they would commit suicide rather than be POW's. The Marines didn't care. It saved ammo and time. This was war at its worst now. Even though I was not in the direct line of fire, the beachhead was a dangerous place. Mail call came.

My Dear Ethan, Nothing much new here, work, sleep and take care of Todd. He is so cute at sixteen months. I have pictures of you and me and all of us around the room and he seems to know who Daddy is when I show him. Honey, I feel like a prisoner in this apartment. Sometimes it's like being an unwed mother hiding so I don't embarrass the family. I walk down the street by myself and some stare. I don't wear my wedding ring much because it gets dirty and scuffed up at the mill. Guess I should. Maybe it is just my lopsided feelings but you returning to Pearl made me sad. Please be safe my love, Duluth is starting to get casualties. I am so scared and I wonder what would happen if I lost you. Ethan I am weak, I come on strong but I'm weak and not much good trying to be happy when I'm not. God bless you my dream come true, love Missy {I will dream of you tonight} Xoxoxo

After I left the island, Commander Flynn said I could expect a new and different duty.

"Plan for the worst," he said.

"A desk job? Oh, Sir, no," I said, only half kidding.

"Vanderbilt, this is no desk job and no joke. But what I can tell is you a desk job might look good."

"When will I know, sir?"

"When I tell you, Ethan. Try to find some nice woolly warm gloves."

"Where in the hell am I going to find them in the Pacific?"

"Chief that is all."

The Forgotten Battle

In February, I boarded an oiler bound for Puget Bay that was heading for dry dock. I would report to an amphibious unit for further instructions. After only one amphibious landing, I wished that I had a ship to call home . . . sea duty never looked so swell.

Upon arrival in Puget, I went to the Northern Pacific Force, which to me meant nothing. I had never even heard of it. Admiral Thomas C. Kincaid was the commanding officer. He had served on some well know ships like the Pennsy, Arizona and USS Indianapolis. I reported to Lt. Commander Jackson Randolph, a forty-year-old career officer. He had never married. He was an arrogant kind of person, very cold too. He deserved duty in a cold wet place like Puget. He came right out and told me that we would plan the landing invasion in the Aleutian Islands. The Aleutians were on American soil. This was a military action largely unknown by the American public. This was the Forgotten Battle of the Aleutians. By the time I left this campaign, there was one sailor who would never forget it.

The Navy must have had its act together when it came to mail because shortly after I arrived at Puget a letter came from Missy.

Hello to my love and from Todd the home wrecker! I wish this child were a little more of a slow learner because now that he can walk and he is into everything. My mom has had to rearrange her house for when she watches him and he still finds things. Better that than being a crying brat. Work has been good and I am catching on real quick on crane handling. The mill is turning out record amounts of steel to beat the hell out of those rat bastards. Like my language darling? These steelworkers cuss like crazy and they say the "f" word in every sentence! I won't say that word and ask them not to use it around me so they just say "f" you and walk away. Someone told me to give them the finger but I forgot which one.

I miss you so much Ethan and wonder just where you are. Can you give me a hint? I won't tell anyone. Please my sweet husband—boyfriend and lover, be safe and pray for an end to this madness. Always yours, Missy

P.S. I got my childhood teddy bear out, put a sailor suit on it. I call it EA! LOVE YOU SO MUCH. Xoxoxo and more!

Soon all of us knew why we were in this cold damp place. When the weather broke around May, we would invade a beach in the Aleutians to drive the enemy off. Then the Army could concentrate on taking back the rest of the Pacific.

I felt the need to ask a dumb question. I asked Chief Nigel Ware.

"Wonder while we wait for the weather to change if leave will be available, Nigel?"

"I doubt it, not with this first class jerk from hell. Where would you go, Ethan?"

"Duluth, Minnesota, man!"

"Heck, that's colder than here."

"Not when I get there. We know how to stay warm!"

"Oh, that's where your wife lives. I see what you mean but don't get your hopes up, maybe after the mission."

My wife wrote and said she was getting some nightlife in with her sisters and girlfriends. Missy assured me she would never dance with another man. I had no problem if she did. I wrote and said if it is some GI leaving for war give him a dance and even a kiss on the cheek. Tell him you'll pray for him too. She wrote back and said okay, but not the kiss. I am sure someone did ask her to dance. Man, if I were a homesick GI, she would be the one I would ask to dance. Gosh, she could dance! The USO for me was only down the street. I decided to wait because only my baby would do.

In March, training for the invasion began. It seemed to be a simple one. However, we were short on landing craft. We were also improperly equipped for cold weather duty too. The Navy knew this, and still was hell-bent on getting the enemy off American soil.

With May a whole two months away and my wife only two days away by train I thought maybe we could meet half way to spend a few days together. I will just ask the Commander. I was sure he would go along with it.

"Commander, I need to ask a question."

"Sure Vanderbilt, but the answer will be no."

"Sir, you have no clue what it is, so may I ask it?"

"Vanderbilt, I know you are a newlywed with a child and want some leave . . . I must say no. You're needed here and some of the people sent to me for this mission are, to be frank, idiots. I need you because you can handle small craft better than most. This invasion might be like a low budget "B" movie, in regards to the little amounts of good equipment we have. It is so bad we might have to swim to shore with the supplies on our back! Ethan I know you think I am a cold miserable old salt, but I understand. When we are relieved in the Aleutians, you can get leave and see your wife and son. I will promise you that."

"Yes sir, thank you for your time and confidence in me."

I sure hoped this guy kept his word.

Pin up girls posters were everywhere back then. Some were already known actors or models. One newcomer that caught my attention was a gorgeous woman named Jeanne Crain. I'm not going to say she looked exactly like Missy, but there were similarities. I wrote her about this. I was sure my wife would have something to say about it, I loved getting her goat.

Dear EA, so you have discovered Jeanne Crain eh? That's all I hear at work and even from my Daddy. Gosh sweetheart, I guess I'm not your #1 drool anymore. Honey thanks for the compliment but I don't hold a candle to her and anyway she is only 18 years old! Cradle robber! Yes, she is beautiful but would you really want her over me? Don't think on that okay? Anyway, all is well and your little boy is just fine and so much like you. He is so sweet that when I get teary over you, he comes, pats me on the back, and hugs me just as you would do. Ethan my senses tell me you are close and that makes me feel sad but also happy because if you are in the States, you are safe. Know that I love you so much and miss you and that sweet way of yours. Must go to work, dream of me, honey, and Jeanne too. Why would I say that? Hah! Love, your wife, friend and love. Mystic Anne Marie Vanderbilt. I just love writing that. Good night cutie pie. Missy Xoxoxo!

Man, I hated that war.

The weather started to break. Soon the action would begin. We got busy with invasion preparation. Japan on US soil was an eerie feeling although they were on a string of worthless cold islands and many miles from anything significant. Still they had to be taught a lesson . . . go home to your own island and stay there!

In May 1943, we began our invasion with a group of naval vessels and support ships. Our mission was to land the 10th Mountain Division. The 10th was a cold weather mountain division fighting along with Canadian units. To say the least, we were not ready for what was to come. The landing area was not as we had trained on. Beaches were rocky and not like Hawaii at all! I had spent my whole career in warm places. I was not use to it at all. As the invasion unfolded, we met no opposition as had been predicted. With no casualties during the landing, we did have our problems getting men and material ashore. It was a joke, not enough landing craft plus inexperienced small craft handlers. I piloted many landing crafts to the beachhead myself.

At the end of May 1943, the island was under US-Canadian control and my mission here was over. I headed for Fort Ord, California to prepare for another invasion with the promise of leave tossed out the window. It wasn't Commander Randolph's fault, but it disappointed me a lot. I was getting tired of being such a valuable asset, but when duty calls . . . duty calls.

Missy's letters were coming in at a rate of two a week and in order so we were keeping up on events in our lives.

Dear Ethan, Well guess who is now divorced? Not me silly, Allison! She is a free woman (not that she ever wasn't) (gosh that is rude of me), and her and my goofy brother are going to shack up and make this situation even worse. Allison says she is not sure if marriage with Thomas is the right thing to do now. It is their lives but I say it is the wrong thing to do. Honey, could you have ever seen us living in sin? It is too easy for one or the other to jump ship. Anyway, Juliet is a sweet little doll and Todd gets along with her real well.

My grandmother is now in her final days, it is sad but at eighty-two, she has had a good life. Grandma Victoria was always rather cold and showed little affection but without her, my Dad would not be here. Anyway must close, will write soon like in a few minutes! I love you so much and so does Toddy, be safe, read my Bible and dream of me and maybe our dreams will hook up and you can mess my hair up! Missy {Ms. Lonely}

When we got to Ft Ord, we had liberty call for two days.. No leave was granted. It was made known that reassignment was to happen soon. I thought about calling Missy but was that a good idea? Maybe hearing each other's voices would be nice but then again maybe the pain of being so close yet so far away would hurt more than it helped. I decided to sleep on it and pray, as Missy would say.

Long distance calling

I decide to call. I figured six p.m. would be a good time to call. Finally, it was time. I was nervous and for the life of me, I had no clue why. I felt like at times knowing Missy was just a dream, maybe it is.

"Operator I want to call Tuxedo 2—1978 and reverse the charges."

Now, the longest thirty seconds while the operator place the call. Annikin answered the phone.

"Yes, we will take the charges, Missy telephone for you, Missy right now, I'll take the baby."

"Who would be calling me on a Saturday evening? Hello, Missy speaking?"

"Hi sweetheart. It's me, your sailor man!"

"Oh Jeepers."

Then I heard a loud noise with her Mother yelling, "Girls! David! Missy has passed out. Ethan is on the phone!"

"Well for heaven's sake! C'mon daughter, wake up! The meter is running, why is this kid so damn dramatic!"

"David, stop it and quit worrying about the money. Just get her up and on her feet! What did you expect from her?"

Finally after a bit Missy got on the phone and said, "Oh Ethan, where are you? I can't believe I'm hearing your voice."

"Honey, I am in California. I had to hear your voice."

"I'm so sorry I fainted . . . I went into shock. You know me, never a dull moment."

"Missy, these are the things we can tell our grand kids about. Being married to you is never a dull moment! So how are you and how is the little guy?"

"Oh, he is great and such a beautiful little boy. He is so smart and funny. Why are you in California? I am coming out to see you."

"Hold on now. We are leaving soon. I requested leave and it was denied. I want to see you so bad. It's just not going to happen right now. You must hang in there, make steel and raise Todd."

"Ethan, the heck with making steel, I want to make . . . I can't say it on a party line!"

"I know, hot stuff, me too."

We talked for one hour and Toddy said hi in his own little boy language. It was so good to hear that giggle of hers plus all of the bizarre stories she told me. At the end, we spoke about how much we missed each other. We said goodbye with tears. We were both so heartbroken. Talking to Missy was fun and better than letters; still, let it left me blue and homesick for her.

Light at the end of the tunnel

June 1943 I received orders to head for the Solomon's to prepare for another amphibious landing with the US Marines. I left on a transport heading West under full speed with destroyers and subs keeping an eye on the enemy.

When I arrived, Commander Jackson Randolph said our job was going to be a lot of island hopping. These landings would be all different. We could have some close contact with the enemy. The enemy was dug in well on these islands. They were well trained, equipped and determined.

August, we hit the beach and eventually took New Georgia. Then off to the Solomon Islands. After one month, the mail finally caught up with us and there were many letters from Missy.

Ethan my husband, boyfriend and other things that the mail censors don't need to know, I hear the war now is going our way and you see it in the people's faces by the way they act. Good, that means you will be home soon and we can be normal again. I got promoted at the mill and now operate the overhead crane pouring the molten steel into molds. It's kinda scary but a beautiful sight with the bright orange steel flowing like water and so hot! Like you dear, hot! Back to business. I got a crane cab that was so filthy and smelly that during a down period I cleaned it up and painted it too. Now they call it Missy's Perch. Some very off color jokes have been made like this is a brothel. Men have such dirty minds! But not you, right? Hah! Anyway, Toddy is great. He is talking in his own way . . . so bright and funny. Allison and I are becoming friends and she is a nice woman but has had a rough life. Juliet is a sweet little girl and Brother Thomas is still a jerk. Allison doubts if they will ever marry. She is going to move out to live by herself. Shacking up never works out. Honey I love you and need you home so bad, please be safe and pray a lot! You're my sailor man and you know that. Love, your wife the steelworker, Missy

November, 1943, our forces landed in the Empress Augusta Bay. This was the starting point of the Battle of Bougainville. As usual, my job was to supervise the landing. The Marines needed every tool to kick their butt. We would give them everything they needed to end this madness.

In the Gilbert Islands, we would engage the enemy at Tarawa. This was to be one of the worst battles in the war. Before the landing, we all got mail and all of us knew that some were reading or writing the last letters of our lives. Before I read Missy's letter, I wrote to explain that this was going to be a real bad one. I told her I was in a good position to avoid any real danger. Before that letter, I had never lied to her in my life.

Hi sweetheart, Guess what! I am going to audition for—a modeling service with a clothes designer from Chicago. My sisters are also and we will wear some very nice outfits from p.j.'s to gowns and shorts plus swimsuits. I want to do hand and foot modeling. You always said I have great hands and cute footsies, right Ethan Allen? I am so excited and it pays well. I told them NO risqué posing so don't worry you won't see me on a pin-up calendar! I would send you a pin-up pose but I wouldn't want you to laugh yourself to death!

Missy the model, wow, you just never know about my strange cookie! A pin-up picture, sure why not! Then again, maybe not such a good idea. I had seen what some of these pin-up posters look like after a sailor is done with one.

Commander Jackson met me on the deck right before the invasion and said this will be our last mission together. I asked, "I don't understand sir. Last mission?"

"Yes Vanderbilt, it's called personal rotation. You, me and others are going home for thirty-day leave so stay alive. You will be with your family very soon."

I almost fell over. I thought this must be a dream and who knows maybe it was. I decided not tell her I was coming home as to not get her expectations up.

Tarawa November 1943

Several days before the invasion it seemed like a quiet calm had come over the transport we were on. Many men were visiting the chaplains and praying because we all knew this was going to be rough. Marines were a tough bunch. Facing death is something you have no idea how to handle. I was no different. I spent hours looking at Missy's picture along with my boy's, wondering what would happen to them if I didn't make it. I daydreamed about our meeting for the first time and our wedding. I thought of everything we ever had done together. In just a short time, we would be thinking about how to stay alive.

The day of November 28, 1943, was going to be the last time for at least a few days we would have a mail call. That was more important than eating steak. I was really hoping to get one from my wife, as it would make me so much more at ease to at least read her words and imagine her speaking. Mail call came and I got one.

Hello my love, Everything in Duluth is fine and no bad news to report. The little boy is being a little boy and I am working at the mill five days a week for twelve-hour shifts. Honey I am bushed but this is what I must do to win the war and get you and others home. However, guess what! All of us are going to be in Collier's Magazine in a modeling piece called "The Bay Sisters of Duluth." We are wearing some of the new designs for "44" and are they gorgeous! I modeled one outfit, they asked me to take a drag of a cigarette for the pose, and I almost choked to death! Gosh, how can people do that? Anyway, I will be buying up all the copies of Collier's when it comes out in June. I'll send you some pictures that they gave us so you can see how beautiful we are. Honey, try hard to focus on me and not my sisters! Hah, I know you only have eyes for me.

Ethan I know it must sound like things are fine but darling I am so lonely without you and miss you so much. I try not to sob but I do. I hear the war is going to get very bloody. I am so scared, please be safe and pray a lot that this evil will leave soon. Your wife that's so in love with you, Missy

Missy always tried to make bad look good. I was happy she was having some kind of fun. *Wonder how she will look in Collier's, bet she out does those sisters of hers!* I thought, daydreaming her into different outfits, smoking that cigarette. *Also, hope the bright lights do not take her away from me. No, I think I am deep in her heart. I know it is awful to say . . . this is one heck of a time to be in love.*

November 19th was a night of preparing for the invasion. No one would sleep well that night and I was no different.

Precisely at 2:15 a.m., we prepared for D-Day. There were worship ceremonies for all faiths that evening. At 5 a.m., seven US battleships let loose with hundreds of salvos of fourteen and sixteen inch projectiles. We believed that nothing could survive that. For a short while, our aircraft bombed and strafed the beach. Then we hit the beach. It was awful. Our LST did not have enough armor. The Higgins boats, which I was in, were stuck on reefs. We were like sitting ducks. Men were dying everywhere, boys drowning from having heavy backpacks. It was utter confusion. I told the boatswain to zigzag and come in fast on the beach. We landed, but instead of dropping the gate, we climbed over the side keeping low. The Japs were slamming us with machinegun fire. It was hard to fire back. A Marine Lieutenant was in command now. No one is ever ready for this. Bodies started washing ashore. You could smell gun power and blood. While lying pinned on the beach, a young marine stuck his head up for air. Seconds later, he got shot through the head. Finally, a second wave of troops came. After some time passed by, the beach was declared secure. I began my job of securing supplies and setting up a naval command post for re-supply. At dusk, I was back to the ship reporting to Commander Randolph. The initial landing had been a complete disaster.

With Tarawa in our hands there was a feeling we were getting somewhere in this war. Commander Jackson asked to see me . . . my fingers were crossed.

"Mr. Vanderbilt, a job well done! So what are you waiting for, man? Your leave starts when you step on US soil."

"Yes sir and thank you and also Commander when I return I request to serve with you again."

"Ethan, you do need a leave. Nobody has ever wanted that. See you when you get back. Maybe we can end this mess once and for all."

The Beautiful Mistake

Man, what a shock that was! I never thought the promise of leave would happen. I was not going to question it. I headed for the officer in charge to pick up my orders. I would travel on a converted luxury liner to Long Beach USA then take the train to Duluth. I would be home for Christmas. What a present this was for the both of us. This would be a surprise visit due to security reasons.

5,100 miles

A week later, I was on US soil. Of course, I wanted to see my family in Lincoln; however, they would understand that getting to Duluth was the more important thing.

At Christmas time, the trains were packed and running in multiple sections. The train left at 4 p.m. and off to Minnesota we went. I ate, drank a Coke, headed for the sack and slept until morning. We arrived in the Twin Cities around 7 p.m. on the day before Christmas Eve. I realized that I needed to get Missy and Todd something. I headed over to a department store. I found something nice and made it back to the station before my train left.

Near Duluth, the train broke down. I survived fierce combat, ate sea rations, froze in the Aleutians and fought tropical heat for this to happen? Now I knew what S.A.F.U. meant. It sure was F.O!

The conductor said that a replacement engine was on its way from Duluth, but that would take awhile. We would arrive there about three hours late. This was starting to stress me out though there was not much I could do other than be patient. Finally, we got going again. When we got in, I called Thomas hoping he was at his apartment so he could give me a ride.

"Hello?"

"Hey Thomas, how are you doing?"

"Who is this? The voice sounds familiar but . . . no way, is it you, Ethan?"

"You betcha! Right here in living color and also in Duluth!"

"Hell man, I didn't know you were coming here or maybe I am just in a gin fog."

"It needs to be a surprise. I suppose the family will have the big deal tonight at the house. How about picking me up and see if we can get Missy to faint or something stupid like that!"

"Good idea, I will be over in fifteen minutes. Wanna come over to clean up?"

"Cinder's, sweat and bad breath will have to do for now for your sister! The dirt comes off later!"

"Somehow, Ethan, I just can't see Missy giving you a bath. But then she is *my* sister so . . . see you in fifteen! Bye, now."

Thomas arrived and not in fifteen minutes! It was 45 minutes . . . typical for him. I could have been mad but figured that's what I got for calling on him of all people.

"Sorry man, I got delayed but it is real good to see you! How are you, Ethan?"

"I'm fine but how is Missy doing and be truthful. I worry so much about her."

"She's good. She seems to have lost some of that spunk. With a job and Todd I guess she's under a heavy load. I know my sister and she'll bounce back, she is one tough cookie."

"I hope you're right, this war can bring a person down. So you off now while the Lakes are froze up?"

"Yes, but they want us back to work sooner than usual because the mills are running low on ore. I keep busy with my daughter and shipyard work."

"And Allison?"

"That's over, she is . . . no . . . I'm not ready for marriage."

"Was it love at all or just sex? She is one fine looking woman and it would be hard to know which came first."

"Sex did. I know I'm probably blowing it, maybe someday. Well sailor, we are here. Your dreamboat and son are just one hundred steps away."

"Yes, five thousand miles and one hundred very long steps."

Christmas Eve was the Bay's big bash at the house with family and friends. I had never been to one. I heard it was all about Swedish tradition. The glogg was no doubt flowing. The outside Christmas lights were on and you could see a big tree all lit up. The place looked like a home should at this time of year.

Thomas and I had devised a plan in the car to surprise Missy. We went up the long path to the side entrance. When at the side door Thomas went inside and asked Missy if he could see Toddy for a moment. He told her he wanted to show him something in the sky that might be Santa and his reindeer. He got the little boy, brought him into the side entrance, and said, "Todd do you know who this man is?" I waved at the little boy and put my finger over my mouth to tell him not to yell.

"My daddy," Todd whispered.

"How do you know that at barely three years old?" I asked, beaming.

"My Mommy has "pitchers" all over the house of you and my Mama kissing."

"Good. Now take this package and tell your Mama that Daddy gave it to you for Christmas. I'll go with you," said Thomas.

Todd went running into the living room and yells," Mommy, Daddy got this for me!"

Then you heard Missy say, "Todd Allen what are you talking about! Stop taking presents from under the tree and I mean it little boy! Now follow me and do not do this again. If you keep this up Santa won't bring you or me anything!"

Missy knelt down to take the package from him. Then I moved in and said, "Merry Christmas Mrs. Vanderbilt!"

Missy looked up, her mouth opened up and she fainted. Dad and her sisters ran in screaming.

"What's the commotion, did the tree fall over again?" Annikin asked.

"No dear," David said. "Ethan is home from the war and Missy has passed out cold, now poor Todd thinks his mother is dead. Put another place setting on the table. Ethan, how the hell are ya?"

"What are you talking . . . oh my there is a Santa Claus and look what he brought Missy!" Mrs. Bay said.

After a few short moments my wife came into my arms . . . we kissed, hugged and she cried. I picked up Todd and stared at my family almost speechless. Annikin chased everybody out so we could be alone. After talking some, we went into the living room and were hugged and kissed by everyone there at least twice. We had dinner, answered a million questions and then cut out early to go home to start our own Christmas Eve.

On the way over, I drove the '40 Ford because Missy was in 7th heaven. We chattered like two lovers, held hands with her almost sitting on my lap. We kissed between red lights. With the little boy in her lap, we got home without wrecking or stopped on suspicion of DUI. We got home; I made

Todd walk while I carried my beauty through the door. I was home! All of us were together. For thirty days, it would be just us. World War Two would have to go on without me for a short time. I would spend every minute with my Missy and a little boy named Todd Allen Vanderbilt.

Santa Claus is coming tonight

"Ethan, this is home. It is not much, but big enough for us. Cheap, too, like $35 a month."

"This is real nice. Cozy warm and safe. I like it. I worry about you living alone."

"Cutie pie, you have enough to worry about. We're safe and my daddy keeps an eye on us."

"Come here, you doll, and give me a kiss. Let me put my arms around that beautiful body of yours!"

"Ethan, let's put Todd to bed. I will give you more than a kiss and lot more than a hug!"

"Looks like Todd is in bed already. What does he do, put himself to sleep?"

"This kid is ready for college. He is potty trained and feeds himself. We have some little child, EA. Watch what you say around him. He is like a parrot. He heard me say 'shit' one day when I burnt toast. He repeated it in Sunday school!"

"Yeah, I believe he is a genius. These are two presents for you. One is for tonight and one for tomorrow. I hope you like them."

"Thank you dear, the bedroom is straight back. I will pretty up and see you soon. If you need something, the ice box is full."

"I'm only hungry for you and close to starvation at that. You always look beautiful, so don't be long."

"I'll be quick. Sure not much on me to feast on."

"Oh, I will find something to munch on."

"Ethan, such a dirty mind . . . I love it!"

I went back, tucked Todd in, and waited for my wife. I had dreamed of this moment for so long to say good night to my boy. Soon I heard Missy say, "Honey, this is a beautiful nightie but kind of indecent."

"I think that is the general idea."

"I know, just kidding, how does it look?"

"Wow!"

"Are you nervous about tonight after all this time away from me? It is sort of like our wedding night," I said.

"A little, are you?"

"No . . . I am one ready woman! I am so at ease now that you are here. You are my husband and my love. Ethan, I am just a sucker for you. I love you so much."

"Missy, I look at your picture and sometimes think this is all a dream. Even now, it seems so unreal. The day I saw you at the beach in that brown bathing suit with that brown hair blowing in the wind I just knew you were the one!"

"My bathing suit was blue but . . . you know I think it *was* brown. Oh well. Are we going on a camping trip?"

"What are you talking about?"

"Your pole is coming through the sheets—looks like a tent stake!"

"My pole? I like your dirty mind too! Yeah, it hurts too!"

"Pain is soon going to change into pure pleasure very soon Ethan."

We woke up on Christmas morning with Todd still asleep. We chatted and savored the moment of being together.

I asked, "Is this kid in a coma, how on earth did he stay asleep after all that noise we made! You are some woman . . . last night was just the way I wanted it to be."

"Darling, there is no man alive that would or could make me feel like you did. I cannot picture anyone but you ever in my life. This is what love is all about—you, me and so much more. Now remember, Todd slept through Pearl Harbor. He is a real good sleeper but he should awaken soon. Then he will be up all day. Let's get dressed and I will make coffee the way you like it!"

"Ugh, the attack, how could I forget that day?"

"Ethan, I'll never forget that day. I can still smell the smoke, hear the sirens. Years from now those memories will still be there. However, it is Christmas Day, you are with me, and our son is waking up. Let's open presents!"

We got Todd up and gathered under the small tabletop tree watching the glow on his face as he dug in on what little Santa Claus had brought. This moment was that words could not describe.

"Sweetheart, here is the other gift for you."

"Oh it is beautiful and very much in style but expensive. Such tastes you have! This blouse will match so many of my things. Now for yours, I was going to send you these. I hope you like them."

"Collier's Magazine with you and the Bay babes. Wow, these shots of you are beautiful!"

"Ethan, I could just cry I am so happy. This is the best Christmas ever!"

"Now son, this is for you!"

The kid dove right in and opened the package. He was so excited to see what it was.

"It's a boat like Daddy owns! Thank you, Daddy."

"He has good manners, Missy. If I owned a warship like that, this war would already be over."

"Ethan, no war talk. Here is the other present."

I opened it up. There were all the shots taken of her and the sisters that did not make the magazine. They were beautiful shots. Her sisters are gorgeous . . . but Missy is pure beauty, inside and out.

We ate breakfast and watched Todd play. By some miracle, he fell asleep. We continued giving and receiving presents that required no unwrapping of paper. In the afternoon, we went for the family Christmas. By the end of the night, I was ready for a powder. Missy was too. This had been one wild day.

She went to work the next day and told her supervisor that I had returned from the Pacific Theater. That meant the company would grant her leave as long as I was home. While she worked her last day, my little boy and I played with his toys. We had fun! I really liked having him to myself for the day. We went down the street for lunch, took a walk in a nearby park where we made a snowman. After a long day, we took a nap. Before he fell asleep he said, "Daddy, when I wake up will you still be here?"

I said, "Yes I will and Mama too. We will be all together."

"Good," he said.

A little later Missy the Mill Hunkie was home.

"Hi everybody. I'm home from the mill . . . where are my men?"

"Mommy, Daddy and I ate hotdogs and ice cream then played in the snow. I peed on a tree like big boys do!"

"Gee, Ethan, now *that* is bonding with your son, peeing behind a tree. What next, picking up chicks?"

"Maybe, hey the boy needs to learn how to do these things. How was your day?"

"Good, I am off now till you go back so let's plan what we want to do. I think we should take the train and see your family on the last week of your leave. What do you think?"

"We'll see. I need to think about it."

"Ethan, you know how I feel about you keeping distance between your people. They have a grandson and he needs to know them plus I love your bunch too. Figure on going, EA."

"Yes, Adolf. Oh by the way, whose men's clothes in the dresser? Are they your boyfriend's?"

"First of all the men's clothes are yours. It gives me security for them to be there for when you return. Number two . . . look at these pants darling, only you would wear a pair of pants from the 1930's! Now are you satisfied?"

"Oh, I'm teasing you. I know there is no other but those pants are my favorite pair."

"Off to the men's store tomorrow, Mister. That is an order!"

Ms. Style took me to town and put me in up-to-date clothes. Of course, she just had to pick some things for herself! She bought a nice New Years Eve dress. It was a seductive one. The conversation of New Years Eve came up with Missy asking, "Ethan, I know you love spending time with our son, but for New Years can we let my parents keep Todd while we go out and have dinner and dance? Then come home and mess up my two dollar hairdo, please?"

"Sure love . . . two dollar hairdo, man you're expensive!"

"Wonderful. I will make reservations at only the best. That is cheap for a 'do. Nails are 75 cents now!"

On New Year's Eve, we ate at a real nice restaurant. After a nice long candlelight dinner, we headed over to a club. Missy had a drink and I stuck to ginger ale. The band started playing and they sounded good. When the crowd got bigger, we danced. It was so nice to have her in my arms. Some of her friends happened to drop in and sat with us for a while. Finally, the clock struck midnight. The drunks were grabbing every girl around for a kiss. Some woman that came out of nowhere kissed me. A person hugged and kissed my wife. I think this might have been and old boyfriend. I asked her and she smiled and said sort of.

"So honey, miss the old kisser?"

"Ethan, we dated six months in 1939. He was a real nice guy. Never a possibility for a romance, we soon went our own ways. Then I went to Hawaii and met the man of my dreams, who's around here somewhere," she said laughing, and held her hand over her eyes as if searching deep in the crowd. Her gaze finally landing on me, she smiled, grabbed my hand and kissed me on my lips. "Now let's go home and bring in 1944 our way, ok?"

"Sure, I was sort of jealous when he kissed you."

"Jealous, eh? Thank you. That makes me feel good. Why, I have no clue. Nobody has ever been jealous over me."

"I'm not so sure about that. No way did a nice pretty woman like you go totally unnoticed."

"Ethan, did you notice that redhead lady sitting next to us? Is she a Navy WAVE?"

"Yeah, she is a WAVE."

"I thought so. Pretty hairdo but her outfit . . . so blue and boring. It needs some glitter or something to break it up."

"Ms Fashion, she is wearing a uniform not an outfit. They aren't for fashion."

"Don't get me wrong. I admire her sense of duty. If we did not have a child, I would enlist too. Ethan, do you think the war will last much longer?"

"Please. You stay home and make steel and raise Todd. The Navy will do just fine without your help. Lovie, to answer your question, I think from what I hear the war in Europe will be over soon."

"What do you mean the Navy will do fine without me? Anyway, Germany isn't the war I meant. I'm talking about Japan."

"Japan is another story; it will be longer but let's not talk about it. Let's talk about us."

"I'm sorry. It's just, sometimes I get so scared I'll lose you and that just can't happen. So many boys from this area have died. It is so sad. When I see a Western Union car I cringe."

"Just put those arms around me, and let me whisper in your ear. I am coming back to you and Todd . . . no doubt about it. So Happy New Year, Mrs. Vanderbilt!"

"Happy New Year to you too darling. Would you mind if I had a cigarette in a while?"

"Now you know I don't like women that smoke and especially you. Why would you start that habit?"

"I don't intend to puff away like a blast furnace, I just want one after we make love, that's all. They say it settles you down, okay?"

"Where on earth did you come up with that? I guess so, though I don't get that one at all, settle you down after making love. I thought sex was to help settle you down. I thought I smelled smoke on your breath when I got home. This is another reason I hate this war so much . . . it changes people . . . usually for the worse!"

Happy New Year 1944

Nineteen forty-four was here, I was in bed with my wife . . . things could not be much better. All I wanted to do was get as much living in as I could. In my racket, things could change in a split second, I gave Sleeping Beauty a kiss. She woke up with a smile.

"I'm hungry,"

"What are you hungry for?" I asked.

"Food first, but you're next."

Ah, I loved her honesty. We got up and made some coffee then she whipped up some eggs bacon and waffles. The rest of the day would be at her parent's house for New Years Day.

At the house, I ran into the bleach blonde bombshell Allison.

"Well Happy New Year, Ethan! How are you tonight?"

"Same, Allison, how are you tonight? You look so charming."

"Thank you Ethan. You are so sweet to say that. Still messed up, wrong man again, living with my mother and trying to raise my baby by myself as I was. Sorry to dump on you, sailor. On a brighter note, your wife has become one of my best friends. She has given me so much of her time to help me get straighten out. I love her so much . . . she is a real sincere and loving person. The Bay's have been so good to me too. I guess they could have thrown me to the curb. I am certainly not in their class."

"Allison, you are in their class. My upbringing is different from Missy's too. I am from a poor uneducated family and as far as they knew, I could have been a bum. The way I know this family now, I know they are just plain good Christian people. If my girl thinks you are okay, that means you are."

"Thank you sweetie, I just wish Thomas wasn't Thomas and I sometimes wish I wasn't me."

"Love him, do you?"

"I could but he thinks I'm just another lake port whore and maybe he's right."

"No, you just need someone to love you for what you are. The rest will work itself out. Now let's go party. Give me your hand, let's go."

After the party, we headed back to our place and talked on the way home, mostly about the Allison—Thomas affair. Missy believed she could do better. I thought if her brother would grow up some, they could get together.

"You aren't mad we kissed, are you?"

"No Ethan, of course not, but who kisses better?"

"It's a tie, dear, but I love you so who cares?"

"I'll show you sailor who kisses better. Come here!"

"Ok, you are better and I smell smoke on your breath! I thought you told me this smoking was to only calm you down after getting laid!"

"Allison and I had a couple outside. Honey, this might be the only way to keep my nerves steady while you are in a war zone. I will stop when the war is over, I promise. One other thing—we make love, we don't get laid!"

"We won't let this get in the way of our short time together but I don't like it at all, Missy Anne. You have not been truthful with me. Guess I can thank working in the mill for this."

"No, Allison suggested it, but it was my decision to start. I am sorry that it makes you unhappy. Ethan you don't know what it's like at night alone and worried stiff about you. It's like a relaxer, only not a drug and better than me becoming a boozehound. There are nights I think I'm gonna lose it."

"Hope you don't learn any other of her bad habits like dating men while married."

"Ethan Allen, really. I can hardly handle you."

"Sorry, I see your point. Some people bite their nails and like you say, some drink. As for me, I just stare into space or look at your picture. So smoke if you want. I hate this war so much."

War and separation would cause people to do strange things they would normally not do. Some women left behind would leave their husbands or boyfriends. Some had affairs. When he would return nobody would know the difference. Others turned to alcohol and some even committed suicide.

With the holidays behind us, we needed to decide how to spend my three remaining weeks. Gas rationing limited how much we could move around but public transportation was good and cheap. Taking our son to places like the zoo had its limitations with the cold weather. In those days, there were not many things to do anyway outside the home. Families stayed home and played games, read and listened to the radio. You had to use your imagination and we always thought of something.

"So Missy, are we still going to Lincoln?"

"No Ethan, we are going to visit your family that lives in Lincoln. In other words . . . our son's grandparents, my in—laws and your parents. Now I know you have a problem. I really don't understand why . . ."

"I have no problem going, but we should stay in a hotel."

"No, your parents have a new home and would want us with them. Now I know you are embarrassed of the way you had to grow up. It doesn't matter what kind of a house you lived in. Your parents are fine people and I love them the way they are. They also raised a fine son."

"Navy raised me."

"Ethan, do you want one of my sharp heels in your foot? Stop the crap! Listen. Yes, I did come up with a silver spoon in my mouth. I never even knew there was a Great Depression. My parents kept us away from seeing soup lines and lake sailors begging for work. I got an education and thought everyone was like me. You did something about your situation and joined the service. Your parents did the best they could and I respect them for it. If I have to sleep on a bed stuffed with straw and use an outhouse, I will! Quit blaming them for your lost youth. Our children will always be a part of their life and I will too. Now stop the pity party and join this blessing we have . . . your family!"

"Silver spoon in your mouth? Maybe so, you also sure have a big mouth at times . . . Ouch that hurt!"

"Heels are a woman's best weapon, now are we going Pullman all the way or coach?"

"Pullman dear. And I never have slept on a bed stuffed with straw, feed sacks but not straw. You know it is going to be damn cold there. I would hate to see that cute bum of yours get frost bite on a trip to the outhouse!"

"Frostbite? Well, I'll make the trip very fast. You're right, though, my bum is kinda cute."

The Beautiful Mistake

The last week before we were to leave for Lincoln, a letter arrived from Edith Timken. I looked at the envelope thinking couldn't be good news. Handwriting of hers was jittery and the stamp was on crooked. I read it, and then told my wife.

"Lloyd is missing in action somewhere in the Pacific. No real details but . . . This ain't good."

We both cried and held each other. When little Toddy saw us he put both of his arms on us and said, "Don't cry Mama and Daddy." We hugged him and said nothing. Tragedy had hit us for the first time in this war. I knew what was on my wife's mind. Perhaps to say nothing was better for now. I did not know what kind of mission Lloyd was doing. It no doubt dealt with some kind of commando operation. In that sort of work, anything can happen. If luck was on his side, maybe he'd end up with friendly islanders. I prayed for the latter and I prayed hard.

Missy wasn't saying much. She sat and smoked a cigarette, then another and another. I held Todd in my lap while he napped. Finally she spoke, only asking if I was hungry.

"No, but I'm getting hold of the commanding officer in Chicago to request orders back to the fleet."

"Why Ethan, you have two more weeks left."

"I lost a friend. It's time we end this madness for good, duty calls!"

"No, damn it! You are not going off half-cocked and fight a war by yourself. What about us? In two weeks, fine, but not now. This war is much more than just you or Lloyd. It will take a concerted effort to beat the Japs, not some hothead wanting nothing but revenge. Please don't do this."

"You're right, pray. Let's put the baby to bed then you and I cuddle."

"Ethan, I have a million feelings right now. Edith must be so scared and confused. You might have lost your best friend. Today we have lost some of our innocence and I feel so bad she suffers while I'm in your arms."

"Sweetie, we have lost some of our innocence. This is the way things are in a war. We won't give up on Lloyd. He's very good at what he does. he's too arrogant to die, remember? I'm on leave to be with you and the boy. I am not going to sit around and be miserable. We are going out every day and have fun and be a family."

"That is what I would expect you to say. You see, you are my dream come true, strong, and loving. Ethan, let's get on our knees and pray for Edith and Lloyd and our country."

"Our knees, why not pray here? We're in bed already, nice and warm."

"Ethan," she said, pulling my arm down with me in tow, "get on your knees and pray with me or else. Dear Lord, send comfort to our wonderful Edith in her time of need and protect her with your warmth and love. Wherever Lloyd is, Lord, keep him safe and in your strong hands. Be with our nation and help put an end to these lunatics from across the sea and bring our troops home soon. We ask this in your name through your Son Jesus Christ. Amen."

"Amen. Missy, my goddamn leg got a Charlie horse. Give me your hand, please."

"Really Ethan . . . swearing and using the Lord's name in vain after a prayer! Shipmate, I have a lot of work ahead of me with you. Please God let me persevere with this nut."

"Sorry but I said it with a small "g.""

We did exactly as I promised, had fun. We prepared for the journey West to a home and people that I have not really seen or been close to since 1932. Missy was very family oriented. I had to remember the old adage, "GO ALONG TO GET ALONG." After all, maybe it was time, as she said earlier, to "quit blaming your parents for your lost childhood." She was right, they did do the best they could.

Lincoln, Nebraska

Our train was scheduled for 9 a.m. departure. Her parents came over earlier and we all went out to eat. Missy's mother was near tears. I asked my wife, "Why is she in tears? You'll be back in a week?"

"Ethan, she is crying for you, dummy. My Mom is crazy about you and worried, just like me! Now hug her and tell her everything will just be fine. Don't you understand women yet?"

"The only woman I need to understand is you, and that might be harder than beating the Japs! Sure I'll hug Mom, she's cute!"

"Jeepers, cute as in how?"

"Cute as in being cute, that's all."

It was time to board so we all hugged goodbye. Missy was in tears too. Why, I will never know, but she always said she enjoyed crying. Todd was excited and dirty already from when his Grandpa took him up to the steam engine. He had to touch the tender smeared with coal dust! We boarded, the train gave two blasts on the whistle and rang the station bell, departing for the Cornhusker State. Missy sat down in our compartment, cleaned off the kid and sat quietly.

The train was packed with civilians and servicemen. Chances are most of these GI's were battlefront bound. You could tell that the country was out to get this war over with by the numbers of new enlistee's on board. The draftees were so young now. Many eighteen year olds were going to service. These men were the ones that had the least chance of living through the first days of hardened combat. I felt so heartbroken knowing many would never know the real joys of life.

Finally, it was time for dinner in the diner. Missy who never missed a meal in her life and never gained a pound headed that way. Our son could eat like a starved dog also. We had a table to ourselves until a Marine sergeant came. We started talking some and of course, Missy told him our life story. When he heard I had been at Tarawa his eyes lit up saying he was on the first assault too. As he spoke about that horrid day, he asked me what my name was. I did not want to tell him but if I did not Missy would.

"WO Ethan Vanderbilt, USN."

"You were on the first assault, right? Aren't you the one that turned the Higgins boat broadside? Then pulled drowning Marines that bailed out of a sinking boat? Madam your husband is quite a sailor and a hero in my book!"

"Gee honey, you're full of surprises. Thank you, Sergeant, for the kind words."

With dinner over, we headed to the compartment. She asked me about what the Marine had said.

"Well, he pretty much told it the way things went that day. It was a duesy."

"So Ethan, what happened with you "safely out of harm's way" and being honest with me? You get mad at me for starting to smoke. I guess that all along you have been in danger. Now I do have a reason to smoke!"

"I didn't want you to worry is all."

"I am disappointed in you. You're my husband and I need to know these things. You have not been truthful and I don't like it at all. I feel betrayed, Ethan."

"Missy, it's not like I was sleeping with another woman or nothing. I was trying to make life easier on you. You have enough to do with working and raising our kid. I would never betray you so damn it woman stop the drama! I do things for a reason with you in mind. There is very little honestly in war and that's why I hate it so."

"All right I can accept that. If you are a hero, you think I should know? Ethan, I am so proud of you, upset a little but o' so proud! I saved an injured squirrel once. Saving someone else's life is a thing I can't even imagine! Just tell me from now on, what's going on. I am in awe over this. I might just cry, Ethan you are a truly unselfish human being. I am so proud of you! "

"I still worry about you. Missy, I'm no hero, only a guy doing his job. Now that you know my real job how will you handle this?"

"Pray more and probably smoke like a blast furnace. Kidding, dear."

We decided to head for the lounge car. We ordered some root beer. The little one lapped it down real quick. A few minutes in, we noticed Todd rubbing his eyes so I picked him up and we headed for our room.

Missy laid him in the top rack.

"Let's have some sneaking sex tonight, sweetheart," she said, turning to me. "It will be practice when our house has many little ones. Then we have to be sneaky!"

"I agree we should get some practice in! Since there is so little room in this compartment, you strip first, then me and we'll get this Pullman a rocking."

"Strip? Yes Sir, Mr. Vanderbilt!"

A little later Missy said, "Gosh Ethan that felt so good." Being sneaky is great but . . . having a wowie zowie is no fun without some noise!"

Actually the hard part is putting our clothes back on."

Soon it was announced "Lincoln Nebraska, next stop in fifteen minutes." I had to try to put the past away as to start a new relationship with my family. Missy was all smiles and told our son that he would soon meet his other family. I popped off saying, "Gee, let's show him how the other half lives."

"Ethan Allen, enough, now put a smile on your face. This is going to be the best week of our time together. "We will have fun . . . understand, sailor?"

"Yes Your Royal Hind Ass."

"Shape up Mr. or my Royal Ass will be off limits!"

"Now you wouldn't do that now, would you?"

"Probably not but why push it."

The train pulled into Lincoln. There was many passenger's getting on and off. I said, "let's not be pushy as in wait our turn." Missy, holding Todd, looked at me, sighed and blew air from through her bangs. I loved to piss her off sometimes! Finally, we got off with every damn relative I had. They surrounded her and the boy with Missy all smiles and Todd looking for a way out. My Mom came over and we hugged. My wife seemed please. I shook hands with Dad and he said, "Ethan you look good . . . the Navy should be glad to have a man like you!"

When we got to my parents' new house, my jaw dropped. It was a Craftsman design on about two acres with a dining room, living, four bedrooms plus a real big kitchen, my parents must have been doing very well!

"Mom and Dad, how did you swing this? This is a nice place and such a lay out."

"Well, we wrote and told you. Maybe the letter got lost. Anyway, your mother got a good job at the University as a Professor's secretary. As for me the elevator has gotten so busy they built two new sites and I manage the one on the north side of town."

"Great! That is great! I guess the war has had its good points."

"No it doesn't Ethan, because if we lost you this bit of success would mean nothing at all to us. Remember we are the same simple people now as before. You mean more to us than all of this."

My mother went into the other room and brought out a "keepsake" from long ago. When I saw it I about died, it was a pair of pants I had as a young boy made from a feed sack.

"Mom, why show this thing?"

"Ethan, when you joined the Navy at 17, you did what you had to do . . . you have done well. You have a good position, now this wonderful wife and a beautiful son. I found these pants after you left and said I will keep these for a reason. That reason is to show your children someday that you can become somebody no matter where you begin. I want you to have them now show your kids someday."

"Ok I will, but couldn't you have come up with a better keepsake?"

"No dear, this is how bad it got back then for us . . . this is the best symbol of those days."

"Ethan, I never realized how bad you did have it. Honey, I am so humbled by this. Your life before we met means so much to me now. Owning all those clothes and shoes of mine makes me feel stupid or uppity. You all must look at me like I am some rich brat."

'Honey, you are a rich brat, your Dad said so!"

'No he did not, Ethan Allen."

"Don't feel that way, Missy," my mom chimed in. "'Feel good about how you had it as a child. You and Ethan as a couple will raise fine children from mixing both sides of life together."

"Thank you for saying that. I told him the other day I know I was born in a different world than he. At times it makes me feel awkward at times."

"Don't feel that way around here, dear" my Mom replied.

"Yes remember, Missy, everyone around here feels awkward so you'll fit right in," I replied.

Did I get a dirty look on that one from Mom and Missy!

So what do you do in Lincoln, Nebraska in 1944? Well not much but my wife was hell bent on tracing every step of my life from birth until I joined the Navy. I hated to disappoint her but there was not much to show her. My first home no longer existed. Since I was born at home, there was no hospital to visit. I attended school until the eighth grade. It wasn't much, built on one level with five classrooms.

Missy in her cute way asked, "Where is the gym?"

I grinned and told her we got our exercise by walking two miles to school. Then went home and worked. She truly looked puzzled. My sweet innocent wife was looking at life through a very different spectrum. This was not Duluth in a nice neighborhood lined with Victorian homes with cars in the driveways. However, she seemed very interested in my past.

Missy could have and probably would have married a man of her own peers. She might have lived a good life. It sure would have been a more predictable one, kids, taking care of a home and PTA meetings. With us, it had been a rushed romance and a short time living in paradise together. Now it was war, separation and not knowing what tomorrow would bring.

We headed to the grain elevator where I worked for a time sacking feed and loading it onto railcars or local farmer's wagons. The sacks always ran at least fifty pounds and were clumsy to handle 'em. And the dust—grain could kick up in a storm and choke you good. In those days, ventilation fans did not exist. If they did, our company was too cheap to buy them! You wore a bandana across your mouth. At the end of the day, you coughed up dust. A typical workday would last from 7am to 5pm with few breaks. Hard, dirty work was the order of the day, everything was manual labor. I noticed some improvements since I worked there but a grain elevator is still a grain elevator.

"So did you like that part of the tour?"

"Ethan that is a horrible way to make a living. {Missy screams} What was that?"

"That was an employee. And one that seems to have been here awhile."

"That was a damned rat! Get me out of here. An employee . . . What a crock, Ethan Allen!"

Missy looked like she had seen a ghost. It was probably the first time she had ever seen a rat. Those critters usually became pets, and in a way were cool. All she did on the way back was dust herself off too make sure one was not in her hair. At five pounds, it would be hard to know if one was even on her with all the hair this woman had. When we pulled in, Missy headed for the shower.

"Need some company?" I asked, trying to sound helpful.

"No!" she said, and slammed the bathroom door.

Girls just wanna have fun!

"EA, why don't you, your dad and Todd go to your brother's farm while you're mom, Amelia and I go to town for a little girl fun?"

"And do what, if I didn't already know?"

"Oh maybe take in a "weepy" and then have lunch, that's all."

"Aren't you leaving something out Miss Bloomingdale's?"

"If they want to, sure we could do that. Good thinking EA, which is why you are a US Navy Warrant Officer!"

"Listen woman, Mom and sister are country girls and know little about style. They can make dinner out of prairie grass and use every part of a steer for something. These are poor plains women, so don't go making glamour girls out of them, understand?"

"Ethan, you don't even know them so how can you say that. All woman love to look their best, and it does not cost a fortune to do it. I will not make them do anything. If they want to, I am going to pay for it as my gift to them. Why your coarse attitude towards them? These two women have lived a hard life. If they will accept my generosity then I will be happy to do it."

"I guess there ain't no stopping you so have fun. Go easy on the bank account. You are some kind of woman. You are so unselfish and want to make people happy. I guess sometimes I am a little dense."

"Thanks. I love you and them so much. Kiss me and have fun with your dad. You are not dense, just stubborn. Get this rift over with between you and him. Life is too short. Now on the money, sweetheart, this sounds awful but like your family, this war has put more money in our pocket than you can imagine. With your pay and me working, we are fine. But as the Lord is my witness I would give all the money back if it would end the war or could save just one life."

Steve Zingerman

My Dad, Todd and I hopped in Dad's 36 Ford driving twenty miles south to Wilson and Jeremiah's one section of a nice laying spread. They were still single, 22 and 20 years old. I knew them really very little because they were only kids when I entered the Navy. It looked like they too had prospered well because of World War Two. They said more opportunity lay ahead for them in agriculture if that is what they wanted. Wilson was running a breeder hog operation on the side and Jerry was the executive of the farm. It was, according to Dad, a match made in heaven. This was a first class operation with modern John Deere tractors and big plows to cover a lot of acreage.

Todd was in heaven. Willy took him for a tractor ride while my Dad and I talked.

"Ethan, it sure is good to see all of you. This has been so good for your Mom. She sure misses you, as do I. I know you hold a lot of resentment towards us . . . I would too. Because of the Depression, you lived in the middle of a mess that made you miss a lot of your growing up. Having to work at age 13 was not fair. You must know that your sacrifice saved this family. Jerry and Wilson were so close to ending up in a county home. At one point, we couldn't even buy food or a roof over our head. I'm sorry son."

"Dad, I understand . . . it's water under the bridge. The loner person I was ended on the beach at Waikiki. Missy has taught me much about family. I need forgiveness too, Dad. I can't stand this distance we got, it ain't right. I'm a happy guy right now except for this war. When it's over I can promise you and Mom that we all will be much closer than in recent years."

"Good Ethan, this is good. Let's go up to the house . . . bullshit and wait for the girls to come home."

"Let me warn you, Missy is on a mission with them and it might not be pretty! She knows how to shop."

"I know your Mom and Amelia are so excited about going. Burton and I are prepared. I am afraid that I have not given your mother an exciting life. Now if they would come with new clothes and a little high . . . Well then, good for them."

"I don't think Missy would get her and Amelia soused . . . new clothes I can guarantee."

We expected them by five for dinner. There we were, waiting for our wives. Seven went by, then eight, and finally they showed up. Laughing and loud, they came in barefooted and smoking cigarettes. Mom and Amelia, being Baptists, had never smoked. Apparently my wife could do anything.

"Hi everyone, we're home and did we have fun!"

"So Delores, what kind of fun did you have, other than all three of you are ginned up?" Dad asked.

"Well we went shopping, then to a movie, then lunch and some dancing at the hotel."

"No Mommy-in-law, we went to lunch, then saw a weepy."

"Oh whatever Missy, I'm a little too high to care. Ethan, this is a real fun woman! This woman can shop, drink and dance . . . . almost all at once! Now I know why you married her!"

"Missy, what did you do now?"

"Nothing . . . just being me. You know how to have fun, right?"

The giggle girls told us the whole story. Evidently, my Mom talked them into going dancing which lead to some boozing. Missy got them some new clothes and accessories.

"Why did your shoes not make it home?" I asked

"I guess we took them off dancing and forgot them," Missy said. "Don't worry cutie pie Ethan, we bought new ones anyway. Gosh, I was wondering why my feet were so cold."

When we woke up the next morning, vomit breath kissed me saying sorry about last night. I wasn't really mad. The three women had bonded into a friendship, becoming like sisters. Missy was right about coming to Lincoln.

"Ethan, I know you're not gonna wanna hear this but it is Sunday and we are all going to church."

"Oh for the love of God, you are kidding!"

"Yes Ethan, for the love of God, and I am not kidding, so hit the deck, sailor, turn to!"

"No sailor talk and why church? We're on a vacation, sorta."

"Does God take a day off from watching you on the shores of Montezuma?"

"Missy, Montezuma is in Mexico. Gosh, you are so beautiful this morning, honey. Come here, sweetheart."

"Up. Flattery will not get you out of it, when you see your mom, sister and I all dressed up, well you'll see."

We all went to church. True, they were all raving beauties.

I would be leaving Tuesday at noon. Missy and Todd would be leaving later on in the afternoon. My family decided we needed to spend our last two nights alone. They booked a suite at a very nice hotel. It was a good idea however Todd would be with us. I wanted it all in the last few days.

That evening we worked on getting the little boy that never naps to bed. We needed to have some time alone, not only for romance though. Since Missy knew I would be in the middle of the toughest fighting the Pacific had to offer, I wanted her to know that if I did not make it back, she must move on someday.

"Ethan, first of all I know you are coming home and in one piece so *stop the drama* as you tell me," she said, waving her hands in front of her. "Now I have something to say, Popeye, I feel alright about you going back to the war. I don't want you to go, but it's you and others that can end this nightmare. We can start where we left off. I really believe we are going to grow old together and have wheelchair races at the old folk's home. I'll be sad when you get on that train. I will cry but I am strong and ready for the last chapter of this mess. So cutie, let's forget about war for a minute, put the *do not disturb* sign on and pull the blinds down." She grabbed my shirt collar and pulled me close to her.

"I am proud of you, sweetheart. Now I can return to end this knowing you feel that way. You are a brave, wonderful woman. How lucky I am to have found a beauty like you? You're the best, Missy Anne Marie."

After we made sure our boy was sound asleep, Missy asked me if I'd seen the bathtub. I took a peak and man was it something else! It was huge, big enough for a steer to wallow in. Missy looked at me and I looked at her. Before you know it, the hot water was running and we were peeling each other's clothes off like ripe fruit. We had never had a bath together because we never had a bathtub. This was our moment to sit next to each other and just relax. Man, was this nice. This was better than making love. We talked about everything under the sun. I got out of the tub to check on Todd and when I came back in Ms. Hollywood was wearing her sunglasses smoking a cigarette looking like, well a movie star I guess.

"So what are you doing? You look like a giant praying mantis on with those sunglasses."

"Hop in Ethan and shut up. You'll never meet a bug as gorgeous as me. Relax, let's talk some more. Come here, sit close, and kiss me. Ethan, I know you always miss me, now what do you do when you really miss me? Like, in wanting to, you know . . . have me?"

"I have no clue what you are talking about."

"Ethan, you know darn well what I'm talking about . . . so?"

"I am godsmacked dear. You sure you have not been around the world, if you get my drift?"

"Be serious. I know some stuff and I did not learn that in health class! Sometimes the loneliness gets to me so . . . ."

"Missy, if you think that'd help, and then do it. Make sure Todd is sound asleep. Play some soft music on the radio, remember safety first—keep the radio away from the tub because if it falls in, well, no more Missy"

"Good advice, cutie pie . . . that would be a double shocker! Ethan never ever let anyone know about this conversation. If you ever write memoirs of us . . . keep this part out, okay. And where did you hear of the hot bath, soft music stuff?"

"Probably the same place you did, sugar lump. As for me missing you . . . Well, that's all in my hands."

The next day was for our boy. We did whatever we could think of to have fun with him. Around five p.m. we headed for the hotel for our last evening together. The hotel was the place to be a on a very snowy Nebraska night. There was going to be a lot of snow. I stepped outside, picked some up. It was of the right texture to build a snowman. I said, "Follow me, let's put the kid in a snowsuit and have some fun!"

The snow was falling even more now with at least six inches more than before it started. Missy showed Todd how to roll the snow up in to a ball and soon we had a snowman. Couple of sticks for arms, rocks for eyes and we had a real nice looking greeter for the hotel! Missy started a snowball fight. She had a darn good arm! Todd was picking up the art of throwing very well too. Missy and I got close and threw a few and both of us tripped falling down. We started laughing. I looked at her, our eyes met then we kissed . . . nothing like kissing her cold sweet lips. Of course, Todd thought kissing was not a part of being outside.

"No kissing Mommy and Daddy," he said, reprimanding us. "Just throw snow!" Kids rule so we played some more. Then Missy said time to go in and warm up. How does one make the most of this being the last night before you leave for war? Neither of us had a clue. Our son was getting tired. This was both good and bad. Good that he would not interrupt our farewells and bad that this was the last night for a while.

I suggested we start with a nice hot bath to relax after a cold day in the snow. Then do what any other couple would in this circumstance. Missy agreed, however she had one other idea.

"Ethan my dear, we are going to have a slumber party which means we will stay up all night, talk, mess my hair up . . . have fun!"

"Slumber party and stay up all night, sounds good but what if we do get sleepy?"

"Ah good question, I am going to call room service right now and order a big pot of coffee. Good idea?"

"Ok I guess so. When you drink a lot of coffee Missy, you get jittery and never stop talking!"

"Are you saying I talk too much? I know I ramble on sometimes. How about the nice things about me, like the cute way I wiggle when I walk. Or these great legs, Ethan Allen?'

"You're turning me on girl! Go call room service . . . I will meet you in the tub."

If Missy made it to midnight, I would be surprised. This woman was not a late night girl. I heard the little boy get up so I gave him a cookie and some milk putting him back to sleep. I headed to the bathroom. Missy was in the tub with that gorgeous brown hair piled up on her head and green eyes glowing. She had her lipstick on, looking for love. Well guess what, she had come to the right place. It might be a long time or maybe even never again I would be with my wife. Maybe we did need to stay up all night.

"Missy, Todd woke up but I got him to back to sleep. And what are you trying to do?"

"I'm trying to blow smoke rings."

"Smoke rings? Oh brother. I wish you would give this smoking crap up. This can't be good for your health putting that in your lungs."

"Honey, we have already talked about this. I said when the war is over, this is over too. Anyway, I don't inhale so quit being crabby. Now get in her with me and let's talk about when we first met. Hot water stimulates the brain and relieves the body of stress, so let's get moving, sailor!"

"Ok . . . you're not going to make tiny bubbles in the tub are you?"

"Bubbles? Get in the tub!"

Man was this life, a fancy hotel with a tub built for two. After tonight, that would all end. It was back to ships sailors and combat. Missy, too, would have it rough—back to a steel mill and taking care of our very active son.

"Ethan, when we're settled and rich someday, let's buy one of these for our house."

"By the time we have money for this we'll be too old or too fat to fit in it."

"We'll get one anyway. It would be so neat to have a place we both could come and relax."

We started the "slumber party" with goofing off like a pillow fight, hide and seek and other weird games of hers. Finally, it came to the adult stuff. After that she said, "Honey wake me up in a half hour, I need to rest my eyes." I rubbed her back and let her doze off. Missy was done for the night. As much as I wanted to stay up all night, I knew to let her sleep. We spooned . . . I was as close as I could be with my Sleeping Beauty.

"Why did you fall asleep?" she said a few hours later, shaking me awake.

"You fell asleep. You were so content and pretty laying there so I cuddled up."

"What time is it? Wanna start all over again, sailor man?"

When duty calls . . . duty calls! But when the sun came up it is as though we were in Cinderella and the ball was over. We looked at each other, smiled, and hugged. Todd would be waking up soon and, like most kids, hungry. He woke at nine a.m. We knew then the honeymoon was over.

We headed to the restaurant and all of us ate like pigs. I told Missy I could understand why we were so hungry. She smiled and kept eating. It was snowing like crazy. I wondered if the trains would be on time. More time here would be nice. It would delay the inevitable. My mother wanted us to come over for a little good-bye dinner. I balked at the idea when Missy mentioned it.

"Don't even start, Ethan Allen . . . you have patched up things between them. It would break you mama's heart if we shoved off without seeing them."

"I'm going . . . I wasn't complaining. I just had a pain in my back that's all"

"Sure Ethan, I never have heard you complain about your back. You hit the beaches of Tarawa with courage, and then want to hide from your own family. You aggravate me so much sometimes about this."

At their house, my mother asked if she could speak to me in private.

"Ethan, you look down, don't be. I am proud of you and always have been. Things have happened for a reason and look at the results. You got a great family, you're successful in the Navy. I know we missed a lot not being close." She sharted shaking her head and waving her hand in front of her face, looking down. "Okay, that's it. Give Momma a hug before I cry. Go spend time with your family, unless you want to peel potatoes."

I hated peeling potatoes but did anyway. Things had come full circle in our relationship.

When dinner was ready we all sat down, prayed, then dug in. Missy and I sat together with Todd. I told them I had something for the three party girls.

"Mom, Amelia and especially Missy . . . did you know that shoes are being rationed at three pairs per civilian per year?"

"Yes husband, what of it?"

"Since they are I went back to the dance hall and found your shoes so here they are. Now Missy how did you buy three pairs of shoes for them and three for you?"

"I have my ways, sweetheart, and it is all legal. I trade cigarette coupons for shoe coupons on a trade of three to one."

"Missy, you smoke now, remember? So what are you going to do for your little puffing habit?"

"I don't know, I'll think of something, maybe trade gas or meat coupons. Maybe I'll become a vegetarian and ride a horse to work. Ethan, we are in a war . . . self survival is everyone's job"

I called the rail station. It was time to head that way. The snow had stopped. We arrived at the station at five, checked the baggage and went into the waiting room. Missy was starting to look pale . . . I was too.

"Honey, you all right?"

"Yes Ethan, I'm fine just . . . You know, a little nervous."

"Maybe use one of your sedatives?"

"You know I don't take those, I'm not that bad. Yet."

"I mean the Lucky Strike sedatives."

"Oh, right. Smoke in front of Todd so Honest Abe Junior will go report back to my mother once we get back to Duluth. Anyway, let it go. Let's only talk about us and be close."

"Come here, give me a kiss. I remember our first kiss, I knew that you were the one for me and I was right."

The Beautiful Mistake

"Ethan, I love you so much. I want to be strong as I told you I would. Darling I am so weak, especially now."

"I'm weak too baby. But we'll get through this together."

My mom suggested we say our goodbyes to them now. The three of us took a walk down the station platform to show Todd a troop train. All of a sudden, we heard a cat call and Missy turned red.

"Ethan, was that for me?"

"It had better be or the Army is getting desperate for recruits."

"What am I suppose to do?"

"Wave and say thank you then blow them a big kiss!"

She did . . . those soldiers went nuts! I would have too!

"See you do get noticed and why wouldn't you anyway, your gorgeous!" She smiled. We sat down to let Todd run around while we waited for the train to arrive. My wife seemed in a daze. I asked her what she was thinking.

"Oh, just thinking about all the really fun and wild stuff we did in Hawaii. This boring dirty old depot is so full of people like us. Some are saying goodbye for the last time and don't even know it. Not us though, right Chief?"

"For Christ's sake, that's a morbid thought."

"Ethan, don't use the Lords name like that. I'm just thinking of our days in Pearl, I miss it so much. These people have their memories too. I hope they are thinking of more happy days too. I pray everyone will come back."

"Missy, you okay? You are rambling."

"Yes. I'm fine, a little nervous. No, so nervous I might get sick."

We both started talking about Hawaii . . . the daring fun we did have. We went skinny dipping in a very secluded pond up in the mountains once and even at the beach. We were nuts, though I'm glad we did all that. Once she dressed in Navy men's dungarees after being told not to go to the PX in them. I heard about that one! Missy once drove through the main gate at Pearl without stopping. When chased down by the Marines with weapons drawn she said, "I am late picking up my husband so get out of my way. My husband could send your butts on a slow boat to China!" That one almost got me sent there! Yes, our first year was fun . . . it will be that way again soon.

Todd came over. We told him what was going to happen. Missy had that special soft touch with children. When she began to tell him that

Daddy had to go back to work, Todd looked perplexed. She told him that I would not be gone long. She handled the whole thing, as I knew she would. Todd put his arms out to me, gave me a big hug, and kissed me on the cheek. He said with a frown, "I love you Daddy and I will take care of Mommy."

This was a special little boy. I really felt like crap! Said it once and I will say it again, I hate this war! The clock now was 5:45 CST and the train was getting near. Missy was sitting as close to me as possible with our son on my lap. We were a family even though a train and a war would soon take me away.

"May I have your attention please . . . train number15 will arrive in fifteen minutes for Hastings, McCook, Denver and points West. Boarding is on track number 2."

That was my call. This was it, back to the front. I motioned my family over to say our goodbyes. They moved inside to give us privacy. Then the train pulled in, shaking the platform, throwing out steam. I asked the conductor how long is the station stop. He said not long, for they were running late. Two cars away was my Pullman car. We strolled that way. The porter took my bags saying stay close to the car. We began our goodbyes.

"Honey, this is so hard on me. I know for you also but I can make you one promise . . . I will come home to you and as soon as I can. You and Todd are the reason I will make it back."

"Ethan, I have all the faith in God that you will come home. I know to ask you to let some others do the job instead of you is dumb but darling please be safe, do your job and do it well. I am so proud of you, I love you so much."

"Missy, I love you too and I will pray. I know you will take good care of Todd. Take care of the new dog coming too . . . okay?"

"I'm always doing that Ethan. As soon as I know, I will let you know when the puppy is coming. I'm trying to be so strong, for you and for our son but . . ."

"Let it out if you have too, I'm sure Toddy will understand, right little man? Now Todd, you take care of Mama and give her all the love you can, okay?"

"I will Daddy. Mommy, don't cry . . . it will be all right."

"Ethan please hold us tight, I love you so much. You know you are my dream come true."

"Honey dream of me. Soon I will be dreaming with you, holding your hands and kissing your sweet lips. Then one morning you'll awake and there I'll be, then your dreams will have come all so true."

"You're not only a wonderful man, you're a poet! Kiss me, sweetheart, and tell me something I love to here."

"Missy, I love you and that is all I know."

With Todd holding his mamas hand we kissed and hugged and kissed again until we heard, "ALL ABOARD!"

I boarded, looked back one more time and watched my parents come out. I got to my compartment to take my last glance. Missy put her head on my mother's shoulder. They both embraced. My dad was holding Todd's hand. My son looked baffled. Two blasts of the whistle . . . train bell ringing and the train whose name I have forgotten pulled out slowly from Lincoln Nebraska on January 25, 1944. The train's final destination was San Francisco, but mine was unknown. I shut the door of my compartment and closed my eyes.

1944—Back to the fight

The train sped across the snow-covered plains of the Cornhusker State. I was in a fog thinking of what I had left behind. My thoughts turned to what lay ahead of me, not in the next few days but weeks. Soon I would be in South Pacific where it was hot and sunny but full of who knows what. The war was now in full swing and with the Germans almost beat we had all of our sights on Japan.

Several hours later, we made a stop in Hastings, Nebraska to pick up passengers. It was a very short stop. Soon again, this hotel on steel wheels was rolling at a good speed. I heard the conductor tell this woman that he was sorry because they sold her a ticket for an occupied compartment. He said she would have to sit in the coach until we hit Denver, and then a room would become available. Like the nice guy I am I said to him, "Do you want me to go into coach till morning and let her have the sleeper?"

The conductor said, "Let me go up a few cars to see if I can find her a compartment shared by a female."

I told the woman to have a seat until they could figure this out. We talked. I found out she was a singer headed for the Bay to join a troupe of USO entertainers going to Pearl. Her name was Bobbi from Hastings, Nebraska. After about a half hour, the conductor came back and said, "Madame, please walk to the fifth coach up for all spaces are taken. The Union Pacific apologizes for this inconvenience."

With all honorable intentions, I suggested that if she thought it was appropriate she could share the sleeper since it had two beds. Bobbi said thank you and accepted the offer. I stepped out and told the conductor what we were going to do.

"Fine with me ,sailor, like they say any old port in the storm."

"Listen, my home port is in Duluth. This is all on the up and up. My wife would cut them off with her nail clippers if I pulled a stunt like that!"

After some small talk, we went up to the dining car. We ate, then went to the lounge car for some conversation. I showed her a picture of Missy and my son. Bobbi had a boyfriend. He was in England with the US Army 82ND Airborne Division. He must be some rugged person because they only took the best. Bobbi showed me his picture, saying he was a great guy. He wanted to marry, but didn't take too well to her being a show girl singing and dancing around in front of horny servicemen. She wanted to be a big name singer someday, and act too. I thought to myself dream on girl, you and fifty million others. Heck, what do I know? Maybe she had what it took and might make the foot lights. Better than singing at weddings or dreary smoke filled nightclubs and state fairs.

We talked exchanging stories. I was trying not it make it look as though I was flirting. What if I had been a single man? Heck yeah I would have put the make on her. She was mysterious and sultry . . . pretty too! Around ten pm we headed for the sleeping car. I asked do you want the top bunk or bottom bunk. Bobbi said the top and smiled. I thought to myself, *why didn't something happen like this when I was single?* I left the compartment while she got her clothes changed. I hopped into bed with ALL of my clothes on. Then the thought came over me . . . how would Missy view this setup?

I knew what she would say, *Ethan I would expect no less than gentlemanly behavior and I trust you did.* She would ask, *Dear was she pretty?"* I would answer by saying, *Hon, she was very cute but if the two of you were on Waikiki Beach the day I saw you I still would have picked you.* Missy would have replied, *Sailorman, you're so full of it.* I would be sure to write about this strange episode in my next letter to her to cover all the bases.

The next morning we were in Denver. Bobbi got her own compartment. She thanked me then gave me a little peck on the cheek. Bobbi wished me the best saying she would pray for my safe return. That was it.

Submarines, Flying boats and PT boats

A day later, the train pulled into San Francisco. I reported to the duty officer. They put me up at the army barracks for the night. About an hour later I was awakened the US Navy Shore Patrol. They said I was to go with them. Soon I arrived where our ships tied up. I figured one of the troop transports was for me. I was lead down the pier past all of the ships and finally to my ship . . . a damn submarine! I hated submarines and never in my career wanted to serve on one.

"Chief Warrant Officer Vanderbilt reporting for duty sir, as ordered."

"Welcome aboard, Chief, I'm Commander Bob Griffin, how was your leave?"

"Great sir, but I am puzzled why I'm on a sub and not a transport. After all, I am in amphibious service."

"Well it's like this. A huge landing operation is going to happen soon and they want you on station ASAP. That's all I know, Chief, so we'll give you a quick lesson in sub operations. Anyway, you'll have no real duty so just enjoy yourself."

"Sir, I must let you know I am claustrophobic."

"Vanderbilt, aren't we all? You'll get used to it so please relax."

"Mr. Decker, prepare to get underway."

"Aye, aye Skipper, alright men up on deck and standby to cast off all lines!"

Around midnight, we slivered out the Bay under the cover of darkness. We ran on the surface until daybreak. By morning, I had enough of doing nothing. I spoke to the skipper and volunteered for watch duty too past time more quickly. Since this area of the Pacific was patrolled by air cover, we ran on the surface as much as possible. We ran on the surface a lot.

It sure was better than running below surface. When submerged the air was stale and the smell of battery acid and grease was everywhere. I felt a bit less claustrophobic on the surface. My opinion of the "silent service" remained the same: it stunk!

Captain Griffin told me at breakfast that in eight days we would rendezvous with a seaplane. They would take me to a troop transport. I must admit all of this special treatment of me with subs and seaplanes was very amusing. This was really something to tell the grandkids someday.

Soon my sub ride ended. Right before dawn, we surfaced and met up with the seaplane. In a matter of minutes, we were skimming across the smooth ocean surface then lifted into the sky as the sun broke. That was really a beautiful sight. I was thinking it was so peaceful up here except for the roar of the engines. Only miles away was the real estate of two very powerful forces fighting for a bunch of stupid islands? Soon the only way any of us would find peace whether Japanese or American was maybe to be dead. I had no intention of that happening to me!

I started to get airsick from the high-octane fuel smell. I moved up closer to the cockpit. The flight engineer motioned all the crew and passengers to look down and see what was below. In all in my years of service, I never saw so many ships in one place. They were ours. It was a mass of battleships, carriers and everything the US Navy had to offer. This was the task force of all task forces. The Imperial Japanese Navy would never stand a chance against this armada.

A few hours later, we landed in choppy waters. We pulled into a PT boat base in the Solomon Islands. I reported to an officer on duty and he had someone show me to my quarters. It was getting late in the day so I figured this would be my layover place until the next day. Besides the heat and humidity, this was really a nice base. Small with only PT boats on a small inland tender, it would remind me later of McHale's Navy, the sixties comedy. This was war tough and there was no friendly prisoner of war or Captain Binghamton. When these boats went out, it was to fight and not make beer runs like on TV!

By now, it had been about three weeks since I left the States and mail for me had arrived. How this woman works a job, takes care of a youngster, and writes me ten letters is beyond me.

Ethan, I am writing this wondering where on God's war—scorched earth you are. News about the war is vague and that worries me. I assume you are safe . . . you know I miss you so much. Our trip back to Duluth was to say the least horrible. Todd became almost unbearable. I at first I couldn't figure out why. All he would tell me is that he hated trains. Why I asked and he would just say the same thing. Then he mumbled, "Train takes my Daddy gone." I tried to calm him but he was just plain mean. He pooped his pants twice and has not done that in months. He acted up in the diner and did not obey me. I gave him a good swat on the butt but then he kicked me! I sent him to bed early. When he woke, I gave him a good lecture. He pouted the rest of the way home; even the porter tried talking to him. When we got home, Mom tried to calm him down and he finally did. Of course, he ratted on me and said, "Grandma, my Mama smokes." I had to hear about that for an hour and then just left him there and went home. This poor little boy is so hurt and he is in a way a casualty of this war too. Sweetheart, he is coming around but I wonder if he will ever get on another train! He sees your pictures and it makes him feel assured that you are in our lives.

She closed by saying how much she missed me. Yes, she was right. Our little boy had become a victim of the war. It pissed me off. I wanted blood now and any Jap would do!

The following day at three a.m., I boarded a Motor Patrol Boat (PT boat) with four other boats heading out across the vast Pacific Ocean. We were to meet up with a task force for an operation to take back a Japanese-held island. This was like motor boating on a large lake with a bunch of boats having fun. Loud motors, fast sleek craft, but instead of girls and beer on board, there were guns and torpedoes. PT boats were not much bigger than some pleasure craft. These boats made of wood would take on large ships made of steel!

I asked the Chief if we were in dangerous waters and his reply was, "Shit yes we are, take your choice, subs, small warships and fighter planes. Is this your first time in combat, Mr. Vanderbilt?"

"No, I was at Pearl, the Aleutians, Tarawa and the Canal."

"Oh, I see."

With the sun hitting us in the face we got word that enemy aircraft were in the area. Soon after the report came in, they hit from the west. We couldn't see them until they passed us. The squadron turned south. We banged off rounds, sending one down. With three to go, the enemy came in low and dropped a bomb missing every boat. Then, out of nowhere, came the US Marines flying the F4U Corsair. This was one of the finest fighters ever built. The enemy nicknamed it "whistling death" because of the noise it made as it came out of the sky. The Zero's tried to out run them,

The Beautiful Mistake

and thankfully the Marines knocked them out of the sky in minutes. One Japanese pilot bailed out. We went over there and picked him up. The Chief said, "Watch out, these guys never surrender, he might be booby trapped!" The crew fished him out and carefully stripped him, declaring he was clean. He wanted to surrender. It had been a very interesting day in this "mans navy!"

I met up with my task force and Commander Randolph Jackson. It was back to business right off the bat. He told me we would be hitting the beaches of the Marshall Islands. This would be a large operation. We had good intelligence that this would be an easy place to land. That was good news because the landings I had been on did not go well. It really bothered me to train so much only to see our landing tactics were not good. Dying on the beach was one thing, but drowning was so senseless.

On February 1st, we hit the beaches of Kwajalein in the Marshalls after a massive naval and air bombardment. This was a textbook landing with little causality. Air strikes kept ahead of us. I stayed on the beach getting more troops and equipment to the front. By the end of the day thousands of troops had landed successfully. Another good day!

By February 4th, the battle for Kwajalein was over and that meant the amateurs could handle my job from here. I went back to the ship and the first thing I wanted to do was shower and shave. That felt better than snuggling up to my wife, at least for now. I got into a clean uniform and ate like a pig, then headed for a staff meeting for our next assignment. On the way to the meeting, I met up with several Underwater Demolition Technicians, now called SEALS. I asked them about Lloyd Timken. One knew of him and knew he was missing in action though nothing more. However, their CO was to arrive by PT boat and might have the answers I needed.

Commander Jackson wasted no time getting to the point at our next meeting.

"Gentlemen, our next mission is to capture all of the Marshall Islands. I want to see raised hands who can name every island in the Marshall Chain. No one, eh? Doesn't surprise me, I can't either, but that's where we're going now so listen up."

We went to lunch and I purposely sat next to the UDT officer to do some intelligence work myself. His name was Ed Braddock, Lt USN. He looked like a swim jock from some expensive Ivy League school. Well built with blonde hair, he was what the frogman navy was looking for—a glory hunter. He was a 1939 Olympic swimmer and a silver medal winner.

"Lt. Braddock, I need to find out if you have any information on WO Lloyd Timken, a navy diver, Would that be possible? He is a very good friend of mine."

"Chief, I will do what I can. I have two friends that are MIA. Who knows, maybe they were on that mission. Anyway, I'll look into it. This UDT Navy is operating under some heavy security. Saying they are closed lipped is an understatement. I promise you I will try."

I was surprised he was willing to help me. I judged this guy as some cocky swim jock . . . I was wrong.

By surprise, I got some info on Timken's mission. He did a UTD mission in the Solomons which was to gather information from native coast watchers. That is all Lt. Braddock could find out. I still had faith he was alive. The islanders were very pro American and would do anything to help us.

Soon after my briefing with Braddock we had mail call. I had six letters from Missy, three from Lincoln and one from Allison. I had read all of them except for the last one from my wife. I wanted to save the best for last.

Ethan! Oh honey, there are miracles and we have received one! Lloyd is alive and well! Moreover, he is back in Pearl with Edith and son Michael. Sweetheart I know you already know this because you are so in touch with all that secret Navy stuff. Just bear with me while I write this letter with so much excitement, this is so wonderful. Praise God a billion times! I found out in a letter from her that I received the same day I started writing this one. He cannot give the details of his past few months due to security reasons. Edith is of course so relieved. Now darling don't you disappear and scare the living poop out of me, please? I love you so much and miss you, Missy. PS, Todd can write his name . . . I think we do have a genius!

Yes, this was exciting and very good news. How did she find out about Lloyd before I did? *What gives,* I asked myself. *This is just plain ass backwards. Does my wife know we are heading for the Marshalls too?* I wondered, *perhaps a Duluth version of Tokyo Rose!*

The invasion was fast approaching. Tension was in the air because we all knew this was a major invasion. The Navy was getting mail in and out for the troops because who knew what lied ahead. I got one letter on a rainy gloomy Saturday . . . it was from my wife.

Dear Ethan, This letter only brings bad news. Thomas was on his boat getting ready for the ore season and there was an accident. A boiler they were testing exploded. Six men have died and four were injured. My brother is severely injured. He may not live. He has many injuries. If he does make it, it will be only by the grace of God. He is in a local hospital but needs more care than they can offer, but transfer isn't an option for now. Since the ore boats are under defense contract, the Coast Guard is sending their medical staff. The other men hurt are just has bad too. My Mama is, to say the least, in great distress. Daddy is trying to keep her in one piece. He has seen this happen before, saying cold boiler starts are dangerous. I have no idea what he means by that. Allison has been by his side and has been so strong and loving towards him even with the rift between them. Darling I am so scared and so remorseful about the things I have said about him. I love my brother. We are so close and in many ways very much alike. It is that he makes me so mad at times by being so careless and cold to her. God forgive me. The war has come to our back door and it is frightening.

I have contacted my congressman. They will forward any information about him to you immediately. Toddy and little Juliet are fine and with Idonea and Eira. The kids know something is up and are showing it. These two little bright stars are smarter than we give them credit. They wonder and ask where Uncle Thomas and Daddy are and we are running out of, well, lies.

I must go for my bus comes soon to get over to the hospital. Etha,n I have had enough of this war. I did not used to judge all people by the action of a few sick bastards but honey, I hate the Jap's and Germans! My faith in humanity is being questioned. Please be careful and come home soon but get the job done before you do. Kill one for me and make him suffer. They are making so many good people in the world suffer. Pray for my brother and the other seaman and stay safe, I love you so much, Missy Xoxoxo

This hurt and bad. Thomas was a reckless immature person but deep down a good man. I'd never heard her talk like that before. Missy does not get mad often, but when she's had it, she's really had it. Was she still a Christian acting like a hypocrite? No, she was mad at two nations that took it upon themselves to rein terror against some that didn't even have armies! Now she was even more upset that the war in its own way had reached home. My wife had every reason in the world to hate these monsters!

We continued our push into the Marshalls with little rest and little mail. We ferried in supplies and carried out the wounded back to the ships. After that, my command headed for the Philippines.

Steve Zingerman

To the love of my life, YOU Ethan, First of all Thomas is going to make it but they had to take his left leg at the knee. It was so crushed even those fine doctors could not save it. Even still, he's not out of the woods yet. He took it well and is making jokes about it, can't he ever be serious! He says his new nickname is peg leg. The children think that is so funny. Darling guess what, Allison and my brother got married in the hospital. I guess it took this to bring him down from the clouds. We did the ceremony in the room and Allison wore a pretty off white dress (real off white, sorry that was rude) plus a different hairstyle. I picked out her dress and did her hair, you know I always have to get involved in that stuff. She looked so beautiful and both were so happy too. Juliet seemed to know what was going on and seemed tickled to bits. She was the flower girl also. He will be in the hospital another month and they will live in Duluth near where I live. This has worked out well, my brother is alive, married to a great woman and has grown up a lot. Well not all the way, he asked the hospital if Allison could stay overnight. Gosh, he almost dies, losses a leg and the only thing on his mind is sex! The hospital said no, but I think a night nurse arranged something for them. Oh, before I forget the other injured men survived too, God is good! Peg leg and Allison Jeannette Bay say hello and send all their love. Peg leg, can you believe that goof?

Now for some more good news . . . I am going to model again this year. My sisters were not asked but for good reason. I will be modeling maternity wear, it looks better on me . . . Moreover, I get to keep the clothing after the shooting is over. Might need it soon Ethan Allen. At least we won't have to buy it. Might wear it to church tomorrow to show them off. I'll get a snap shot of me in it and send it to you. Cutie pie Ethan I must go, I am a little tired, I can't seem to figure out why, can you? Your loving wife and my dream come true, Missy. Many long kisses to you sailorman. PS. Wondering though, did we leave the diapers in Hawaii, I need dust clothes to clean in. Love you sweetheart. Todd can count too. He is so much like you, love you and miss you! Missy . . . why am I so hungry for stuff I hate!

That was about the most dramatic drawn out way for her to tell me we were going to have a baby. That is my wife though, so dramatic. Of course, I was happy though not surprised. I was sad in one way because this child would be born without me being there. Missy would have plenty of support. Still I needed to be there and there was not way for that to happen.

With all this good news, I could concentrate on my job. We were now involved in some major battles and the enemy was feeling our wrath.

The Beautiful Mistake

Recapturing the Philippines would really be a moral rouser for our country and a big blow to the Japanese. Many perished in the Bataan Death March. The enemy was still a formidable force and we knew it. Things though were looking good here, not so good on the home front.

Hi sweetie, I have been getting your letters almost every day. I read them over and over again. Thomas was home for a while but was back to the hospital because of infections. He is progressing but slowly. All of us are on the edge of our seats over him. Allison is so brave; she just keeps smiling and will not leave his side for a minute. This is a special woman. She amazes us with her devotion. I guess she knows how to handle life's ups and downs. I'm feeling fine. Things are going well. I will soon be leaving my mill job and in a way, I hate to. It has been a wonderful experience. I made some good friends. The baby will be born in late September. I hope you are here when she comes. Yes, I said she, call it intuition. How does the name Marietta Lovisa Vanderbilt sound?

I am having problems with Todd. He wakes up at night crying. On many nights, he ends up in bed with me. With my brother being hurt and losing his hero (you!) and seeing me cry, this poor little boy is feeling the horror of war too. I hate to bring this to you but you are my husband and I need to share this with you. I am getting wary of this war and want an end to it and soon. Ethan I am so tired both physically and mentally. Sometimes I wonder if this is just a nightmare. When I wake you and I will be on the beach at Waikiki fishing and making out! Gosh, honey could I use that. Well time for a bath and bedtime, I will be thinking of you. Oh Ethan, they are playing our song "Always." Good song to take a hot bath with, I love you so much. Many kisses and say your prayers. Missy Xoxoxo

I received orders that I was to be a part of an operation of great importance. The mission was to go into the Leyte Gulf and under the cover of night rendezvous with Filipino resistance fighters. We were to pick up information for MacArthur's return to the Philippines. I would scope out the beach to see if it was suitable for a landing operation. We would go by PT boat. When the moon was not visible, we would land in a rubber raft. This would be the most dangerous assignment yet. We were to make sure our personal business was in order. There was to be no mention of the mission in letters to home. My last letter to Missy before this mission would be the usual, small talk, kidding around and "I love you." My girl knew me too well. I hoped she would not sense something was up.

The mission to the Philippines began on June 6, 1944. Ironically, the same day Allied forces were invading occupied France. We were up at nine p.m. to begin getting ready for our own little invasion. Soon a PT boat pulled up to our transport. Off we went for a four-hour trip across enemy infested waters. At around three a.m., we arrived safely on station. I got our landing party into the small rubber raft. It took one half hour to reach shore. According to my chart, we were at the right spot. Man it was dark and creepy! How they would find us was beyond me. They had no radios and asking aloud was asking for a visit from the enemy! They gave us one hour on shore . . . that was it. Five minutes would have been enough for me! Out of nowhere came two Filipinos men that were talking loudly.

"Hey guys, keep it down, want the Japs to hear us?" I said.

"No worry, Captain, no Jap's here, they're all asleep . . . forever, bolo sharp and quiet," the Filipino said with a strange laugh.

"Yeah, nothing like a sharp bolo, now let's get to what the devil I'm here for."

"Lots of time Chief. You have a couple of Jap beer, took from dead. They no need now!"

"Save it for VJ-Day," my Gunners Mate replied.

The OSS took the information. We checked out the beach, stepping off some measurements. I got what I wanted and then I ordered us off the island. Our Filipino friends had one request. They had a very sick member of their force that needing medical attention. I agreed to take him. This poor kid was very sick. Maybe a ruptured appendix or other internal injuries but he needed a doctor. When back on the PT boat the hospital corpsman checked him out agreeing it was a ruptured appendix. The corpsman said, "This guy will die before we get to the transport, but I'll do I can."

Two hours later, this brave young kid died in my arms. He quietly slipped away. The PT skipper said, "We will take him to the ship and give him a proper burial." We did not know his name but the OSS man promised he would get it to notify his family after we retook the Philippines. That is the way it was in WW2, everybody was a comrade in arms.

Back on board, we gave our reports then hit the sack. I was up around ten a.m. to attend the funeral of our fallen mate. Off into the deep blue sea he went for his eternal rest. Mail call came and never was I so glad to read letters from my family.

My Mom wrote and said the winter wheat was going to be a bumper crop. That was good for my brothers. Mom was in college part time, learning to be a librarian. She seemed happy to be learning more than how to make bread out of nothing or sew up a shirt that needed pitched. She was on top of the world! My Dad was doing well at managing the elevators. My sister was having her share of problems with polio but her spirits were good. Burton was still somber and making good money on the railroad. All seemed well in the Cornhusker State.

Missy on the other hand seemed fine though her letters showed more than she was telling. She was lonely and trying to hide it. She was suffering for more reasons than just my absence. Her brother's accident affected her so much. I believed that if she could survive World War 2, she could survive anything.

The battle to take back the Philippines began on October 21, 1944 at Leyte Gulf in the Philippines. It started out as a true Naval sea battle. Battleships, heavy cruisers, destroyers and airplanes. The battle only lasted three days. In the end, the mighty Imperial Japanese Navy and Air Force were finished. We took hits too, lost plenty of sailors and ships. With the US being able to do whatever it wanted to do on the high seas and in the air; I knew my time over here was nearing the end.

As the sea and air battle waged on, we made plans to land in Ormac Bay, in the Philippines. As it always seemed that when we got into a major offensive, the damn mail stopped showing up. My last letter from her was in early September. By all accounts our baby should have been born. I asked Commander Jackson if he could send out a message to find out. Jackson was very good at saying no.

Finally, on the second day of the battle, mail came in and I had twenty-one letters from Missy.

My darling, and so far father of just one child, Things here in Duluth are good but not great. Ten more names were in the paper today. Most in European battles. I knew one that I went to school with. Idonea knew one also. She said they went out one time but she said he got fresh with her and that was the end for him. He was a real hell raiser and always liked motor cycles and fast woman. Idonea, fast? I doubt it. The boy I knew was just the opposite. He was in the Third Armored Division with General Patton, the crazy one. Honey I am really near the end with being pregnant. I need to have this baby. Since I cannot work anymore, thinking about you is all I do. Todd is being such a good boy and loves on me when I get teary. He is so excited about the baby and thinks they can go play when he or she arrives. Todd always is bragging about you to his friends. To him you are everything a boy can imagine. My brother is doing better but will not see an ore boat this season. Doctors say next spring, but Allison says never again to sailing. I think she is the boss and he seems to like it that way. I guess that is it. A letter just came from you and I will read in before I close. I am sending a cutout picture of Jeanne Crain and me. Now look and you will see I am no Jeanne! Do not even resemble each other! Wish I was but I am just homely skinny me. Cutie pie Ethan I can do anything they can and more, come home soon and you will see! You know these Hollywood beauties do the same things as the rest of us women. When they go to bed at night, they tie up their hair in rags and put cold cream on. When they wake up, they look like crap and have bad breath just like the rest of us. Get it, sugar? Loving you so much, Jeanne! PS, The rumor is Heddy Lamar likes girls and men!

That night as I laid my weary self down to sleep, we had mail call. My Chief Petty Officer brought my mail down and there it was.

"*Hi sweetheart, we have a beautiful baby girl! Marietta Lovisa Vanderbilt was born October 10 at four a.m. weighing 7 pounds and three ounces. She is fine and I am good too. Everyone in Nebraska knows and I hope this letter gets to you soon so you know. Todd is in amazement over her. He will make a good brother. I find it hard to believe that four years ago we were alone in this world and now have two beautiful children. Who would have imagined that our walk down Waikiki Beach would lead to this? Four more kids to go Ethan!*"

Man, a daughter. Missy will have fun with her! Now I will have two fashion nuts in the house, and boys to chase away! Then again, she might be a tomboy. It would that be funny and ironic in a way.

The war nears its end

With the bloody sea and air battle over in Leyte Gulf, the invasion began of the Philippines. This time I was on board the transports overseeing loading and discharging men and material. I felt safer here than on land. That didn't last long. At noon, a kamikaze pilot hit us. The aft of the transport burst into flames with heavy dense smoke. A bunch of us headed back there to begin fighting the fire.

The Jap plane had disintegrated upon impact except for the tail section. The pilot died. If he had not, I would have finished him even if he had begged for mercy. Not many sailors were hurt on the deck. Some appeared trapped on the deck below. The fire was out quickly. Now began our search for the ones below. There was an entrance to the below deck that had the ladder blown away. The only way down was for someone was get lowered in to bring the four men out. The six sailors there with me stood six foot and big like football players. Even though I was tall, I was skinny so I would go down. We got some line and away I went. It was a ten foot drop and hotter than hell. The men below were hurt with one in very bad shape. I tied him up and the men above raised him to the main deck and fresh air. It took forty minutes to get everyone out of there. When I came up, I passed out from dehydration. I woke up in the infirmary an hour later with some burns and one heck of a headache. The next day I was back on duty, hurting some but there was no way I was making a hospital bed my new duty station!

General McArthur was to come in by boat to the beachhead. My orders were to follow his staff in another boat. There is a picture of this event showing Commander Jackson and I directly behind the General. He was everything people say his was . . . a towering giant who let you know he was in command.

Steve Zingerman

My wife had gone back to work at the steel mill. Her mom and sisters did the babysitting. There was no talking her out of working. It made her feel useful by helping the war effort. Daily life in the States was getting a little easier. There was a suspension of some types of rationing. Shoe rations were soon to be over also. I'm sure Missy was overjoyed!

The Leyte Gulf was in our hands in December, 1944. We were on roll now with our spirits high. The Jap Navy was sinking faster than you could count and their planes fell from the sky like at a pigeon shoot. Time flew by and before I knew it, February of 1945 was here.

Iwo Jima

No doubt, the most famous battle of the Pacific was to begin. Iwo Jima was a small island with beaches made of volcanic ash. We wanted it to provide a landing field for our B-29 bombers. This would save many aircrews on long distance flights.

The shore bombardment of Iwo began in February. Our Navy hit that rock with everything they had. It was like July 4th with gunfire lighting up the night. How the enemy could live through that was beyond me. The pounding went on for hours and soon landing operations began. I was to be in the second wave with the anticipation of a secured beach. At 7 a.m., I took off in a landing boat and an hour later, I was on the beach. What a mess, nothing was where it was supposed to be. The enemy did not even seem fazed by the pounding from our ships. Our Marines began taking heavy fire. They were taking so many causalities. My group was only taking up space so I asked the Marine Captain should I load up some wounded and head back to the ship.

"Chief grab a gun off a dead man, take a position and fight like hell!" was his answer. I told my men we were under his command. Find weapons and keep your head down! Getting a weapon was not hard to find, the dead were everywhere. My men pulled a wounded sailor to safety. The young man died. I grabbed his Browning automatic rifle. I banged off some rounds. Soon we made our way back to the boat unloading more ammo. More boats were coming in so I got the captain to release us to help unload supplies. Word got to me to start bringing wounded back then return for more. After awhile, the Marines started making progress on the beachhead. The Marines were inching their way up the island making more room for badly needed supplies. As Marines went up, our dead came back for identification. Missing limbs, heads and some only in piles of flesh. A lot of the wounded wanted to stay and fight. These were the bravest men I had ever seen. Most were not much over twenty years old.

As night fell, I found us on the beach stranded for the night with the possibility of snipers creeping up on us.

By morning, we headed back to the ship. We were allowed to eat and get some sleep before starting up again. That day was somewhat easier, but seeing so many dead and wounded made me sick. They say two thousand of our people were either dead or wounded on the first day.

On March 26, 1945, Iowa Jima was ours. We had 23,000 US Marine and 2,800 US Navy causalities. I felt ten years older and now was beginning to wonder how much more could I stand. I wondered even though the war was almost over, was I going to survive or be normal ever again.

A letter from Missy, April, 1945

My sweet Ethan, I am getting your mail but the letters you write are not in order. What is going on? We hear of the fighting on Okinawa and some place called Iowa Jima. Honey I am scared out of my wits, are you okay? Please write me a long letter, I need to read your words and see your handwriting. Betsy Vetzy, my friend, says maybe you are a prisoner of war or taken by the enemy for medical experiments done on you. You aren't are you? My brother said no because your letter is post marked FPO San Francisco and the Krauts are the ones that do human experiments. I must settle down and realize you are busy.

Smoking doesn't even settle my nerves anymore. I take a sip of glogg at night after our children are in bed. I feel that it might be taking me over. I pray all the time. Now I am keeping my head covered with a scarf. This represents that I am in continuous prayer. Sweetheart I am so confused and I am afraid when you come home I will not be the women you fell in love with. I love you so much and hope you will love me too. I cannot pretend anymore, Ethan, I am a nut waiting to crack. If you find that I have changed too much when you return and cannot stand me, I will give you a divorce. Our children will always be yours to be a part of. I hope none of this happens and we can start where we left off. Please be patient with me and never stop loving me. You know you are my dream come true. The kids are fine and the baby girl Marietta is so cute. Todd is such a good son and is like at times a little man. Honey I cannot write anymore because my tears are wetting the paper or is it the rain coming from my open window? Maybe it is both. Please be safe and pray like hell! Your wife Missy Xoxoxo

Me divorce Missy, there was a better chance of me becoming a priest! I really felt empty and so helpless. There was nothing I could do besides feel bad and write her a long traditional "love letter." I did.

In the letter, I told her to dump Betsy. She was one the girls that went to Hawaii when I met my wife. Betsy Vetzy, even in the forties believed in flying saucers, reincarnation. She was a vegan. She was nuts, very homely and never stopped talking. Betsy kept a 4.0 grade average in college but had no idea what to do with all that knowledge. She was of Jewish decent whose father was an eye doctor. I heard her mom was a nut too. I had to laugh though . . . me a prisoner of war or better yet a human guinea pig. If they dissected me there would be little to learn about. The Jap's thought we were full of shit anyway and that is what they would get from me . . . shit!

May 1, 1945 the Third Reich that was to last for a thousand years ended. I guess Adolf was not the right person for the job. The plan now was to send troops from Europe to the Pacific to finish off the other bunch of goons. We were all feeling good about Germany's defeat. Then we heard what could happen. If the Japanese did not surrender, we would have to attack the mainland. This could take two more years to end the war. In addition, it might cost two million lives both, Allied and Japanese. If this war lasted two more years . . . Well, it could not.

A victory letter

Hi sweetheart! I guess you know the Huns have had it! We celebrated in the streets of Duluth and had so much fun. I stayed sober. I danced with my sisters and Allison. We stayed up until midnight. Now to finish the Japs off, and I know that will be soon. I am making a bet with Betsy that it will be over by July, '45. When all of this is over the party will be even bigger and I hope we can celebrate it with our own big bang! OOPS! I hope the censors don't read that, ah the hell with them! Love you cutie, Missy Xoxoxo

While still on station, Commander Jackson summoned me to his stateroom.

"Chief, Iwo Jima was a success from the landing standpoint even though a lot of causalities occurred. Now hear this . . . you have heard about a secret weapon that we have that could end the war in one airdrop over Japan. No one really knows much about this bomb or gun or whatever it is. We do know this the war must end. The War Department said we would invade the mainland if we have to. Here's the role you play. In the near future, you will return to the Philippines and help with organizing landing operations for the invasion of mainland Japan. How you get there or when is up in the air. For now, I will try to keep you out of the Okinawa campaign. There is much to do here at Iwo with the cleanup and building of the airstrip. By then, the picture of what is going to happen will be clearer. That is all and that is enough!"

One Sunday I took a ride up into the island to see what we had won at Iwo Jima. Iwo Jima was no island paradise. This hole had rock for terra firma with few trees even before the bombing and negligible wildlife plus little if any fresh water. I rode up with a US Marine captain in a Jeep. He was showing me the caves where the enemy had hid out in. As we rounded, a curve there was a ridge, which sat off to the left of us. We heard nothing but when we saw the dust kick up, we knew we were under assault. We stopped the Jeep and ran for cover. He said there were some Japanese that were still around. Sniper fire from stragglers was to be expected. If I had known that my Navy ass was gonna be a target, I would never have gone on a Sunday ride in the country. I pointed out where the Nip was while the Captain fired back. I fired back too, however the Nip had us pinned down. The captain sneaked back to the jeep and grabbed his radio. He called in our position, and then told me to keep down and wait for the fireworks. The soldier kept firing. About ten minutes later, which really felt like an hour, a low flying Marine Corsair, came in. With his wing guns firing, he dropped a napalm bomb. That was the end of the enemy holdout. We spent one hundred seventy five dollars to kill one dumb soldier. He could have surrendered . . . gone back to Japan and lived to see grand children. Who knows maybe this soldier would have become became president of Toyota. War is so sad.

May also brought the death of Franklin D. Roosevelt. Historians say he got us out of the Great Depression. I think the Japanese might have had more to do with it than him. FDR was a very inspirational man. I would have never wanted to be president in these times. Even then, he had his critics like all presidents do.

In July, I got orders to board the USS Indianapolis, a cruiser. I was excited about sailing with her because some of my friends were serving aboard her. Commander Jackson and the rest of the staff would be with me too. This would be a nice peaceful cruise.

As my luck would have it, my travel arrangements changed. The "Indy" was all booked up. I would instead sail on a stinky troop transport heading for Leyte Gulf. This vessel was a real gem, as in a lump of coal. Because this ship was in such bad condition, my life jacket was always in sight.

We left from Iwo Jima on July 25, 1945 and steamed towards the Gulf at a very slow speed of fifteen knots. The Indy left Tinian Island with the remainder of our staff. In a few days, both ships would meet again.

I have done every job in the Navy imaginable. As a young seaman, I did galley duty, painted bulkheads, cleaned water closets, and steered the ship many times. After awhile you know when a ship changes course, even if you can't see it happen. Call it a seventh sense. At first, we were on a zigzag course to avoid enemy subs. Then we started steaming on a straight-line course. Reports came in that one of our ships was hit by an enemy sub. The ship was the *USS Indianapolis.* My heart sank. I expected the worst.

The next morning we arrived at the area where Indy went down. Debris and oil was the only thing we saw for awhile. Then we ran across men floating in the sea. These poor souls covered in oil looked more like seals than sailors. The skipper of the ship sent launches into the water picking up survivors. Some other ships also appeared and joined in the rescue. Once all of the Indy crew aboard we found out what had happened.

In the early morning of July 30, a Japanese torpedo, sent from by a sub, sank the Indy to the bottom. A survivor I spoke to believed that almost the whole crew got off the Indy alive. The first shocker for me was the sinking had gone unnoticed for four days! Why? How? This was so atypical of the US Navy to make such a blunder of this size. After a day or so, we found around one third of the crew. What happened to the rest? Most did get off the ship alive as mentioned. Sure, some died from jumping overboard. Some died of exposure, lack of water and sunburn. Survivors said that many were taken away by sharks. We couldn't believe our ears. This was one of the saddest events in Naval history. It shook my confidence in my Navy. The horror of what I saw would haunt me for years. I thought how blessed I was not to have been on that ship but still saddened that I lost at least twelve friends. In that twelve was Commander Jackson Randolph. Chief Gibson and I were the only two left. Disillusioned, our ship headed back to Guam and awaited what to do next.

August 6th 1945 . . . who is sorry now?

August 6th we got word three B-29 bombers took off from Guam heading for Hiroshima Japan. One bomber dropped the secret weapon we had been hearing about called the A-bomb. I didn't understand how it worked or even cared. The damage it caused practically leveled the whole city. This bomb was supposed to end the war immediately but didn't. This didn't surprise me one bit. One little bomb on one Japanese city was not going to stop these fanatics.

I received orders to board a Landing Tank Ship and prepare for the invasion of mainland Japan. This was very disappointing news for all of us but it looked like the only way. The Japanese Imperial Army was getting beat everywhere.

August 9th I set sail heading for a larger task force. We got word a second Atomic bomb hit Nagasaki. This time we were hoping this did the trick. The bomb did not seem to faze these bastards one bit. *What would it take*, I wondered. From August 8th until the 14th, we hit them with air, surface and subsurface strikes. They hit back with kamikazes and even torpedoed my old ship, the USS Pennsylvania, but the old girl stayed afloat.

Tojo says, ok, I have had enough

A letter came from Missy.

Dear Ethan, The war is over, as you know. Thank God! Most from Europe aren't even home yet. Why, I ask? Can't you just tell them you miss me or shed a tear (yes dear cry, I always got my way with Daddy). We are so excited and your son has you all planned out. He wants to fish, ride bikes and learn how to play ball. I want just you. Please save some energy for me! I cannot wait to wake with you every morning with bad breath cold cream and my hair in rags. I miss our mornings we had in Hawaii, drinking coffee together, talking and listening to the singing birds . . . being together . . . alone! Ethan I just remembered we have two kids . . . forget the above! Sugar you will love having them in the morning . . . they are a real joy! Todd cannot wait to go outside and play. Marietta is somewhat of a crab until she is changed and fed. Todd eats barely enough and "Etta" eats and eats and eats! Our life has changed some with them but it is a good change and I know you will love it too.

Ethan, please no surprise arrivals. I want to look beautiful for you. I need time to get my hair and nails done and get that sexy dress I promised to wear! Come home soon, I understand it might take time. So impatient for you, love Missy, Todd, Marietta plus every person in the USA!

Only my wife would be concerned about her appearance! I could care less how she looked. As long as I could wrap my arms around her and kiss those perfect lips, that is all that mattered. I wanted to see my children. I think in some strange way I was more homesick now than in the beginning.

As the details of surrender were being worked out, we heard that an occupation force was being formed which would require Naval and Army personnel. I wrote my wife urging her to be patient. I never shirked from duty. This time I hoped some other person would get the glory.

We now needed to land on several islands that we had bypassed during the war. Men on those islands were our POW's. We wanted the war criminals of Japan too. I received orders to steam with a task force to make a landing on Wake Island. This had been the second target after Pearl. The Japanese captured our forces, sending them to work camps. Throughout the war, they did forced labor for the enemy. The enemy would surrender peacefully.

They did. The Japanese left them to fend for themselves. They were starving, dying of disease and more than happy to surrender. So desperate for food, they had eaten every bird, lizard and rodent this worthless atoll had to offer. I felt sorry for them, in some ways.

After being on Wake for two weeks, I received orders to board a destroyer to head home by way of Pearl Harbor. The trip to Pearl would take several days. Calm seas, sunny skies with no enemy to worry about. I daydreamed of Missy. I wondered how it would feel to see her everyday and be a married couple with two kids. I wondered if there would be readjustment problems. Had war changed me? Yes, it had. What about her, had war changed this funny high-spirited goofy beauty? Writing letters is a way to stay close but it's not like speaking to each other in person. I had to believe all would be fine . . . it had to be.

Pearl Harbor, 1945

Entering Pearl filled me with mixed emotions. Happy as heck to be there . . . sad to think this is where it all began. The base looked good again. The USS Arizona's hull was at the bottom with many of its hands entombed forever. Oil still leaked from her telling us she was still bleeding. Then again perhaps she was saying I am alive . . . do not ever forget me.

We tied up near where the Pennsylvania used to dock. After a bit, I was free to leave the ship. I walked down the pier. To my surprise, Lloyd Timken was waiting for me, leaning against the hood of Yellow Baby. We shook hands and headed to his house. Lloyd asked, "Ethan, want to drive past where you two lived?"

"No, I am homesick enough. That would make me feel worse. Right now, my mind is with her and my body is here. I need to get home faster than some transport. I feel sometimes my honey has been all nothing but a dream."

"No man, no dream. I have seen her myself . . . she is real. Someday this war will be like a dream and not the nightmare that it is. I wish the Navy could get you home on one of those new jets that are entering service. I did check on flights back to the States. Only the ass kissers are getting dockets."

"I know. Thanks anyway. The war is barely over and already the Navy we know is becoming obsolete. The big battleships are being replaced by air power with carriers, they're king. Even the backwater Navy is a dinosaur. Change is in the air. I hope not much has changed in Duluth."

We pulled into their driveway. Edith was standing there looking very good. Missy must have had an influence on her with style—didn't look like a drab old missionary woman anymore. Their little boy, Michael was there. Edith looked like she maybe was working on number two.

"Oh Ethan, gosh you look good, handsome as always. God has been so good to us. The war is over and you and Lloyd are home. I got letters from Missy. It must be fun being she, so much spirit and quirkiness. Where does she get all this zip?"

"I don't know. She is her worst enemy at times. Missy can cause a ruckus. No doubt when I get home, something will happen. I hope she has some zip left for me."

We sat down and talked for hours about what we each did in the war. From what Lloyd told me he had seen most of it in a diving suit aboard a submarine. He had done some scary missions.

I stayed at their house that night. The next morning we sat drinking coffee. Lloyd asked me how eager I was to get home.

"Lloyd, I really would do anything to get home faster but I must be patient. Its four thousand miles to Duluth . . . at one time I was seven thousand miles from home . . . things are looking up!"

"So you would do anything to get home faster?"

"Yes. I would do almost anything."

"Well sailor, in two hours you are boarding a sub. It is heading for Long Beach California, so pack your bags!"

"A sub, I hate subs, you know that!"

"Ethan, here is your choice. You can be in the States in ten days by surface ship or six days or less underwater. In eight or nine days, you will be in your birthday suit with Missy all sweaty and happy. The choice is yours."

"I'll take the sub!"

Edith with tears said, "I mean not to get emotional, excuse me. I will miss you two so much. Will we ever meet again, EA?"

"Edith, Missy and I wouldn't have it any other way. You can count on it. Lloyd, I thought only my wife cries. Women and emotion sure go together."

"I know what you're saying. It's a part of everyday life for women. I think Edith learned it from you know who."

"I know what you mean. Missy is like a spreading virus sometimes. I caught it on Waikiki Beach and haven't gotten over it yet!"

Lloyd had everything to do with this ride on a sub for me. We had an emotional goodbye. Edith was a damn good woman. Missy and I loved her so much. Lloyd was like a brother to me. He was what he was and I hoped he never would change. We promised to stay in touch. The war was over and sadly, many things in our lives were over too. Some friendships would last. Some would fade away.

"Ethan, here is five hundred bucks for the car. Sign the title over to me. This might be the first legal transaction I ever make."

"Lloyd, please do me a favor. Keep this car. At least until we return to Pearl for a visit."

"I will do that. You can count on it. Please come back soon. So long, sailor . . . I'm gonna miss you."

"You too, man."

As I waved good-bye, standing in the conning tower of the sub, a tear came to my eye, or was it a splash of seawater? It didn't matter. It was both a happy day and sad at the same time. As we pulled out of the harbor, we passed the vehicles of war. Before December 7, 1941, most of these ships did not exist. I hope that they would never have to see war again. Too many good men had died. It was a just war, fought only after we had no choice. Would this be the end of tyrants, troublemakers and thugs? Would they finally learn not to start something they cannot finish? I hoped so, though deep inside I knew that it was only wishful thinking.

Fifteen miles at sea the command *DIVE DIVE* was given. The sub slipped quietly under a smooth, blue and peaceful Pacific Ocean. I went to my bunk looking at a picture of my family daydreaming until I dozed off. In a short time, we would all be together forever.

Back in the United States of America!

Arriving in the United States felt strange. As we tied up in Long Beach, I immediately sensed that we were a nation at peace. Even the air smelled good. The sailors on shore helping us tie up were in high spirits. As I hit dockside, I picked up a handful of small sea gravel putting it in my pocket. I promised myself that this gravel would travel with me to Duluth. I would have my wife put in a decorative glass piece. It sits on our mantle.

I wasted no time in picking up my orders and travel arrangements to begin my long agonizing trip back home. It would be the same old long train ride. If there were a way to put me in a Rip Van Winkle sleep until I got home, I would have done it. I sent Missy a telegram.

Honey in US.—Arrive Duluth 9-20-2pm—Love Ethan

Missy would receive this in a few hours . . . I would be home in two days. She had said, "No surprises Ethan. I want to look beautiful for you." She could show up in dirty mill clothes, it would not make any difference to me.

I took the night train out of Los Angeles. Surprisingly it was light on passengers. It was nice to have the whole train to myself. It gave me time to relax. I awoke in Gallup, New Mexico. The difference between the deserts compared to the oceans was this . . . nothing. Nothing is nothing!

I had little to do on the train but think. My thoughts took me back to the first day I saw that skinny brunette on the beach. I thought about our first date when I took her to dinner eating real Hawaiian food. I remember our walks down the beach. I always said I hated shopping with her but really, I did not. This woman shopped with such intensity you would think she was performing brain surgery. I loved that free spirit of hers too.

As we neared the Twin Cities, more serious thoughts came. Suppose both of us were very different now. Maybe after awhile we realized we needed to go our own way. It was going to happen to some couples as it always had before. I took a pen and paper to it and figured out how many days we really had been together. It was around seven hundred fifty days. Since the day we met, it had been a total of 1,506 days! I had been away a little bit more than half the time! I was lucky, many men were away longer and of course, some never returned. The nearer we got to Duluth the more anxious I became.

"The train will be one hour late for the Twin Cities due to track work," The conductor announced.

"Just my luck but I'm almost there."

"Where's home, Chief?" asked the conductor.

"Duluth. That will home for a while. I can't wait. My wife and two little kids are waiting for me. The ride to Duluth seems to take forever!"

"I have done that Duluth local, worst duty on the railroad but you take what they give you. Coming from the Pacific?"

"Yes, been there since 1932 more or less. I am sick of it. Next duty station better be good."

"Hey Chief, I got a question. If a Marine got killed at Guam, will they bring the remains back as the government promised?"

"Yes, they will. I saw them doing it at Wake Island before I left several weeks ago."

"My wife will like hearing that. Thank you Chief."

I shook my head, closed my eyes and thought to myself, God give me the strength to endure all of this. How many of those stories would I hear? Should I feel guilty that I survived without a scratch?

"Minneapolis—St. Paul, Minnesota is coming up, Mr. Vanderbilt. We will exit from the rear of the car. Your sea bags will be in the station. Good luck sir, and welcome home!" the Pullman porter yelled.

"Porter, here is a little souvenir from a Jap that will never miss it. They tell me it is a medal for courage. It might be worth something someday so hang on to it. Here also is a ten-dollar bill I found on Iwo Jima. I don't know whose it was, hopefully he is wondering what the hell happened to it."

"Thanks skipper . . . this is the best tip I ever got"

If it was not one thing, it was another. The Duluth local, due to a derailment of a freight train, now would be late. The stationmaster announced the railroad was gathering up some cars from the coach yard. How long this would take was anyone's guess. I was starting to feel more defeated than when Pearl got it!

The Brunette with Red Lipstick wearing a Yellow Dress

I decided to call Missy to let her know of the delay. I went inside to get some change. I saw a woman facing away from me that could be Missy's twin. This woman had a hat so I knew that was not my girl. I got change from Travelers Aid, and then headed for the phone booth. Then she turned my way . . . my jaw dropped! That woman standing there in a tapered, yellow knee length dress with expensive Spectators and white wrist gloves was Mrs. Mystic Ann Marie Vanderbilt! With her were a handsome little boy and a beautiful blonde baby girl. our children. I stared for a moment in awe. She had not noticed me yet. For a brief second I wanted to absorb this beautiful moment before it happened.

How do you describe a moment like this? Those first bursts of high energy when you see each other will only last for a few minutes. This exact moment will never happen again. I was spellbound and at the same time a bit scared. This was my family. Here was the moment both of us had been waiting for. I guess I was being silly in the head. I will never forget that moment.

"Missy, I'm right here. I don't know why you're here . . . man I'm glad! Gosh, you look good. I don't know what to say . . . I'm shaking like a leaf. You are wearing a hat and the kids . . . Oh my. Now I think I might faint!"

"Oh Ethan, Ethan my sweet Ethan, you're home, you're really home! Kids, Daddy is home . . . your daddy is home and will be forever! Gorgeous? Yes . . . I feel so gorgeous. The hat . . . why not? I needed a change. Now don't you dare faint! That is my gig. Kiss me, sailor, just kiss me and tell me this is not a dream."

"Maybe it is . . . hey buddy, are we dreaming?" I asked a stranger standing nearby.

"No sailor, she said kiss her. So kiss her!"

We looked into each other's eyes. Our lips met. I ran my hands through that beautiful brown hair. We hugged and kissed so passionately. Then I picked up my son Todd and little Marietta. I hugged and kissed them. I was home. Yes, I was really home and this time to stay!

"Missy, I can't seem to say what I want to."

"You are saying it right now. Ethan, words cannot say it right now. Just hold me and let me feel you against me. Look, these two little darlings are ours . . . isn't that amazing. Let's sit for a moment."

"Missy, they are beautiful. Hi Todd, do you remember me?"

"Sure I do, Daddy. When can we go fishing?'

"Soon Todd . . . real soon. So, you are Marietta. Wow, you are a cutie. Missy, you sure can make beautiful babies!"

"Ethan, we make beautiful babies and maybe more sometime soon. The car is outside. Let's go, I don't want to see a train station for a long time."

We got into the '40 Ford. Missy explained how she ended up in the Twin Cities.

"Honey, I couldn't wait any longer. Gas rationing is pretty much over and I had extra coupons. I am kidnapping you before we go to Duluth. I rented a place on a lake near here. There are no phones. There is plenty of room to play with Todd and Marietta and . . . me! I brought fishing stuff and other things to play with the kids. What do you think?"

"You should be a vacation planner! Good idea, baby. Let's go start honeymoon number three!"

"Yes, but can we make this the last honeymoon? From now on, let's be a normal married couple, though never boring?"

"Yes, that is what I was thinking. I got a feel it will never be boring."

We got to the cabin in record time. To me it was like a house. To Missy anything with less than ten rooms was a cabin! The house set slightly elevated surrounded by pine trees with wooden steps leading to a dock. The dock stretched out twenty feet into a nice midsized lake. There was even a decent looking boat that we were could use. Missy could row while Todd and I fished! My honey had made a good decision coming here. This would be a good place to relax and get to know my children.

When we got out of the car, we embraced. I think this bothered my boy and he let us know it. Missy looked at him and giggled. We kept right on staying in our strong embrace. We saw nothing wrong with it. The kids needed to see that Mama and Daddy belonged and loved each other.

"Missy, isn't Marietta at the age where she should be walking?"

"Yes, she is behind but don't worry. I really believe Etta waited for you to come home so you could see her walk."

"Daddy, let's go fishing!"

"Now Todd, why don't we wait till later, Daddy might be tired."

"Honey, it's okay. Let's all go down to the dock and fish for a while. I don't mind, really."

"Ethan, you are going to make a fine dad! You know you and I are going to play second fiddle now with two kids so I guess we might as well get used to it. I'll take the baby, then change into my new sun suit. You'll love it. My short shorts are so . . . short."

"Missy, stop the tease or I might have to put away the fishing poles and get my . . . .

"Ethan I know what you're going to say so don't. Remember there are little ones here with big ears and mouths too. I'll be back real soon."

She showed me her new outfit. What a hot cookie! We fished awhile then moved into the house where she began dinner. We had steak, man it was good! After dinner, we took the kids for a long walk. At bedtime, I read the kids a story I made up. It was all about a person that comes home from work and turns into a boogieman if his children will not go to sleep.

"Daddy, why does he want them asleep so bad?" Todd asked

"Answer him, Hans Christian Andersen." Missy said.

"Who?"

"Sweetheart, I'll finish the story. Boogiemen at bedtime! I guess you don't want them a sleep at all."

With the little ones in dreamland, it was time for us to do what two people should do after twenty-one months of being apart.

"Missy, I have been thinking . . . how about if I figure how those short shorts come off?"

"Sure. Honey, are we done with honeymoons."

"I sure hope so."

Like my wife, I hoped there would be no more honeymoons, only a normal life. Absence makes the heart grow fonder. It made me love and appreciate my wife so much more.

"Ethan, good morning time to wake up."

"Why? We're not going anywhere and its only 7a.m. Time for a quickie?"

"No sweetie, from now on, night time probably will be the best time for whoopee. These two don't nap much. Maybe no early morning fun but we can always say, "I love you" in the morning, right?"

"You know it, you 100% octane doll! I am so glad to be home, I missed you so much. You are everything to me . . . Sorry I must have a slight cold."

"Oh you have tears in your eyes. Like I have always told you, to cry some is good so Ethan, let it out. First, I need to thank someone. Thank you, God, for bringing my Ethan home to us, amen." As she was finishing up, Todd poked his head in the bedroom with Etta crawling behind him.

"Mama, can we come in bed with you, please?"

"See what I mean. Sure you can but Mommy and Daddy want some kisses and hugs!"

"Sure, Daddy, can you help me take the training wheels off my Flyer?"

"I told you that your son has your whole life planned out."

"That's fine with me, beats the heck out of landing invasions. We'll do it right after breakfast."

Pine trees and a tranquil lake surrounded this beautiful place. We did something different every day. One day it rained and we played kids games in the house. Missy with that soft unique voice would read them stories or help Todd with his reading and writing skills. When they were doing their own stuff, Marietta and I would play. She had become a Daddy's little girl. Some days we would take the boat out and explore the area. We fished a lot and caught some nice ones. We ate those. Todd had learned how to swim so all us except the baby took a dip. The water was not very warm but with warm clear skies, it was nice. Missy had a bathing suit she had bought in Hawaii and it still looked very good! One night we got the kids to bed and she and I took a quick dip.

Back at the cabin, we checked on the kids and ran into bed. We were both shivering so much even cuddling did not help. I made a fire in the fireplace that made the room nice and warm. After awhile we started to warm up and stopped shaking.

"Warming up now?"

"Yes some . . . hold me sweetie and tell me something I need to hear."

"How about . . . your headlights are on!"

"Nuts! I will go shut them off. Be right back."

"No, those headlights."

"Ethan, Not much has changed . . . I'm naive as heck and you got a dirty mind. Okay, then warm'em up sailor!"

"You are the most amazing woman in the world. Never lose anything about you, you are perfect."

After a week at the lake, we headed to Duluth.

We pulled into home around six p.m. Even though her flat was small, it felt like home. The mail was stacked up. There was big packet for me. My wife looked at it in an uneasy way asking me what might be in it. I told her probably a new duty station when my sixty-day leave was over.

Missy said, "Open it up and let's get this over with."

I opened it and read the orders. I thought with the suspense she would light up a cigarette but she didn't. Then it dawned on me . . . since I had been back she had not smoked at all! Man I must have been in a fog.

"Honey, what do the orders say?"

"First sugar, have you given up smoking?"

Yes, you haven't noticed? When the war was over, I quit as promised. I wish I had never started. My clothes smelled and my breath did too. Now the orders and if it is bad news I might start again."

"You ever have been to New York City?"

"Oh you mean all of us like all four of us? A home, you and all of us every day together like a real family, Ethan. "

"You got it you honey, just the four of us! Now you'll see if you can stand me every day or I can stand you!"

"Oh Ethan, I know I can stand you. But me, well, I'll try not to drive you nuts. New York City, Bloomingdales, Tiffany's and Macy's—this is a dream come true! Broadway too. This is swell!"

"Listen, we are going there to raise a family, not to go shopping."

"This is great, goodbye Duluth, hello New York City!" I think my love really meant it when she said goodbye Duluth.

"Missy, you look happy. I love to see you smile."

"EA, I am in a beautiful cloud. No war, Thank God."

Three little mobsters

I took Todd to the garage in town to get the Ford checked out. We could make it a father and son day. Missy asked if she could tag along and I said no. I knew what the fashion queen had in mind. This was a man's trip and nothing more.

At five years old, he had the vocabulary of some adults I knew. We talked all the way to the garage getting to know each other better.

Todd was hungry even though he had already eaten. We went to a diner down the street to get something. He said he would pick up the tab.

"And how'd' you plan on doing that, little man?"

"I'm the richest kid in town, Daddy! Mama gave me this quarter and I also have a piggy bank with one dollar in it."

"You are rich, little man. What did you have to do to earn that quarter?"

"Keep my mouth shut."

"Shut about what, Todd. Is it a big secret that no one is to know?"

"Yes everyone knows except you. That is what I ain't allowed to tell you, Daddy."

"You can tell me. Right, Todd?"

"I guess but don't tell Mommy. One day the policeman came and took Mommy away in a real police car."

"When was this, honey?"

"Daddy, I ain't no honey, I'm a big boy. Mama and Marietta are honeys."

"Okay big man, so when did this happen?"

"About fifteen years ago I think."

Fifteen years ago, Missy would be about twelve. Something did not add up.

"Hi my men, did you have a nice day, is the car ready?"

"Yes we did baby, a very nice day and the car is in A1 condition. Todd and I talked about world politics, women and family secrets."

Missy smiled and kind of ignored the comment. We ate dinner, went for a walk with the kids and returned home. After the kids were asleep, we decided to turn in early to talk.

"Ethan, what family secrets could a five year old come up with?"

"You tell me, the kid is very bright."

Missy started to sob. She told me she needed to come clean with something. I got that sick feeling in my gut.

"Ethan, please love me and don't get mad. Everything has been resolved . . . the matter is over. Here goes, three months ago I got a ticket running a stop sign. When the police officer came up to cite me he asked why I had all these ration coupons in a shoebox. I said, 'My two friends and I pooled all of our extra coupons and give them to charity.' He said, 'That's nice, lady, so why's there a bundle of cash with the coupons?' The box must have fallen off the seat when I stopped. I was shocked to see money hanging out of the shoebox from a false bottom in it. He placed me under arrest for suspicion of illegal distribution of government property. He cuffed me and hauled me to jail! Daddy came down bailing me out. It was so embarrassing. I did not know a thing about the money, honest! Now . . . Wanna fool around?"

"Not so fast, Missy Anne. Who was the money launderer if I didn't know all ready?"

"It was Betsy Vetzy. Donna was innocent like me."

"So how did you get out of this? Surely the US government had something to say?"

"Yes, the US Attorney's office and FBI looked investigated it. They let Donna and me off. They fined Betsy one thousand dollars and one year suspended sentence. Her dad, who's a lawyer, got her off."

"How many times have I told you what a nut that lady is. She has too much brains and no common sense. For you, Ms. Missy, you're lucky you're not in prison with a bunch of women who would love some new meat!"

"What do you mean by meat?"

"Missy, damn it. Lesbians, you over-educated brat! I come home in one piece and you might end up in the river! You had to know something about money was involved. How can a grade-A student with almost a

The Beautiful Mistake

Masters Degree be so blind? This is so unbelievable. This must be a bad dream."

She started to cry while I went to the living room, stewing. I hated Betsy for doing this. I came back in the bedroom even more upset.

"Ethan, you're yelling at me, stop and please come to bed. Be mad if you must. I'm sorry and I know what could have happened. It was only to help families with lots of kids get more food. Donna and I meant not to get rich off this. I might be book smart but I guess I flunked at life. You are not going to hit me are you?"

"Missy, you've got my bowels in an uproar. No, I would never ever hit you. "

"EA, isn't it fun being married to each other?" The sooner I got this family to New York, the better.

As Scarlett O'Hara said, "there is always tomorrow" and this one came like a typhoon. At nine o'clock, the doorbell rang. It was the county sheriff. Missy was in the shower. The kids were playing. The sheriff's deputy had a warrant to arrest her.

"Why, what's this all about?"

"Well I'm sure you know about the ration coupon ordeal."

"Yeah we were just talking about that last night, actually. I just got back from the war."

"Well, the county DA's pressing charges again."

"Okay, uh, let me go fetch her, she's in the shower." I went back towards the bedroom and called in to her quietly.

"Honey listen, the DA is filing charges on you three and the sheriff is here to take you down for booking. You need to be strong and control your emotions in front of our children. Now get dressed and I'll be down to make bail."

"What? No! Ethan, the Feds closed this case. I will not go through this again! Oh, Ethan, no—I can't stand all this, please do something, call Timken and do something! The babies . . . Suppose I go to the big house and don't come out till I grey?"

"Settle down, go through the formalities and we'll have you home by noon. We'll get this taken care of. We need a good lawyer, Timken can't help."

"Deputy, she is ready to go but can we forget the cuffs please?"

"Sure Mr. Vanderbilt, we can do that. Madame please let me walk you to the car."

"Yes, sir," she said like a scorned child.

Apparently, this DA was new and wanted to make his mark. Mr. Vetzy said it was a weak case. We needed to plea-bargain this. The trial would begin in two weeks.

Missy was a wreck and so was I. Annikin had a brother who was an attorney that lived in St. Cloud, Minnesota. He said he would come down to represent Missy.

She started to smoke again. My little naïve wife was in a pickle and if this got out of hand all three could do time. The picked a jury. The day of the trial, all the lawyers went in the courtroom. Soo, everyone came out. After lunch, they went before a judge.

"Ms. Donna Yurka, Ms. Betsy Vetzy and Mrs. Mystic Vanderbilt, do you understand the charges brought against you and the agreement you have made with the court?"

"Yes, your Honor, we do." They said it in unison like it was the Pledge of Allegiance.

"Then I sentence Ms. Yurka and Mrs. Vanderbilt to three days in the county jail plus a fine of two hundred dollars each. Ms. Vetzy, I sentence you to one week in the county jail with a five hundred dollar fine. Madame Bailiff, take the prisoners across the street and process them. After processing, family members will have fifteen minutes with the prisoners. This court is now adjourned."

At the prison meeting room, we said our goodbyes.

"Ethan, look at me, these prison outfits are hideous! Stripes, I hate stripes!"

"Missy, stop the shit. You are lucky this isn't goodbye for years. If we didn't have two little innocent kids I would leave you and never come back!"

"Sweetheart, please don't say that! I love you and I know this is embarrassing. Please stick with me. I need you now so much. Don't divorce me over this, please."

"I'm very mad, but . . . No, I would never leave you. I was just lashing out. Life would be boring without you. Come here and let me hold you, everything will be okay."

"Honey please tell the kids I love them and to remember me always. I must go now and do my time, goodbye my Ethan, I love you."

"You sound like you're in some dumb weepy. Missy, as your dad would say, *Damn it daughter, stop the drama!* You'll be home in three days!"

The Beautiful Mistake

Then Betsy appeared.

"Ethan, Missy, I am so sorry that I got you involved you in this. It's my fault. I know this has put a damper on your homecoming. Missy, please don't cry. It's only three days and we will be all together in jail. Think of it as a slumber party!"

"Betsy, shut the hell up for once in your life," my wife said.

"Okay I will," she said solemnly. She paused a moment and then added, more chipper, "Can we still be friends?"

"No Betsy, go away." I said. Find a man or at least go out and get laid!

"Okay, Ethan. I get it."

The three little mobsters headed off to jail. I headed home and played with the kids. I packed for our trip and Missy's things too. When she got home, we were heading out of Duluth before anything else could happen.

The days went by fast and soon Missy and Donna were out. She got in the car with her head down and sobbed. I didn't tell her that she had a musty jail smell about her. If she knew that, she would have run into Lake Superior for a bath! She lit up a cigarette took a few hits then chucked it out the window. She never smoked again.

"Ethan, I am so sorry for this. Please forgive me. You must be thinking, *what I have got myself into*. I promise I will become a regular housewife and no more than that. I'm done being me."

"Sweetie, it is water under the bridge. Only promise me this: you will always be you, the girl I married. Now, in two days we leave for a visit to my family. Then we will take a nice calm leisurely trip to New York City."

"Thank the Lord above, I am leaving Duluth and will never come back again."

Whatever she meant by that comment I had no clue. I guess she had her reasons. Maybe in ways she was in as much of a need of a change as I was when I left Lincoln. This trial might have been the sealer. All I wanted to do was be with my little family and live our version of the American Dream.

Leaving Duluth

The next morning we had breakfast with her folks. Before we left, her Dad said,

"Ethan, like I said, the day Missy and you headed for Hawaii, she's all yours." I laughed because I knew what he meant. After five years of marriage, I was ready for more of this Duluth beauty! I suppose you could say we were starting all over again and I couldn't wait.

The girls cried and said goodbye. Missy was in a pair of Navy dungarees with a pink top and of course those sunglasses. She sat close to me and held my hand. The kids sat quietly in the backseat with the windows down.

Leaving town we saw the city limits sign, "Leaving Duluth." Missy smiled then stuck her arm in a backwards position waving and saying, "So long Duluth!" She sure seemed glad to leave.

The trip to Lincoln took one long day. All of us seemed so content to be in that small hot Ford. We were one happy bunch!

My Mom was up and waiting.

Ethan, thank God, you are home and safe. Missy, it's so good to see you. I just have to see those beautiful kids."

"They are in the back seat asleep. I will get them into the house."

The next morning their grandma already had the kids fed. Todd remembered my parents and he was begging to go to my brother's farm. Marietta had never met them although she might have got her start in life in the second bedroom on the right. We talked for hours. They asked little about the war. Dad wanted to know what was ahead for us. I explained my new duty station. We kept Missy's recent trip to jail quiet and prayed Todd would not say anything. He did. After we told the story, my parents laughed so hard I thought they would throw up.

"Missy, why doesn't this surprise me?" Mom said. "Don't feel bad. This is something you and Ethan can tell your grandchildren. We don't have to see Red Skelton and Ann Rutherford movies, we've got you!"

"Maybe your son is right. I should be an actor. Everyone calls me a drama queen anyway."

My mother was excited about her new career. She gave us the grand tour of the university campus and showed us how Lincoln was growing. The university impressed Missy so much that she mentioned that after my twenty was up we might consider settling there. I did not want to put stakes there.

Everywhere we went, Todd had to let people know that Mama was, an ex-con. Missy being Missy took it like a good sport. We finally sat him down and said to stop it. At five, he could not understand why because she taught him to be sociable and truthful. He was both. Todd had the gift of gab and if he or anyone else did wrong, he would tell you.

Soon it was time to leave Lincoln. This time the emotional trauma was less severe. Both of us had never seen much of the USA so this would be an adventure for us.

"I can't wait to get to New York. This is so exciting, I feel like I'm on cloud nine."

"Missy, right now you are probably in the Bloomingdales ladies department. Now you know we will be living in Brooklyn."

"I know we are. I checked it out and they have subways and trolleys that take me right where I want to go! When will we be there?"

"Don't you want to see some sights on the way?"

"No, I mean sure but like what?"

"I don't know exactly but we will be going through Kansas City, St Louis, Indianapolis, Pittsburgh and Philadelphia."

"I've heard KC is known for great steaks, St Louis for music, Indianapolis for racing and of course Philadelphia for history but Pittsburgh? Probably not much there but a lot of steel mills, and this girl has seen her last one of those, let's just bypass there."

"We can't Ms. Stuck Up . . . the road goes right through it."

"Ethan, I'm not stuck up, I only want to get to our new home and be normal. You know like dinner on the table for four instead of three, have you all the time . . . I'm not stuck up!"

"Now simmer down, I was kidding. I guess it will take three days to get there."

"Good. I feel like a kid before Christmas!"

On our first day, we made it to St Louis, Missouri. We had completed our first day of travel with no incidents. That night we stayed at a nice downtown hotel, ate a good meal and even had some time for a walk. We got the kids to bed then we had some good old fashion pillow talk.

"This is so swell, Ethan. The Vanderbilts in St Louis. Gosh, this is a big city with probably a lot of fun things to do. However honey, I never saw so many Negros in my life."

"Missy, does that bother you?"

"No, I didn't mean it in an insulting way. Duluth hasn't got that many because of our cold weather. I never really knew any until I married you."

"Sometimes you come up with the silliest comments. Cold weather has nothing to do with where they live. Maybe you fair skinned Swedes don't want them there. Being in the Navy I lived around every color and nationality there is. "

"Listen, I know you. You are not going to corner me into looking like some Aryan super race Nazi. I am a Christian woman that accepts all of God's children! I know I should not have said anything about any of this to you. You love to tease me. Good night!"

"Missy, now that is not what I was doing. What you said came out funny and sometimes you leave yourself wide open. Now kiss me goodnight . . . . There that's better, I love you sweetheart."

"I love you too. Why is your hand in my pj's," she asked.

"They're cold, remember they were in Duluth too."

Pittsburgh, A spot in the road

When we approached Pittsburgh about four p.m., it looked like nighttime. The sky was grey. Cars had their headlights on. We had plans on staying at a hotel there so we began our search for it. This city was not an easy place to drive in. We stopped at a fire station for directions. None of them could agree on which way to get us there.

"Follow me," one of them said finally, breaking up the argument. "I'll just take you there."

A soon as we got checked in, we made peanut butter sandwiches for the kids and then went for a quick stroll to stretch the legs after being in the car all day. By 6:45, it was time to start the bedtime ritual.

"Okay, kids time for bed," Missy said, pulling back the blankets on the hotel bed. "Tomorrow we'll be in Brooklyn and in our new home."

"So Missy, what is your opinion of Pittsburgh now?"

"I like it, dirty like Duluth was. I must say they have nice stores. Ethan, have you ever heard such pronunciation of the English language? Saying words like "haus" for house or "dauntawn" for downtown. And what about "uins", what the heck does that mean?"

"I guess it's where they all came from. Seem to have melted all the foreign languages together. You have that typical nasal sounding Minnesota accent."

"Which is what, may I ask?"

"Like when you say soda, you say soooda."

"I do not . . . I speak with a normal accent. Here listen to me say, "Ethan, you're full of it!"

"See you drew out the word full, you said "fooool."

"Goooood niiight Eeeeethannn."

'Hey sweetie how about . . ."
"Nooooo not tooooooooooonight I'm toooo Tirrrrred."
"Missy, I get the point."
'I'm glad you doooooo, gooooood night sweetheart."

Brooklyn Naval Station

After I signed in, we headed there for our new residence. It was an apartment building with four units. The place was empty so we were had the choice of which flat we wanted. They were all nice.

"So what do you think of it?"

"It's great, Ethan, I am so pleased. Moreover, to think we got this place without Lloyd's help. We did, right?"

"Yeah, Lloyd's good but not this good. We can get all unpacked today and tomorrow take a tour of the big city."

"O' sweetie that would be so much fun, Macy's Bloomingdales, Gimbals and so many more!"

"Missy, I was thinking of the Empire State building and the Statue of Liberty."

She just stuck her tongue out at me and grinned.

That night she wanted to talk about a few things.

"Honey, will the day come when we own our own bed and furniture? Take this bed. It is nice and clean but you don't know what has happened as in, you know."

"This bed was no doubt owned by an admiral. They do not screw anybody except sailors like others and me. I suppose we could start buying some things. We'll start with our own bed."

"Good. I would love to have our own bed. That to me is a special place for us. It is where we talk about simple things like what are our plans for tomorrow are. It is a place to be close. Does that sound corny?"

"No, not at all. I feel that way too. I like your definitions of a bed."

"Ethan, wait we need to talk on something."

"What, now? At ten p.m.? I know this is going to spoil the mood!" I sighed. "Go ahead Professor, what is the lecture about tonight?"

"We need to discuss our plans for future babies. Right now, I don't want to get pregnant. Therefore, we need to use protection at times for at least a year. Then we will decide what to do next."

"Missy, I hate raincoats; it's like . . ."

"I know darling I do too. It must be this way or the Catholic way."

"What the hell is that?" She explained it to me.

"I understand now why Catholics have big families. I'd never make a good Catholic."

"Ethan, you don't even make a good Lutheran, though we are making progress."

Chief Acker volunteered to give us a tour of New York City. Our first stop was Battery Park in Brooklyn, then over to the Statue of Liberty. We drove through Wall Street and then over to the Empire State Building.

"Missy, are you going up with us?"

"Ethan, enough with the dumb questions. I do not fly on airplanes so what makes you think I want to go up there. Furthermore, the children stay down here with me. Etta weighs twenty pounds and Todd is thirty-five. They would blow away like tissue paper."

"That's dumb. Come on. I'll get the Chief to take us to where all the stores are. Chief, don't ever get married and if you do, have her fill out a questionnaire."

She changed her mind, going up scared to death. Missy got airsick then vomited on her dress. We cleaned her up then headed to Gimbals. She walked out of there with three new outfits for herself and some things for us. Missy had fallen in love with New York City. She would never be the same.

We both did get into the charm and excitement of the Big Apple. Once we figured out the subway system, we saw everything the city had to offer. Once a month we took in a Broadway show. We really liked off-Broadway shows too. Missy starting cooking ethnic dishes like Jewish, Italian and others from recipes you gathered from the neighbors. We had become successful transplants to the City.

All I can say is . . . why?

"Missy I'm home. What a day. We brought three ships in for dry dock. I think they need scrapped. Some of the newer ships are junk. The war was rough on most."

"In here with the kids, Etta's asleep on the sofa and Todd is playing. Dinner will be soon so. Ethan, speaking of ships did you heard about this Naval Inquiry on a ship that sunk near the end of the war?"

"Yeah, I did."

After the kids were in bed, Missy came to in the living room. I was sitting there in a stare not even realizing she sat down.

"Honey if you stare at the wall much longer I'm sure it will do whatever you want it to do."

"Yeah, guess you're right. I don't feel good . . . I am tired."

"This *Indianapolis* tragedy is big news . . . gosh someone is it big trouble. Here it is if you want to read it."

"Night, Missy."

"Ethan, what is the matter?"

She came in with her clown face of cold cream with a hair net. I could have done without this look!

"What is the matter, are you mad at me, I don't understand."

"Don't ever mention the *Indianapolis* ever again. There is no use talking about it."

"All right, no . . . not all right, you need to get something off your chest. Now if you cannot talk to me this will not get any better. Why does the *Indianapolis* irritate you?"

I explained the tragedy of the *USS Indianapolis*. At times, I broke up. I also told her at times I wished I had died that night with my shipmates.

"Ethan, let me help you through this. I don't know what all you saw. Please don't feel guilty for coming home. Honey, many have come back alive and you have come back for a reason. In the bedroom down the hall are two reasons. I'm one too. I won't ever pressure you into telling me what you did or what you saw over there. If you ever want to tell me, I'll listen. Ethan, I am your wife and I will be here for you. That is a part of our love also—listening."

"I know this will take time. The island battles I can handle. I knew what to expect at Iwo Jima and others. Now some innocent men will get all the blame for something they could not have prevented. Let's just pray on it as you say."

Through the next couple of months, I did tell her some things.

Some experiences I did not want to share with her or anybody else. One was at Guadalcanal. After we had secured the beach A Marine captain asked me to wait before I took my landing craft back to the ship. He said some "grunts" were to bring six Japanese prisoners back. They needed to get them to the ship for interrogation. When the Marines arrived, there were no prisoners present.

"Sergeant, are you the detail with the prisoners?"

"Chief, some things just don't work out as planned. You know how war is, right? Chief, you run the boat back to the ship and we'll take care of the rest."

One Leaves the Nest . . . sort of

In September, Todd started first grade. I don't remember my first day of school as a child. I hear it is usually an emotional day for the mother. I had an emotional wife in some respects so I thought this is something I had to see! I believe Missy's tears began even before she woke up.

"Todd, today you are going to school and you will be in the first grade," she said, forcing a smile so big it looked painful. "You will be there longer than at kindergarten. A bus will pick you up and bring you home. There will be teachers there to help you so do what they tell you. Here is your lunch and money for milk." At this point she was weeping and Todd just stared at her, confused, as he ate his toast. "Anything you want to ask me, honey?"

"No. Umm, well, will it be hard?"

"Not for you, my little genius. But you'll learn a lot, and you'll make friends and have a lot of fun."

That night we were lying in bed talking about our son. We were happy that his first day of school had gone well. Todd seemed excited to be there.

"Ethan, he's growing up. Soon he will be gone and making a life for himself."

"Missy, he's a long way from that! Don't worry . . . he will be fine. I bet he does real well in school. Don't cry baby . . . just think someday he might head off to college or join the service. One day he will get married then have a family of his own. I guess you have a lot of crying for joy ahead of you."

"Ethan, my boy will never join the service."

"Okay you have hit a nerve! What is so wrong with that? It's been pretty good to us."

"I know that but war is awful. I don't want him in one. He can do more with his life than that."

"Listen, I didn't join the Navy to fight World War Two. I joined to get my next meal! There was no war then. There is more to the service than fighting wars, you know that. What was I doing when we met? Anyway, Todd will be the one to make that decision. He doens't need you or me deciding for him. And what does *he can do more with his life than that* mean, Ms. Blue Blood?"

"Good night, I wish to say no more to you tonight. I am not a blue blood!"

"At times you sure are. Pout all you want. I thought on our wedding night we made a pact never to go to bed mad."

"I'm not mad, I'm being a mother . . . And I am not a blue blood either!"

A little life and a little change

Missy was to have our third child in February, 1947. We were excited about this because there was a chance this might be the last baby. We picked out two names. If the baby were a girl, her name would be Genevieve. If a boy, he would be Matthew.

This child coming meant so much to me for one reason: I would see every stage of growing up the child would go through. I missed certain parts of Todd and Marietta's, which disappointed me.

On January 10th, Missy went into labor. She was one month early. The Navy always took could care of its personnel and their family. This was no exception. They brought in some top OBGYN's, which meant so much to us.

Three hours later she gave birth to a little baby girl. Her vitals were good. Things could go sour quick.

"Honey, you okay?"

"I'm fine Ethan, very confused how this all happened. Have you seen our baby?"

"No, they said in awhile. Captain Ralston and his wife had an early arrival baby and she is in a spelling bee so . . ."

"Sweetheart, I want you to know that I realize she might not live. I don't want to lose her. I know after all the death you saw in war this is like a nightmare. She is in God's hands. We have good doctors and nurses—"

"Honey, I know," I interrupted her, not wanting to talk about it.

"I'm worried about you. I know having her means so much to you. Somehow, I know this will all work out and you know how I am about things sometimes. Now we need to give her a name. Is Genevieve Bay all right with you?"

"Genevieve Bay sounds beautiful," I said after a deep breath. "Sure is a mouth full. How 'bout Genny for short?"

"Well how about Genny-Genny for a nickname?"

"Have they got you on sedatives? Genny-Genny is harder to say than Genevieve."

"In times of trouble we need to just be goofy. Even when you were overseas didn't you have a good laugh once in a while?"

"Yeah. I'm not sure I know how anymore."

"Ethan, when we get through this, I'll teach you to smile and laugh again."

The next two weeks were all up for this little gem. Now it was time to tell the wife of our upcoming move to Florida. After a month, Genevieve came home. When we all got home, I popped the news.

"Missy I have some news for you. I'm not so sure you are going to like it."

"Honey as long as it is not sick kids, war or you wanting a divorce, I can handle it."

"All right then, in a couple months we're being transferred to a small navy base in Florida called Mayport on the Atlantic Coast."

"That sounds like a nice base to retire at. I do love the beach. Honestly I will miss New York City."

"I am sure you will, especially 5th Avenue."

Mayport, Florida

Mayport sounded like a nice place for us to live. Jacksonville Beach, better known as Jax Beach, was close with all the crazy stuff beach areas have. Carnies, hot dog stands, pinball machines and of course beach bums. Mayport was close to Jacksonville, which was a nice mid-size southern city.

May 3, 1947, we left New York. It was close to summer. I had concern whether the baby should travel over one thousand miles in a non-air conditioned car. Genevieve was a fragile little thing. Missy agreed. We decided that they would take the train. Todd and I would drive the Ford down.

"All right Ethan, remember Todd is only six. He needs to eat right, sleep in a clean bed and keep himself tidied. He says his prayers every night . . . unlike you."

"Listen, he is a man, only little. We love to eat and get a good night's sleep so we can have more fun the next day. He'll be fine, trust me, sweetheart."

"You mentioned meals and sleep but nothing else. Now I expect you to stop at clean restrooms when he needs to go. Ethan, none of this going on the side of the road stuff! It is a three-day trip, so stop at a nice motor court and bath him. Ethan, this child knows to tell the truth so I will ask him when I next see him. I don't want him to grow up and be a rowdy."

"Don't worry, he's my son too—he'll be fine. He's a boy, boys love to rough it. I don't want you making him into a sissy. We'll have a trip that he will never forget!"

"Ethan, I don't want to make Toddy a sissy. I do want him to become a decent polite young man. I know you want to have fun so have fun but make sure he brushes his teeth. Speaking of, let me do mine then let us have some mid week fun? Want me to put on some lipstick and fix my hair?"

"Why bother, hot stuff, it will just come off real quick."

Highwaymen

The day came for us to say goodbye to the Brooklyn Navy Yard. I took the girls to Penn Station, putting them on the train for Jacksonville Florida. We would drive almost nonstop. Toddy would get his teeth brushed but probably no bath until we got there. I would make him say his prayers and I would pray with him too. My prayer would be, *I hope Missy doesn't ring my neck for disobeying her on some of her requests.* Hell, we were out to have fun. She would get over it.

As my wife and daughters headed down the Eastern Seaboard, Todd and I were doing the same down US Route 1. No interstates back then and not much traffic either. In those days, four hundred miles of travel by car was a good day. We stopped to eat lunch outside Washington DC, and then had dinner south of Richmond. We slept in the car, waking at four a.m. Todd was wide awake and eager to go. We grabbed some breakfast then headed south. He fell right back to sleep. Soon we were in South Carolina. Man it was hot! A big thunderstorm roared in, cooling things off very nice. Before we knew it, Georgia was in our sights. Jacksonville wasn't to far off. We could be there by midnight. The girls were already there and in a nice clean hotel.

Maybe Missy would be half-asleep. I hoped that she wouldn't look at the clock. We arrived at midnight. The bellhop helped me with my bags and I carried Todd. Missy answered the door. Luckily, she was very much in a fog.

"Gosh, Ethan, you're early. What time is it?"

"I don't know sweetie. Let me get him to bed. We are early but not by much. Let's get back to bed before we wake all of them up. How are the girls?"

"Fine . . . Need to sleep."

There's no fooling mothers. When Todd woke up, Missy was feeding Genevieve. When he hugged her, she knew this kid had been roughing it. She said, "When I get done feeding your sister, you are getting a bath. Ethan, I need to speak with you."

"Coming, mother."

"Did this child get a bath on the way down?"

"No, we were too busy."

"Did he eat, use a proper bathroom, brush his teeth and pray before bedtime?"

"We ate at only good places, he did use a bathroom when possible and we both prayed together."

"Why did this kid not get a bath?"

"That's simple . . . the car doesn't have a bath tub."

"Ethan Allen, where did you highwayman sleep at night?"

"In the car, and before you go off the deep end, we slept in a safe place and I had my gun. I changed his clothes and beside that we had a lot of fun."

"Your gun! Now that is comforting. Was it loaded?"

"Missy, what good is a gun if it isn't loaded?"

She shook her head in disgust asking, "Todd, did you have fun with Daddy?"

"I sure did, Mama! Dad is so funny and cool! He's more fun than you or my grandmas!"

"All right then. I'm glad you had fun. Daddy is very cool all right," she said, rolling her eyes. "Ethan, maybe you should be in charge of him and I'll take care of the girls."

We headed to the base and I reported for duty. Then we went to housing to find out where we would live. The sailor who checked us in was a career man. In a similar way, he was the East Coast version of Lloyd Timken. He told us where our quarters would be. The "back water" Navy was alive and well!

"We got the key and address, so here we go," I said.

We soon realized that this base was a great place to raise our family. The Mayport area was a quaint and quiet place.

After what we had been through lately, we really needed some time alone. The base set us up with a good babysitter who lived in base and we were free to take a few days to ourselves to do some site seeing as a couple, making up for lost time. Missy wanted to see Miami and I always wanted to see Havana. Once in Miami, I would suggest a side trip to Cuba, though I knew what her answer would be.

Perfidia!

We took off for Miami by train. Miami had some great clubs, restaurants and neat art deco buildings. The train arrived in the late afternoon and we checked into our hotel. Miami looked different than anywhere we'd lived before—bright paint on the buildings, palm-treed streets and a Spanish look to everything. That night we ate at a good restaurant that had a band playing from Havana. They played one song with that great Latin beat and Missy and I took to the dance floor. The song was "Perfidia!" It was the music of romance. That is why we came here.

"Ethan, this is so much like Hawaii when we were newlyweds," Missy said as we walked back to our hotel. "I love being a parent but we do need this. This is such a great idea coming here."

"Yes it is. You know, we separated for almost four years. I figure it will be awhile before we aren't newlyweds."

"You got a point, honey. Let me go brush my teeth and we can be newlyweds all night long."

"Why don't we just be this way for the rest of our lives, Missy Anne?"

"Three reasons, Ethan Allen: Todd, Marietta and Genevieve. You melt me, you really do."

"If that melted you I wonder what I'm going to tell you will do."

"OK, shoot."

"Wednesday you and I are going to Havana for two days."

"Havana! Ethan, you are kidding, that is like the most romantic place on earth! I can hear the music now and see us doing the rumba, tango and cha—cha! Now I can't sleep!" This was not the response I expected at all but I wasn't about to challenge her.

The Beautiful Mistake

Cuba was ninety miles across the water. In order to save time and see more we would fly there. My wife had never flown and said she never would. She would this time, I just couldn't tell her.

The next morning we had breakfast on the veranda. The morning was cool with a gentle breeze. As we went into the lobby, to the right of us was an advertisement of Pan –American airlines flights to Cuba. If Missy saw that, well that could be it.

"Ethan, see that poster over there?"

"No I can't see that far," I lied. "I don't have my glasses on."

"You don't wear glasses! We aren't flying, are we?"

"Yes we are. In order to give us more time there we must and will fly . . . understand?"

"Yes, dear," she said with sarcasm in her voice. "Whatever you say."

We went down to the harbor where the flying boat parked. It was a good-sized airplane with four engines. There was a crowd waiting for the flight to Cuba. Missy was all dressed up and pretty as ever. I thought I heard these two young women say, "Isn't that the woman a movie star? Gosh she is pretty, let's get her autograph."

"Hey honey, those two gals over there think you are a movie star and want your autograph."

"Me?"

I knew she must be getting edgy because she didn't seem all that interested in the situation. It was about twenty minutes before boarding time. She started picking at her fingers with nerves. I guess this woman would do anything to be in Havana. All of a sudden, Missy noticed that this plane could land on water as well as land.

"Why doesn't this plane just go like a boat to Cuba instead of fly?"

"Because it is designed to go to places without landing fields, understand."

"Ethan, is that the pilot over there talking?"

"Yes Missy and you stay put . . . he's busy with important stuff."

"I'm going to ask him why we can't float to Cuba. Excuse me sir. May I ask you a question?"

"Sure Madame, go right ahead."

"Thank you, since this plane can float like a boat and since Cuba is only ninety miles away, why don't we go like a boat?"

"Are you afraid of flying?" he asked, smiling.

"Yes Captain. I'm not sure I can do this."

"I have a way you can overcome your fear. When we board the stewardess will give you something to settle your nerves."

"A pill?" asked Missy.

"No, a stiff drink," he laughed. "You'll be fine. It's about an hour flight and a lot of that time is taking off and landing. Just relax and enjoy the view from ten thousand feet."

"I'll try . . . Ten thousand feet, you say?"

We boarded, taxied out into the harbor and took off with a lot of noise and Missy buried in my armpits. She looked liked a scared kitten. When she couldn't take my armpit odor anymore, she sat up and looked around. After awhile Missy seemed to like it and took the window seat. Before we knew it, Cuba was beneath us.

At noon, we ate at a real Cuban restaurant. I can't remember what we ate, but it was spicy. Missy drank a little alcohol. At lunch, her rum drink hit her. She was a giggle box. Missy wanted to see the Havana tourists don't see. I knew this was a bad idea. The area we headed into was residential. Then I started getting a creepy feeling. I told her we are turning around and heading back to the main street. Just then two dirty looking Cuban's came right up to us.

"Are you lost, Americanos?"

"No, we're fine."

"We are sort of," Missy said, still tipsy. "Can I offer you some money to point us in the right direction?"

I knew what was coming next.

"Senora and Senor give us all your money and rings and we won't hurt you. You and your pretty woman can go then."

"Listen, you piece of shit," Missy said, "My husband is a US Naval Warrant Officer! We will give you nothing. Ethan, show them your gun!"

They were not showing any weapons though who knew what they might do. They backed up some then asked for a few dollars for a bottle of liquor. I gave then two bucks to ease the situation but a police officer showed up and threw cuffs on them, then the officer asked us for a tip. I only had a few bucks left but there was nothing to be done. We walked out of there and I wanted to give her the ass chewing of her life.

"You sober up and think about what almost happened. We could have got hurt. You might have been raped! Money is nothing when it comes to your safety. We are going home on that plane tomorrow."

"Please Ethan, no. I love it here and we are having such fun. Please, honey. Please?"

"You sound like a little kid," I said, easing up before I really wanted to. "I'll let you know in the morning, now back to the hotel."

How could you stay mad at a woman like Missy? She knew what happened could have turned bad, so there was no point yelling more and ruining our vacation. Back in our room, we cleaned up and went to dinner for a night of music and dancing. We did some innocent gambling. The evening was fun. We were like newfound lovers taking in the entire Caribbean atmosphere. Back at our room, we slipped into some nice silk sheets then talked.

"Gosh Missy, these sheets are like being on ice . . . so smooth and slippery. By the end of the night we may slide all the way back to Miami."

"Better than flying on that rattletrap. I guess we're getting on the plane, eh?"

"Yes, we are. You liked it when we got airborne so what's the difference going home?"

"Nothing I guess. I have caused you enough problems on this trip so I will get on it and pray. Now to us, Ethan will you give me one of your fantastic massages?"

"Sure, roll over on your back. So kiddo, how about doing what blows my socks off!"

"Ethan take your own socks off," she said with a smile. "I'm good but not that good."

At the dock where the clipper would take off we saw the two same teenagers who thought Missy was an actress. They approached us asking her for an autograph.

"Sure girls, I would love to. Shall I say something special?"

I whispered in her ear, "Tell them you are a fraud."

"There girls and thank you, have a nice day."

"Thank you so much, we just love all your movies."

"Missy, why did you do that?"

"Ethan, chances are they will never meet a real movie star so what does it hurt?"

"I really hope no one on this plane finds out you're a former steelworker and an ex-con from Duluth."

"You are right, we better not fly home."

"Get on the damn plane Missy, and keep quiet!"

Say Goodbye To The Forties!

New Years Eve 1949 would be a special celebration. This was the end of a remarkable decade. A world at war now filled with a remarkable peace.

All dressed up, we headed for a party at the base. Everyone seemed to be ready for a good time and happy to ring in the new decade. We danced to our song, setting the mood for us bringing in the New Year.

The New Year was counted down, we kissed, and both could tell we were not the party animals we once were. We headed home before the party was over and talked about the last ten years.

"When you said hi to me at the beach I almost was going to say nothing and keep walking. Then I thought, maybe I should hang around. Because I was a jaded women didn't mean I should give up," Missy said.

"Jaded? I thought you never really had a boyfriend. Missy, what do you mean by *jaded*. What brought this up, a New Year's resolution to come clean after ten years of marriage?"

"No. I need to tell you about this. This is so embarrassing. This is the reason for me not wanting to live in Duluth. It was serious, ending so painfully for me. I haven't lied to you. I was very humiliated by it. Ethan, you were the first man who ever really loved me. You know that you were the first man to do anything with me."

"I know all that. I don't understand why you never told me about this. So let's hear it though it doesn't change anything."

"We got engaged the night I graduated from college. My parents never liked him. Eira was out one night dancing with her boyfriend and saw him with another woman. I didn't know her but my sister's boyfriend did. She was a real floozy. I confronted him about it. I forgave him, Heaven knows why. One month later, he dropped out of sight. I never saw him again. Word was, he moved to St. Paul with this girl and she was pregnant by him. My brother read a St. Paul newspaper saying a woman by the same name died. The police arrested the quack for doing abortions shortly after she died. We assumed it was this girl. His parents were so upset that they moved away. The creep supposedly joined the army. That is why I never want to live in Duluth ever again."

"Gosh Missy, what a story. If he is long gone and it's all behind you, why won't you live there again? It all worked out."

"Maybe, but there is another reason . . ." She said, hesitating. "I can't stand cold weather anymore!"

"Heck, I love keeping you warm!"

"Yes sweetheart, you sure do keep me warm. Now that brings me to another subject."

"Please, no more sad stories! It's three a.m. and soon we will be looking at three hungry kids."

"I think you'll like this . . . we are going to have a baby."

"You told me no more babies."

"Sailor boy . . . what can I say? Guess my doo-dad isn't good at catching fast balls . . . Happy New Year!"

"Catching fast balls . . . never heard it put that way. Wow, four kids, a wonderful wife . . . what possibility could go wrong?"

Oh, God, please not again!

It was a Saturday morning in late June. Florida weather was very hot by then. A cool breeze blew into our bedroom. Missy was up with the kids fixing breakfast, trying to keep them quiet while I got some extra sleep. Through my window, I saw Todd go out to bring the newspaper in. Everything was a normal as normal can be.

Marietta darted into our room jumped in bed with me screaming, "Daddy, you awake?"

I said, "If I wasn't I am now, little girl. Gosh, you have a loud voice. You should be an opera singer."

"Mama, Daddy is awake. Mama wants you in the kitchen right now."

"Morning honey, what's up? Which kid needs a talking to?"

"None, Ethan look at the newspaper headline."

"Ok..."COMMUNISTS INVADE KOREA!"

"Ethan, what does this mean?"

"War."

Missy started to sob, "Oh God, please not again."

Todd, Marietta and little Genevieve hugged her and said, "Don't cry, Mama. It will be all right."

The Korean War was not a war as we had gone through five years ago. This was more of a police action. North Korea and China invaded and the United Nations did not like that. This was the start of the Cold War.

After a couple of months it became clear I was not going to Korea. I had no idea what kept me out of there and no intention of asking.

This was such a relief for me, my kids and a very pregnant wife. We didn't have air conditioning. It was a very hot summer and fans did not help much. When this baby would come in the world . . . I was heading to the doctor's office for a little adjustment just south of my belt buckle!

Medals

September came and we had our last child. Missy gave birth to a boy right on her due date of September 7, 1950. He was the biggest baby we had, weighing in at ten pounds and twenty-one inches long. Missy told me in her own mysterious way that this child would be a handful when he got big. That would be the most accurate prediction she would ever make! We named him Matthew David Vanderbilt. Years later we would joke that we wished we had never seen a baby! My saying would always be "Fighting in the Pacific was easier than having kids!"

Rumor was that the Navy was getting around to decorating personnel from World War 2. I was one of them. We did have one sailor who would probably get the nation's highest award, the Congressional Medal of Honor and it would not be I, thank Heavens.

"Honey, on Saturday the Navy is having an awards ceremony on the base at noon so get the kids dressed in their Sunday clothes."

"OK. I will go shopping and get something nice."

"I'm sure you will. I will be in my dress whites."

"Ethan, are you going to get some medals for your service in the war?"

"Probably a service medal but nothing big so don't get excited, I'm no hero."

"Yes you are, sweetie."

Saturday came. Missy was dressed in a new light pink dress with a black border and her new black sling-back shoes. She had gotten her hair styled shorter. The kids were dressed in church clothes. Marietta was a cloned Missy. At six years old, this kid knew what she wanted to wear. Genevieve at three was dressed up, as a little girl should be. She would have been as happy in her diaper or nothing! We could see this kid was a tomboy. In the interest of sanity, Matthew had a sitter.

The program began with the base commander giving his way-longer-than-needed speech. As I suspected, they pinned the usual ribbons and medals on the men who served in the war. The admiral of our fleet appeared and began his words of praise.

"It has been determined that these fine representatives of the United States Navy are given special recognition for service above and beyond the call of duty. The following personnel step forward; Gunners Mate Second Class Bradley H. Simmons, Machinist Mate Chief Petty Officer Clifford M. Jenners, and Chief Warrant Officer Ethan A. Vanderbilt.

Then it was my turn. Missy already had tears in those radiant green eyes.

"Warrant Officer Ethan A. Vanderbilt; you are awarded the Navy Cross for your unselfish service at Guadalcanal during landing operations 1943. The landing craft you were aboard landed Marines unknowingly in deep water and came under heavy fire from the enemy. You took command of the craft after the coxswain panicked. You then steered it broadside, protecting the men in the water. Then you and several others pulled drowning Marines, saving twelve lives."

The ceremony ended. I turned around and walked toward my family. Missy came up to me smiling. "I don't know what to say, darling. I know that this shouldn't surprise me. You are an unselfish man. For you to have done this makes me so proud. I wish the children were older to really understand this. I will tell them of your courage when they're older. Honey, I know you are a modest shy man so I won't flood the place with tears."

"Cry away, baby, cry away."

That night as we talked about the day's event, Missy gloated. I told her of that day in all the detail I could remember. All the horror of it came back in living color. I wanted her to realize that saving someone's life was indescribable. I let her know there were young Marines that none of us could save. We kissed good night falling asleep in each other's arms. This was a tough night. I needed my girl, but not in the usual way. That was fine with me.

That night, I had a nightmare of that day at the Canal. These events would come to haunt me from time to time for many years to come. The price for others was worse.

We got a letter from our old friends, Edith and Lloyd. He got out of the Navy in 1950. They now had two boys. Edith informed us that Lloyd received the Navy Cross for his part in intelligence work as a UDT

The Beautiful Mistake

man. Edith said Lloyd and a UDT team swam to Tokyo Bay. They did their dirty work under the cover of night with the Jap's never knowing anything. Now that took guts and my friend had plenty of that!

In 1952, my twenty-year hitch was up. There would be no big deal made of it. Getting out was similar to ending a job. Clean out your desk, turn in any gear that the government might want back, and sign some papers and then head out the door.

I got up at seven a.m. got dressed and waited until it was time to leave. The kids and my wife got up at the same time. She fed the little ones, got them bathed and dressed. I wondered why on a summer day they were all in their nice clothes.

"Hey, are you taking the kids somewhere special?"

"Yes, and you know where, so don't act dumb."

"No Missy I . . ."

"Stop right there! Ethan, I know what you are going to say . . . *I went in the Navy alone and I am leaving alone.*" she said in her classic "Ethan" voice. "Well guess what, sailor—if you've forgotten, there are four kids and one little wife who want to share this as a family. Now we are all going down together, that is the end of that!"

"All right, Missy, but no tears. Once you start, Marietta starts then Genevieve and sometimes the boys. Todd is too old to cry."

"Ethan, that is so stupid. Too old to cry? Don't let me ever hear you tell him or Matthew that! There is a big difference for crying like a brat versus showing emotion. Now let's head to the base, come home then take the kids to the Jax Beach before we pack for Lincoln. Stop rolling those bright blue eyes of yours too!"

The drive over to the base was quiet. I got out, went over to the tug pier and said my goodbyes to my crew. I went to the office to take care of my final business. It took about one hour. I walked out feeling good in some ways and sad in others. From now on, I would live the life of a normal family man. I made some good friends, saw a lot and did a lot. I truly was better off joining than not. It saved my family from more harm during the Depression years. World War Two had been something I could have done without. I saw the greatness in men and I saw how ruthless the enemy could be. My eyes witnessed the horror of war, which would be in my mind forever. I will never forget the ones who did not come home. Everyone sacrificed something to win. The ones who died sacrificed it all. In retrospect, the US Navy was the best job in the world. I am proud I served and would do it all over again.

Chief Warrant Officer Ethan A Vanderbilt . . . departing

Morning came quickly. I was ready to go and so was Missy. She would never admit it, but getting out of the Navy was fine with her. I don't blame her. It is no place for a couple trying to raise children. Some marriages made it; sadly, most did not.

I gave the order for all kids to make sure they had something to do in the car while traveling. We double-checked the house for items left behind. The kids and I went to the car. Missy came out last.

I said, "Hey, Todd, here is a tablet and pen to write a journal of our trip. Write down anything you find interesting, okay big man?"

"Sure Dad I'll do that. You mean anything funny or dumb like what Mom might do?"

"You got it man, especially your Mom."

Missy came out of the house telling me that everything was out. The power and water was off and the key under the step. I told her to count heads to make sure we had everyone. She did saying there were four in the back seat.

"Missy if there are four in the car then who is that crying inside standing in the window in the house?"

"Oh my, it's the baby! I counted four heads. I'll go get Matthew."

"Mama, I think you counted my Tiny Tears doll," said Marietta.

Todd said, "I will jot that down. Dad, I thought that people that go to college are smart and come out even smarter."

"Your Mama is a smart woman, only a little . . . different at times."

Off we went, one big happy American family driving into the "Fabulous Fifties!"

The Easy Decade

Driving from Mayport to Duluth is one heck of a long drive! You could not trust my wife to drive for the simple reason that she didn't believe in speed limits. However, Missy was very good at keeping the children occupied with things to do. Watching her interact with them was such a thrill for me. This is what I had always dreamed of: family.

One night in Duluth, we left the kids with her family and went to the big rock where I had proposed almost twelve years ago to the day.

"Missy, the rock is still here . . . it seems so long ago. That night when I asked you I was so certain you would say no. Did you know I was going to ask you?"

"Ethan you cutie, a woman knows. I knew in Hawaii. I never prayed so much for us to marry. Even if I knew for sure a war was coming I would have married you."

"I knew too. I never wanted anything so much in my life."

During our stay, I received a long distance call from no other than Lloyd Timken. He called me from Hawaii and said the whole family was coming to Los Angles to sign a deal to get his own Chevy dealership in Honolulu. Of course, he wanted us to come and see them. When I told my wife, she immediately said yes.

We arrived in Los Angles by rail one day before the Timken's did. Missy decided we should do some touring. Our tour around town took us to Beverly Hills. We had never seen such richness and "gaudiness." Why people needed so much space to live in was beyond me. I will bet some of these folks didn't even know what they had! The streets had mansions with statues, pools and big fancy gardens. However, we saw no movie stars.

"They're probably out trying to pay for all of this indulgence," I said to Missy.

"Ethan, wouldn't it be so nice to have all of this?"

I shook my head no.

Out reunion was emotional to say the least. Missy and Edith had not seen each other since March 1942. Both looked very well.

"I can't believe it's been twelve years since we last saw each other! In that time, there are now six kids between us. You and Ethan look so good and happy," Edith exclaimed.

"I've missed you so much. Those days in Hawaii before the war were so much fun. Such fond memories, Edith, I really believe that we might have lived in the greatest time in our country. I know the war was horrible. It almost put me over the edge, somehow we made it."

"Yes we did . . . we have witnessed a lot!"

Three Twentieth Century Foxes

We all wanted one good night out. The hotel concierge fixed us up with sitters. This night would not be cheap. Dinner was the best in cuisine and would cost ten dollars per person. Drinks would be fifty cents and everyone from the door attendant to the bathroom attendant was tipped.

"You know, hot shot, this food isn't cheap. In the morning it will be gone," I told Missy.

"Ethan," she shook her head, "Hold it for a couple of days. Will that justify the cost?" The band was music of the forties and fifties. I hope that this evening would be like some of the nights we remembered in pre-war Honolulu.

We headed out to the restaurant. There were the people hoping to get a glimpse of someone famous.

"Man, what a place, this is fancier than the ones we went to in New York. I still have sworn off booze. You three do want you want to."

"Ethan, I had to give it up too. I did some lung and stomach damage due to extended diving in the war. It makes me sick. You girls drink up for us."

"Maybe one drink. I have four kids to face in the morning and that can be similar to a hangover," Missy replied.

"I'm a missionary woman so I must behave. Waiter, I will have an Old Fashion and make it a double, please."

"Edith, this is why I married you—old fashioned and always a lot fun. Not stuck up like some of your Bible thumper friends!"

"Lloyd, now be nice. They are good people, just a little square. Missy, what is that you're drinking?"

"Gin and tonic . . . only one or two then Ethan and I will dance it off. Right, sweetheart?"

"I can't dance well but I love dancing with you!"

"So, man, now that you're out, any ideas on your future? Staying in Jax or around the mariner scene?"

"Hell, I don't know anything. I am so confused. Missy says whatever makes me happy will be fine with her. Staying in the Navy would have made this so much easier. Something will pop up."

"Move to Hawaii. It is growing and you can pick your job. Pearl is getting bigger and it is using many civilians to run it. Want to sell cars?"

"No, I'm no car salesman. Moving to Hawaii might make one certain brunette happy. It would be so far from family. Believe it or not that has become important."

"I know; Edith's parents are retiring and moving near us. Since I really have no one, her parents have become my family. Man, remember when we were just drunk sailors looking for port whores and nothing more?"

"Lloyd, I remember being drunk . . . real drunk. You know I never bought a whore! Missy was my first and last. There always has been something special about that!"

The band came back on and the girls showed up. The leader announced to the audience that while in Korea he had met a talented young woman. He hired her and then they married.

"Ladies and gentlemen tonight our singer will sing requests so don't be shy. I know you will enjoy her. To start things off, she will sing that great melody, 'Always.' And now I present, originally from Hastings Nebraska, Ms. Bobbie Hagen!"

Missy said, "Ethan, she is singing our wedding song!"

I sat there trying to act normal though it was hard. This was the same Bobbie I "slept" with on that packed train in 1944. Since the club was packed, surely I could be anonymous.

They played for twenty minutes then rested for ten. Missy excused herself and headed for the bathroom. While gone we all talked. Lloyd and I laughed as Edith slurred her words from too much liquor. Then the band cranked up, however my wife had not returned. Then the band took another break. Finally, Missy showed up.

"What happened honey, did you fall in?"

"No, I bumped into somebody. She wanted to meet my dream come true. Ethan, Edith and Lloyd may I introduce you Mrs. Jeanne Crain Brinkman. Of course we all know her better as Jeanne Crain, actress and my husband's other dream come true!"

"Hello, so very nice to meet all of you. The band is playing a great number. Ethan, shall we dance? Excuse me Missy, would you mind?"

"No go right ahead. As far as we know, Ethan has a strong heart."

I about pooped my pants.

"Ethan, relax, I'm a regular person and from what your beautiful wife says I should be the one in awe. Missy told me of your accomplishments and service in the war. You are a very good dancer. Most men I've known hate to dance"

"Thank you Mrs. Brinkman or whatever you want to be called."

"You can call me Jeanne."

We talked and danced through two numbers. I told her I always liked her movies and compared her in looks to Missy. She laughed and saying, "Ethan, Missy looks like Missy. She looks so much in love with you, too. She is a lucky woman. In Hollywood I am afraid some of us don't know what love really is. Hollywood is like being in a war everyday of the week."

"I can imagine it is hard with all the bright lights and trying to be normal at the same time. So many opportunities . . . at times it must be so tempting. How anyone stays married in your racket is beyond me."

"Well said Ethan . . . so very true."

When we stopped dancing, she gave me a little kiss on the cheek and a hug. Ms. Crain wished us all then left.

It came time for the night to end so we headed for our room. Missy checked on the children then slipped into a beautiful negligee.

"Wow what an evening, the type that dreams are made of! I sure am in the mood."

"Sailor, you are always in the mood but tonight I bet you really are! After all you have been in the company of three great women."

"Tonight as always I'm with you and no one else."

"I believe you."

"For tonight though . . . don't kiss me on the left cheek, okay?"

"Don't push it, Ethan Allen or else I'll take this flimsy thing off and wear my teddy bear flannels with footies! Now do the things you do so well to me . . . and remember what my name is too!"

"Missy, making love to you is like being at a smorgasbord . . . where do I start?"

The next day it was time to leave Los Angles and our friends. It had been a good visit. Lloyd was like a brother to me. Edith and Missy shared something unique that few people would ever experience.

In the lobby, we went through the process of checking out. The desk clerk promptly went to working on our bill when there was a light tap on my shoulder.

"Excuse me sir, did you say you are Ethan A. Vanderbilt?" When I turned around, I knew who it was . . . none other than the singer from last night and my bunk buddy Bobbie Hagen.

"Yes I am. How are you doing, Bobbie? My wife and friends saw you perform last night, we loved your singing."

"Thank you so much . . . what a small world, yeah? We're off to Seattle for a show then to our home in Kingman, Arizona for a rest. I guess you're out of the Navy by now, Chief?"

"Yes, last month. Now I am figuring out what to do next with my life. I see you didn't marry that Ranger."

"No, he was killed at Normandy on the first wave. He is up for the Medal of Honor for sacrificing his life. It was very hard to lose him. I found love again though."

"I'm sorry, Bobbie, for your loss. I've heard this story way too often. I'm glad things have worked out for you."

We talked about that night, having a good laugh over it. Missy came over and I introduced them.

"Nice to meet you Missy. Oh, such beautiful children you have! That's gonna be our next gig, working on a family."

"Bobbie how do you know Ethan? He's never mentioned you."

"I'll tell you the story, honey," I interrupted, hoping to smooth it over some so we wouldn't get into it in the middle of the hotel. "See in '44 when I left you in Lincoln, the train was packed. The railroad oversold her Pullman so she slept with me in my compartment. She was on top and I was on the bottom." Missy just looked at me, wanting more detail. "That's about it, sweetheart."

"Let me get this straight . . . you're on the bottom and she is on top?"

Bobbie started to giggle. She explained the event with more detail than I could and Missy seemed satisfied. We all gabbed some then it was time to get a cab and head to the rail station.

Once on the train Missy gave me a good, long stare.

"So why didn't you ever tell me that very strange story?"

"I planned on it at the time. I just forgot is all."

"Ethan, me being on the top will never quite be the same! Maybe from now on I should be on the bottom." Her quick wit had got me again. Was Missy mad? No, she knew nothing happened that night. More importantly, I knew nothing was going to happen. Missy and I rarely fought and when we did, it always cooled off quick. Since the war, I was even happier to have Missy as my wife. I don't know what would have happened to me if I came home to a life of arguing and bickering. We all got comfortable in our double compartment and headed east. It was dark but through the window the ocean descended to the past, and the mountains grew and shrouded the dim view, blanketing us in tree-shadow and the moon peeping out way above us. As usual, our final destination was unknown.

Now that is a good idea!

We were both tired of riding these damn trains! The pressure was on both of us to find a place to settle down. On our last night before our return to Lincoln, she had a great idea as to our future.

"Ethan I have an idea."

"Shoot, because I am more confused than ever. I feel like I am in limbo. I don't want to end up letting you and our children down. Sometimes I start feeling like some sailor who never made third-class petty officer."

"No Ethan, you could never let us down. I know you well enough and you don't ever give up. To the kids, you are bigger than big. Now, how about this? We need to be near family. Why not put down stakes in Lincoln? It's a nice town, midsized with good schools and not far from Duluth. You need to get your high school diploma. I could start teaching school while you go to school at night. In the daytime, you could watch the kids making up some of the time you lost with Todd and Marietta. When you get your diploma, I am sure you can find work or maybe go to college. The GI Bill will help you with this. If there is one person who deserves it, it's you. So what do you think about, sailor?"

"Missy, I would look silly with high school kids. I am an old man! College, yeah that's me all right—frat boy with a sweater tied around my neck!"

"You didn't hear a word I said, huh. High school would be at night with men your own age. Ethan, you will do so well in school and we're all already proud of you but you'll be proud of yourself for getting a diploma. Maybe go to college or learn a trade. Yes, you are starting life all over again. Heck, after the war everybody had too. You can do it!"

"Ok, we'll give Lincoln at try. In a way, this next chapter is scarier than being in combat. Hell I survived that, I should be able to survive this."

I received my high school diploma and with good results. Offers came in for various jobs. None grabbed my attention. They were in law enforcement and government jobs. I was never police material and I sure as hell didn't want to be trapped in an office.

Something would come along.

The Teacher

My wife always said I had talent to be a writer. In the war, I had written poems. She thought they were very good. While I waited for an opportunity to come, she suggested I take a creative writing course at the university. I balked at the idea, but in the end I was under orders by the strict boss with piercing green eyes.

My teacher was a young attractive woman around twenty-five years old from Grosse Point, Michigan. At first, she seemed aloof. You know the type, dumb hairdo with wire rimmed eyeglasses. After the third class, she realized the class was a bunch of prairie dogs that had talent, although in a different way. We wrote as we spoke—plain, to the point and in simple English. Once it sunk in, I think she liked our style.

My works met with praise from her and the class. I wrote some stuff that I never thought I could do. She also helped me organize my thoughts on life from when I was in the war. It came just in time too. The paper I wrote them on in the war was deteriorating.

Jennifer Kieslowski, my teacher, had an effect on me that I will never forget. I admit I had a crush on her though not in the way you think. The idea of having an affair with her was totally out of the question. I loved my wife and really, what would a young woman want with a thirty-seven year old man? It was like a crush a young schoolboy would have with his first pretty teacher. Jennifer opened my eyes to a completely new world of expressing myself. She got a job in Pennsylvania somewhere and I never saw her again.

Things begin to work out

Soon things did become to click. I got a job at a concrete yard doing everything. This gave me good experience working in the private sector. I also was getting tired of being a stay-at-home dad.

One day my boss asked me to stay after work for a chat on things he had on his mind.

"Ethan, it is like this. I have three businesses'nd they're all small. They all could be big but I cannot give time enough to all of 'em at the same time. I wanna sell one. Concrete is my baby. Petroleum is growing. Metals will too. Lincoln is gonna grow. I wanna sell off the metals and petroleum. Would you be interested? The price'd be right. You would get all the support to run it. I'd be able to work with you until you're ready to take over. In six months or so, you could be on your own. This is a piece of cake with a good Navy man like you. No rush, Chief. Think it over."

That night we got the little ones to sleep while Todd and Marietta stayed up playing Monopoly. Missy came in the living room looking ready for bed. I told her I had something serious to discuss.

"Do I need to be half crocked for this?"

"No, but just . . . Remember all that talk about opportunity and all that crap? Well, listen to this." Then I went into my story.

"Honey, if this is what you want then let's do it. You know I know you'll succeed. You have my support. Do you know which business you want to own?"

"Yeah, the steel service business."

"All right, negotiate a price and I'll get the money from my trust."

"No Missy, I'll borrow the money from a bank. It's sink or swim. No easy way for me. That money is for the kids' education."

"I knew you would say that."

The Talk

Todd was sixteen years old now. He was growing into a very handsome young man. He noticed girls, and they noticed him! Missy would have been happy to see the kids stay in diapers. With Todd hitting the age of manhood, she was a little uneasy about the whole thing.

"Ethan, I think you need to have a talk to your son about sex. I'm sure he hasn't kissed a girl yet, but it will happen and then more might happen. So let me know how the conversation goes."

"What am I gonna say? Nobody told me about whoopee. Chances are he already knows, so let's wait and see."

"Wait and see for what . . . a pregnant girlfriend? No, he needs to know. Or at least you find out what he does know and fill in the blanks."

"Maybe I'll buy him a rubber like your grandma did. She seemed to have the right attitude on sex."

"Ethan, I was twenty-one years old, not sixteen! Why not buy him a motel room and a case of beer too! Sometimes you drive me nuts with that mid-Western laid-back philosophy of yours!"

"Stop the drama, woman. I'll talk to him."

I did what she wanted me to . . . Well, sort of. Todd let me know that he knew. That was good enough for me. I reported to the queen bee and she seemed satisfied.

One day at work, I got a phone call from Missy. Man she was in an uproar!

"Okay, Missy, okay. I'm sort of in the middle of a shift here, do I really need to come home?"

"You bet your ass you do, mister!" Whatever it was, I was partially to blame. I took off work early, heading into the storm of 1956.

"Ethan, this is what I found in Todd's closet! This is disgusting. I can't believe our son would look at this!"

"Calm down. It is only a girly magazine. Naked women showing off a little skin, what is the big deal? There is not a kid in the world that hasn't seen one of these. I know you were not cleaning his room . . . the children clean their own rooms. You were being nosy! Why, Miss Nosy?"

"So what! Thank heavens I was! A naked woman in a magazine is nothing for a young boy to see, or anyone for that matter. How did he get this crap?"

"Ask him, he's coming up the sidewalk. Be understanding now, he's only a kid. As long as he didn't buy, it I could care less."

"Todd Allen," she started, storming the sidewalk before the kid reached the door, "Where did you get this magazine?"

"I got it out of the trash down at Dad's plant when I was there last week."

"Todd . . . as your mother I resent you bringing this filth into our home. This is disgusting. You get your driver's license in two days. Now it's two months! Next time use better judgment."

"Yes Mama. I'm sorry. But, two months for this?"

"Yes, and you're lucky it's only that. Now take this to the burn barrel and think about what you've done! Ethan, to the kitchen!"

That night in bed I told her I thought the punishment was to rough. There was no arguing with her. To go against her would put me in the doghouse too. I reminded her that in the war we all saw pin up girls. The only difference was they kept their clothes on back then. I also reminded her that she sent me a couple sexy poses of her while overseas. Of course that made no different, Todd had to wait for his license.

PTA meetings, Capri's and a tight sweater

Missy always knew how the kids were doing in school. She went to every conference the school had. She was a card-carrying member of the Parents Teacher Association. I went, though Missy had to push me. It's not that I wan't interested in their education. Some people were there for the right reason, but many were there just to impress and it bugged me. The men who attended wanted to talk sports or business. The women seemed more interested in gossip and their wardrobe—frankly most of them could not dress a Thanksgiving turkey let alone themselves. We went and tried to avoid all of the social climbers. One night my wife went alone.

"Ethan, I don't have time to eat or change into a dress for tonight's PTA meeting. Do I look all right?"

"You look fine, dear. I always like you in Capri's even with your slight weight gain. That knit sweater is firing me up!"

"Down boy, maybe later. I have to go. Dinner is in the oven. I will return as soon as the meeting's over and w— hey, I did hear you call me fat?"

"No, I said slight weight gain. There is a difference between that and fat."

The next day after work, I came home to a very upset woman. I asked what the matter was. I figured Matthew had been bad which he was good at doing.

"No, not Matthew or the girls. Not even you! Ethan, when I went out last night did I look provocative or improperly dressed for a woman my age? Or maybe looked a party girl?"

"No you looked fine. What's the problem?"

"Some of the ladies complained Capri's aren't the dress for a PTA meeting. I guess they want all of us women to wear print dresses with orthopedic shoes and look twenty years older than we are! I don't try to dress like a teenager but I will not look like an old hag! They have a lot of nerve judging me. I will never go to another meeting."

"Now honey, calm down. You always look your age even though you don't always act it. I am never ashamed of the way you dress. You are who you are and I love you the way you are. As far as the PTA, go back with a smile on your face, a new dress with shoes, matching purse and 'do."

"Ethan, I think your right! It took nineteen years of marriage for you to get it but by golly, you got it! Tomorrow is Saturday and it's gonna to rain. Let's go into town, just the two of us, and have fun shopping."

"Oh boy, now that sounds fun."

Measuring Curtains

The next few years flew by quickly. Before we knew it, Todd had graduated from high school. He had excellent grades. He announced his plans to apply for the US Naval Academy. Deep down inside Missy was not thrilled. She knew if there was one thing that could end our marriage, it was standing in the way of his desire to attend the Academy. After awhile she got used to the idea.

The process of applying to Annapolis was a long drawn-out process. My service to the Navy had very little to do with it. Finally news came he was accepted.

Todd left for the Yard two weeks before we would leave for our new home. They wanted all midshipmen there for orientations. We packed up and headed Annapolis in our Pontiac Safari. With five of us in a two-door wagon, it looked like we were on safari. Luggage was strapped to the roof with not much room for us inside.

Missy seemed to be in another world as we crossed the plain states of Iowa, Illinois and Indiana. I knew what she was thinking. Todd was on her mind. She was losing her first born to the world. She knew this would happen one day. That "one day" came too soon.

The US Naval Academy was really something to see. The campus was big and beautiful. Annapolis was a first-class operation. As far as educational benefit, it surpaseed any state or private university. Whether the kid would make the Navy a career or not, he would have an education bar none. I didn't care if Todd wanted to make the service a career or not—that was up to him.

We met our son at an auditorium were all the first year midshipman were waiting. Todd came up and gave his mom a hug and a kiss. We shook hands and then he hugged his sisters and tickled little Matthew. Todd had the famous boot camp haircut. He looked sharp in his whites.

"Nice haircut, Toddy, I mean Todd. I haven't seen you this bald ever."

"When you were born you even had hair," his mamma said.

"Todd you look like a spaceman we saw at a drive-in movie," Matthew said.

"Yeah Matthew, it isn't one of my favorite things here but its regs."

We walked to his dorm. Todd walked with his mother arm in arm. As the cadets walked passed, I could see then raising their eyebrows. I knew what they were looking. We went into his dorm room and the girls started checking it out. Matthew thought it was cool. I could see Missy measuring curtains even without a tape measure.

"Ethan, when we were walking to his dorm were those young boys checking me out? I thought they were going to trip over each other."

"Sorry dear, not you . . . Marietta was getting the eye over."

"Marietta, she's only fourteen! Those boys should be ashamed of themselves!"

"Honey, for one moment look at her as if you don't know her. Etta looks at least eighteen. She is a little girl in a woman's body. She is a beautiful girl. From now on getting looks by boys is going to happen. Now before you say anything, have you told her about the birds and the bees?"

"No I don't know how to describe sex to my daughter. Are you sure they weren't looking me over?"

"Positive. Sorry honey, I'm afraid those days are over. But I still check you out."

"Sure, Ethan. Boys checking out my baby, gosh I feel old. You're right, I gotta have a talk with her. I'll borrow a health book from school."

"Good idea, a health book works every time."

The next day all parents had to be off campus by noon. We all went out for breakfast. Missy took it all in stride and Matthew could not wait to head home. He was going to have his own room. At breakfast, Todd mentioned that his roommate would like to be pen-pals with Marietta.

"Todd, does this boy know your sister is fourteen?"

"Yeah Mom, I told him but he says that's okay with him."

"Guess what, the answer is no and I mean no."

"Mom come on, he's cute and seems real nice. Please? Daddy may I?" Etta chirped in.

"Your mother said no, so let it go. Four years is too much of a difference right now. What about that kid in Lincoln?"

"Daddy, he is a little kid. It's not like I can get pregnant over a pen-pal!"

My wife almost lost her breakfast!

It was time to say goodbye. Todd said his goodbyes to his little sister and brother. He hugged Marietta and then turned to us.

"Here goes, Dad. Hope I don't disappoint you. I'm gonna to try to be a sailor like you were. I need to protect that Warrant Officer Vanderbilt legend. Dad, I'm going to miss you."

"Todd, no legend to keep here, make your own. Anchors aweigh."

"Mama, I know this is hard on you but I want to do this. I'm going to miss you. You are the greatest mom on earth. I love you Mama. Oh, now, please don't cry."

"Todd, you used to say that to me as a little boy. When I would cry from missing your Daddy you always said, *Don't cry, Mama*. Todd, I am going to cry because that is what I do best I guess . . . Bye, Toddy. I love you."

"Mama I saw you measuring for curtains . . . I will let you know if I can hang them. I hope I can."

Todd was a special young man and to his mother he was the world. We turned around and headed for the car. All of us were so proud of him.

We started driving towards Lincoln Nebraska. It would be a long boring drive for us. Todd's journey would be long and hard. His journey would be anything than boring.

Betsy Vetzy comes for a visit

After Thanksgiving, she invited Betsy for Christmas. I rolled my eyes and agreed. What could I say?

Betsy arrived by train and looked like the nerd she was. Dumb-looking cat's eye glasses, a short haircut, a below-the-knee dress, and tennis shoes. We all went down to the station to meet her. Betsy rode coach all the way and looked it. Frumpy and disheveled, she ran into Missy's arms and they hugged. She was louder than the locomotive!

"Daddy, is that Betsy?" Marietta asked. "Gosh, are those tennis shoes?"

"She looks like a girl Frankenstein," Matthew said.

"Now kids, let's be nice, this is your Mama's friend."

That night, after everyone went to bed, the giggle session between them began. I cannot believe there was that much for two women to talk about. I worried maybe they would use up all the oxygen in the house and we would all suffocate.

"Missy, its two, what could you be yapping about?"

"Ethan, you know I'm gabby. We have been having so much fun. It's like we're back in college. Betsy is a sweet woman, offbeat is all. There's a sad side to her, though. She told me that she wished her life had turned out differently. No kids or husband to love and now she's all alone. No man ever proposed to her."

"I wonder why," I said under my breath. "Honey, are you sure she isn't mentally ill?"

"Aren't we all a little bit? I think she does need a leveling medication but that stuff is so unpredictable. Betsy is better not taking those medicines. What she really needs is a boyfriend!"

"Betsy, a boyfriend? Never happen."

Christmas dinner 1961 would be a dandy. It would be a small affair this year. We all gathered around the table and Missy asked someone to say grace. I was never a public grace person so I kept a low profile. Betsy volunteered. She gave a nice pray. The strange thing was, it was a Christian prayer.

"Betsy, that was very nice but if you now want to say a Jewish prayer please do," my wife said.

"No, the one I said is just fine. It comes from my heart. I've been thinking it over and I'm going to convert to Christianity. I never felt right in Judaism. There are many reasons that I don't wanna discuss right now. However one is when I die I want to be in Heaven with my best friend: you, Missy."

"Betsy, I don't know what to say, I'm speechless. I'm happy for you and I know God is happy too!"

"Thank you, best friend, now I have one more thing to add. I've accepted a job at the University here in Lincoln. I'm moving here to start teaching in the fall," she said, bouncing up and down. "I'm so excited!"

"Betsy, this is so wonderful! Praise God! Isn't this wonderful, Ethan?"

I thought to myself, *World War 2 wasn't so bad after all*. My whole world flashed before me. I really had no use for Betsy.

The American Slide

In 1962, we elected our first Catholic president, John F. Kennedy. He was young, attractive, and energetic. Moreover, he was a Navy man. He saw action right where Lloyd Timken did. I could never see why all the commotion over his religion. Missy was Democrat and I was Republican. We never discussed politics much. I'm not even sure she ever voted. When JFK ran against Nixon, I voted for Nixon. On Election Day Missy forgot to vote. It had been a busy day for her and time ran out. Her day included a nail job, hair salon and a sale at her favorite dress store. If she had any interest in politics our marriage would not have been as good as it was. That said, Missy would have made a good politician. She could be tough when necessary.

In my opinion, the American slide began on November 22, 1963 in Dallas Texas. When President Kennedy was assassinated, America lost what innocence it had left. I was at work with a sales representative from US Steel when he told me over the phone. I couldn't believe it. When I announced it to my employees, the place fell silent. Missy was teaching school. She called me.

"Have you heard the news? What's happening now, this is like Pearl Harbor!"

"I'm going to close up shop and come home. Try to keep calm and get home in one piece. If school lets out, I'll see you all then. I love you Missy Ann . . . I gotta go."

I was in tears that day, like many people. This only happened in foreign nations like Colombia or Rwanda. When I got home, Missy walked in behind me, crying. The kids came home right behind her. They were confused about the whole ordeal. We explained that this was terrible though nothing was going to happen that could harm them. That night we ate grilled cheese sandwiches while watching the news. Missy prayed for the Kennedys and our country. Matthew asked me if there would be a war. I said no. We fell asleep in the living room. Missy and I woke up and threw blankets on the children. We headed for our bedroom. We held each other close, kissed and cried. It had been a hard day for the whole country and us. It took time for our country to heal.

When things settled down, I expanded my business when I bought into a scrap yard in Lincoln. It would compliment my steel service business. For reasons I could not explain I was always intrigued by scrap! Missy continued to teach. She was one of the five top teachers in Nebraska. Marietta started college by going to a small school in Illinois. Our daughter had blossomed into a very beautiful young woman. She was talented in art and design. She had gotten her looks and love of clothes from Missy. Genevieve was a typical teenager. She was a tomboy and a star on the school's basketball team. Matthew was another story. He was only thirteen but already, like his mother, he was always in some type of scrape. Thankfully, being a typical boy, it was mainly things my brothers or I had done as kids, or at least trouble small enough for Missy and I to handle.

Ensign Todd Allen Vanderbilt, USN

The highlight of 1964 was when we piled into the car and headed for the Todd's graduation from the US Naval Academy. He had done well. We had seen little of him in the last four years. Missy was so eager to see him she drove many of the miles. In Indiana, she was speeding and pulled over.

"I need to see your driver's license please."

"Officer, what was I doing?"

"Speeding Ma'am . . . you were going eighty in a fifty zone. That is way over the limit. I am going to give you a citation. You must be in some kind of a hurry."

"Yes, we are. My son is graduating from the US Naval Academy. We haven't seen much of him lately, I miss him so much."

"Ever had a ticket before?"

"No speeding tickets sir. By the way blue is your color! I went to jail for running coupons during the war but I was innocent. My friend Betsy took money. I ran a stop sign. The FBI dropped the whole thing but the county DA recharged us. My husband came home from the war and almost divorced me but changed his mind. My little boy Toddy, who is the one we are going to see, cried that his mama was a jailbird. We did three days in jail . . . meaning Debbie, Betsy, and me. My husband, son, and our little baby girl jumped in the car and left town. Other than that, no, I have never had a speeding ticket, officer."

"Guess what, lady. You will not be getting one today either. Just slow it down. Mr. Vanderbilt, I presume . . . Good luck."

Luckily for us, the kids were asleep and did not have to hear about Missy's misadventure. I took the wheel. She never drove another mile on that trip.

When the Navy wants to show off, they do it big. Ship christenings, award ceremonies and graduations were no different. Missy was dressed to beat all and the kids all had new clothes. It was hard to get Genevieve and Matthew in their best. The youngest were in a different generation when casual wear was becoming popular.

The ceremony lasted about two hours. An admiral gave the commencement address. He gave an excellent speech on why we serve. I believe the admiral was speaking right to Missy and she finally got it.

After the service broke up, Todd came over and hugged his mama first. She had tears in her eyes and Todd did too.

"Toddy, let me call you Toddy, no one can hear us. I'm so proud of you! You are so handsome and look so much like your Dad. He was always so proud of his uniform and the Navy."

"Mama you make it sound like Dad is dead!"

"Yeah Missy, wishful thinking? Todd, job well done, we are all so excited. Proud, too."

"Ready to head home for some leave time?"

"Yes sir I am. Do you remember Donna Bryant from school and church? We have been writing each other for a year now. She's pretty cool, I like her."

Missy and I looked at each other and smiled. We both knew what was brewing.

Wings, War and the Generation gap

The sixties brought more changes to our family than ever before. Todd graduated from flight school. He would fly fighters off carriers. His first mission would be to steam in the Mediterranean, keeping an eye on those pesky Russians. Before he left, he married Donna, his dream come true. Happiness glowed from them. I remarked to Missy that they reminded me of us. She agreed.

Of course, what would our lives be without a war? Vietnam slid into the 60s like a poisonous snake in the grass. Some of the country was against it. I didn't know what to think. My war was fully justified. Korea was debatable, but this one was so different. The biggest worry I had was that our son would end up there. Our military was handcuffed by political bullshit. That meant he would not be able to fight to win. That's how men were killed for no reason.

Though they lived over an hour away, one afternoon my son and his wife came over to visit without notice. I had an idea what they had come to see us about. It was either to tell us they were going to have a baby or he was going to Vietnam. Maybe it was both.

"We need to tell you what will happen very soon. We are going to Long Beach where I will meet up with my squadron. We will be sailing on the USS Bon Homme Richard, an old World War Two carrier. Our mission is ground support with Marines in . . . Vietnam. That's the scoop."

Missy put her head between her legs. Todd tried to comfort her first. I followed and she held both of us by each arm. Donna said, "Mama V, It will be all right." After a bit, Missy wiped her eyes clear and spoke.

"You Navy men always doing your duty, there is no way we can stop you. Your Dad did his job and did it well. Toddy . . . Do your job well too, but please come home safe. You have a wife and a wonderful life ahead of you. Come home to her as your daddy came home to us. I love you so much, little boy. Excuse me. I need to cry alone."

"Mama V can I come with you?" Donna asked.

"Yes, but remember I can outcry anybody!"

As always in the end, my Missy found some way to crack us up!

Fender Bender

Missy was a smart woman, not a good driver of an automobile. She seemed to think cars were like tanks: indestructible. The '40 Ford was pretty much that way, so that's what she knew. After the war, cars became fancier in design and cheaper in quality. If Missy needed to squeeze the car through a tight space, she did it. One time, though, she had a fender bender—no, a bumper bender.

"Ethan, I'm home from school. Honey, I need to show you something I did to the car."

"Now what, is my Safari a wreck?"

"No sugar, it's not a wreck. I would not hurt your baby car that you love more than me. It's my car that has the problem."

We went out to the garage. The car looked fine until I got back to the rear. The big—and I mean big—chrome bumper had vanished.

"Where's the bumper . . . how did it fall off?"

"Now Ethan, please don't fly off the handle and scream at me. You know I'm sensitive and . . ."

"Oh, cut the crap. You may bring the water works pretty easy, but we both know you're tough as nails when it comes down to it. Now where's the damn bumper, Mystic Ann Marie Bay?"

"There you go again, getting angry, calling me *Bay*. I was leaving school when I snagged the bumper on something and the bumper flew off. Honey, the bumper is there, I moved it out of the way. We can go now and put it in the car. Not to worry honeybunch, who would want a bumper?"

Someone did, because when we got there it was gone! A man walking his dog said he saw a pickup truck get it. I hoped it was a scrapper.

That week a scrapper came to the yard with an assortment of junk. In that load, thankfully, was her bumper. We paid the man for his scrap and I put the bumper in the building. That night I announced Missy's punishment.

"I got the car bumper back. Tomorrow you and I are going to the yard to put it back on."

"Tomorrow is Saturday, sweetie. Your mother and I are having our hair done. Take Matthew. He loves stuff like that."

"No, you are going to help. Maybe next time you will think before you act. Sometimes Missy, you are an air head."

"All right, but do you still love me even if I am an air head?"

"Yes, I love you. We start at seven a.m. Even those bedroom eyes will do you no good tonight. Now we need to get some rest, it will be a long, hard day in that cold, dirty building."

We got there by nine a.m. because she couldn't find a thing to wear. I found her a pair of dirty coveralls. She pissed and moaned about crawling under the car and really was little help. This two-hour job turned into four. We did have some fun though—never necked under a car! That night I took her out for dinner. I drove.

Can't fool your Mama

We knew that Todd had to be flying bombing missions over Vietnam. He was flying the A—7 Corsair. The plane flew low level, low speed bombing runs. Donna seemed tight lipped in her phone calls to us. His letters to us never said much other than the usual.

"Dear Mama and Dad, I hope everyone is fine. I'm doing good and enjoying my time as much as I can. The ship is a great place for our operations. Moreover, this is a well run ship. The weather has been bad since I got here so missions have been few. When we fly, we stay clear of enemy positions. The F-4 Phantoms and B-52's are doing the bombing for now. They say we might not do any runs because we are not precision equipped.

Keep in touch with Donna. She will be arriving back soon to Lincoln. Love for now, Todd.

"Ethan, are all of you Navy men told to write letters fibbing to your wives and families? He is writing the same letter you wrote to me in our war. Why? Why not just the truth? He is in the thick of it and you know it too!"

"Sweetheart, he wants you not to worry. Anyway, his missions are secret. Todd is a good pilot and well trained, he will come through this."

"I could have lost you back then and now we could lose our son. I was scared when he left . . . Now I am petrified. I can't bear any more wars. Will you pray with me, Ethan?"

"Yes, I will even lead us, alright?"

"That would be nice dear . . . and a first for you! You have made God and me smile. After that I'm going to write Todd and tell him he can't fool his mama!"

1969 was a lukewarm year

With the Vietnam War in high gear, it seemed as though everyone had an opinion on it. I continued to be an observer; being a Navy man myself, I tried to keep an open mind and keep my ears open to all sides of the debate. Missy worried about Todd as I did. Matthew, still in high school, had formed his own opinion and he wanted no part of it. He said he would serve if called on, though. With his grades, he probably would be. I told him, if you want to stay out of the draft, volunteer for the Navy or Coast Guard. Better yet, get those grades up and get into college. He took my advice. The next semester he had a 3.5 grade average.

When Genny got out of high school, a huge change occurred. She dumped her feminine dress for jeans and sweatshirts—the sloppy look, as her mother called it. She applied for nursing school. Genevieve would make a good nurse because she was a very sweet compassion woman. Regardless of what her mother thought of her wardrobe change, Genny was changing for the good, a little more outgoing and dating some.

Todd was fighting in an unpopular war. With all the anti-war stuff going on, I felt sorry for our boys in service. I began not trust our intentions over in Vietnam. If I were to lose my son because of silly rules of engagement, I would never forgive the government. Missy hated war. She had all the reason to hate it.

"Ethan, maybe I'll become a war protester. I love my country. I love our boys in uniform . . . I'm not sure we should be there."

"You're entitled to your opinion. You might look good in hippie wear. Some of those chicks look good with no bras on. Come take off yours and let's see what you look like!"

"Be serious, I wouldn't go braless in a million years! Those kids really need a makeover. That includes our son. Such behavior . . . not like our generation was."

The Beautiful Mistake

"Our generation had crazy stuff like this. We had swing music, wild clothes. We even had opium dens, weed and heroin. This will all pass. Thing about these punks is they believe they invented all of this. I think many of these rebels are clueless. Some have had too much too soon."

"Maybe our kids did too," Missy replied.

Matthew decided to attend a college in Denver. He wanted to try living away from home. Missy was getting used to the chickens leaving the coop. Only Genevieve was here with us now. It was nice in a way, peace and quiet.

One early morning, we received a phone call from Donna. She was living with her parents in Lincoln now. It was rare for her to call on the phone. Donna always came over for a visit especially when there was news on Todd. She said she was coming right over. It was seven a.m. Donna came up the drive looking like she had been crying. I cornered her in the drive. I asked her if there were bad news, so I could deliver it to Missy myself.

"Oh no, Chief, Todd is coming home! He has completed all his duty and will be in Long Beach in two weeks. This is good news, now let's tell Mama V!"

Missy came in the kitchen looking bad! Pale, shaking and tears in her eyes.

"Donna, tell me and no beating around the bush."

"Mama V, Toddy is coming home and soon! He is on the ship now heading this way! Oh my, I'm going to faint!"

"Okay! Like these kids say, far out man!"

"Gosh, Honey, I love that hippie talk, you're turning me on . . . Get it, turning me on?"

"Ethan . . . I get it."

We were never so relieved to hear the good news. Being a parent, I was more concerned for his safety than I ever was for mine during my war. I was beginning to see the value of prayer. I must have thanked God so much, my prayers probably were getting on his nerves!

Saturday morning, not a dark cloud in the sky

It had been a very hard week in the steel business. The mid-west was in a slow period. Matthew was in college, demonstrating about everything from the war to why life is not fair. Of course, he always knew who was paying his tuition: we made sure he did not forget it! If he played at college and had bad grades, that was it, he would return to Lincoln. I would put his sorry ass in the scrap yard. There he would work in the conditions I'd known all my life.

It was a Saturday late spring morning, birds singing and a warm breeze. My wife was out of the house getting her hair done. I liked being alone sometimes. This meant I could eat peanut butter—jelly sandwiches, and drink chocolate milk. I could do whatever I wanted without Miss Manners getting in my face. If I were too lazy to tinkle in the toilet, I would go behind her rose bushes! She hated that! All hell was about to break loose. I saw my daughter with my sister Emily coming up the walk. To see Emily here on a Saturday was a little strange to me.

"Hi Daddy, is Mom home?"

"No she is getting beautified and won't be back for hours . . . I hope," I said, joking. "Hi sis, what are you doing here?"

"Genevieve asked me to go for breakfast."

"Daddy I need to talk to you. I am in trouble. Please don't hit me."

"Hit you? I never even spanked you when you were little . . . So spit it out. I won't get mad as long as you didn't murder someone or become a stripper."

"No I haven't murdered or become a stripper; Daddy . . . I'm pregnant. Mom is going to kill me. Do not throw me out of the house or disown me. I'm sorry."

"Come here, Genny. Now calm down. Holding you in my arms is all I am going to do. Now tell me the story . . . Here, wipe those tears."

"He's a guy from work at the hospital. His name is Howard. He left for army boot camp two months ago. We have been dating for six months."

"Do you love him?" Emily asked.

"I don't know. I think I do. I wrote him a letter telling him. I haven't heard back. Maybe he's deserted me."

"Well kid, I figure you asked Aunt Emily for support because this happened to her, right?"

"Yes. I wanna die, Daddy. I've disappointed you and Mom . . . Myself, too."

"No, you don't want to die and none of us want you to either. Your mother has this picture perfect view of the world. Mom has stepped in shit a few times. I will let her tell you those tales. You realize she'll be hurt. Might even become angry and dramatic. Honey, Mom has a right to be mad. I know her better than anybody does. After she calms down, all she will really want to do to you is help you. Remember though . . . She has a right to be upset. Emily, if you don't mind, would you stick around?"

"Sure Ethan. I will do all I can to help. If Mom and Dad didn't kill me in 1937, I'm sure Missy won't kill you now," she said, rubbing Genny's back.

My daughter was hurting. The poor kid always had problems getting dates because she was taller than most boys were. She was into all sorts of sports. With that, some people start to wonder about things. Genevieve was pretty, but a tomboy.

Soon D –Day arrived. Missy walked into the living room. She seemed surprised to see my sister. Genevieve was in her room. I told her we needed to talk. I called in Genevieve and she sat down next to Aunt Emily, looking at the floor.

"This sounds serious. What have I done now," asked my wife.

"Honey, we have a problem to solve. I need you to listen and remain calm."

"Daddy, let me tell Mom," she took a deep breath. "Mom, I'm pregnant."

"Pregnant, I see . . . With whose child? I didn't know you were even dating. I don't know what to say other than I am . . . Excuse me, I need to be alone for a moment."

Missy left the room. You could hear her sobbing, though not going nuts. She came back in a few moments then sat beside our daughter.

"Genny, the only thing important right now is making sure you know that I love you. I am not happy . . . I don't understand why you let this happen. Are you two getting married soon?"

"Mom, he's in the Army and seems to have disappeared. Unless I hear from him, I can only figure the worst. When the baby is born, I plan to put the child up for adoption. I want to finish my training and forget the whole thing."

"Genevieve, you can't 'forget the whole thing'," she said, wiping the air as if erasing some invisible error. "You will never forget the whole thing! You are giving life to an innocent baby. You are not chalking some mistake up to a day. I cannot believe your attitude! If you are so lackadaisical, why not just go get an abortion and then pick up a gallon of milk on the way home! You are not acting the way you were raised."

"Mom, I won't have an abortion. If I chose adoption then at least some good comes out of this."

"Ethan, are you going to say something? This kid has gone crazy! Genevieve, you're grounded . . . for life! Go to your room."

"Missy she's almost twenty-one, you can't ground her." I turned to my daughter. "Now you go to your room and let's all calm down. We'll work this out. Things like this have a way of doing that."

Emily went in and soothed Genevieve. I headed to help Missy out. I explained my feelings. Yeah, I was disappointed, but I wasn't going to crucify my little girl over this. Missy needed to know that this could happen to anybody. She knew happened did to Emily and she raised three great kids. I told her to look at Allison and Thomas. That was the most reckless irresponsible couple who ever lived. She probably screwed more men than Thomas had screwed woman. They came out fine and raised three beautiful kids also. Missy seemed more upset because there was no father on the scene. I told her that she needed to accept the situation and go to her. This was no time for drama.

"I know. I will go to her and put my anger behind. Ethan, that baby has Bay-Vanderbilt blood in it. If Genny will not raise the baby, I will. The child stays in our family. Agreed?"

"I think this will have a good outcome . . . I have lots of faith in her."

That night we talked to our daughter. Everybody's nerves had calmed down. Emily had done one heck of a job helping Genevieve. Missy began to understand some things. Emily knew all the questions and had all the answers. The main point my sister made to us is this was not the end of the world. How you handled it from here is what counted.

When I turned in for the night, I suggested that Missy call her mom in the morning. She agreed. Annikin was not a judgmental woman. Having a son like Thomas, how could she be! She would be supportive and compassionate like always. My mom would be of great comfort too.

Around midnight my wife came to bed with wine on her breath. She woke me up and wanted to talk.

"Did you and Genny celebrate the coming of our first grandbaby or get smashed to forget about it?" I asked.

"A little of both . . . of course I didn't let her have any. We watched an old movie on TV. Ethan, of all the movies to see it was 'People Will Talk' with Cary Grant and Jeanne Crain, you know, the one you still really love. It was about a young girl that gets pregnant by a soldier going off to the army! We had a good giggle though. She told me the whole story. It seems they were two of a kind, meaning they never had a lot of experience with dating. It got out of hand and one thing led to another. I'm glad he was no Romeo. Genny would be such an easy target for a fast talker. She's so innocent and naïve. Like me when I was young. I still would have never let this happen to me."

"Missy, how the hell do you know that? Grandma Bay only gave you one raincoat! If you had been fooling around, you would have been in trouble for sure. Back then you were so dumb about sex."

"Oh, Ethan, get off it. My morals were higher than kids have these days. Our generation wasn't out doing whatever the heck they wanted to. Don't they call this the Pepsi Generation? Moreover, what do you mean, *dumb on sex*. I remember us having a very sensual wedding night. I remember both of us a little naïve."

"Listen, if I had been living in Duluth and we felt the way we did back then, something could have happened. Hormones, baby, hormones and when two people . . . click . . . things can happen. I might be wrong, but if you had stayed one more week in Hawaii, we might have made love. You're older now, you look at it different."

"Maybe . . . Yes it might have, but it didn't. My parents would have killed us girls if this had happened. Thomas got away with it because he was a boy. I will have my angry moments from time to time, however, I will be there for daughter. Ethan, did we do something wrong or different with raising Genny and Matthew compared to the others?"

"No I don't think so. It's the way things are. Movies, TV and a loose society brought all this on. Blame it on LBJ and his so called Great Society."

"I guess . . ."

There was nothing left to say, nothing to do but watch nature take over and time pass us with the urgency of war or love, too fast for us to control, which was at times a blessing in itself. We both wanted the best for our children, but what was the best besides being there for them no matter what. We turned off our reading lamps and slept close, dreaming the sun to rise again.

The dark secret

Missy called her parents and, surprisingly, they didn't criticize. Her dad asked if coming down to Lincoln would be helpful. Missy said sure. Her parents loved seeing us for any reason.

When they arrived, we got word Matthew was coming in by train for a long weekend from college. His grandparents had not seen his "new look." This might upset them more than their pregnant granddaughter.

After dinner, Annikin asked if all of us could sit in the living room to talk. We did the usual family small talk gig. Then she asked if she could have the floor to tell a little story. Missy asked her, "Mama, please no boring Swedish stories of old."

Annikin replied, "Missy, this story is not about some Viking. It is a story for our Genevieve and for you, too." There was silence.

"Genevieve, what has happened to you has happened many times before and will happen again to many people. What you did is wrong. Sometimes our emotions take over. Then we make mistakes. How you handle it from here is up to you. I know being the smart woman you are this will work out. You have two wonderful parents who will stand right there beside you. So will your brothers and sister. All of us will. We love you and want only the best for you. Now I want all of you to know something that few people living know. Before I left home, I told Thomas, Idonea, and Eira this same story. When I started dating Grandpa David in the twenties, it was a time when if an unwed girl got pregnant, you would think the world had ended. Back then, girls either married quickly or were sent away. Some girls would try to get an abortion and usually ended up dead. Genevieve, two people in love always are like a loaded gun with a hairpin trigger. Some do and some don't . . . Grandpa and I did."

"Did what, Mama?" Missy asked after taking a sip of wine.

"Missy, your Daddy and I were in love. Through our love, we made a mistake. You were conceived before we were married."

"What! Oh God, I am illegitimate! Mama, Daddy . . . how could you do this to me?"

"Missy, settle down. That was decades ago," I said.

"Now let me finish the story. We told our parents. Yes, they were very upset. The only thing going for us was that my parents liked your dad and his liked me. We wanted to get married. They said no. We were only eighteen. Our parents said that if we still loved each other in one year from your birthday, they would let us marry and then help us out to get started. When I was carrying you, your dad was there for me as if we were married. When you were born, he was there. We were married two weeks after you came in to this world. It has been the best years of our lives. The point is, Genevieve, do not rush into anything. If this young man is not right for you, or you are not ready to marry, do not. For now, take care of you and that baby . . . all the rest will fall into place."

"Thank you, Grandma. That was a beautiful story. I will remember it forever," Genny softly replied.

"I know I'll never forget it! Mama and Daddy, I cannot believe all of this. I always knew I was different."

David fired back, "Missy, you have been different from day one, no matter what the circumstances are. Now you know so how about some pie and a good glass of milk! You're different all right!" He rolled his eyes.

"Pie and milk, Daddy? I need a damn drink!"

"Missy," I whispered, "Watch your language around your parents."

Missy stared at me with those green eyes, which had turned red.

We all had a good laugh—well all but Missy, who went into the kitchen, poured some milk for David and a stiff gin and tonic for herself. The dark secret was out. I must admit when I heard my wife was born out of wedlock, I almost busted out in laughter!

The dark secret was out. This one was dark. However I had seen darker tales in my time. My family had a murderer in the clan. Missy met him, too. I will never say who it was. To me, that is water under the bridge.

Matthew vs. Genevieve

Matthew always had a big mouth. He tormented everyone. He especially had in for Genny. We had a big dinner before Missy's parents headed back for Duluth. Matthew was under orders not to say anything nasty about his pregnant sister.

"Matthew, you learning anything in college other than how to demonstrate about anything not tied down?"

"Dad, it's like this. I look like a hippie and sometimes I do have opinions. Mostly this is a big act. You see, at student demonstrations there are tons of babes. That's where I get dates. I would never burn our flag or spit on police. It's just a happening."

"Matthew, you're a pig. Are girls all you think about? How about you learn something useful and become somebody? You're a big fake, and a phony too," Genny exclaimed.

"All right you two, stop it. This is no place for you two to act like that," Missy said.

"Sorry, Mom. Genny, let's change the subject. I guess I'll be an uncle, huh? That sounds cool. I was never sure about you but I guess you do like boys. For a while there . . ."

"Shut up, just shut up Matthew, and leave me alone! Excuse me everyone, I feel sick."

"Matthew, out. I mean it, get out of here. You apologize to everyone here then go to your sister and apologize. She has been through an awful lot. You don't know the half of it. After I cool down, maybe I'll consider *letting* you stay in school. Remember there is always a cutting torch at the scrap yard with your name on it. Now move and I mean move!"

That night I asked my wife if she needed a sedative.

"I do. I don't know what would work best. Hold me Ethan; I need to feel love. I feel like I was dumped on my parents, not ever really wanted . . . This is too much for me to handle."

"For God sakes, Missy that is so stupid. Sex was the act but love was the reason. Didn't you listen to your mother? All that was wrong was the timing. Same thing with our little girl, it was not as if Genny was some whore. Go to sleep. No, listen, now that you have me wound up, how about explaining a few things for me. Lately you have been offish, moody, and short. Our love life is pitiful. We are not close anymore. A kiss on the cheek is rare. Why? You in the mentalpause? Another man maybe?"

"No other man, darling . . . and the word is menopause. I already did that . . . Came through it fine. Lately I've felt very stressed. Having nightmares . . . Thoughts of not wanting to live anymore. Ethan . . . I think I really am going mad. This has been building even before Genny announced her pregnancy."

"Okay . . . We will get you help."

War wounds never really heal

Dr. Miles prepped us when we sat down in uncomfortable office chairs in a small examination room. This was our second time meeting with him in this room. The first time I waited outside most of the time while Missy talked with him and he checked all the possible medical factors. This time, Missy asked me to join her.

"Okay Missy, this is what we do know. Blood work is fine and all organ function is very good. Medically, there is nothing wrong with you. You could pass any physical that I know of. I know that you and Ethan are the same age as me. I have a theory. Some questions first. Did you serve in the armed forces during the war?

"No. Ethan and I married in 1940 and lived in Hawaii during the attack. Ethan went to fight and I came home with our son and worked in a steel mill. We were more or less separated during the whole conflict. We had our second child in '44 when he came home for a short R&R."

Missy went on to tell her life story and mine up until now. Dr. Miles suggested we see a psychiatrist to confirm his opinion. He believed my wife was suffering from post-traumatic stress. We back then called it shell shock or battle fatigue.

What I should have had didn't happen to me. However, my experiences along with her experiences during the war had rubbed off on almost entirely on her. This was not uncommon for wives, mothers and other people close to servicemen during the war.

After two months of testing, it was determined that Missy suffered from post-traumatic stress. As our lives progressed through the years, events piled up. I was part of the problem, too. I never told her much of my wartime experiences. She let her imagination run wild, and she had a big imagination.

"Gosh Ethan, I've been a college student, wife, mother, steelworker, model, teacher, and now a certified nut! Aren't you glad you married me?"

"Yes. You are not a nut. However, you need a change. You know, love, you have been steady steaming since you met me. You have been through a lot since 1940. A war, separation, having four kids and all the stuff that goes with life. It's time for a break."

"What about you? You've done your share too. They are not putting a straight jacket on you.

"Not yet. Listen, I have seen strait jackets and you wouldn't look good in one. Let's take a couple days off and figure this whole thing out. I want my Missy back."

"I want to come back. I have been sharp with the kids. I have been distant to you. I want to feel good again. I miss you, Ethan, even though we're together every day."

In war, I could see men getting bad in the head. I felt awful that I couldn't see it coming in my wife. From that moment on, nothing would get in my way of giving her all I had to help her.

Good news did come and right in time. Todd and Donna were expecting. He had the opportunity to bring into the fleet the replacement fighter for the aging F-4 Phantom. This meant shore duty for them. Todd was also in review for a promotion to Lt. Commander. That seemed to relieve Missy of some anxiety.

Things were going to change for Marietta too. She announced her engagement to be married. His name was Jeffrey and we were a little skeptical since our daughter had always caught the eyes of all kinds of men. But we met him and he seemed nice and more importantly, they seemed to care about each other.

Missy's anxiety subsided. Missy would come down to the plant, bring me lunch, and hang around. I liked having her there, at least sometimes. She did some church work too. For the first time in her life, she watched soap operas. She planted flowers, made great meals and of course shopped. Missy put a baby nursery together. She was a regular Mrs. Cleaver. Of course she could still cause trouble, though, as part of her design.

One busy day at work, my crane operator had called in sick. There wasn't anyone else I trusted to run a large overhead crane. This was a new customer and we needed to get this order out. I was in a jam!

I talked to Missy on the phone about it. She said, "I'll be down in awhile to you bring lunch." About three hours later, one of my men came in and told me the order was loaded and out the door.

"Chuck, who ran the crane?"

"Your wife. I asked her if she knew how. She said yes. I asked if I should check with you. She said, *Oh, let's surprise him.*"

Then, she walked into my office in a sundress, hair all done up, looking as she usually does.

"What the devil have you been doing?"

"Loading trucks, sweetheart. Needed done and now it's done. Here's lunch. Eat, you look pale," she said, patting my cheek.

"I should be pale. You could have gotten hurt or hurt somebody. Missy . . ."

"Ethan, just say thanks and eat your tuna fish salad. You can take the girl out of the crane . . . you cannot take the crane out of the girl! Now here, drink your Dad's before it gets warm."

"Yes, and thanks for the help, I guess."

"Now want me to do something else? Tom is cutting that steel plate. Can I help him?"

"No! Sit there and be still!" She rolled her eyes and smiled at me as she grabbed a bite of my sandwich. She knew that I knew she'd been a huge help, even if I couldn't admit it.

The first of eleven

Babies never arrive when you think they will or when the doctor says they will. Genny was due in two weeks so, stupid us, that's what we figured. We needed to know if she wanted to do this alone or have one of us in the delivery room. Genny never said much about any of it. It was enough to make one explode in rage. She finally opened up. We had climbed into bed when there was a knock on our bedroom door.

"Mom, Dad. Can I come in? I need to speak with you guys."

"Sure, what can we do for you?"

"I'm sure this baby is coming soon, like maybe by this weekend. I'm scared, Mom, would you mind if you are with me in the delivery room?"

"Honey, I will be with you through the whole thing. Having a baby is scary, if I did it four times, you can do it too. I'll be there."

"Thanks Mom. Daddy, I thought about asking you but I thought maybe you would feel uncomfortable."

"Good thinking! I'll be outside the door waiting."

"One more thing. Can I sleep with you guys tonight?"

"Sure," Missy smiled and remarked, "Better lie on my side of the bed. Your dad has roving hands even when he's sleeping."

"Gross Daddy!"

Genny crawled her big belly into bed and fell right to sleep.

I whispered to Missy, "I'm glad she asked you. It would have been very strange to view my daughter's below the belt parts."

"Ethan for heaven's sake . . . you used to change her diapers and give her baths. What's the difference now?"

"Honey, she's a grown woman now. That's the difference."

"If you've seen one vagina you've seen them all. Now sleep. We might be in for a long week."

"Missy, what did you say?"

"Sleep!"

After two days and seven hours of labor, eight-pound, four—ounce Lurline Mystic Vanderbilt came into the world. A healthy and wide-awake soul she was. Genevieve forgot her apprehension. She had a typical Missy delivery . . . quick. Our daughter also decided to keep her baby.

"All's well that ends well. Genny is fine, the baby is fine and before I forget, what kind of a name is Lurline?'

"Lurline is a Germanic name. The name comes from Lorelei, which is a myth character. Lurline or Lorelei was a beautiful woman who had an unfaithful lover. She killed herself. Legend says she became a siren. Sailors said they heard her singing among the rocks on the Rhine River. The singing lured them to their deaths. Genny says her nickname can be Lura. Lurline is also the name of the boat—I mean ship—that took Toddy and me home during the evacuation from Pearl. Isn't it a beautiful name?"

"Why not just Nancy, Linda, or even Maureen. Why some man-hating ghost . . . Also, what is a siren?"

"Honey, it's the seventies. Get hip. I'll explain what a siren is when you're a bit older," she said, rubbing my back. "Is it okay to be excited about being a grandma now?"

"I'm excited to be a grandpa. Does that answer your question?"

"It sure does. Tomorrow I go shopping for Lura."

"Am I invited?"

Missy threw her head up as if looking for something high above us. Maybe for whatever flying mythological creature Lurline had conjured that had cast a spell on me to even suggest I come shopping, or perhaps for what part of the ceiling had fallen on my head.

APO San Francisco

The mail came one day while I was washing the car.

"Was our war mail marked APO or FPO?" Missy asked, looking at the mail as she brought it over to me.

"FPO is for fleet and APO is for Army. Who do we know overseas? No one I can recall. Who's it from?"

"It's for Genevieve. I'm guessing it's from this Howard guy." She held the letter above her head and squinted at it.

"Probably. Missy, quit putting it up to the sun light to read it."

"I'm not."

"Sure you're not. Like when we were first married you tried to see what I bought you for Christmas."

"Ethan, you must be thinking of someone else. I hope this is good news for her. I hate to see my Genny hurt."

Genny took the letter to her room. Awhile later, she came back.

"Mom and Daddy, I've been reading this letter over and over. I have my own opinion but let me read it to you and see what you think."

We read the letter. He explained how his chopper crashed from enemy fire the first week in 'Nam, he got hurt and his mail never went out. I knew how it was out there in the trenches, it did happen that way sometimes. The letter sounded sincere and written from the heart.

"Mom and Daddy, I know Howie well . . . He's telling the truth."

Several months later, I came home from work to a strange car sitting in the driveway. I came through the garage into the kitchen. Missy was fixing a snack.

"Who are the snacks for, that dumb squirrel, Consuela?"

"No. I already fed her today and do not call her dumb. We are buddies. Look outside on the porch," she said, motioning towards the window with her knife. "That's Howard. He seems like a nice young man. They've been playing with Lurline. I saw them kiss. Honey, he is a cute guy."

"Saw them kiss, eh? Have you been watching every move they make? Spying?"

"I have to spy a little. I'm a mother."

Howard had scarring from burns on his arm and walked with a cane. Sadly, it brought back some war memories. It reminded me why I hated war so much. We talked awhile. Then he, Genny and Lurline went out to dinner.

"I agree. He does seem nice. I have to say he looks like Howdy Doody though. I never saw a kid with so many freckles and red hair."

"That's terrible to say, he's a darling. Now don't say anything to Genny. If she loves Howdy—I mean Howard," she said, smiling, "and that's all that matters. Gosh Ethan, you got me saying it. There is a similarity though. Anyway, if they marry it will be good. Genny will have a husband and Lurline will have a daddy."

It didn't take long for them to tie the knot. All ended well. Our tomboy daughter even wore a wedding dress and cleaned up real beautiful.

Matthew graduated college by the skin of his teeth. Four years of a liberal arts education did little for him. He had learned very little that he could use for a career. When he came home from Denver, it was like nothing had changed. He got his room back, three square meals and his laundry done. He had no job and acted like he had no plans to find one. We gave him until the fall to get his act together. Missy and I never babied any of our children. It was not going to start with him.

After his little vacation he relented, asking for a job.

"Dad, you win. I'll work. Can you fit me in at the plant?" he asked one morning at breakfast.

"Sure son, report to the scrap yard Monday morning. We'll teach you how to cut up metal. It's hard hot work. When you prove you're worth more we'll talk about moving you up."

"Cut scrap? Come on, Dad, how about something easier like weighing in the trucks or doing office work?"

"Cut scrap or be your mother's helper and get paid nothing."

"I'll be there Monday. Anything is better than being with Mom all day."

"I'll remember that when you're hungry at midnight or you need a shirt ironed on short notice," Missy fired back.

"Mom I'm kidding, lighten up. I don't want to do women's work."

"Then cut scrap. In the war, I worked in a big steel mill running a crane. There was no time for *women's work*, as you put it. All work was everyone's work."

"You, a steelworker? Sure, Mom, like I believe that."

Matthew was another kid of ours who never brought any of his girlfriends around. At dinner one night, he asked if a girl he was dating could come for a visit. She was a farm girl from a small town in eastern Colorado. We said sure.

"What's her name? Is this serious or only a passing ship?"

"It might be serious, Mom. She's pretty cool, a lot like me. Her name is Rachael Harris, but she goes by Shangri La. That's her earthly name." There was a long silence as we just sat there looking at him, both of us mid-chew. "You two look puzzled."

"What the hell is an earthly name?"

"Well, she majored in pharmacy science. Shang believes what the earth provides can heal better than medicine as we know it. To her, life is like Shangri La, as in paradise. Understand? Look at it this way, Mom. Your name Mystic is an early name, and you're no mystic. You're just a mom." I just about slapped him across the head but Missy caught me.

"Matthew, you really don't know that much about me, do you? Rachael can have Marietta's old room. No funny business . . . I can see through walls."

"Yes Mom. Thank you for letting her visit. So Mom, what else have you been in life other than being a steelworker and a mom?"

"Read your Dad's memoirs someday."

When Shangri La walked through the front door, she was what we expected. Long straight hair, wire rim glasses and goofy-looking clothes. She had beads around her neck and buttons protesting everything from war to eating bananas. She stood about five-foot-six, pretty and built. She did wear a bra and unlike some hippie chicks, she looked clean too.

"Mom and Dad, this is Shangri La though you can call her Shang."

"Nice to meet you, dear. I suppose you prefer to sit on the floor. Want a Pepsi or something else to drink?" my wife asked.

"Mom, we'll sit on the couch. Sit on the floor? I get it Mom. You're not funny."

The Beautiful Mistake

"A cup of tea would be nice, if it's not too much trouble. I don't drink soft drinks or alcohol. I believe they have been pushed on our society to make us unhealthy so the medical industry will thrive."

"Then tea it is," Missy said, changing the subject. "So, are you going to work as a pharmacist?"

"Yeah, I need to make a living and it's pretty interesting to me. Not all conventional medicines are bad. It is that some things such as herbs and roots that can be used rather than pharmaceuticals. We have a society now that believes in pills every time someone sneezes."

"So Rachael, you have come to realize there comes a time when we all must leave fantasy land to make a living?" I asked.

"Rachael, I agree with you completely," Missy said. "Matthew's dad ate roots, weeds and prairie grass when he was a kid. It didn't hurt him so maybe it is good for you."

"Wow, Mr. Vanderbilt. Like, is that so cool and primitive or what! Man that is really far out. To answer your question: yes, sir, I know we must all live in the real world."

"Yeah, it was far out. I did and to this day, I do not eat oatmeal or spinach. Anything that does not look like meat and potatoes is off the menu! Now my wife ate steak during the Depression. She lived on the other side of the tracks."

"Rachael, I did not just eat steak during the Depression. Plus I'm from Duluth . . . Not the other side of the tracks."

"Where's Duluth, Mrs. Vanderbilt?'

She was strange. I had the impression she was like our son—a wannabe hippie and not an anarchist.

That evening, Missy and I took a walk to hold hands, talk and enjoy some fresh night air. "Missy, I wonder if Matthew has a weird hippie name. If he does, it's probably Shit For Brains."

"That's terrible to say. As you get older, your mouth gets worse. Matthew earthly named would be Spoiled Brat! I really hope he does not bring a pregnant girlfriend home. They say this generation drops their pants for any reason. A very sad state of affairs, I believe."

"Yes sad . . . in a way"

"I know what you're thinking, sad our generation wasn't like that. This bunch has its fun and then when the fun is over they toss whatever it is away starting all over again. Innocent babies treated like throw away soda bottles. If I would have ever gotten into trouble I would have paid the price."

"Simmer down, sweetheart. Genny did the right thing. If it did happen, I'm sure they would do the same. If it had happened to us we would have done the right thing."

"I know we would have. You're a good man, Ethan Allen. Too much swearing, but a damn good man! Let's walk back to the house. I made some really good peach cobbler with fresh peaches especially for you."

"Good, I love your cobbler. And your peaches."

"You do, do you?"

A Vacant Nest

Shang and our son became serious. He straightened up, working for me. Love had hit the earthly couple. The moonbeams were engaged to be married. Soon there was a wedding.

"Ethan that was the strangest wedding I have ever been to. I thought Betsy's was strange. Under an apple tree with bails of straw as seats? Where'd be pick that up? Now I've seen it all. At least the reception will be in our house."

"That's what they wanted. At least they had a preacher and not some guru. If they're happy, that is all that really matters. I like Shangri La. She always has a smile on her face and isn't afraid to get her hands dirty. She might do Matthew a lot of good too."

The reception was nice. Some of their friends were vegetarians. Hell, when I was growing up I was a vegetarian too. We didn't call it that, though, we called it meatless Tuesday. Growing up, my family went meatless for weeks, but because we couldn't afford it, not because of some revelation on hierarchy in the animal kingdom.

All of our children but Marietta were married now, her engagement dragging out endlessly, but she had long ago moved into her own apartment. Tonight we would go home to an empty home. Since September 1941, we had always had children in our home. Tonight, all of that changed. Missy and I were now on a different journey. Even though the house would be quieter, life would never be dull.

"Honey, they're all on their own adventure—like we were. I'm going to miss all of them. Like they say in the Navy, a job well done."

"We did the best we could, Ethan. I'm proud of them all. If the war hadn't gotten in our way I would've had more. Another reason to hate war."

As we began to get comfortable in our bed, there was a knock on the front door.

"Who could that be at one a.m.?"

"I'll answer it and see. I think to be safe I'll get my .45."

"Be careful, it might be a guest or one of our kids."

"I will."

After a few minutes, I returned.

"Who was it?"

"It was the newlyweds. They were going to have their wedding night under a tree. You know, that natural hippie crap. It's raining like hell outside. Matthew wanted to stay in his room. I said no. I gave them fifty bucks for a hotel room in town. I told him no dumps for Rachael, get her a suite, she's your wife, she deserves only the best. I gave him my credit card too. Now that I think of it maybe I should have let them stay in the house and we go to the hotel."

"No, you made the right move. In the morning, our home will be in the same shape as when we went to bed! Now let's cuddle and enjoy the silence of having only us."

I could hear Missy sniffling as she nestled her forehead into my chest, and her tears beginning to sweat against my bare chest. It was starting to settle in that the kids were not only gone, they were grown up and had families of their own, they no longer needed her the way they'd needed her for over 25 years. It was hard on me, but she had a stronger bond with all of them. When I was in the Navy, it was the children she could focus on instead of the war, the children she attended to when she dreamt of my impossible wounds. They were all gone now, and now there was us, finally alone, and in the dark I held her tight as she wept the real tears of loss.

How the years fly by

Missy turned sixty. For me it was only a number. For her it was pure drama. In my eyes, she was the same beautiful, sweet, off the wall girl I had always known. A few wrinkles with a little grey hair. She still had that cute giggle, that warm smile. In short, Missy was still Missy, only now sixty.

I told the girls to plan a party. The party was not going to be a surprise and neither were the honored guests, Lloyd and Edith Timken.

Everyone had something special for her that day. I did too, though not of the material kind.

"Honey, this isn't the usual birthday present. I hope you like it still."

"Ethan, you don't have to give me anything. I have it all and it is right here, my kids, grandkids, and wonderful friends."

"That's true. This is something for you and especially our kids. I wrote a letter to you in '44. It would have been mailed if I had not returned from combat."

There was silence.

"Ok, here goes."

To my dear wife Missy, Tomorrow we will engage the enemy on a tiny little island that none of us have ever heard of, Iwo Jima. It is going to be a tough landing. We will take many casualties especially on the first wave. I will be on the second wave. Honey, I intend to make it. I have so many reasons to do so. First . . . You. I have never been happier in my life. You mean so much to me, more than I can ever put into words. Having two kids with you is like a dream for me. Knowing that you are their mother makes me feel good while I am over here.

Sweetheart, things can happen in a war. None of us are exempt from danger, whether on a big ship or on a beachhead. If something were to happen to me, I would want you to know that it was fate. I would want you to move on with your life. You would have to do what would make you happy. I would want the kids to know that their dad loved them so much. Missy, you have so much to offer a man. If love would cross your path again, please go for it. I will put tomorrow in God's hands. If he sees fit to bring me home, we will start where we left off.

"The letter closes with some mushy stuff," I broke off.

"Ah c'mon Dad, it can't be too mushy, look who wrote the letter! Read it, Dad."

"A'right, you asked for it, Matthew."

If I make it home, the first thing I want to do is hold you in my arms, smell your beautiful brown hair, kiss those perfect sweet lips and whisper in your ear. I love you. After the little ones are fast asleep, we will turn out the lights, play some Glenn Miller, and then become one again. See you soon, my dream come true, Ethan.

"I can't picture my parents . . . Well, I suppose when I have kids they'll think the same thing someday," Marietta said.

My kids looked a little unnerved by the closing of my letter.

"How on earth did you think the four of you got here, by the Union Pacific Railroad?" my wife blurted out.

"I think that letter is so romantic. Matthew, you've never written me a letter like that," Shang said.

"I think if I did, Dad would have to write it for me. He's good."

"Had you not returned I doubt if I would have ever remarried," Missy said. "I think love was different from now. People these days, for the most part, kiss their spouses goodbye for the day as they go off to work. They expect them to return. When I said goodbye to your father in '41 and '44, it could have been for the last time. True, people can get killed driving to work, but there are so many ways of dying in war. From an illness to an accident to some sniper picking you off even after the beachhead is secure. I wouldn't've even had a body to say goodbye to. Most were buried where they died or at sea. All I would have had was a telegram and my memories. His death would leave me hanging in limbo. In other words, there would have been no real end. I married your daddy for many reasons. The biggest was that I plain loved him. Now let's have some fun and pass us ladies the Kleenex!"

Timken makes me an offer

"Ethan, you ever figure we would end up this way? Married, or should I say married to the same woman after all these years? Kids, grandkids, successful businesses, what a way to end up!"

"Yeah, pretty unbelievable Lloyd. I do think of the ones that didn't make it. I know it's been a long time. It eats at me sometimes. Especially the *Indianapolis* incident. That one bothers me. It was so senseless. I still have nightmares."

"Buddy, there is something you can do to ease any pain you still have. Last month I flew with a group of volunteer forensic experts and veterans to Guadalcanal. With the help of military historians, we look for men hastily buried in combat. The forensic people identify them, and then we contact the families. The families either have their remains shipped back for burial in the US or intern them in military cemeteries in the Pacific. It brings a lot of satisfaction for everyone. There's no pay, it's strictly an act of compassion. I dunno, man, it's helped me sleep a bit better and that's pay enough for me."

That night I talked to Missy about it. Personally, it didn't interest me.

"Honey, why don't you? This might be what you need to put some of your feelings to rest."

"Not me. I want no part of the Pacific ever again. That's not to say I don't admire Lloyd for doing it, though, I really do."

The next day I told Lloyd no. Missy seemed disappointed in my decision.

"How about this idea, Ethan? When the bodies return to the US, the Defense Department notifies them. You act as a liaison between them and us. We only recover about twenty bodies a year so it's not a full time job. Right now, we're looking for a person to cover the Upper Plain states. Think about it. I think you would find it very satisfying."

"Lloyd, we'll do it. I'll do it even if my husband won't. But Ethan, this will be good for you," she said as if I'd already succeeded to her.

"You should have sold cars with Lloyd, woman. Okay, I'm in."

It didn't take long for an assignment to come in. Our first was a soldier who died on the Bataan Death March in 1942. His name was Albert Christopher of Minot, North Dakota. He was eighteen years old. Single, he joined up before the war because he needed a job. Albert reminded me of myself.

All of his next to kin were living, including his parents. They were both very old and in bad health.

We contacted the family to tell them their son was coming home. Missy and I held hands as we walked up to their modest farmhouse. Albert's sister opened the door.

"Mama and Dad, this is Chief Warrant Officer Ethan Vanderbilt and his wife Missy. They are here to bring Albert home. They have come from Lincoln, Nebraska."

In a very low tone, Mrs. Christopher touched my hand saying, "Thank you. I knew he would come home some day. You have made this old dying woman so happy. Here is a picture of him in uniform the day he left for the Philippines. He always wanted to be a soldier."

Then his dad spoke. He had recently suffered a stroke. You could hardly understand him. Missy sat with Mrs. Christopher talking to her like an old friend. We told them what we knew of Albert's final days.

The next day, a US Air Force C-130 landed with the body. With Air Force personnel, I helped this fallen warrior onto American soil for the first time in forty-three years. We took his body by military escort to a local funeral home. They placed his coffin in a room and draped a flag over him. His parents, both in wheel chairs, paid their respects. The family surrounded their parents and wept.

That whole day there was a public viewing. All of his relatives were there, along with some old schoolmates. Missy and I went outside for some air. What we saw was so unexpected. Minot is not a big town. The airbase probably has more personnel than the town has residents. The line to the funeral home stretched for at least a mile. Military personnel and their families were there. Minot is close to Canada too. Several World War

Two Canadian veterans came, some in their uniform. It was like a funeral for someone famous.

The next morning, we read the local paper. It said that over two thousand people visited the funeral home. The owner kept the home open late for any stragglers. Minot, North Dakota did not forget PFC Albert Christopher.

After the funeral and graveside service, I presented the flag to his parents.

"Thank you for bringing our son home," they said, smiling. "The Marines never leave anyone behind, so the saying goes."

At a reception afterwards, I took Missy's hand and kissed her.

"You were right, doing this does help. You're a hell of a woman, Missy."

"I know, because you're always telling me that, sailor."

We said our goodbyes and headed home. This had been a wonderful day.

War Stories

Captain Todd and family came to Lincoln for a thirty-day leave in June, 1984. Their new duty station would be Meridian, Mississippi.

One day I sat outside on the patio. Our grandson Ethan showed up. I had a feeling I knew what he was going to ask.

"Grandpa, will you tell me all about your Navy days? I am doing an assignment for school. Dad says you might not want to talk about it."

"Ethan, some people like to talk about it. Others have reasons not to. I guess the biggest reason I never said much is because of your grandma. When your dad was a few months old, the war broke out. When they evacuated Pearl, I was brokenhearted. Those two were really the only family I had. From then on, my only thoughts were of them. After the war, my only focus was being with them. I placed that part of my life away."

"Rough. You don't have to talk about it, Grandpa."

"Son, for you I will. Get a sharp pencil and paper. We'll start at the beginning. While you are in the house, grab a couple of root beers. This may take awhile. I have a lot of bullshit to tell you."

I heard Missy yell to stop the bad language.

"Sorry, honey. I thought you were still out," I said.

"Ethan, no sailor stories. He's only fifteen."

"It's okay, Grandma, Dad cusses sometimes. What kind of sailor stories, Grandpa?"

"Well once in Melbourne, me and this . . ."

"Ethan Allen!"

After I told him what he wanted to know, he said that when he got old enough he hoped there would be war for him to fight.

"Son, war is not like in the movies or even how I described it. There's a lot I can't talk about. Young kids not much older than you, dead or dying, are the real face of war. Ask your grandma what it was like for her, too. You won't ever want any part of war. Sadly, war is necessary at times. There's no honesty in war and really no winners. Yes, we stopped two nations from taking over the world, but look what they took. Millions of lives, billions spent on weapons and wasted time. Their cities destroyed almost beyond repair and for what? Ethan, I'm afraid you will get your chance to be in one, though I pray you have the choice not to."

Ethan continued taking notes for a few more seconds, then leaned back in his chair and looked at me. I tilted my root beer to him and we clanged bottles and chugged.

Admiral on board

After a congressional review, Todd became a rear admiral. All of us were proud of him. I thought making Warrant Officer was an accomplishment! In my twenty years of service, I had only shaken hands with admirals. Now we had one in the family.

We threw a makeshift party. Betsy was there with her husband Professor Arnold Teatop –what a pair! And all the kids with their families. Marietta had come alone, which had started to become par for the course. We didn't bother her about it, as she was a pretty private person who was easily embarrassed about things like that. As far as Missy and I were concerned anyway, it was for the better. We'd never tell her to break up with him, but if she told us she had, we'd tell her congratulations.

As we were sitting around gabbing, Marietta asked what Missy had done during the war. She shared with them our days in Pearl Harbor, working in a steel mill and the loneliness from being separated from me during the war years. Then, after one too many Tom Collinses, she spilled the beans.

She told the story of the Three Little Mobsters. The kids and grandkids were in complete awe. They didn't know whether to laugh or keep silent. Missy confessed that she, not Betsy Vetzy, was the one who had been the ringleader of the group. It was true that the coupon operation was for the needy. When the cop stopped her for running a stop sign, she panicked and told the cop what she thought he wanted to hear. Betsy confessed, saying she was the ringleader. Betsy knew the war was ending. She knew I would be coming home soon. Instead of Missy getting the longer sentence, she took it so my family could be together.

Betsy said it was the least she could do for her best friend. She said most people always tried to avoid her because she was different. Missy always stuck with her. I was seeing another quality of my wife: loyalty.

"Thank you, Betsy. I really mean it. I had no idea. You're real true blue."

"Ethan, I thought that day on the beach in 1940 you were going to flirt with me. I'm glad you didn't. Missy was the right one for you."

"Me too," I said and gave her a hug. To myself I added, "Me too, a thousand times over!"

Todd said he had some news and a suggestion.

"OK, I need your attention please. First, Donna and I have an announcement. Pearl Harbor will be our new duty station. This will probably be where I retire from the Navy. Now I have a suggestion to make. Next year is the fiftieth anniversary of the attack on Pearl Harbor. It's going to be a big deal, as it should be. I would like for all of you to attend this event. I know not everyone can come but I would like to see all of us go. To my Grandmas, we know you can't come though I wish you could."

The Grandmas both said, "Us? Toddy we're old, not dead. We'll be there."

That night as we climbed into bed, Missy with her unique intuition knew I had reservations about going.

"Ethan, tell me why don't you want to go to Pearl with us?"

"Never said I didn't, did I?"

"After fifty years of marriage, I know you like a book."

"I was there, remember? It's history I don't really wanna relive."

"I was there, too. I have tried to put it out of my mind. Remember when we helped return remains from the war to the family that didn't want him? They buried him at Pearl. We are the only ones who remember him. We must at least go to put flowers on his lonely cold grave. We owe it to the fallen to go. Look it like this, Warrant Officer Vanderbilt, this is your final mission. Get it through that stubborn self of yours and prepare to head for Hawaii next December, and give me a big loving kiss!"

"Trying to seduce me, Mrs. Vanderbilt?"

"Yes I am, I will succeed and you know it, Popeye."

"You win both ways. Happy now?"

"Yes I am. We are going to have more fun than you can imagine. I am planning it in my head. This will be something else!"

"That's what I am afraid of."

I still didn't want to go, but there was no arguing with Missy. Maybe it would be nice to revisit Hawaii, to see how much it's changed or stayed the same over the years, how they've rebuilt it. And maybe it would be nice to re-leave Pearl together and on our own terms. But really, I'd worked 50 years to put that all behind me, to move past the nightmares and make sure that despite Pearl Harbor, despite the Japs trying to kill me and my family, we survived, we grew, we succeeded and now there are more generations of us to defend this nation and our freedom. I didn't need to go to Pearl Harbor to realize that, but I did need to make Missy happy.

Mission: Pearl Harbor

As soon as we got off the train, we knew we didn't like LA at all. What a mess—people everywhere, traffic and confusion. No one seemed to speak English.

The next morning we would fly to Hawaii. I could tell Missy was getting nervous. At dinner, she had two glasses of wine, then asked me if she could have a cigarette to calm her nerves.

"Honey no, do what you always tell me to do: pray."

"Can I pray and smoke one too?" she said with a smile. I shook my head and gestured to the foot of the bed.

The next morning we boarded the Boeing 737 and sat toward the back of the plane. Missy was quiet and played with her bracelet.

"Is that the Lutheran version of rosary beads?" I asked, trying to get her to smile.

"Funny, real funny," she said with a blank face.

Soon we taxied to the runway, then the engines throttled up and within seconds, we were headed west. It was perfect weather for flying. Missy ordered a drink, Gordon's gin and tonic. In our fifty-one years of marriage, I never saw her take a drink at nine in the morning. She calmed down. We held hands and talked. Missy drifted off to sleep. The gin and tonic worked.

Flight time from LAX is five and a half hours. Missy slept two hours, waking up to blue skies and a big ocean below. She blurted out, "Oh my gosh . . . it is beautiful. I feel so close to God. Heck at this altitude, I *am* close to Him. I wish we had done this before. We could have gone to Europe or South America."

"Missy, no shit. You never would trust in me on flying. Now we're over the hill and too old to travel."

"Not me, I'm going to Sweden and England. I have relatives over there."

"They're probably all dead or heard what a crackpot you are and have gone into hiding."

"I love you too, sweetheart."

We made our approach on Hawaii. From the air, it looked like the same Hawaii I left forty-six years ago. I am sure it had changed and probably for the better. This time it was what it was suppose to be—a paradise, not a war zone.

Todd and Donna met us at the airport. Todd looked like a real Hawaiian. He wore a Hawaiian shirt, shorts, and sandals. Donna looked good too, all tan and wearing shorts and a top I never figured she would ever wear. Todd brought the car around and whisked us away for the forty-five minute drive to the beach house. Missy and I were in a fog. I think our minds drifted back to a different time. We stared out the window and would smile or giggle at nothing. Nothing looked familiar except the trees and general landscape. Todd tried to talk to us. I saw Donna motion him to be quiet. She knew we were in a different world.

The beach house had been in the family of a pineapple plantation owner for the past sixty years. Some of the renters had been high people in government and movie stars like Kay Francis, Clark Gable, and Sinatra to name a few. This place was big, bright and with an ocean view. The rooms were decorated in seaside colors. Most of the furniture was wicker. The porch wrapped around the house. Big trees and native plants surrounded the place. The walk to the ocean was about two hundred feet. This place was a beautiful!

Our first night in Oahu we rested. We waited for some of our family to arrive. Marietta got there last. All looked travel-dead except for our mothers who were rip roaring and ready to go. Both were in amazement to be here. Missy and I were, too, though for different reasons.

The next morning, Admiral Todd and his family came over to give us our itinerary. He was all about detail and good at giving orders. This kid had all the qualities of leadership.

The main reason for our visit was the Pearl Harbor anniversary. When that was over, we would tour the island and have fun. I wondered if I could have fun. Many memories, both good and bad, were ahead of us.

After Todd gave us our itinerary, he said he had something for his sister.

"Marietta, I have an escort for you at the ceremony."

"Todd, you should have asked me first. I don't want one and right now, I am not interested. You need to tell him I'm sorry."

"He's someone you know and he's dying to see you. Remember my roommate from the Academy, Robert Ellsworth? The one that wanted to be your pen-pal? He's a Captain, single and nice."

"Sorry Todd, no."

After dinner at the admiral's house, Missy and I decided to hit the hay early. We talked about being here, wondering would it have an effect on us for the good. The other topic was Marietta. She had been along long enough to get back in the swing of things. She was a woman who had so much to give. She was a beautiful woman, sweet and kind, talented and very lonely.

"Ethan, I know she's scared to date. An escort is not as if she has to marry the guy. I'll talk to her in the morning and see if I can change her mind."

"Don't be pushy. She needs to decide for herself."

"Me, pushy? Another thing—have you noticed our kids don't show much everyday affection with they spouses? It's like they've forgotten how to be lovie-dovie. They seem so dry and bored with each other."

"Yeah I sort of noticed the same thing. Maybe some good Hawaiian beach time will loosen them up. We may look like old dried up prunes. I think we do pretty darn well for old goats."

"Ethan Allen, I feel young and alive at my age. And you still turn heads, sailor."

I leaned over her and gave her the best kiss I could to make up for our kids' lack of spirit. We were in Hawaii, after all, and had some memories here that we still needed to create, that we weren't given the chance to fifty years ago. These old bodies of ours were certainly alive.

December 7, 1991

The kids headed for the base in a rented car. We rode with Edith and Lloyd. Lloyd and I were in our dress whites. For two old swabbies, we looked good. We talked about everything except what happened fifty years ago. I think we all were avoiding the subject. Lloyd, who was always a cool and collected person, seemed edgy. I decided to break the ice.

"Okay, so are we all nervous about today or what?" The unanimous answer was yes. This was different from a high school or family reunion.

When we pulled into the base, I didn't even recognize the main gate. The base was different and bigger too. When we got to where the ships moored, it all came back to me. The parking areas for the fleet had not changed that much. In my mind, it was very clear as to where my old battlewagon, the USS Pennsylvania, was dry-docked. I remembered where the California, West Virginia and Maryland were. Of course, when we arrived at the USS Arizona Memorial it hit me hard. This was where the ship was during the attack and was still there after all these years. I paused and stared.

"Daddy, are you okay?" Genny asked. I shook my head yes and filed into the seating area for the service.

As the speakers began, I drifted off. I'm not even sure if I heard one word. The whole attack came back in my mind as I looked over the harbor. How long we sat there, I have no idea. When it was over, Missy and Edith cried quietly. Most of the veterans and their wives were doing the same. I took my wife's hand and walked further through the Arizona Memorial, even though I had never served or visited the ship. That didn't matter. We looked over the side into the very blue harbor water and saw bubbles of oil come to the surface.

"Honey, she's telling us that she is not bleeding from her wounds. Arizona is alive in her own way. She is the overseer now to those entombed.

Those are some of our finest down there. When I die, I want to be buried at sea."

"Ethan . . . I want to be next to you. I am your Arizona . . . right now my heart is bleeding for those poor souls."

As the audience began to move around I realized I didn't recognize anyone. Then again, after fifty years, it would be hard to. I did hear one marine say he was there that day. He said he lied about his age to join the Corps, telling them he was seventeen. He was really only fifteen. I saw some men who had been in their forties in *1941*. These men could have served in World War One. It was a mixed bag of veterans including Korea, Vietnam and ones serving now.

People of Japanese decent were everywhere. Some were American citizens from birth and others were from Japan. Maybe some were veterans of World War Two. Some might have been pilots who attacked us that Sunday morning. As they walked by, they bowed to us. It felt like they were asking for forgiveness. Missy was not in the forgiving mood.

"Ethan, they have a lot of nerve coming here on this special day. I hate what they did then and I hate them now. They took you away from us for way too many years. Many of your friends died. Some of mine did, too. They don't' even teach that history in their own schools about the war. Then they invade us with Honda cars! Forgive me Lord . . . I cannot forgive them. Before I do any forgiving, they had better ask God for forgiveness.

"Honey, it's been fifty years . . . You must rid yourself of this. It is not healthy to hate for so long. We made it all up honey, so many did not. Our lives have been good. Japan paid a horrible price for messing with the U.S. I have forgiven, though I'll never forget. Please try . . . For yourself and God."

"I'll try real hard."

After the ceremony, we had lunch and headed to the commendation ceremony. I honestly didn't want to go another one of these. There was no use complaining because I was outnumbered. I had an idea as to what ribbons and medals I might receive. I got that sinking feeling that many of my mates I did know decided not to come to Pearl or were already dead. I hoped that they survived the war and had a good life afterwards. There was the possibility that some had died in the line of duty. I didn't want to know. Then it was my turn for the awards.

"Chief Warrant Officer Ethan Allen Vanderbilt, for exemplary service. While at Pearl Harbor, you manned a tug to begin rescue operations even while under attack from the enemy . . ." My mind went back fifty years, remembering every minute of the attack.

With the service over, my kids came up and hugged and kissed me.

"Ethan, I am so proud of you," Missy said. "You are my hero. I love you so much. However, sweetheart, you've been keeping secrets from me. I never knew this happened, of course what else is new. I think I understand why you never told me. Even couples can have some secrets from each other."

"Honey, those are the only secrets I have ever kept from you. If I had to do it over again I would have done it different. It is my fault you had those problems in 1969. No one in war wants to hurt anyone more than they have too. Still, I'm sorry. Guess Pearl is a good place to confess my sins."

"The way you have with words. I share the blame too. I know I'm a loose cannon at times, as my mama always said, *that is just the way she is*. Now . . . Edith and Lloyd say they have a surprise for us. Let's see what it is, and then have some good old Hawaiian fun. Oh you know what, I overheard Marietta tell Todd that she would like to meet Robert Ellsworth."

"For an old lady your ears work very well. I know he was at the ceremonies although I wouldn't know him from Adam."

"I know who he was. He was the officer who could not keep his eyes off her. This guy is nuts about her."

Lloyd keeps a promise

We met Lloyd and Edith in the parking lot. "Remember what you asked me to do when you left Pearl in '45?'

"Sort of Lloyd, you will have to refresh my memory some."

"Okay, let's do it this way . . . Close your eyes and open them when we say so. Honey, go get you-know-what."

About two minutes later Lloyd said, "Open your eyes. Here's your surprise."

What a surprise it was! Before our eyes was our 1940 Studebaker Deluxe sedan "Yellow Baby" and in mint condition! I had asked him to keep it until our next trip to Hawaii. I never heard him mention the car in the past years we had seen them so I never brought it up. He kept his word. On top of that, he had his mechanics restore it from bumper to bumper. Missy and I smiled at each other. I know memories of it went dancing through our heads.

Missy whispered, "That car has so many memories . . . most very good. Perhaps some more before we head home, sailor."

"Aye-aye, Captain," I said.

Lloyd gave me a wink as if we were kids again, driving off to the beach to go necking. A good thing about the trip was that, despite all the war memories, it also brought back a lot of memories of the four of us together hanging out, and it felt like we all got a bit of our spark back that we lost that day of the attack.

Tracing our steps

We piled into the cars the day after the ceremony to show our kids exactly what happened. Our first stop was to the place where we had gone fishing that fateful morning. The beach had not changed much in all those years. Missy explained to the children all the details. She explained what she saw in the skies. Missy kept looking around at the beach.

"Honey, you look as if you are looking for something," I said.

"I am. Those were brand new surf rods we lost that day!"

We all laughed.

Our next part of the tour was what we did once we realized they were Japanese. I showed them how we drove close to the tree line as to be not a target. Then we entered the base and drove to where our "mud hut" used to be.

The house no longer stood, however, the lot had remained vacant. The huge tree that shaded our home still stood in all its glory. Both of us shared stories about our lives in that little house.

Edith and Lloyd arrived to share their experiences with them. I explained that Lloyd and I headed over to the fighting while Missy and Edith decided what to do next. Edith shared her story with tears in her eyes.

"Kids, what I am going to tell you is very hard for me even after all this time. We heard rumors that the Japs had invaded Hawaii. I gathered up your mom and brother and headed for the hills. If the enemy had caught us, our future was bleak. I knew what they had done in China. They would have killed Todd instantly. Your mother and I would have been comfort women or executed. I wasn't going to let that happen. I was prepared to do something I am so thankful I never had to do. I hope you can figure out what the something was."

My kids were speechless. Shangri La started to cry. A shiver ran down my spine too.

My wife then opened up a tote she was carrying.

"Kids, this is the uniform your dad wore when he went to Pearl. On these clothes is the grease, dirt, sweat and blood of that day. Most of the blood is not from daddy . . . it is from men he and others tried to save that day. I'm going to donate them to the museum here at Pearl for all to see."

I never knew she had these. My kids, one at a time touched the clothing. With the uniform between Missy and me, we hugged.

At this point, we needed some funny remembrances.

"Got a good story about your mother. One day I came home from the base asking what your mom did today. She answered, 'Edith and me took a ride down where the hookers hang out. I had never seen one. You see Ethan in Duluth we do not have prostitutes.' I said, 'Missy . . . Duluth is a port city . . . where there are sailors . . . there are hookers!'"

"Darn right Duluth has hookers," Matthew said with too much enthusiasm.

"Ethan, I don't remember that!"

"I also remember when you busted through the main gate in Yellow Baby," Edith broke in, "and the Marines ordered you to halt with guns pointed! You told them you were in a hurry to pick up Ethan. You got a fifteen-day suspension from the base!"

The kids were starting to realize their mother was once young and wild.

We headed over to the base. I explained what I did during the attack. Lloyd gave his story too. He also explained the salvage operations after the attack.

When we returned to the beach house, Missy had something to say that had been bothering her.

"This is for all you kids. I have noticed something while on this trip. I know you all love each other. But you all seem rather . . . bored with each other, at least in front of us. I mean, like, holding hands or a little kiss for the heck of it. Your father and I have always tried to keep the fire alive. I don't mean whoopee necessarily, I mean like a little TLC. Fifty-one years of marriage have flown by so fast. It seems like yesterday we were newlyweds living in Hawaii. I guess it's different for us since we had years of separation. Only Donna and Todd have experienced some of that. Never be ashamed to show you love each other. I realize you live a faster-paced world than we did. Please ignore some of the worldly nonsense and give more of yourselves to each other and to your kids. All of you are now forty years and over, but the honeymoon is never over. It never should be over. If I'm wrong tell this old woman to mind her own business."

She wasn't wrong and the kids knew it. The all looked bleakly at the ground, at their feet, their hands. They peered up at their spouses and smiled a little. They fondled their wedding rings. I didn't feel it was my place saying anything, but Missy never gave a damn about where her place was. She was also their mother, even if they no longer lived at home, and this was her way of letting them know that she as still keeping an eye on them.

Saturday Night Fever!

Without hesitation, we told the kids we were going to spend an evening alone and we were taking Yellow Baby. Marietta wanted to know where we were going, what time we would be home and why without them.

"We're adults and it is none of your business," Missy put it simply. "We'll be home shortly after dark."

"All right but please be careful, no getting yourselves in trouble. You're not kids anymore and you need your rest."

"We will get all the rest we need when we kick the bucket, so let us enjoy the time we have," I replied.

Missy then remarked, "Honey, why don't you and the Captain go out to dinner to have some fun. I like him and I know he likes you. Now run along and get lost!"

Our mothers were having the time of their lives. We hardly saw them after the Pearl Harbor ceremonies. All they did was book bus tours to see the sites. They went to see Don Ho too. We wanted them to have fun and that's what they did. Missy tried to slow them down.

"This is our last hurrah so don't nag!" Annikin said.

It made me feel so good to see my mum having so much fun.

"Son, if somebody during the Depression told me I would visit Hawaii I woulda said, *In a book, maybe.* Back then hardly we hardly saw a book!"

Edith told us one of our favorite restaurants was still around. We met with them at seven. Lloyd looked like a seventy-six year old surfer boy with shiny grey hair instead of Beach Boy blonde. Edith wore a summer outfit that made those beautiful blue eyes shine. Missy was the most ravishing, of course. She had on a black top with a white border and matching black slacks. She was still one of the few women I knew that could wear red lipstick and look stunning.

The restaurant had changed as I expected. The food was still superb. This had always been a Navy oriented place. Not a bar where Marines and sailors had fist fights over women but a place where the brass took their wives out. Some of the pictures of ships and airplanes still hung on the wall.

We stayed until about nine then said goodnight.

"So I guess it's back to the house to check in with our chaperone, eh?"

"Ethan honey, we got the whole night ahead of us. Marietta is probably on a date. The rest, I hope, are renewing their love for each other at the house. You know, playing checkers, charades or watching cable news," She said with a chuckle.

"Maybe playing with each other?"

"Yes that too, for their sake I hope so. It's healthy for couples to be intimate. They are at times drier than a popcorn fart, as you say."

We headed up into the hills where we used to go on hot nights. Up there it was cooler and quiet. Many things had changed on the big island but up there was still about the same. The road leading to the hills was still crooked and barely one lane in places. It took a half hour to get there. Like a hound dog, our noses lead us to the exact place. The parking area had not changed either, except it was now a state park with signs posting hours: open from Dawn to 11pm.

"We'll be out of here by then," Missy grinned. "If not, what are they going to do, put us in jail?"

We pulled in and set the parking brake, turned off the lights and rolled all the windows down. A nice breeze greeted us. It felt so good, a mix of sea and mountain air. There were several other cars there too. I'm sure they were up to no good too.

"Honey, it seems like only yesterday we were here. Not much has changed. Still quiet and so dark . . . Be a nice place to die."

"Sailor, I have no desire to do that but I get your drift. I always loved it here. I came here in the daytime with Toddy when you were training. We laid out a blanket and picnicked. Not far from here is where Edith took us to hide out during the attack. Do you think Edith would have really done us in if the Jap's would have come?"

"Yes, she would have. I would've, too. Those bastards would have done unspeakable things to you two. I saw what they could do. Fifty years ago, they were masters of death and now they are the masters of automobiles.

The Beautiful Mistake

How ironic that Mitsubishi builds great cars now. During the war, they built great fighter planes. Oh well, I still like my Mercury and I love this Studebaker probably the most."

We talked some more, trying like hell to stay away from war stories. It was hard, though. That time in our lives was the biggest event except saying "I do" and having our family. Missy and I had such an exciting life in the first two years of our marriage: our whirlwind romance, a wedding and our ocean voyage. We had the luck of living in a true paradise, having a baby and witnessing the attack. Loneliness as we both had never known and no guarantees we would ever see each other again, too. World War Two had been hard on us, especially Missy. Being a young mother of two and seeing Western Union deliver telegrams of bad news daily. She always wondered if Western Union was going to knock on her door next. For us it all worked out well. I couldn't keep from thinking about the ones that never came home to fetch the American dream.

"You know, Todd might be on to something about collecting old cars. This car is something else. Look at this car, long hood, big steering wheel with seats like living room couches! Steel thick as armor plating and the chrome, real chrome, not that crap they spray on today's cars. The room this car has. You could start a family in that back seat . . . it's like a bed!"

"Ethan, we did start a family in this car! Toddy got his start in life on the hood, roof, or back seat. Remember?"

"I remember. I can still feel the hood ornament digging into my feet! Gosh, that was fun– you full of zip, me being very able. I miss the able part."

"Well sailorman, let's jump in the back seat to let history repeat itself. What'aya say, Chief, wanna try?"

"I know the only thing I can do is get into the backseat. I don't want to disappoint you sweetheart. Standing at attention for an awards ceremony is something I can do. However a part of me . . . might not."

"Ethan Allen, you have never disappointed me. To be close and to have you hold me in those mighty arms of yours is all I need. Whatever happens, happens. Let's leave it at that. I love you and that is all I need to know. Now maybe this will help. Let me whisper this in your ear . . ." and she went on with the sweet nothings a wife knows will get her husband going, sometimes nothing really at all.

"That worked . . . holy shit . . . would you look at that!"

"Shssh, sailor boy"

I woke up first with every limb of my body feeling numb. The backseat was big for many things though not for sleeping two adults.

"Oh poop," Missy said, waking up. "Are we in big trouble now, its daylight!"

We were in big trouble. Our family was awake and no doubt frantic as to our whereabouts. At first, we were worried, and then realized we are adults, damnit! Missy combed her hair and I tucked in my tee shirt.

We started home for the ass chewing we knew was coming. As we proceeded home, we turned on the radio. AM was the only stations we could receive, which was fine by us. The music was our kind of music. It was like being in 1940 all over again. Then the news came on. The newswoman said:

A family visiting from Nebraska is desperately worried about their parents who went missing around eight pm last night. They went out for dinner and have not been seen or heard from since. Ethan and Mystic Vanderbilt, in their seventies, are driving a 1940 bright yellow Studebaker. Any information, please call the police.

"Wow Missy, we're wanted. Now that is what I call exciting! Don't you?"

"Honey, you forget? I did that gig already once in my life!"

We turned and started laughing, as we had not done in years! I told her that maybe McGarrett and Dano would pull us over telling Dano, "Book'm Dano!" Then we started humming the theme song to Hawaii Five-O. We were having a blast until red lights appeared in the rear view mirror.

"Morning officer, I suppose you're looking for us?"

"Yes sir, are you both okay?"

"Yes sir we're fine. We had way too much Hawaii, I guess."

"I'll bet you did. We love happy tourists. Now follow me and I will escort you to your family."

I followed the officer to our rental.

"There is a cop car in the driveway!" Donna screamed. She assumed he was there to deliver bad news.

Marietta came running, saw us, stopped and blurted out, "Where have you been! Are you all right, why didn't you call! Officer, are they in trouble?"

"Not with me, but I'll bet they are with you. Have a nice stay on the island. Aloha."

Marietta chewed us out for scaring the heck out of them. Todd was relieved we were here. The rest came out laughing. They knew what we had been doing.

"Have fun?" Matthew, the smart-ass, asked. "Looks like you had a rough night. Well I'm going fishing!"

Our kids never called their mom "mother." The older kids called her mama because that is what we called our moms. The younger two called her mom. It was a generation thing. When Marietta started calling Missy "mother" we knew she was mad!

"I want a full explanation of what you did! What about our feelings, we were scared half to death! Look at you, Mother . . . you are a mess! Your hair is uncombed, clothes wrinkled, and you look half-dead! Here, let me straighten you up . . . there is smoke on your breath! Daddy . . . your belt . . . fix it! What have you been doing all night?"

"We will apologize for scaring you. What we were doing is none of your business. Simmer down. We are going to bed."

As we walked away, we heard Todd tell his sister to bug off. We felt sorry for her. Marietta was so lonely and in some ways jealous, even of her own parents.

After a nice nap, I went down by the pool and sat under an umbrella to work on my memoirs. I had decided to make the trip to Pearl the endpoint for these writings. My ability to write was getting harder to do with my old, worn out fingers. Donna said she would retype my story and if I wanted to, get it to a publisher for print into a book.

"Only after grass the grown over my grave," I told her. "I wrote them so my children and their children would have a record of our lives in a very different era than they were in. This was also my way of showing how wonderful my life had been since 1940 with that skinny brunette I met fifty-one years ago named Mystic Bay."

After lunch, we decided to go down to the beach to relax. Matthew and Shang were down fishing. They seemed to be having such fun. He was showing her how to surf fish as I had taught him and his mother decades ago. Genny and Howie came down the path, headed for the beach and holding hands. He was shirtless. His war wounds had scarred his back severely from burns, and he was always so conscience of it. Maybe it was the easy Hawaii lifestyle, but he seemed now to accept what had happened. Genny never minded, she loved him for who he was. Todd and Donna let their Navy hair down. They were playing beach volleyball. Our kids had taken the hint: marriage is a beautiful mistake and one to make together.

Missy and I enjoyed the warm sea air with the gentle surf hitting the beach. It was a good day to be alive. She read a book and I watched Matthew fish.

"Holy cow, what a sight to see! Apparently I haven't been to the beach in a while!"

"What sight? Oh, Ethan, put your eyes back in your head. Those women should be ashamed to be in public like that."

"That's your opinion. Would you wear a bikini like that in the forties?"

"No and that is a little less than a bikini. Now put some oil on my back, then hop in the surf to cool off before you have a stroke! Why don't you do some work on those memoirs you're writing?"

Marietta came down to the beach in a nice flowing summer dress, wearing sunglasses and carrying her shoes. She looked very happy.

"Hi. I am going out with Robert for dinner. I won't be home until late. Mama and Daddy, please, *please* hang around the house tonight. We leave on the nine a.m. plane and must catch it or we are stuck until Monday. Have the Timken's come over or something."

"Honey, are you and Robert an item perhaps?"

"Maybe, Mama. We're going to keep in touch. He's gonna visit me in six months, after his retirement. We shall see, I suppose," She added listfully. "I admit it . . . There is something there. Well I'm off. You two stay put!"

With Missy wearing those Wayfarers, I looked at her saying, "So the Captain is coming to Lincoln for a visit. Sounds like somebody I know . . . Boy meets girl in Hawaii, visits girl, then marries girl."

"Yeah, it does sound familiar. Maybe it will work out for her. It did for us. I hope it does. Now that the watchdog is on a date, whaddaya wanna do, Sailor?"

"First I wanna take a nice long walk down the beach holding hands. One thing first, do you want to move here? I know you always liked Hawaii. The weather is so much better on our old bones than Lincoln."

"No Ethan, I want to go home. That is where we belong. Our family is there. It is where we made this beautiful life. Hawaii was our first home. This is where we started. December 7th, 1941, changed all of that. Here is only a memory—a good one but still, only a memory. Lincoln has been good to us. I miss sitting in our garden in the morning, drinking coffee, talking or reading the paper. I even miss telling you not to pee in my rose bushes although it does seem to help them. Now . . . let's take that nice long walk on the beach at Waikiki, hold hands and talk about what to do with the rest of our lives. Ethan, I love you."

And I loved her. She didn't need me to tell her, but I did anyway. I grabbed her hand and put my old feet to that hot sand. To me, it didn't matter where we'd met, or where we'd lived or raised our kids. Where I lived, and where I would spend eternity was with her. Wherever Mystic Bay was, I called home.